# AQUILA

Into The Light

# AQUILA

### Into The Light

## T. L. SEARLE

authorHOUSE®

*AuthorHouse™ UK*
*1663 Liberty Drive*
*Bloomington, IN 47403 USA*
*www.authorhouse.co.uk*
*Phone: 0800.197.4150*

*Published by AuthorHouse    11/06/2014*

*ISBN: 978-1-4969-9430-1 (sc)*
*ISBN: 978-1-4969-9431-8 (e)*

*Any people depicted in stock imagery provided by Thinkstock are models, and such images are being used for illustrative purposes only. Certain stock imagery © Thinkstock.*

*Because of the dynamic nature of the Internet, any web addresses or links contained in this book may have changed since publication and may no longer be valid. The views expressed in this work are solely those of the author and do not necessarily reflect the views of the publisher, and the publisher hereby disclaims any responsibility for them.*

*For my children*

*Depart from me,*
*ye cursed,*
*into everlasting fire,*
*prepared for the devil and his angels:*

*Matthew 25:41*

# Prologue

I'd thought I'd known the world around me. I'd thought I'd known the man I loved.

On feathered wings we'd flown, united. Together we'd declared our heart's to the other. We'd given our souls completely.

But as I lie caged in iron, captured and taken from the ones I love, I find a single fact above all others the hardest to consume:

The cold, steel shaft of the arrow in my thigh bears the unique sigil of that same, handsome man I love.

Liam.

# · One ·

There's a new numbness in my heart, acquired in the unconsciousness. I can feel it settling like snowfall, slowly. It's melting slightly on first contact but if I let it continue, pretty soon my heart will be as cold as the deepest winter and as unfeeling as ice. I've felt this numbness before, swore I never would again. Now, I welcome it.

I try to fight my new reality, keep my eyes closed, attempt to sink back into oblivion, but the din in my ears increases until I'm almost convinced that there's a swarm of locusts somewhere inside my head. There are other sounds too, faint sounds leaching in around the buzzing: the squeal of our convoy as we traverse steel tracks, gentle snoring, and a voice I recognise shouting my name – but my muddy brain can't place it.

"Liam?" I murmur out of some deep-rooted hope that I'm waking from another chest-crushing nightmare.

The voice sounds confused by my comment. "No, it's Brue," he says. "Are you okay?"

Brue? His name is relatively new to me, but I know who he is – a dragone – one of my captors.

My breathing is surprisingly even. I inhale slowly. The air is damp and stale; the scent of dirt permeates every pore. I choose to squeeze my eyes more tightly closed. I don't need to see to know where we are. The cage which holds me is wrought of iron. The engine which powers us is not mechanical, a dozen dragone pull the thick chains. Dragone, strong dark creatures swathed in black and as swift as the wind. The air is damp because we are no longer above ground. And my heart is breaking, not because I find myself captive but because of what's lodged so deeply into my thigh.

"Aquila?" Brue calls my name again.

I still refuse to open my eyes. Stubbornness is embedded into my DNA – along with a few other things.

I can picture Brue clearly, despite only knowing him a few hours. He's just a child: small, rough around the edges, and nursing an injured stomach courtesy of a punch from me. I find it hard to believe that the concern in his voice is for my benefit.

"Hey, fake angel!" Brue shouts at me again. "Wake up, we're nearly home."

Home? I almost laugh. Wherever they're taking me is not my home. I'm not even sure if where I came from is my home. My friends are there – my family are there, but it's never felt like home. Celthia is an impressive city, carved into the rock of a mountain, with only the monolithic golden doors visible to the human world. The angeli of Celthia are a proud and regimented people and fierce enemies of the dragone. Liam is the fiercest of them all. Liam...

"Aquila, wake up or Clyst will have to carry you," Brue yells.

Clyst? That name is not familiar but I can guarantee I would not want to be carried by the owner of it. I may have been stripped of my freedom, but I can at least attempt to maintain some of my dignity.

With a groan, I force myself to sit. Brue's impatient face is what greets me when I pry open my eyes. His jet black hair is as scruffy and unkempt as I remembered. It looks as though he's attempted to cut it himself, with some kind of garden shear. His face is pretty, obviously youthful, with a small button nose, but it's hidden beneath a layer of grime and sloppily applied black face paint. His stunning yellow irises are flashing bright against the dark of the tunnel.

All of the dragone have luminous eyes and excellent night vision. The pitch black of the tunnel is no problem for my captors. Then again, the darkness is not a problem for me either. My bright amber eyes hold the same mystery ingredient – another element embedded into my DNA.

Brue visibly relaxes when I make eye contact. It makes me smile, though I have no idea why. Perhaps it's the way he's suddenly changed his response to me. When I dived into this cage to protect my mother, the dragone looked more frightened of me than I was of them. Brue especially, after I tackled him and sent him sprawling into the dirt. But now that he's been tossed in here with me, the real Brue is starting to emerge – streetwise and world savvy. I'm not afraid to admit I like the boy, despite my circumstances. He reminds me of August, and August is one of my favourite people in the world.

A soft moan from the other side of the cage draws my attention. The recently snoring form of my mother is rousing from her impromptu slumber. I passed out, she fell asleep willingly. Although in her defence, she's been a prisoner of the dragone for months now – not hours. Plus, she's as high as a kite on peyote, the dragone's drug of choice, to keep her compliant and amenable. I can't seem to muster the appropriate level of anger at that fact. The truth is, I'm glad she's partly out of it. I don't know how I would handle an emotional reunion with her. I was furious she showed so little feeling when I practically surrendered myself to save her. Now I'm just glad she's safe, that we're together again.

She sits up slowly. Her ochre hair is a mess. She usually has it shorter. It's grown in the time she's been missing. Her skin is darker from the regular sun she's been enjoying. We very rarely had sun in England. Our small farmhouse at the foot of the Quantocks was generally floating on a puddle of rainwater. I loved the rain. I used to think of it as home, before Liam...

"Rise and shine," I murmur.

My mother's head snaps around. "Aqua?" Her eyes attempt to focus in my direction for the first time. I mean properly focus – like the veil has lifted and clarity now rules. I guess it's been a while since they last dosed her. She can't see me in the dark. Her eyes wield wildly, her breath comes in short pants.

"Hi, Mum," I answer. My voice still sounds off. It's tinged with the uncertainty, and pain, that I'm trying very hard to suppress beneath the increasing snowstorm. I cough to clear the gravel from my throat. I can't think about that yet. I can't think about who and what I left behind to come here for her. I definitely cannot think about what the dragone plan to do now they have me. So, instead, I focus on my mother and her soft features.

I forget sometimes, how young she is. She's not quite forty, but she's wise and talented – in the kitchen especially. I have missed my mother's cooking, the smell of her baking wafting around the thick stone walls. I have missed her more.

Her sweet face falls in horror. "What are you doing here?" she gasps. I can barely hear her voice; even with my heightened senses it's just a whisper.

"I came to rescue you," I answer gently, afraid to upset her.

I'm past being upset myself – that was before I passed out, before the blessed black of unconsciousness beckoned me, before my heart went into self-preservation mode. Now I'm focused on her, I'll deal with me later.

"It didn't quite go to plan," I add.

"Honey." She moans her favourite endearment. "You shouldn't be here."

I refrain from agreeing. I know I shouldn't, there are many other places I would prefer to be. But since the moment the dragone raided our house and stole her in the night, leaving my best friend broken and bleeding to death on the floor, I have vowed to get her back. I do not regret coming after her. I very much regret what I have lost because of it. Liam... I open up to the snowfall a little more, to let it bury Liam.

"I couldn't have stayed away," I whisper.

She moves then, stiffly after her doze on the metal bars of the floor, and finds me in the darkness. At least most of the moss they used to disguise the trap is riding with us. It makes our journey slightly more comfortable.

Folding me into a hug I feel her tension release, and suddenly torrents of warm tears are pouring down the collar of my leather vest. My mother sobs violently against my neck as I hold her. I let her cry. I've been here. I felt this pain the night my world was whipped out from under me. I descended into a haze of depression soon after. I won't let that happen to her.

"It's okay, Mum," I soothe, talking into her hair. "I'm here now. With you is where I need to be."

Brue is watching us with interest. He witnessed my outburst when I was first caged. When I yelled at her because of her lack of emotion. When I found out my captive mother has actually been sunning it up on a beach sipping cocktails.

My mother's arms are around me, her fingers dipping into the feathers on my back. I feel her stiffen as she registers that I have them on display.

"Aqua," she gasps. "What are you doing?"

I know what she means. My mother is human. I was raised in the human world, hiding my wings under sweaters my entire life, almost eighteen years.

"Don't worry, Mum, it's a bit late for secrets now." That secret, at least, I have plenty more I'm hanging on to.

"Aqua," she questions. "What's happening? I feel like I'm waking up from a nightmare, except I'm still in it."

I've been there. "I know, Mum. I'll explain everything I know when I can." I can't now. There are too many inquisitive glowing eyes turned in our direction. Even the pace of the cage has slowed as the dragone strain to listen. I look at Brue then, his are the most inquisitive eyes of all.

"Where are we going?" I ask him. I know he'll answer.

He shrugs nonchalantly. "Our home, Hantiem."

I'm more than a little surprised by his answer. The angeli told me the dragone live somewhere called Gravinwart. Then again, they said it was underground. I don't think there are many beaches underground. I nod anyway, filing away the information for later. I've lost track of the turns in the tunnel now. I was cataloguing them as an escape plan, but passing out scuppered that.

Axion, Brue's brother, looks up every time Brue speaks. He's at the front of the pack, pulling the longest chain and flanked by the monster brute – the one who gave the order to kill my mother. He's the one I'll kill first, if I ever escape.

"I don't think your brother likes you talking to me," I state.

"Axion doesn't like anything I do." Brue grins, flashing his crooked white teeth. "He didn't want me to come."

I smirk. "Well I'd have to agree with him. What would you have done if it had come to a fight?"

My protective instincts are stirring. I really should rein it in. I'm sure I'm not meant to care about the fate of my enemy. Ha, and I thought my mother was the one with Stockholm syndrome. Incidentally, I don't know if she is listening to us as she's still sobbing ferociously against my shoulder.

"I can handle myself," Brue huffs.

There's a palpable flash of fire in his eyes. I'm quite sure he believes he can, although it didn't take much for me to bring him down. The dragone are supernaturally strong and incredibly fast. I ran from China to England in one night, last night actually although it feels like decades ago, utilising the added strength my lineage provides. I don't believe my captors are party to that particular secret yet.

"I believe you," I offer. "But still, that didn't stop the brute almost leaving you behind."

I can't help smiling at the dragone boy, though it's more of an instinctive face movement than the result of emotion. I'm putting a lot of trust in my judgement of character, but I really can't envisage Brue as a threat. The monster brute, on the other hand, will never receive a civil word from me.

Brue frowns. "Axion isn't a brute."

"Not him." I can tell he isn't. He looks soft. "The other one, taller and fatter."

Brue's face turns iridescent as he descends into a fit of hysterical laughter. It's a melodious sound, full of innocence and promise.

He snorts as he tries to talk. "That's Clyst," he sniggers.

"Oh, then I'm glad I woke up." Although, if I pretend I've passed out again, I could stick my dagger in his gut when Clyst carries me. No, not his gut – into his heart.

Brue shrugs. "I told you, they couldn't leave me. My dad would kill them. They were just messing with you."

I raise my eyebrows but don't reply. He didn't see the sneer on Clyst's face when he rolled him in here with me. That man is evil personified.

Something else grabs my attention, then, and my conversation is forgotten. I nearly drop my mother too, in my eagerness to push myself against the bars of the cage. I can smell the ocean. Salt and seaweed, brine and life – everything I associate with water.

Water is my safe place. I could live beneath the waves indefinitely, another of my secrets. One that nobody else knows, not even Liam.

"We're nearly there!" Brue almost bounces in his excitement. Just another thing about him that reminds me of my brother. I have to force down the urge to vomit, let the snow speed up. I promised August I'd never leave him. He was my tie to Celthia – one of the few. I'll vow now, to myself, that I'll return to him. I can focus on that.

The smell of the ocean is getting stronger, calling me. "I can smell it," I sigh.

"Smell what?" Brue asks.

I forget the dragone don't share all of my abilities – like heightened day-vision, smell, hearing and flight.

"The ocean." I grin, a genuine grin.

Brue huffs. "I wish I could do that."

I shrug. Those gifts come from my angeli half. My *supposed* father, Marcus.

I can almost taste the water now. My skin is tingling with anticipation. I can't wait to see it. Claustrophobia is an issue with me. I hate walls, any walls. I crave open space. I need water like I need oxygen. Although, needing the water is one thing. Being held captive so close to it and being denied it is another. It just occurred to me that being taken to an island, as a prisoner, may not be a good thing.

"What will they do with me, Brue?" I blurt.

Brue looks at me strangely as he processes my question. Perhaps it was wrong to ask him. He's so young, I bet not even a teenager. Maybe he's too innocent to provide a real answer.

"My dad will kill you," he responds.

Or maybe not. "Kill me?"

My mother amps up her wailing, squeezing me so tightly I can barely breathe. Brue's father won't need to kill me; my mother's doing the job rather effectively. I prise her arms away from me gently. I am much stronger than a human, so it doesn't take much effort.

The numbness is hastening, snowfall an inch deep, cloaking my heart from the horrors of the world, protecting me from the hurt. I know I should feel terrified right now. After all, I'm a bird in a cage. Brue looks apologetic at least.

"Why would he do that?" I ask.

"Because you're an angel." He shrugs again, though I see a twinge in his eyes.

"Only half," I correct. My voice holds no emotion.

He frowns slightly. "I don't think that matters."

"Worth a shot."

I'm definitely having some kind of episode. I'm sitting in a cage, discussing my pending execution with the son of my would-be executioner. Brue grins at me, my mother wails and Axion stares dumbfounded. All of their faces disappear though, when I look ahead.

The end of the tunnel is approaching. We are on an incline. Light is beginning to seep into the darkness. It affects my vision as I switch from night to day mode. The world turns hazy, until I'm blinded by white. I know my captors are suffering the same affliction – the cage shudders as they stagger from the mouth of the passageway and into the light. I'm sure my eyes adjust more quickly, because I gasp a good second before Brue.

I can understand his reaction, and he lives here. Hantiem is beautiful. It's not the bare gray walls of Celthia, or the lush green hedgerows of England. It's pristine white sand and sapphire blue ocean that disappears into a blurred line with the same coloured sky. The air is breathtakingly moist, and wonderfully hot. It almost burns my lungs as I breathe it in. I don't care.

I love the heat and the droplets of moisture sticking to my skin. I'm dehydrated from my run earlier. I only drank mouthfuls of rainwater during my several thousand mile marathon.

We've appeared out of the side of a small hill, a stones throw from the beach. The metal tracks sweep around to the left, gifting me with a view of the coast. A seam of pure white dissects the centre of my field of vision. To my right, the blessed ocean goes on forever. To my left, rows of grass huts are nestled in abundant green vegetation and bordered with colourful exotic flowers. The tracks weave in behind them and climb up the bank to the next level.

The same huts edge our passing. These are slightly bigger, though still woven from the same dried reed material, and standing on wooden stilts. The dragone pant as they pull us. We have travelled a long way from England tonight. I can't help wondering why they went to all the effort, when they plan to kill me anyway. At least I have survived long enough to see this view, to feel this warmth. It could even warm my now frozen heart, if I allowed it.

Brue and my mother are watching the landscape with the same look of wonder on their faces. The view seems to have helped my mother forget how we came to be here, at least for a few seconds. I relish the quiet after her tears. If not for the bars of the cage, I could imagine living here. Browning my pale skin under the sun, exploring the marine life around the coast, sleeping under a reed roof with the smell of dried grass, fresh brine and fragrant flowers. This could be home.

"You like it?" Brue asks hesitantly, but not in the way you ask a visitor if they like your house. No, he asks me in shock – disbelieving that an angeli could like somewhere like this. It is true, the angeli hate the heat. They relish the high ground, the frigid temperatures of the mountains. They live in the dark, illuminated only by candles. Few leave the city of their birth, few leave the rock walls unless on a special occasion.

I glance at Brue. He's staring at me, watching my reactions. He really is very astute for a young boy.

"I like it," I sigh. "I like the heat and the smells and especially the water."

My mother starts crying again then, her momentarily relief forgotten, so I hug her to my chest and hold her as the cage nears a wooden gate.

It isn't ornate, or overly spectacular. It's just a series of small logs held together with dried vines; but I find myself smiling at it. Wood. Celthia had so little of it. The wood reminds me of Somerset, of Saturday mornings at the course and of chopping logs for winter. It reminds me of Aaron.

"You like the gate?" Brue frowns. He's been staring at my face the whole time. I'm obviously very readable.

I nod. "I like wood."

I watch as the dragone push through, the gate swings steadily until it catches open. The metal tracks run only a little way into the trees which line the path. The dragone grind to a halt, panting and pulling off the black robes that cover their bodies. They are home now I guess. No need to be ghosts anymore.

Although, my eyes widen minutely when I see what little they are wearing. I guess you don't need shirts in this climate. They wear shorts that are relatively snug, cut long in the same fabric as their cloaks. They are wearing heavy boots with thick soles, the kind used for hiking long distances. They each have a single broadsword, fastened to their waists. They are not the vile looking creatures depicted as lizards in the angeli scriptures.

Axion walks toward the cage then, the only one still wearing his cloak. I watch his progress. He has a fluidity to him, a gentle grace. I still can't budge the feeling that I know him somehow. His face looks so familiar. He is their leader, although I have no idea why. He doesn't have the assertiveness leadership requires. There's nothing Alpha male about him.

He stands by the cage, looking unsure of how to proceed. The three of us watch him, though my mother is still sobbing. Brue is huffing out of his cloak, clearly eager to be free of the bars. I'm merely inquisitive.

Axion doesn't hold himself like a leader. I have seen good leaders. Victus is one. Plyrian another. However, Liam is the best I've seen. Master of the Guard of Celthia: my Guard Master, my brother and my boyfriend, all rolled into one stunningly hateful reward. I touch the arrow in my leg instinctively, drawing Axion's eyes to it.

"Can you walk?" he asks.

Walk? I've got a friggin' arrow in my leg and a distraught mother on my arm. But if he wants to let me out I'm happy to fly... I nod and help my mother to her feet. My leg protests painfully. The fire is spreading from the point of penetration. I almost welcome it. It's a feeling I can cope with. The snowfall is at blizzard status, my heart sufficiently numb to protect me from the emotions I can't face right now.

The dragone surround us, drawing their swords in defence. I roll my eyes. I'm not planning on fighting. My plan A, if I can get my mother out with me, is to flee. It's what I usually do.

Brue tenses beside me. He's not armed. I give him a reassuring smile. I really must stop with the niceness. His dad's possibly about to kill me.

I bend my knees in preparation. I could be airborne in seconds, escaping with my mother in my arms. Except shrewd little Brue jumps on my back like a limpet and secures his arms and legs around me, with unbelievable pressure. He's secured my wings. I have to smile. I knew I liked Brue. He may have more brain cells than the rest of the party combined. I still have Plan B.

It takes four of the biggest dragone to lift the iron bars. Clyst is one of them. I watch the veins on his bulging arms as he heaves the side of the cage above his head. Then I step forward, and kick him in the face. It's not as hard as I'd planned, because my leg protests at the movement, but it does the job.

"Aqua!" my mother exclaims at the same time as Clyst bellows an expletive and Brue starts laughing, he's like a cute but annoying musical backpack.

Clyst stumbles backward and I follow, dropping from the elevated platform and landing unevenly, protecting my injury, inside a ring of my captors. My mother shouts my name again but I ignore her. I am single minded, focused on escape. The blizzard in my chest has eradicated the feelings that held me back in the clearing. They hindered me, they prevented me from fighting. It was my heart that brought me here and now my heart is encased in ice.

I move first. Spinning, I kick Clyst in the stomach. He falls backward with an *'ooof'*. While he's down I kick him in the crotch. I feel Brue squeeze tighter as he clings to my back. I ignore his voice; I think he's shouting too.

The next kick is aimed at the dragone who's sneaking up behind me. I go straight for the knee. He lands heavily in the powder-fine sand of the trail. The soles of my feet are suffering, worn raw. The burn of the fire is intensifying, spreading across my whole body. My lungs pant because of it, my heart thumps in my chest. Sweat glistens on my skin and Brue's grip begins to slip.

I roundhouse the next attacker, my fist connects with his nose sending a spray of blood onto the white sand.

"Aqua!" Brue slips then with a squeal of my name. He lands in a heap on the floor, just as a dragone is sneaking up from behind, and takes the brunt of the man's boot to his ribs. He screams in agony.

"No! Not Brue." A red veil descends over my vision. I stop fighting with my head. The dragone who kicked Brue doesn't see my dagger until it's in him, sunk to its hilt through his ribs. I freeze, in horror I think though I can't really feel anything. The rest of the dragone freeze too, watching the man's face drain of colour.

Brue pulls himself to sitting, staring at the dragone who is wobbling unsteadily. My mother is screaming. Oh. My. God.

The man I killed falls hard, like a felled tree, landing at my immobile feet. I can't move. I can only stare and try not to vomit. Even my mother has fallen silent. The ocean breeze whispers through the leaves around me, whispers "murderer," like a mantra. My legs give way, buckling under the crushing guilt. I'm a murderer now.

I'm on my knees before I know what's happening. Brue is there too. I watch as he leans across, shoves the dead man onto his back, and pulls the dagger from his chest. I'm broken. Only the ice in my heart is keeping me upright. I never wanted to kill... Not really...

Brue wipes the blood on his shorts, inspecting the blade when it's clean. I just watch. I'm barely able to process his actions. Like watching a foreign film with no subtitles, the images are there but I can't understand them.

He looks at me then, and smiles. I blink but nothing else. I can't fathom his expression. His eyes are bright and alive. Not glazed, like those of the dead man in front of me. Brue hands me the dagger, or tries. I just stare at it. My brain has logged off, or crashed. So he crawls over and slides it into my sheath. I watch his little fingers as they release the handle and he sits back.

I stare blankly as he says, "Thank you."

I blink.

Hands grab me, strong arms lift and carry me. I don't see whose face it is. I don't even care if it's Clyst. I close my eyes and pretend I'm somewhere else, anywhere else. My body sinks into unconsciousness.

# · Two ·

When my eyes flutter, the scenery has changed. No, it's changing. We're moving. I can hear the thud of heavy boots. There is also a scraping, like something's being dragged. No one is talking.

I look up. The sky is a cloudless striking blue, green palm leaves sway above our heads, and Axion's jawline is incredibly close. My heart rate spikes and then almost stops as I remember.

I'm a killer.

I can feel the fluid gait of Axion's stride. My body bobs with every step. His spicy scent fills my sinus, pepper and chilli. It makes me sneeze and he looks down.

My wary amber eyes lock with his dazzling yellow irises, and in that second something passes between us; a silent communication with a dash of intuition. He's grateful for what I did. I can feel it, but I don't understand it.

I look away first, to study the figures around us, to look for Brue and my mother. It doesn't take long. My mother is riding in arms, eyes closed. Brue is stubbornly hobbling in front, leading the way along the fern lined trail. One of his legs is dragging and he's favouring an arm but I can see the determination radiating from him. Brue will be a formidable opponent when he's older.

I watch our progress. My eyes flutter occasionally in my fight to keep them open. My body feels drained, my mind detached. I'm weary. Not just physically. Everything is hurting: my body, my brain, even my heart. The numbness is subsiding. My ice shield is cracking as my energy levels diminish. Soon there will be nothing but pain; and then I'll beg for the death I'm facing.

Another wooden gate approaches. Above it, a series of buildings begin to take shape. They are all at different heights; a beautifully patch-worked collage of red and white against the bright blue of the sky and the green of the landscape.

Brue leads us into a courtyard, surrounded on all sides by high whitewashed walls topped with red tiles. I watch through drooping eyelids as we make our way across, past plants growing out of terracotta pots and up through the brickwork of the floor. There are several doorways off of the courtyard but none look like a main entrance. The door Brue leads us through is small, we go single file. Axion is careful not to hit me against the doorframe. I frown as my brain tries to reason, tries to explain what's happening. I can't shut it off and it's making it ache.

The passageway is narrow. The floor is beautiful. Bright patterned tiles lead us past more doorways. The colours look even bolder against the pristine white of the walls. This place is spotless, like it's been bleached.

We enter a small room. It has a little window with no glass. The walls are the same white as the corridor, the floor laid with blue tiles. There's a bed under the window, made up with white linen. I watch as it gets closer. I feel the loosening of Axion's grip. I'm lowered carefully, the fabric of Axion's cloak billows softly against my cheek. The bed is softer than I'm used to. Brue smiles from behind his brother.

I watch them watching me. They stand there, staring, for so long that my eyelids begin to droop. My exhaustion is taking over. With little other option, I let myself be pulled back under.

My vision is red. I can smell the ocean swirling around me. I'm close to it, closer than I have been in weeks. When my eyelids open the redness disappears, replaced with the searing light of the sun through a small rectangular window. A beam of light, so strong it looks tangible, lands on my face. Dust motes swirl through the rays like fish in the ocean. My fingers are moving before my mind catches up. They swipe through the beam and the dust motes dance away like fairies.

My body is still stiff, my muscles still carrying the tension of my new location – of my recent actions. But the pain has dulled. My heart is still beating. I'm still breathing. So is someone else.

I look to my right, where Axion sits on a wooden stool against the far wall. He appears relaxed but experience tells me to look closer. His muscles are tensed, his skin taut over the defined ridges. He's not as slight as he looked next to Clyst. His jaw is clenched, his eyes intense. He's still watching me. Guarding me?

My hand moves reflexively, not expecting them to have left me armed. But my dagger's still there. The discovery makes me sit up, too quickly, and the world spins dangerously until my blood pressure stabilises. Why would they leave me armed?

The arrow is still in my thigh. I sigh at the sight of it.

I whisper, "I'm still alive," to convince myself more than anything.

"For now." Axion's voice is as tight as his body. He's still swathed in black but his face is clean of the war paint. He looks even more familiar. I stare stupefied.

"Why? You saw me kill." A lump in my throat makes it hard to swallow my pooling saliva. I can feel the moisture in my eyes. I bite my lip to keep from crying. I must be emotionally wrecked. How embarrassing, to cry in front of your enemy.

Axion doesn't answer. He stands lithely and walks over. He's still armed too. I can see his sword at his hip, below his cloak. He lifts me easily, and I let him. My feet feel cold and damp. I think they've been washed, which is a little disturbing. I attempt a glance at them as he carries me from the room, along the corridor which leads to a larger courtyard. Someone's definitely tended to them, and applied some kind of balm. I'm not ungrateful, just freaked out. We emerge quietly, but the few dragone outside turn to stare. We both ignore them. A fountain bubbles in the middle of the courtyard. I watch the cascading water intently as we pass. The sun glistens on the surface, making it look more precious than diamonds. Perhaps it is.

The sun has moved in the sky. I've slept, that much is obvious. I don't know how long: hours, days, weeks. Time has lost meaning.

The next door is wider, big enough for two. Inside is a foyer: white walls, green tiled floor, wooden desk, wicker furniture, and my mother, sucking from a cocktail glass with a proud paper umbrella. She's wearing a bathing suit and sarong. Her eyes are glazed and unfocused. She's high again.

"You drugged her," I accuse the jawline of Axion.

"We had to, she watched her daughter kill a man. She was uncontrollable." He doesn't glance at me as he sets me down in a wicker armchair opposite the tanned form of my mother.

She smiles when she sees me. I smile back. Huh, maybe they drugged me too. Brue bounces in then, before I can ask if the reason I'm sitting here compliantly is because I'm tripping or because I've lost my mind. I smile at him too.

"Aq-ua!" my mother's shocked voice stutters. "What are you wearing?"

I almost laugh. She's not worried about the metal shaft still in my leg. She's worried about my outfit. I've changed since she disappeared, literally. I now wear the uniform of the Guard. Very different to the loose fitting sweaters and jeans she's used to. I'm now in skin tight black leather and steel armour – although I'm severely lacking in the armour department right now.

I give a tight smile. "I've got a lot to tell you, if I get the chance."

"Have you seen the pool?" she asks, her shock forgotten. I roll my eyes.

I look at Brue then. He's leaning casually against the desk with a dark black bruise covering the right side of his torso. I gasp. He also has a yellowing bruise on his stomach, one I inflicted.

"Brue." I can't speak. His name is barely audible.

He walks over anyway, not an ounce of fear in him. I grab for the bag on my belt. There is no pain syrup left;

I used that in the cage. I have half a vial of heal aid, the other half already used to help Brue's stomach.

I hand him the vial, my last one. "Drink this, it's for healing."

He turns his nose up. "No way, angel poison won't work on me."

I laugh despite myself. Brue is a force of nature. "It already has, on your stomach. Take it Brue, please."

His hands shoot to the bruise on his stomach. He frowns at me fiercely. "You gave me that stuff in the cage?!"

"Yes and pain syrup, this is all I have left. Take it." I force the vial into his reluctant fingers. What use is me having it now anyway? Half a vial won't do me much good.

"Why?" he asks.

I shrug. "To make you better."

"Why did you give it to me?" he asks more sharply.

"Same answer as before."

"Why?" he barks.

I frown at his question. "So you weren't hurting, so you'll get better faster. Why not, Brue?"

He doesn't answer, just frowns more deeply like my question annoyed him.

"I knew it would work on you, I had it on me. It just makes sense." What happened to 'thank you'? Maybe I'm used to the angeli, with their impeccable manners and outstanding grasp of syntax.

His nose crinkles, like a pair of bellows, as he thinks. "How did you know it would work?" he probes further.

Trust shrewd Brue to pick out the only piece of information that I don't want to explain. I smile at him, warmly, because the longer I spend in his company the more I like him.

"Why are we waiting here?" I ask instead.

"To see my dad," Brue answers. His face falls slightly as he considers that.

Brue said his father will kill me. I know now how easy it is to do. Physically at least – one sharp jab with steel and life is lost – but what is the cost? I've seen people die. The dragone who stabbed Aaron lost their lives at Liam's hands, his slick steel sword felling five of them within seconds. He didn't break down afterward. He didn't fall to his knees in horror. He picked up Aaron and saved his life.

And then I fell in love with him.

And now his arrow is in my thigh.

I swallow the urge to vomit.

"Aqua?" Brue's voice cuts in. He is just a boy, sweet; too sweet to be here.

"How old are you Brue?" My mouth is too dry. I need water. I haven't had a drink for hours... days?

Brue squares his shoulders and puffs out his chest, like a peacock putting on a display. "Old enough," he says boldly.

I nod. My eyes are on my mother's cocktail, debating whether it contains alcohol, although I'd take any fluid right now.

"Water?" Axion's amused voice accompanies the appearance of a hand, and full glass, from above my shoulder. I actually jump before grabbing the tumbler and drinking without considering his motive. It could be laced with cyanide for all I know.

"Are you drugging or poisoning me?" I ask, sure it's one or the other.

He smirks. "Neither, yet."

"This is crazy," I mumble as I lean back in the chair. This place really is very nice, like I'd imagine a Greek holiday resort. No wonder my mother's looking for the pool.

"Come on."

I turn at the sound of Clyst's coarse voice. He's standing in the next doorway, his sword in his hand.

My mother jumps up willingly, like he's some sort of tour guide we've been waiting for. Axion pulls me to my feet but doesn't carry me. I have to hop. Coincidently, my feet actually feel much better. I hear when Axion draws his sword behind me. I glance at him, but he simply points me onward. Funny, he now feels the need to keep me at weapon's length. I wonder why, when he hasn't before.

Clyst leads us to a flight of steep redbrick stairs. My leg is more than agonising now. I can't weight bear. I can't fly within the narrow hallways. Even if I wanted to escape, which I can't without my mother who's skipping merrily behind Clyst, I'm unable to.

We descend the brick steps. I slide down on my butt, into another small room. This place really is like a rabbit warren... an above ground, pristine clean one. There are glassless windows looking out over another courtyard, one housing grape vines. My stomach rumbles as I hop on. I'm hungry, too.

The windows could be an option, if I can toss my mother through one first. It'll have to be plan C. A and B are still under construction.

My foot stops. My hand grabs for the wall and I freeze, staring at the doorway in front of me. It's wooden, nothing special about it except the symbols written on it in black paint. I feel Axion's sword against my back as he stumbles into me. The blade doesn't pierce the skin but slices open the leather, there's now a breeze where there wasn't before. Still I stare at the door.

"What..?" I mumble.

"The throne room," Axion answers hesitantly, confused. Clyst knocks. Still I stare.

"The symbols?"

"Our language."

Their language? I can't read it, I have no idea what is says but I've definitely seen it before. I can't formulate any other response. The door opens and Axion's sword pushes me through.

The room is bland. Not how I'd imagine a throne room to be. There are no royal flags, elegant banners or ornate decoration. There are just a lot of people, crowded around a man perched in a wooden high-backed bucket chair. It has several carvings as decoration, but is otherwise ordinary.

He looks up when we enter. He's middle aged, with a shock of jet black hair and an island of tanned scalp. He wears a wreath of black twine around his forehead. His features are sharp and angular, his chin covered in rough stubble. And when his lips pull back in a terrifying sneer, I see a mouthful of crooked yellow teeth.

Clyst strides to the throne. He falls to his knee in front of the king. "Uncle," he greets him.

Axion does the same, except his greeting is, "Father."

This is just getting better and better. The room has fallen silent around us, leaving the king to rise to his feet dramatically. He is a tall man, just as thin and angular in his body as his face. He wears the standard black cloaks of the dragone. No fluff or finery.

Brue has snuck to my side. "Your father is the king."
I whisper.

He grins. "Yes."

"And Clyst is your cousin." I frown at the dragone in
question.

"Yes."

"I don't like Clyst," I state, speaking my thought
aloud. My mouth sometimes has a mind of its own.

"No one does," Brue replies. I can hear the smile in
his voice.

"I wanted to kill him," I clarify.

"Everyone does," Brue answers, without any fear.

The king stalks toward me then. His pace is menacing
and for the first time I feel a semblance of dread. His eyes
blaze with something more than anger – it's hate, pure
hatred, and it's aimed at me.

"You need to bow," Brue whispers.

"He's not my king," I snap back.

I won't bow to him. I wouldn't even bow to Victus. I
know this king is going to kill me at any moment. I can
feel it emanating from him. I can smell it on him. What
good would a bow be, except to make me look weak?

My mother appears from nowhere then, blissfully
unaware of the predator poised to attack. As she crosses
his path, he swipes her aside with a flick of his arm. I
watch wide eyed as he sends her sprawling across the
rough brick floor.

"Mum!" I rush forward automatically but he blocks
me, grabbing my throat inside of his iron grip and
squeezing. My feet leave the floor as he chokes me.

My eyes are on my mother as the world begins to
dim and the black spots appear. My lungs start crying for
oxygen. The burning in my leg disappears under the fire

in my gullet. Adrenalin is flooding my system, making me feel lightheaded, but I don't have time to think.

"No!" Brue yells.

He tackles his father and I can breathe again. I gasp with difficulty as Brue pushes the king away. My breath finally comes in raspy pants as my vision whirls, but my eyes are on Brue now. He doesn't get far. Brue is small, the king is not. It was the single minded ferocity in the king's attack that prevented him anticipating Brue's outburst. The king stalks forward again, Brue pulling on his leg like a police canine on a deranged criminal. The king's step doesn't falter.

"Father." Axion's slightly shrill voice cuts in. "We should question her first."

The king's step doesn't falter.

I don't give him time to attack again. The adrenalin has infused into my muscles. My fight or flight response has cut in, and I can't fly in here. I kick out, turning my body and planting my foot into his chest so hard that he sails backward, leaving a shocked Brue sitting on the floor at my feet. My whole leg catches fire, the agony of the arrow crippling me. I can't put the leg back down. I stand teetering on one foot as the king furiously climbs back to his feet. Brue jumps up like lightening, standing in front of me to face his father.

"Dad, don't." His voice is much stronger than Axion's was.

The king dispatches of Brue in the same way he did my mother, and as I watch my new little companion drop to the floor with a thud, the red returns.

I knew I tortured myself with training for a reason. I use my injured leg to kick the king again, my foot connects with his face. It hurts but I don't stop to watch this time. I follow up with my fists, pummelling them into his chest. I put everything I have into it. All the anger I can muster. I let myself feel for the first time since I woke up. Feel the hurt and pain of Liam's betrayal. Feel the grief of loss. Feel the emotions that have plagued me for the last few months. Anger, pain, loss, hurt, grief, love and, now, sorrow. The king falls to the floor and I go with him, straddling his chest while my fists move to his face. I land a faultless punch to his mouth, splitting his lip and extracting a fetid decaying tooth.

It doesn't last long. Huge hands grab me from behind and lift me off. I squirm in their grip, hopping backward when the dragone sets my feet on the floor and pulls me away. I try to thrash but my energy has been depleted on the now bleeding king. It's nice to know I can make them spill red without my dagger.

"That was very stupid," the brute sneers into my ear. It's Clyst, of course, and suddenly I don't feel so tired. I slam my head back into his face. Pain blasts through my brain but he lets go of my arms, cussing as he grabs his gushing nose. I pivot and bring my foot up into his groin again. Hopefully I have prevented the risk of any future little Clysts. He drops to the floor with a groan.

I'm about to draw my dagger and finish him when Brue calls my name. He's back up, holding his already injured arm protectively. I give Clyst another sharp kick to the ribs before hopping in Brue's direction. I would have done it then, I would have killed him. Maybe my soul is as black as theirs.

I reach Brue quickly. "Are you okay, kid?" I grab him in a hug.

"Don't call me kid," he groans.

My mother joins us, unsteadily, and we survey the carnage. Clyst is rolling on the floor, with his hands clamped between his legs. The king is back on his feet and in a rage. The rest of the dragone watch in shock and maybe fear. None of them have moved to defend their sovereign.

"You've made him mad," Brue whispers.

"You started it," I grin. I feel high on adrenalin and endorphins. I'm hyped up.

The king licks blood from his lip as he walks toward me again. He glances at Brue, who squares his shoulders in response. My mother starts sobbing. She appears unharmed, apart from a scrape on her forehead.

I'm focused on the king. I can see the hate in his eyes, but there's also a new flash of reason. He observes me, almost speculatively as he approaches, sucking his lip like his blood was wine. The lines of his face are hard, but his brow is crinkled in thought. He's regained control of himself.

I stand and wait. I don't think I could kick him again. My leg's gone past agony, it's numb.

The king doesn't stop ahead of me. He circles like a predator, walking around our small group with his eyes planted solely on me. I can still feel it when he is behind me. I focus on not flinching while I listen intently for the sound of metal, in case he decides to put a sword in my back. He doesn't. He completes his circle and steps closer, his eyes dropping to the steel shaft in my leg.

I continue to watch as he reaches down and pulls the arrow from my thigh. The pain is excruciating and a scream rips from my lips reflexively. My whole leg remains numb, except for the red hot poker scorching one spot, burning to the bone. My hand goes to the wound instinctively, stemming the trickle of blood as the king inspects his prize. I cringe in case he decides to lick that, too.

"Speared by one of your own," he sneers. It's the first time I've heard his voice. He has a low raspy tone, the voice of someone who smokes and drinks too much. I can't focus. I'm trying to concentrate but the pain in my leg is frying every synapse in my brain.

I see him look at the arrow, study it. The blood is seeping through my fingers. Not enough to kill me but enough to make me feel woozy. There are drips splashing to the floor. I watch them as my head dips.

"Dad?" Brue's voice cuts into my consciousness.

I pull my head up, with a lot of effort, at Brue's tone. The king is pale. His hands are shaking so violently that the arrow drops from his grasp and clatters to the floor. I watch it in astonishment. My blood is still crowning its head as it bounces twice before reverberating to a stop. The king doesn't attempt to retrieve it. I can't bend down but I want it. I need it. The king's reaction is so disturbing that it must have importance.

"Brue," I whisper, looking at the arrow when he glances. He's smart. He grabs it quickly, stowing it in my thigh sheath with my dagger. The king doesn't notice.

"Take her to the west top," he commands while fisting his shaking hands and inhaling a large breath.

Axion is the only one who moves, although he keeps his distance from me. I smirk.

"Now!" the king bellows and even I flinch.

Axion draws his sword and points it in my direction, his hands trembling. Is witnessing one fight really that drastic? I've already killed one of their own at his feet. He carried me happily after that.

"I can't walk," I shrug. Axion looks lost. His eyes are flicking between me and his increasingly agitated father. Maybe I should just take what I can get. It looks like my execution has been stayed, the west top sounds better than a shallow grave. "Fine, I'll hop."

Brue's unexpectedly under my arm, supporting some of my weight. I look at him, stunned, and he flashes his impish grin. I give him a quick squeeze with my arm as thanks.

My mother follows us like a forlorn puppy as we beat a hasty retreat.

I can't hop. As soon as we're out of the throne room Axion lifts me into his arms.

"What are you doing?" I ask, bewildered.

"Helping."

I stare at his jawline again. It's something I'm becoming very familiar with.

"I don't understand," I finally murmur. I really can't assemble the last few hours into any conceivable order in my head.

Yesterday my life was so different. I've tried not to think of it, tried not to think of him, but it's too late. The fury at the king has diminished, and now I realise Liam *actually* shot me with an arrow. Liam betrayed me... but I love him with every fibre of my being, every beat of my heart. I love him so fiercely I would die for him. Every one of our memories together is engraved on my soul. Every kiss. Our first kiss when he took me by surprise in our classroom, our last kiss, in my room, after forging my now bloodied dagger. He engraved my blade with such care. Liam gave me my sigil, an inverted triangle with water in the centre, to meld with his and make a star.

His sigil, a triangle surrounded by flames, the same sigil that's on the arrow.

I can't control it. The flood gates open. Axion's eyes widen as I break in front of him. My heart fractures in two. Liam was half of me, without him I'm crippled, trapped in an existence of eternal night. I can't speak. I can't think. I'm not even making a sound. But my eyes release a tsunami and I can feel my face constricting, morphing into a physical impression of the pain I feel. I close my eyes to the world, but unconsciousness doesn't save me this time. My mind is too broken to power off. It's like a haunted television set, staying on regardless of a lack of electricity. I can hear everything. Feel everything. It's too much. I'm overwhelmed.

I feel the rush of gravity as Axion's arms release me. My eyes stay closed; I don't attempt to open them. This bed is harder than the last, if it is a bed and not a rug on the floor. The room smells different, more oppressive somehow, like stale cumin and ginger.

Someone touches my leg and I whimper involuntarily. Hushed voices murmur familiar words, I tune them out. Footsteps, followed by banging, and then the sound of running water; I almost open my eyes. There must be a bathroom nearby.

Cold, something cold and wet on my lips. I drink automatically, gulp in fact, ignoring Axion's admonishing.

Dizziness makes my brain wobble, like I'm sliding out of my own body. Someone's touching my leg again. I can feel my brow sweating. My leg is lifted and I clamp my eyes closed with the fresh agony. The sensations against my skin get fainter but the noises intensify, like the sounds are originating inside my ears. I let out a groan.

Quiet footsteps, the click of a lock, and then nothing...

The silence is worse.

My body is numb, paralysed and heavy. Trapped inside my delirious mind I'm forced to relive it all, over and over again I remember. Remember the clearing, where the dragone captured me, where Liam betrayed me. Remember the soulless eyes of the man I slaughtered. Remember the hate on the king's face – immediate hate. Because I killed one of his men? Because I'm half angeli? Does it even matter why?

And the arrow? His reaction to that was dramatic. Why, I wonder. Because of the sigil perhaps, I had the same reaction, though I don't find the thought amusing. What does Liam's name mean to him... and the symbols on the door, strange swirls and foreign text... their language.

I open my eyes. The room is dark. I must have slept. I don't know how long it's been. My eyes take a second to focus. I'm alone. The room is silent except for my own laboured breathing. I sit up, slowly. My whole body feels heavy, my leg especially. The wound has been bandaged; white gauze sticks out beneath tightly-wound linen. It's crude but effective. This room is smaller than the last, though more elegantly decorated, and there's glass in the window.

I stagger from the bed. Not sure what I'm planning to do. A tray of food sits on a small table, it looks like meat. I ignore it. A small bathroom, at the back of the room, has a toilet and sink but no shower. I satisfy myself by shoving my head under the faucet, letting the water soak my face and hair, swallowing mouthfuls. My leg feels stiffer as I shuffle to the door. It's a heavy wood affair with thick iron hinges and an antique lock – the key is on the other side. I rattle the handle anyway, just in case. The window also has iron bars. I inspect it next, looking for weaknesses. It appears solid. The view distracts me. The black and white panorama is breathtaking. Gentle waves lap the shore in the distance. Birds glide across the open expanse of sky. Treetops sway with the tropical breeze. I'm above most of them. This really is the top tower.

I refuse to move. I stand by the window, staring at the ocean, ignoring the ache in my thigh.

The night passes slowly. I do nothing, except concentrate on forgetting. Forgetting what brought me here, to this point. If I let the hurt win, I'll never escape this place. I won't want to. No, I need to focus on my reasons to continue: my mother, who's here somewhere, my brother, August, who's in Celthia with Aaron. They are my reasons for continuing. I'll deal with the rest if I manage to return to them. God I hope Aaron's safe there without me, safe from Victus and Liam. I hope Lucas would protect him. Lucas is my best angeli friend, he helped save Aaron. He helped me cope. He's a good man but he's not in charge. I need to get back for Aaron. I need to work on a plan.

The sun rises slowly over the island, it reaches my tower long after is has kissed the sparkling powder-sand of the shoreline. The sun brings warmth, and colour. It brings the new day.

I twirl the arrow through my fingers as I lay on the bed, devising my next move. I need to get out of this room and find my mother, and then I need to fly. It sounds simple enough. This arrow... this arrow is important. I can feel it. My heart is still divided, torn in two. It's definitely Liam's sigil. He held a bow. I can't figure out how he managed it. He was above me. The arrow hit me in the thigh. He shot me. None of this is making any sense.

I hear the footsteps before the scent wafts under the door. Light footsteps belonging to a child.

"Hi, Brue." I grin as I lay on my back, looking up at the ceiling.

He stops on the other side of the door, but doesn't open it. "How did you know it was me?" he groans in his sweet voice.

"You smell like mint and lemongrass, and you're still dragging your leg slightly," I answer. "How are you?"

"Fine," he grumbles. "I brought you breakfast."

"Really? What is it?" I wonder if his father knows he's feeding me.

"Bacon," Brue answers happily.

Okay, he's not feeding me; he's trying to poison me. "I can't eat meat Brue, but thank you."

"Oh, why not?" He sounds annoyed.

"I inherited my father's stomach." Not that I'm sure Marcus is my father.

"So what do angels eat?" Brue asks inquisitively, he didn't even sneer at the word *angels*.

"Fruit, vegetables, insects, flowers sometimes," I shrug. "Nothing mammal or bird based."

"No milk or eggs!" Brue exclaims. "No steak?"

I laugh at his tone, he sounds like Aaron the first time I told him I was a vegetarian. "No, nothing like that."

"That's so weird," he mumbles. "I'll bring you grapes later. I gotta go."

"See you later, Brue," I shout at his retreating footsteps.

Looks like I may get out of this room after all, perhaps I should have accepted the bacon.

I stay on my back, my eyelids getting heavy as my night at the window catches up on me. I know when I'm asleep because I'm back in the clearing. The thick trunks of Grey's Wood circle me. The sky is getting light over our heads. Axion and Clyst stand in front of me. The cage is there, and my mother is in it. But there's no one else. No angeli in the sky or dragone in the trees. I hear the arrow, but this time I don't move. I'm frozen as it pierces my mother's chest. She screams an agonised howl.

I wake screaming.

# · Three ·

Brue has left grapes on the tray. The questionable meat-based product from yesterday has vanished. I slept through my first escape plan.

The grapes are sweet and juicy. I watch the island from the window as I eat. The black heads of the dragone bob around below me as they go about their business. Children run and laugh after a herd of goats in one of the farthest courtyards. There are a lot of people, but not as many as I imagined there would be. Is this the only dragone island? If it is, their numbers are far less than that of the angeli's. None of this is making any sense.

The grapes are long gone by the time I hear the light footsteps again. And so is part of my sanity. The same questions plague me. Most of them start with, why.

"Hey, Brue," I smile.

"But I was extra quiet," Brue whines.

I shrug and make my way to the door. "Keep trying, kid."

"Don't call me kid," he snaps. I can't see him through the keyhole. The key is still stuck in the other side. I need to get him to open the door somehow.

I slouch against the wood. "Thanks for the grapes, Brue."

"S'okay."

"Have you seen my mum?" I ask. I need to know where she is. I won't have much time once I break free.

"She's on the beach," he answers.

"Stoned?" I don't mean the beach.

He giggles.

"Does that stuff leave any permanent damage?" I enquire casually. I probably should be more upset for my mother, but I'm slightly envious – she's had the longest vacation of her life.

"Don't know," he answers uncertainly.

"That's great." I shake my head before sighing. "Why am I still here, Brue?" Still trapped, still alive, still not putting up more resistance...

"Dad's freaking out about something. I think he's forgotten about you for now," he answers.

Forgotten about me? "Well that sucks."

He leaves a few beats of silence. "It means you're still alive."

My eyes roll. "And still trapped in a tower," I add with a groan.

"Yeah," he agrees.

I let myself slide down the door until I'm sitting against it. "Is this the only island, Brue?"

He hesitates. "Why?"

"There aren't many of you," I state.

"There used to be more."

"I've heard that somewhere before." That's what the angeli said. There used to be more but the dragone are wiping them out. I believed it easily enough after my first run in with them. But this island? The dragone I've seen through the windows are families, workers and children.

"How did your mum meet your dad?" Brue asks suddenly.

"Why?" Now it's my turn to be cautious.

"I'm trying to figure it out. How it happened. How you're alive."

I laugh. "Give it up Brue, even I can't figure that out."

He's persistent. "Do you know? Have they told you?"

I know a lot, but not everything. "I've never met my father, Brue." My answer is honest, whilst still omitting some major facts.

"Really?" He sounds dubious.

Brue is clever, but this isn't a lie. "Really. He was taken by your people before I found out what I was." I don't sound bothered – I'm not.

Brue almost growls. "We haven't taken anyone, Aqua."

He sounds sure. I don't hide the scorn in my voice. "That's funny. There are two people on this island that shouldn't be."

He doesn't answer immediately. "Okay, we've only taken you."

"And my mother," I add. I know they took her, I saw them do it.

"She's a guest," he declares. He doesn't sound bothered by my tone.

"Whatever, Brue," I reply sarcastically.

"I'm not lying, Aqua. We avoid the angels, we don't take them. You don't know anything," he answers angrily.

An impulsive plan forms in my head. "I know more than you."

"No you don't," he snaps petulantly, like the child he is. Maybe this is wrong, manipulation of a youngling... or whatever the dragone call their offspring.

Too late to worry, I need to get out of here. I match his tone. "Prove it."

"I know what my dad's freaking out about," he states confidently.

Even I know that. "The arrow," I state. I need more information.

"Yeah," he mumbles.

"Why?" I push further, playing on his competitive nature.

Brue doesn't notice. "He said something about someone called Rennison, that he's still alive. Then he kicked me out of the room and started shouting at Axion."

"Did you hear anything?" I ask eagerly. Too eagerly, Brue notices.

He attempts to shut down the conversation. "No, we can't hear through walls, Aqua."

"You can hear me now," I grin.

I hear the smile in his voice. "Okay, I heard some stuff but I can't tell you. It's a secret."

"I've got secrets too," I offer. This could work.

"Like what?" he asks.

I keep my voice even. "What's a secret worth to you, Brue?"

He startles for a second. "What do you mean?"

I can tell he's interested, and trying to hide it. "I mean a trade, one of my secrets for one of yours." I hold my breath for an eternity as he considers it.

"Um, I'll think about it. I gotta go," he mutters hastily as his feet clatter off. Damn, I almost had him, and he realised it.

"Bye, Brue," I sigh, too late for him to hear.

The sky is turning dark again when I finally give in and flop on the bed. My leg is throbbing. I can still feel it when my subconscious drifts me away, away to a dark place. I'm back in the clearing. The sky is getting light over our heads. Axion and Clyst stand in front of me. The cage is there, and my mother is in it. Angeli fill the skies. I hear the arrow, but I don't move. I'm frozen as it pierces my mother's chest. She screams an agonised howl. I look up. Liam is smiling. Liam...

I wake sweaty and alert. My breath is ragged, my pulse deafening. How dare my subconscious throw that at me? It wasn't even accurate. I'm sure it wasn't. I've been replaying the moment over and over, and Liam wasn't smiling. His face was as emotionless as marble.

The sky is still dark, the inhabitants of the island silent. The sounds of the waves on the shore are audible if I concentrate on them. The gently swelling whoosh is soothing. My body moulds to the sound, my breathing syncs with the rhythm, my heart slows until it beats in time. I force the image of Liam from my mind. My Liam. His arrow. That is the key, I know it. The key to all of this, maybe to everything. Who is Rennison? Why is the king of the dragone freaking out about it?

I pull the arrow from my sheath and stare at it again. I don't know why. I've stared at it for hours already and gleaned no new information. It makes no sense. It's just a steel arrow with Liam's sigil and fletching feathers the same colour as his, except they're not his. I don't know how I know, I just do. They're someone else's.

The waves are comforting. With my body resting, my eyes close slowly.

I'm back in the clearing. I sigh as I realise I'm dreaming again. A small part of me curses my subconscious. My eyes roam the familiar scene. The thick trunks of Grey's wood circle me. The sky is getting light over our heads. Axion and Clyst stand in front of me. The cage is there, and my mother is in it. Angeli fill the skies. I look up expectantly, Liam is expressionless.

That's more like it.

I hear the arrow. I run toward my mother as it pierces her chest. She screams an agonised howl. No, this is wrong, she's not hurt. I made it. The arrow hit me.

I wake shaking, my mother's piercing howl still resonating in my ears. I'm still on the bed. The arrow has fallen onto the sheets beside me. I grab at it, searching out the sigil with my eyes.

This is ridiculous, night after night, wallowing in my own personal *Groundhog Day*.

I can't put up with this any longer.

I need to see the king.

I bang on the door repeatedly but no one answers. So I go to the window. There are dragone in the courtyards below. Shouting does no good either. The glass is too thick and I'm too far up. I can see my mother, her ochre hair sets her apart from the natural inhabitants of the island. That, and she's the only person wearing a cerise one-piece. She's in the large courtyard, the one with the fountain, drinking from a hollowed out coconut by the look of it. At least she's happy, I suppose.

I wander back to the door and sit, leaning against the wood and twirling the steel arrow. I wait.

I hear footsteps before I smell the waft of chilli and pepper. It's not my little companion come to check on me this time. I re-sheath the steel shaft at my thigh. Axion paces the space on the other side of the door. I listen without speaking, debating what I'm going to say. The pacing stops for a second, I hear him snatch the key from the lock. If he's meant to be covertly checking on me, he's not doing a very good job. He sighs and reinserts the key, and then I'm on my back. The tiled floor of the landing greets my occipital bone with an unfriendly smack.

"Ow..." I groan. The dragone are quick, I didn't register the key turning until it was too late to stop myself falling. I didn't expect him to turn the damn key.

"What were you doing against the door?" Axion accuses me harshly.

I blink away my surprise and start devising strategies. I climb to my feet slowly, glancing around the landing in the process: one window, unbarred, one descending staircase. Axion eyes me warily but makes no move for his weapon.

"Waiting," I shrug as an answer, keeping my voice calm. "Not much else to do in there." My eyes flick to the window again as I wonder how thick the glazing is. I've escaped through glass before.

"Brue won't be coming back," he says loudly.

I tear my gaze from the window. "What? Why?" He'd better not be hurt.

Axion is standing between me and the staircase. "King's orders," he frowns.

I watch him intently. "You thought he'd let me go," I surmise from his expression. "That's why you opened the door, to check I was still here."

His eyes narrow to slits as he assesses me.

I grin. This is better than I'd hoped. Now they can't blame Brue for my escape. "Well here I am. Now what?" I tease him, already preparing myself for a fight.

His eyes widen at my expression and his throat bobs with a small swallow. "Go back in," he orders.

I laugh. "No way."

"Then I'll make you," he says, unconvincingly. Still, he draws his sword.

I pull the dagger from its place on my thigh and bounce on my toes. "Think you can? Try it, see what happens." I goad him brazenly, though I haven't seen Axion fight. The Guard are excellent at posturing, I've been taught by the two best Guard in Celthia.

I watch his reactions. Axion frowns. "I'm stronger than you."

We start circling, like crows around a carcass. I keep him moving, keep his eyes on me as I watch our positions. "I wouldn't count on it." I grin.

"I'm faster," he snaps.

I laugh. "Wouldn't count on that either."

Before he can move I attack, startling him with a series of sharp jousts and jabs, which he barely counters. I have to get close, my blade is much shorter that his. He finally gets his footing, coming back at me with a series of strong blows. I nimbly avoid them all. He's fast, but I'm faster.

"Not like the rest of them are you," he grunts.

"You're quick," I answer mockingly while twirling to avoid another slice of his blade.

"So are you," he answers in the same tone. He's strong, I'll give him that. But his attack is unregimented, barely even instinctual. He's not listening to his own body, or watching mine. He's like I was a few months ago. I could kill him. I could stab him at any time, but I don't want to, luckily for him.

"Are we going to do this all day?" I snigger.

He frowns at me but keeps up his easily blocked assault. "You could give in," he suggests.

I answer as I jump a strike he aimed at my ankles, "Not in my DNA."

"What is in your DNA?" he asks breathlessly. Still, it was too curiously to be a random question.

I sidestep, turning us further and laugh as I nimbly avoid another poorly disguised attack. "What's in yours?" I reply.

"None of your business," he snaps, taking another swipe at me.

I dodge it easily. "Ditto."

I don't give him a chance to answer. I've spun him to the window during our little dual. I turn and run down the stairs like lightening, leaving him stunned behind me. His footsteps start up when I'm almost down the first flight.

I know where my mother is, or was. I can follow her scent if I find it. Then I'm out of here. Never mind about talking to the king... I'll interrogate Liam.

The tower is tall, six flights of dizzying staircases with Axion hot on my heels. My leg throbs as the wound re-opens and fresh blood seeps through the bandaging. It's slowing me down. I burst through the door at the bottom into a narrow hallway. I turn right on instinct. The breeze is coming from that direction and a breeze means an exit. The next door leads into a larger room, and on the other side of the room is an open patio-style folding screen. In the room however, are the shocked faces of the king and Brue.

I don't give myself time to process it. I run for the exit. I hear the king yell, and Brue shout my name. I ignore them both, vaulting over a chair and hobbling into the courtyard. It's not the big one my mother was in. I unfurl my wings and jump, and then scream when something heavy lands on my ankle. I'm already ascending, quickly. The voice from my foot is young but commanding.

"Aqua, you have to go back."

"I am going back, Brue."

"No, back down," he shouts.

"No."

"Then I'll let go," he warns.

"Let go then," I snap. We're high now, higher than the tower. I circle, looking at the island and for my mother.

"Fine," he shouts, and he lets go.

"Damn it, Brue!" I dive instinctively.

He's pulling an Oberon on me. At least when I had to pluck my falling friend out of the sky in Celthia, he had the excuse of unconsciousness. Brue's just being his shrewd self. The trust he puts in me is ludicrous.

I grab him easily, still a few metres from the ground, and secure my hands around his small waist. "You're crazy, kid," I grumble.

He just smiles. "I knew you'd save me."

"Like I said, you're crazy."

I swing my little hitchhiker up onto my back. Brue is small enough to fit below my wings. I wouldn't be able to do this otherwise. His legs clamp tightly around my stomach as he sits on my lumbar spine.

"Don't let go," I bark. He gasps, in shock I think. If he thought I'd just land again, he's mistaken. His hands dig into my shoulders as I circle the island, following the coast.

Hantiem really is beautiful. The island is not as vast as I first thought. The whole coast is lined with grass huts. There is a small port on the opposite side. The centre is hidden under the foliage of large trees. The landscape here is both alien and familiar. The green reminds me of England, but the trees are different. The palms and bamboos I recognise, others are completely new to me. I start to lose myself as I explore. There are lots of dragone below me, shouting and pointing but I don't care. It feels great to be free again.

I take us over the ocean. I'd love to dive beneath the water but it's impossible with my little limpet. Instead, I dip down and let my toes break the surface. Brue relaxes slightly as I frolic above the waves. I even hear a small giggle. It makes me smile.

How easily I put my plans on hold to enjoy this. How stupid I am to have just left my mother and flown off? What are the chances of her still being out in the open when I go back? One move from this little dragone and I'm swayed. One shrewd move and my tactics disintegrate. I like Brue, and I like it here, despite why I'm here.

Perhaps I'm just naturally adaptable? In England I was human, driving and working and moaning about my life. In Celthia, I was angeli, training and flying and falling in love. Here, I feel my dark side creeping in. I feel comfortable, when perhaps I should be afraid. I feel like I'm nearly home.

I follow the fins of a dolphin pod for a while, wishing I was in the water with them. Dragone line the beaches, watching us. I ignore them, none are armed.

"Have you considered my proposal, Brue?" I ask as we circle around to the port.

He's relaxed now, his hands stroking my feathers as we glide. "Secrets for secrets?" he asks.

I nod. "Exactly."

His hands disappear altogether. I glance over my shoulder to check he's okay. He's emanating *Kate Winslet* on the bow of the Titanic, arms out like he's flying... I guess he is. It makes me laugh.

"How do I know you've got anything worth telling," he asks eventually.

"Ditto, kid."

"Don't call me kid," he yells.

I don't apologise. He is a kid. "I have one that I think would interest you. It's about my family," I offer.

He thinks for a minute as we fly over the port. I circle once. No large ships, only a few wooden rowboats. "Okay," he finally agrees. "I have one about my family too."

I continue around the coast, his hands secure themselves back on my shoulders. "You go first," I say.

"Ha ha, I'm not stupid, Aqua." His voice is far too condescending for a young boy, though I'd have to agree with his statement.

"I know that, Brue. It's one of the reasons I like you so much."

He stutters before snapping at me, "Just tell me."

I choose one of my tamest facts. It's not really even a secret, but Brue doesn't know that. "I'm not half human. My mum adopted me."

"So you're a full angel?" he asks sceptically.

I glance at him again. He's frowning like he doesn't believe me. "I didn't say that, kid." I grin. "Now it's your turn."

He shrugs. "Axion's like you."

I have to look away, were coming back around the bottom of the island, over the train tracks. "Pardon?" I ask, my brain suddenly racing.

"He's got wings, he can fly." I can hear the smile in Brue's voice. He knows he's shocked me.

I'm already trying to fit it in to the puzzle in my mind. "Wow. How?"

"Don't know," Brue answers. "Dad thinks it's a sign. It's why he put him in charge."

Oh, that explains that then. Axion is not made to be in charge. "You'd be better than Axion," I laugh.

He exhales harshly. "I know."

"So he's got feathers?" I ask, trying to picture Axion with wings. I guess that's why he never removes his cloak around me.

"No, they're freaky, like dragon wings," Brue replies.

"That's weird."

"I know."

Then a thought occurs to me. "So he could chase us if I try to kidnap you?"

"Would you?" Brue asks, but he's not concerned.

"There's nothing I wouldn't do, Brue," I answer firmly.

"I don't believe you," he responds simply.

I frown. "Shrewd."

My inventory of the island is complete, my mother has vanished. I land lightly in front of Axion and the king. I can't waste an opportunity like this. I want to talk to him. I've always been impulsive; maybe I'm finally getting myself back. They haven't moved while we've been gone. I'm really not sure if they are incredibly stupid or unbelievably clever, though I'm leaning toward the first one.

Brue jumps down quickly, laughing at his family.

"Did you like that?" I ask him with a smile.

"That was amazing, you're so cool," he grins.

"I am cool." I turn my gaze to the king. "We need to talk." I'm not scared of him out here, in the open.

He juts out his chin. "I'm not interested. Take her back to the tower," he commands.

My eyebrows shoot up automatically. "Who are you talking to, your Majesty?" Like, really. Brue is still laughing and Axion looks like he might pass out. The rest of the dragone have scattered.

"Axion," he commands, glaring at his eldest son.

Axion doesn't move.

I seize the chance. "We need to talk about this," I state as I pull the arrow from my sheath. "Who is Rennison?"

The king's face turns furious. "How dare you!"

I shrug. "Easily. I know this sigil, and it doesn't belong to someone called Rennison. So who is he?"

The king's skin turns red as he stares at me. He spits, "That is none of your business, angel." His hands rise like he may attempt to throttle me again. I don't back down.

I stare, unblinking and impassive. "I'm not what you think I am."

"You're my prisoner," he bellows. "You're exactly what I think you are."

"I've had enough of sitting in the tower," I growl. "There's something going on and this is the key." I wave the arrow ferociously, like a sparkler about to burn my fingers.

"So?" He can barely speak a word around his fury. He keeps glaring at Axion, obviously too arrogant to do his own dirty work. Axion is avoiding eye contact – with anyone.

"What is the meaning of this sigil," I continue, my voice intensifying.

He snarls. "It means less than even you, and you are nothing!" But I can see something there, in his eyes... knowledge.

We stand, facing each other, both radiating anger. I clench my teeth and ball my fists, ready to beat it out of him.

"You're just like her," he mutters under his breath.

"Rennison?" I frown. I'd assumed Rennison was a man...

"No," he shouts. "My queen."

That brings me up short. I have no idea what he's talking about. "Pardon?"

He stares at me suspiciously. "You are her double." He barks the words, though his voice has softened slightly. "You have her stubbornness, her aggression and her face. Who are you?" His eyes penetrate mine, looking for an answer. I haven't got one.

"What are you talking about?" I snap.

He growls again, "Axion's mother, my first wife, the true queen. You are her double. I want to know why."

"What has that got to do with this?" I shout, pointing the sharp end of steel toward him. Axion bristles slightly at the gesture. I ignore him.

The king watches me intently. His voice has lowered in volume, but is still harsh. "The night she left," he points at the arrow in my hand, "that mark was carved into the wood of her headboard." His hands shake, with the indignation of answering my question, I assume.

"Why would she do that?"

"She wouldn't!" he yells, his voice as fiery as the pits of Hell. "Dragone do not brand the world with their spurious ordainments, sigils and slander."

"Umm..." He's managed to evaporate the next words from my mouth as I try to understand his meaning. He's talking in tongues.

"The queen was taken," Axion whispers in a breath, only slightly louder than a thought.

My eyes cut to him, standing statue-like beside his arrogant and, frankly, completely stupid father. "Who would take her?" I ask him, scowling.

The king turns red with anger. Boiling with rage, he fixes his demonic yellow eyes on me, like a bull at a matador's flag.

"Axion will take me back to the tower," I state, already backing away from the shaking figure in front of me. I'll get no more information now. His eyes are burning, his pulse is louder in my ears than my own. His muscles have expanded like overfilled balloons. He looks... crazed.

"I will?" Axion gasps, apparently too stunned to notice the rapidly altered posture of his father.

"Yes," I snap as I grab the brainless fool and pull him away. "Brue, find my mother and bring her to us. I need to talk to her, you understand?"

Of course he understands. He's Brue. He nods and runs off.

"Meet on the beach," I yell after him.

# · Four ·

"The beach?" Axion exclaims. "That's not a good idea."

"You want Brue to coerce my drugged mother up six flights of stairs to the prison I just escaped from?" I roll my eyes and march ahead. "Not going to happen." I follow the scent of the ocean.

"Where are you going?" he smirks.

"The beach," I snap, infuriated. I stomp into the first doorway that blocks my path, following the hallway to another open door. The room is small, with no other exit. I spin and veer right along a different passage. Axion follows obediently, a smirk on his face. I ignore him as I stride through another door, into a family living room. A woman yells and grabs for her children as I freeze. Axion pulls me backward, apologising, and slams the door behind us.

"Fine," I concede, "you lead the way."

He hides a laugh under a cough as we spin and head back in the opposite direction. "You sure you need my help?" he asks, his amusement dancing under the surface of his voice.

"Aren't you hot in your cloak?" I snap, ignoring his question.

He doesn't speak again. I follow him through a series of buildings. We emerge from a small door onto a stone path. The sea air hits me immediately, although the expanse of water is still hidden behind a wall of greenery. I speed up, almost running, as I follow the path. Axion's boots clatter behind me.

As the trees thin and vanish, my pace slows. The vegetation disappears to nothing. My feet leave the stone path and sink into the soft white dust. I've seen the beach already: from the cage, the window, the air, but to stand on it is something else. The ocean is the only thing on the horizon – an eternity of water – infinite glistening liquid, the shallows as clear as glass. I walk toward it blindly, my instincts overriding my system.

"Whoa…" Axion grabs me. "No you don't."

"I want to swim," I whisper, almost dazed by my need.

"Swim?" he stutters, confused. "Do angels swim?"

My gaze flicks to his then and an inexplicable smile tugs at my lips. "I'm no angel." I smirk and start walking backward, away from the dragone and toward the water.

"Just stop," he shouts, grabbing my arms. "You know the king's going to kill you, right? And kill me too, for bringing you here."

"Why did you bring me here?" I ask, my vision dimming around the edges as I scowl at him.

"You told Brue to meet us here," he replies, exasperated.

"No. Why did you bring me *here*?"

He sighs and flops onto the sand, taking me by surprise. I'm pulled down with him and land heavily on my knees. I shoot him an angry glower, but neither of us makes a move to get up.

"Because I was ordered to," he murmurs, "by the king."

"Because Daddy told you to," I mock. "Why?"

He looks at me, assessing, and answers hesitantly, "To stop the others getting to you first."

"Who? The angeli? They already had me." He must have known that, I was with angeli when they kidnapped my mother. Liam fought them, defended me.

"No," he sighs, "not the angeli. The other dragone. Rennison's army."

"Who is Rennison?" I repeat, desperately seeking an answer to the question. I don't know why it feels so vital, so incessant that I need to know.

Axion snarls angrily, his brow creasing and his eyes hardening. "He's an animal, sadistic, evil. He's a thief and a killer. He takes and he takes until nothing is left and he has everything. Everything."

"You've met him." It's not a question. I pull the arrow out and run the pad of my index finger over the sharp lines of the etched mark. "What does he have to do with this?"

He glances at the sigil before looking away. "Everything," he answers. "He has everything to do with that."

"Can't you give me a straight answer?" I'm still failing to see any connection between Liam and the disappearance of the dragone queen.

"They said he was dead," he confesses, like it's a crime to even discuss it. "Rennison Jarik." He glances again at the sigil, like he's reading the name right off of the steel. It makes me shiver. "The sigil is his."

It's his? How...? "Why would Rennison Jarik have a sigil?" I whisper, my voice barely audible. *And why would Liam have recreated it?*

Axion laughs scornfully. "Because Rennison Jarik is an abomination, a curse, spawned from the seed of my great-uncle and his angel whore." He shivers with anxious relief as he voices the words, digging the heels of his boots into the sand. His speech sounds old, rehearsed somehow, like a lyric that plays around in his mind more often than it should.

"He's a crossbreed?" I ask hesitantly.

He frowns. "You don't look surprised."

"Nothing much surprises me anymore." My lips quirk up into a slight half-smile, which I consciously remove. "So Rennison has an army, huh? That sounds exciting."

He huffs in detest. "They call themselves *The Fallen*." He laughs humourlessly, digging his heels deeper into the powder-white grains. "Conceited irony," he mocks. "Rennison may have been raised as an angel, but he definitely isn't one."

"Like me." I smirk but I can't force any emotion behind my statement, my voice comes out flat. "I've killed," I whisper, finally ridding myself of the words that have been stewing below the surface. I'm still waiting for the repercussions of that event. I don't understand the look Axion and I exchanged after I did it. I don't understand why I'm still alive. "Who was he?"

He frowns. "Who was who?"

"The man," I shudder, "by the cage."

He shrugs. "He was a traitor. The world is a better place, trust me."

"Trust you?" I repeat his words, bewildered. Trust him? A dragone prince, instrumental in my capture and who's still trying to detain me. Is that what I'm doing right now? Conversing with him like BFFs? "Why should I trust you?" I enquire.

He smiles slightly, his eyes flicking down before seeking mine again. "Because I don't want to hurt you," he answers, somewhat honestly.

"Don't want to?" I echo.

"I can't," he sighs. "My dad's right. You look just like her. When I saw you walking through the trees I thought you were her." He whispers the last sentence like he's repenting his sins.

"That's why you didn't attack?"

He shrugs but doesn't answer. I take it as confirmation.

"But I'm not her," I sigh. "You know that now. So why am I still alive?"

He surprises me by laughing. "Do you actually want us to kill you?"

I snort a small laugh in response, maybe I'm losing my mind. "No, I guess not," I reply. "But I am curious."

"We're not murderers, Aquila, despite what you might think. You've done nothing wrong... yet. You killed Nicholai in self-defence, protecting an heir to the throne."

I look at him, stunned.

"Don't look so shocked," he grins. "You yelled at him for hurting Brue before you stabbed him. Nicholai wasn't a good man. He was a Fallen. He claimed to have switched sides; I never believed him."

"But I killed him!" I screech. And I'm not sure if knowing his name makes it better.

"And he deserved it!" he snaps back. "You're acting like you've never killed anyone before."

I gasp, "I haven't."

"What? You're wearing the clothes of the angel fighters." He studies me, looking for the lie on my face. There isn't one.

"I'm a new recruit," I shrug. "I've only trained with dummies and my... Liam." God, *my Liam*? How stupid do I sound? "Raised human, remember. In the house you took my mother from."

"My Liam?" Axion's eyebrows rise in question, an annoying smirk on his lips. I'm not sure he's as stupid as he appears to be.

I attempt to stare him down, chastising myself for being so dense, for sitting here discussing my life with him like he's some kind of pal. He doesn't buckle under my pressure. He waits patiently as I grow more frustrated. "Why do you care?" I scrutinise his face again, nothing there except curiosity. I sigh. Axion seems genuinely interested.

He shrugs, frowning at himself. "I don't know."

"Fine," I snap. "Liam is... was..." I stumble over my own tongue. "Liam is... He... It's complicated."

He schools his expression into sincerity. "Complicated," he agrees, patronising me with his tone.

"He's my brother," I state, ignoring the half-truth of my words. "He was the one aiming this at you." I roll the arrow between my fingers like a pen, staring at it like it might tell me how it ended up in my thigh and not the dragone's.

He scoffs, "Here, I thought the angel fighters never missed their target."

I am... I'm losing my mind. When did Axion and I become buddies? "Tell me why you kidnapped me and my mother," I demand, changing the subject.

He sits up straighter, blowing out a breath. "If I tell you what happened, will you believe me?"

"No," I answer impulsively.

He smirks and tells me anyway, "We didn't take your mother."

I gasp at his audacity, stopping him. I can't form any words. I'm too shocked and too angry.

"The Fallen took her," he adds.

I glare at him, waiting for the punch line.

He carries on without noticing. "We were following them. They were injured, half their number gone when we found them dragging a human toward a tunnel. We fought. We won. Nicholai turned traitor and came with us."

"Stop," I seethe. "I don't want to hear it. I was there. I saw her get taken."

His eyes widen at my proclamation. "You were there? Why did they take her when they were after you?"

I study his face for a long time before answering. "You knew they were after me?"

He clenches his teeth guiltily. "Not at the time." He surveys me questioningly. "You weren't there when we found the bodies." It sounds like an accusation.

I study his face. I can't understand why it looks so familiar; and despite my situation, I can't seem to hate him appropriately. In fact, I want to hear what he has to say. I want to stay sitting here, in the open, listening to him. And deep down, I even want to believe what he's saying. Though, for now, I'll just dig for as much information as I can and try and sift for lies later. I consider my response for a while. "Liam killed anyone who got close to me," I shrug. "Do you know why they want me?"

"Brother Liam who obviously isn't your brother?" he asks, ignoring my question and calling me out on my lie.

I chuckle humourlessly. "Yeah, him."

"He killed five of the Fallen... alone?" he asks sceptically.

"Yep," I confirm. The first time I realised Liam was a warrior was when he'd taken on the dragone at my house. I'd watched in awe until a groan from Aaron had pulled me out of my daze.

"What's he, some kind of superhero action man?" he asks mockingly.

"Pretty much," I answer dryly. Liam is Master of the Guard for a reason. Fierce, strong, sometimes horrible and mean, but no one can deny he's the best for the job. And he's also incredibly gentle when he wants to be...

"You miss him," Axion states.

"Every second," I answer reflexively, honestly. Though for a different reason than Axion probably suspects. Liam deserves my wrath, and it's the opportunity of gifting him it that I'm missing the most.

"You know, advertising your weakness to your enemies is not in any survival guide I've read," Axion jokes, adding a friendly shoulder bump as we sit watching the gentle surf. Worryingly, I don't flinch.

"Missing him is a weakness?" I enquire. "What about you and your mummy issues? Telling me you can't hurt me wasn't a great move either." My voice is light and teasing, and I'm not even faking.

"Touché," he grins. "You going to use it against me?"

"You think I won't," I frown.

"I've seen you fight. I've seen you protect my brother. I've fought you and you didn't kill me. I think I'm safe."

"Do you now?" I smirk. "Your brother is the exception, not the rule. I can't help liking the kid. You should still watch your back."

"Brue does that to people. It's a family trait," he says smugly. I can't help laughing.

"This is crazy," I exclaim. "I'm losing my mind."

"Maybe," he concedes. "Or maybe you've figured out we're not so bad."

"You think your father trying to kill me was *not so bad*?"

He sighs faintly, his brow creasing in thought. "I think his anger was at your audacity to wear my mother's face. He's normally more... calculated."

"Why do you think that is?" I ask, intrigued.

"Because he's in a position of power," he replies.

"I'm sure, but why do I have her face do you think? Honestly, am I that similar?" It's a long shot, unlikely I'd just stumble upon the female donor of my DNA, but life's ironic sometimes. Although, I don't know how it would be possible. A queen is a pretty big deal, not someone likely to have the opportunity to indulge in trysts with an enemy angeli.

"Here," Axion shifts to pull something from a pocket. "You tell me."

He hands me a photo, dog-eared and creased. Obviously something he keeps with him, handled regularly. "Your mother?" I ask, though I really don't need to. The resemblance is striking. Same face, different eye colour, different hairstyle. Her hair is cut in a short pixie bob and hangs almost straight, though it's the same jet black colour as mine. My hair is a mass of messy curls which hang down my back, and I can sometimes tame into a braid.

"Beautiful isn't she? Wasn't she?" he corrects.

"You still think she's dead, now that you know Rennison isn't?" I hand the photo back tentatively. His eyes turn so sad when he studies it that I turn away.

"Yes. I know she is. I feel it." He rolls onto his hip to put the photo back in its pocket. "I don't know why you look like her," he sighs.

I do look like her. And Axion looks like her. He has the same eyes, the same mouth. "How old are you, Axion?" I ask while I study his face. This time I'm not looking for his reactions, I'm looking at his bone structure, his features. He has a man's jaw, but it isn't strong like Liam's or angular like the kings. He looks like a dragone, but he's shorter than his father, shorter than his cousin. "Do you remember her?"

"Why are you staring at me like I'm an alien?" he asks, amused.

"Huh? I'm not."

"A science project then, a frog you've dissected." He smirks at me and my cheeks flush.

"I was thinking you look like her too, but not like your father," I answer honestly.

"I look like a girl?" he jokes, but it's forced. I wait patiently for him to say whatever is skirting around the front of his thoughts. "I'm twenty. I remember her in fragments, images. I'm not even sure which are real or imagined. You don't look like your mother," he comments.

"I know." I pause for a second, remembering why we're sitting here chatting merrily. "Where is my mother?" I stand up, looking the length of the beach, combing each direction for two figures approaching us. Nothing. No figures at all. "Is it usually this quiet?"

"Yeah, I guess. But they should have found us by now." He climbs to his feet too, looking back through the trees toward the buildings I know are there but can't see. "Let's go find them," he suggests.

We amble back along the path. He doesn't seem concerned, so I don't rush him. I'm afraid to say that our conversation has not encouraged me to despise my captors. In fact, I'm warming to them. Well, Axion and Brue. I'm positive I could never like Clyst.

"Wait," Axion commands unexpectedly, slapping his hand across my chest to stop me.

I halt immediately, surprised however instantly alert. "What?" I whisper, scanning our surroundings. I can hear noise through the trees – shouts and footsteps.

"Go back," Axion hisses, pushing me back along the path. "Fallen."

"Fallen what?" I stutter, but I already know.

We hurry back to the beach. Axion pulls me toward the water. "Can you swim?" he asks when we're already knee deep.

"Yes," I answer before we sink below the surface.

He points deeper and I follow, inhaling the salty liquid and letting my gills take over. This is a part of me that no one else is aware of, not even Liam. Axion heads out to sea quickly, skimming the bottom. It soon becomes clear that we share an ability, although he obviously hasn't realised this shouldn't be normal for me yet. We find a natural sand bank and sink behind it, trying not to disturb the seabed. I can just make out the distorted shore through the water. We're deep enough that the ocean shouldn't be clear above us. Axion clearly can't see anything, though he's started staring at me in utter shock. I roll my eyes at his expression, and glare when he prods me like a kid who's just dug up an interesting bug. His eyes widen. I have many witty things I want to say to him, he's lucky we're underwater.

Movement on the shore catches my attention and I indicate for us to get down. Figures search the beach. Dragone figures, though they don't look like the natives of the island. It's hard to describe, but they look burlier – obviously brutishly trained to be soldiers. They look like the dragone at my house. They patrol the area, but only glance at the ocean briefly. After a few minutes they disappear back through the trees. I wait until I'm sure they're gone before I direct Axion upward.

We break the surface. Axion's expulsion of water is much more dignified than mine. My lungs force the water out like a cannon.

"Want to explain what just happened?" he gasps, spluttering in his haste to speak.

"The Fallen patrolled the beach then went back through the trees," I clarify, but my lips quirk up.

"You can breathe underwater," he accuses. "Why?"

"Why can you?" I counter.

"My mother's family are water-breathers," he states, while staring at me like I'm a freak of nature. I am. And that right there is probably one of the reasons why. Axion could well be my brother.

"What are the Fallen doing here?" I ask, changing the subject.

"We should find out." He nods to himself. "This can't be good." He starts swimming back toward the beach and I follow.

"What about my mother and Brue," I whisper when we reach the sand. "Where do you think they are?"

"I don't know," he replies, worry lines marring his brow.

"We should take to the air," I suggest, "to find a higher vantage point." He gapes at me in response. "Why are you looking at me like that? It's basic training."

"For angels who can fly," he stutters.

"Seriously? You're going to hold out on me now? After I just revealed my biggest secret. Take the cloak off, Axion. We need to see what's going on."

I shake the water from my feathers and beat until I'm hovering. I smirk when he begrudgingly pulls his cloak over his head and stretches out his wings. He looks like a bat of some kind, though his membrane-like black wings appear rough and flaky like they're covered in scales.

"How did you know?" he asks as he joins me in the air. He sighs when I grin. "Brue?"

"Quiet dragon boy, we're going for stealth."

We keep low to the trees, circling the clutch of buildings quickly. There are no Fallen sentries around the perimeter, or signs of any of the islanders. They must have everybody inside the walls.

"On the roof," I whisper.

Axion follows me and we land lightly on the red tiles capping the closest building. Axion points to our right and we crawl, keeping low.

"Main courtyard," he whispers.

I nod in agreement and follow him across rooftops, keeping my senses keen. We leap a few gaps until we're overlooking the large stone courtyard that houses the water fountain – and about a hundred or so women and children, one with ochre hair. My mother and Brue are right in the middle of the corralled crowd of dragone, surrounded by a handful of Fallen sentinels holding weapons.

Axion says an incredibly uncouth word as we survey the situation.

"Chances of us taking them?" I ask. I'm already running possible scenarios through my head – none end well for us.

"Slim," Axion cringes. "Where are all the men? And my father?"

"Fighting," I answer. I can hear the ring of metal on metal, hear the grunts of men in battle. "Getting closer, from our left."

"They're coming for the captives," he states. "My dad won't go down without a fight." He pulls his sword from his waist and I grab my dagger.

"Neither will we." I grin, though my knees are wobbling and my stomach turning somersaults. I can fake confidence – I did it in the clearing, though that all went to Hell. I took on Axion earlier – and he sucked. Damn, we're going to die.

The shouts burst through a door below us and dragone spill into the courtyard. The Fallen are still wearing their cloaks, it's the only thing that makes them identifiable in the chaos. Bloodied bodies writhe and struggle across the courtyard. Men attack men, swords swishing with enough force to decapitate a rhinoceros. The shouts and screams of the children, watching their fathers dying, are the hardest to bear. Three of the sentinels move to join the fighting and I have to hold Axion back as he tries to leap. "Wait," I hiss. "Look." I point at the two Fallen left guarding the captives. "One each, think you can take the one on the left?"

He huffs like he's offended, but his hands are also shaking. I imagine Clyst generally does most of the fighting. I don't look too closely but I can't pick out Clyst below us. We shimmy along the roof until we're over our targets. Their attention is on the fighting, they're distracted. I drop first, landing silently behind the Fallen sentinel. I flip my dagger, reluctant to kill unless I have to. I bring the butt of the handle around hard, spinning beforehand to get momentum. The rounded metal end catches the Fallen's temple and he drops hard and fast to the floor. I kick him once to check he's unconscious.

"Hey!" his friend yells as he notices me. Turning to run in my direction he doesn't notice Axion drop behind him, until Axion's sword is sticking out through his stomach. I gulp back the urge to vomit. The Fallen drops to the floor in his pooling blood.

I stand frozen for a second, staring at him and then at Axion. He takes a deep breath, to compose himself, before jogging to my side.

"They haven't noticed us," Axion hisses. "We need to get the women and children out of here."

"Good plan," I mumble, shock kicking in.

He shakes me, studying my eyes. "Snap out of it," he growls. "Freak out later. Brue..." I whirl to look at the kid, who has pushed through the group to get to us. "... lead them through the north corridor, into the trees," Axion orders. Brue nods before rushing off. "We'll guard the rear," Axion directs at me.

I nod, picking up a sword from the ground. Axion smirks as I swing it to judge its balance. "What?" I hiss. My annoyance at his expression sharpens my focus again. We're in the middle of a battle. I need to concentrate.

"Nothing," he grins.

We work together to herd the frightened and sobbing mass through the narrow corridor. The children cling to their mothers, crying for their fathers. We urge them to be quiet but it's nearly impossible. They stampede into the trees like a herd of elephants. We can only hope the men hold off the Fallen long enough for us to hide, since escape seems unlikely.

"Where are we taking them?" I whisper at Axion as we watch for pursuers.

"I'll be back," he says and then rushes off to the front of the group. I glare at his back for a second. Our progress is fast but incredibly noisy. It's hard to hear over the thumping footsteps and cracking fauna, not to mention the screaming. I have to rely on my eyes, sweeping the area constantly.

"To the port." Axion pants as he appears back at my side. "There's a manned ship docked off of the coast."

"They can swim to it?"

"No, row boats," he replies. "We're almost there."

"Good," I exclaim, my voice wavering, "because here they come."

Axion says another rude word. "Run!" he yells to the group. "Get into the boats."

We run. The noise is deafening, hundreds of stampeding feet and the enemy approaching fast. I swing a flagging child onto my back as we break through the undergrowth onto a path. The port is small, constructed of wood. The women start jumping into the boats quickly, pulling their children with them. I hand the boy on my back over to his mother, who already has her arms full with two more. I urge them to hurry, my eyes roaming the dock and landing briefly on my own mother, helping children embark the boats. Someone must have carried her, and I didn't even consider her human speed. Stupid.

The Fallen break through the trees in a rush, heading straight for us. "Hurry up!" I yell above the ruckus, shoving my guilt aside and willing the group to go faster – or the Fallen to slow down.

"Nice knowing you," Axion smirks as he raises his sword. He is standing steadfast beside me.

"You too," I answer, copying him.

We face the men as they barrel toward us. I don't have time to panic. Instead Liam flashes into my mind. Liam, attacking me during training. Liam, teaching me how to fight. I move, fast and precise, dropping into a crouch and forcing my sword up into the ribcage of the man in front just as he swings his sword at my head. I survive. He dies. I can't feel guilty or disgusted yet.

I spin on my knees, pulling the sword from his chest and springing back to my feet as the next blade whizzes toward me. I jump it, slicing the throat of my attacker and landing in the path of a third. His sword slices my arm, tearing a scream of pain from my lips. I kick him reflexively, planting my foot in his stomach and following with a downward arch of my blade. The man falls quickly, landing hard, his blood bubbling from the wound. I gag.

My eyes wield around violently, looking for the next threat. Axion is still fighting, bleeding from a wound on his leg. He falls on his back as I realise he's battling the only Fallen left, for the time being. I can hear more on the way. The Fallen starts to lower his sword toward Axion's supine figure, but doesn't finish. He freezes and lists forward as my dagger buries itself, to the hilt, in his back. I stand at a distance, watching as Axion scuttles out of his way. I blink, hard, trying to erase the last few seconds from my memory. That's all it took, a few seconds, to end four lives. The sword drops from my grip and thumps to the floor.

"Aquila," Axion calls as he rushes toward me, handing me my dagger. "No freaking yet, we need to pull the boats. Now!" He yells again as he registers the approaching footsteps. More Fallen. I scream in frustration and then run for the dock.

The boats are full, all of the evacuees safely in, although they're sitting dangerously low in the water. I follow Axion and dive into the ocean, grabbing a tow rope at the front of one of the boats and then swimming to another. I copy Axion, securing the ropes over my shoulders and opening my webbed toes. I swim fast, faster than Axion. The boats pull together behind me as I become their outboard motor. It takes a second before I hear the faint splash of our pursuers entering the water. I slow only so Axion can pull level. We share a worried glance as we head for open water.

"We're pulling ahead." Brue's voice comes over the front of one of the boats I'm pulling. I glance up to see his sweet face, a huge grin on his face. "Keep going," he urges. "They won't catch us."

Easy for him to say. When the larger ship appears on the horizon I speed up, pulling ahead of Axion again. Brue pushes me on constantly, keeping me updated on everyone's locations.

"They're still following," he yells, "but miles back."

We reach the ship first. I push the boats against its hull, looking for a way to get everyone up. I shake my wings free of water before flying up to the deck. The ship is manned, by dragone. I falter for a second, imagining an attack, but they run to my aid, carrying rope ladders and life vests.

"Fallen," I shriek anyway. "Help the children!"

Then I launch myself back over the side in and ungraceful pencil dive. When I emerge again, I push the already drifting boats back to the hull, so that the woman can reach the ladders that are being dropped. I watch the water where the black heads of the impending Fallen, the dragone sharks, are rapidly approaching. Brue must have meant figuratively, because they definitely aren't miles back. Axion pulls his boats level and ladders are dropped for them, too. Burley men climb down to grab armfuls of young children before climbing back up just as agilely. The older children climb quickly, the mothers scream for them to hurry.

"How long until they reach us do you think?" Axion asks, still floating by his boats.

"Seconds. Will this tub be moving by then?" I ask.

"No," he replies sardonically, watching the Fallen.

"We need more time then."

"We need to kill them," he replies.

Great. More meaningless deaths on my conscience.

"It's us or them, Princess," Axion reminds me, as the first of the Fallen rears his ugly head – bursting from the ocean like the Kraken.

The chaos is deafening as women and children scramble across the wooden boards of the row boats. Screams of fear, heartache and panic rise above the slosh of the battering white capped waves that the Fallen create as they launch their underwater attack. The resistance of the liquid makes any physical move to kick or punch futile. Life or death. Us or them. But my world has never been so black and white and I never want it to be. The sailors splash down from above, like it's raining men. The crack of wood, splintering as easily as a brittle twig, rips from my left. A cauldron of marbled red bubbles around me as the Fallen attempt to destroy the emptying boats.

I rip at them from behind, plucking them away like the leeches they are. I will the islanders to move faster, to teleport, to do anything to avoid the swirling mass of carnage around me. A body floats by as I grapple with a Fallen for his blade. The contour of its chest indicates it's the body of a woman, an innocent. I don't look at her. I can't. I win my battle, barely, and the heavens fill with scarlet mist, blood spurting from the fatal jugular wound I inflict on him.

My eyes rove the scene. A sailor launches himself on top of a Fallen, one who's managed to haul himself into a now sinking row boat. They both disappear below the waves as they topple overboard. Axion hovers above the water on my left, slamming his boot into someone's head. Above, the last of the fleeing captives scramble up and over the railings of the larger vessel. The sailors still on board yell for their comrades to return.

The engines are already powered up, the thrum of the propeller blades create huge streams of pink froth. Blood stained riptides ready to suck in anyone who gets too close. The ocean, seasoned with the fresh scars of death, does not feel like my home today.

I'm distracted by a slash of pain on my thigh. My head snaps down, my eyes searching. There's a glint of silver and fresh crimson below the surface. Two mocking yellow orbs shine up like beacons, lighting the road to Hell. That's exactly where I'm going after this. Hell.

I exhale, ridding my lungs of buoyant air and sink into the thrashing depths. I grab the Fallen fighter's wrist and drag him with me. A sneer etches his lips. I hold his weapon immobile as he attempts to drown me, slamming his other hand on my head and pressing down with the force of a boulder. I kick out automatically, pointlessly, before wrapping my legs around his. His eyes widen momentarily at the move, the sneer drops a little. His mouth remains closed, his lungs still.

I blink in subdued composure, obligated to take his life to save my own. I told August once that death shouldn't be for honour, or a punishment, or taken lightly like it's expected of us. When did we decide that one life is worth more than another? Why should my life be more important than the Fallen before me, thrashing wildly inside my grip, fighting to save his own life now. I breathe the water in, wincing at the taste of copper it contains – the blood of my victims, of all of the victims, not just on my hands but now inside my chest as well. The life leeches from the Fallen as his movements cease. His eyes fixate, stating into my soul and branding it with guilt. Condemned.

I release him and he sinks, descending to the place of the damned. I get to go up, swim back to the surface of this world at least. I release the water from my lungs and take in the sea air. The Fallen are dead. All of them. As are too many of the innocents.

The survivors watch from the cargo boat as the last of the sailors climb back on board. Axion sits alone, atop a raft of splintered wood. His head hung low. His fingers trace the line of a blade that split his arm. I move toward him, pulled by an invisible current. His physical wounds are superficial, as are mine. The emotional wounds, however, are deadly.

His makeshift raft lists gently, a wooden island among a sea of debris. I rest my arms on its surface.

Rising slightly with the tide, I speak softly. "Room on your horse for two?"

His lips quirk. "Beware the Trojan horse," he murmurs, but he moves across to make enough room.

"You telling me there's more hiding under here?" I whimper as I tap the wood. "Because I think I've had enough of the Fallen for one day." For a lifetime.

"Climb aboard, Princess," he motions.

"Why are you calling me that?" I enquire as I heave myself from the water, ruffling my feathers to dry them.

"I thought that was the assumption we're going on now," he states. "We share a bloodline," he assumes, his eyes roving my face. "Your hair, your scent, your eyes… your gills. You're not pure angeli, not a human. Perhaps you are her."

"Who?"

"The baby. My sister the princess." He watches me impassively. Like he's imparting common knowledge.

"What baby?"

He pulls his mouth into a humourless smile. "The queen was pregnant. With a girl, I think."

"Just like that?" I scoff, shaking my head. "A few bits of coincidence and we're just going to throw it out there like it's official. Your mother shacked up with my father and here I am by some divine action of fate."

"Just like that," he mimics with a shrug. His fingers brush the bare skin of my hand and a small huff of a laugh escapes his chest. "Sometimes it pays to just believe in the signs, don't you think? Anyway, you feel it too."

I frown, missing his meaning. Does he think I feel like her or that I feel I am her? I turn my head, away from the dragone prince who might or might not be correct. "They're moving," I comment as we watch the vessel pull away, slowly, like the last vehicle to be towed from the carnage of a fatal collision. "Should we go back?"

"Yeah, we need to get them somewhere safe," he agrees, rising to his feet.

I didn't mean to the boat. "What about the king?" I ask cautiously.

He glances at the island solemnly. "He's still alive. There's nothing we can do, they've captured him."

"But he's your father, we could try..." I mumble, not convinced at my own words.

"The island's lost," he answers. He takes one more glance before we rise into the air and toward the fleeing islanders.

We land on the deck of the ship together, amongst the sobbing figures. My mother runs up, flinging herself against me. "Aqua! Oh god, Aqua."

I wrap my arms around her, holding her up as she wails.

"It's okay, Mum," I comfort her, my own relief seeping through at the sight of her. "We're okay," I nod.

"Hey angel." Brue strides up, looking more relaxed than anyone. "Thanks." He stands scratching his messy hair, more messy than usual. I pull him into a one-armed hug. "Hey," he complains, but he hugs me back.

"Well that was fun," I state, monotone.

Axion laughs sardonically from behind me.

"They just appeared," Brue explains, eager and excited. "Out of the tunnels I guess. I didn't see much. Did you see my dad?"

I shake my head. "No, kid."

"Then he's captured," he nods. "We need a rescue plan."

I raise my eyebrows, judging his determined expression.

"We need to find somewhere safe," Axion growls at his little brother. "Dad will be fine."

Brue huffs. "We need to rescue the king."

"We need to protect the women and children," Axion shouts. "Then we can do something about this." He gestures around, not really looking.

"You're such a coward," Brue yells.

"Hey," I interrupt, standing between them. I sigh. The love of siblings. The atmosphere changed so quickly from hurt to hate. "Brue, Axion saved us. He's not a coward. He's right, we need to make sure everyone's safe and then we'll make a plan to recapture the island."

I shrug off the nausea burning in my gut. I swallow down the bile rising in my throat. I close off my heart, a task that's getting easier the more turmoil I face. I start thinking strategy. Protect the weak, the untrained, keep the group alive.

"Okay... have you got more islands? Somewhere else we can take them that is safe? Somewhere the Fallen don't know about?"

"No," Axion exhales the word on a breath. "The Fallen have already taken everything else. They swore to leave Hantiem for us..."

"Well they lied, obviously. So we need somewhere amongst the humans... or..."

"No way," Brue snarls.

"You didn't hear me out," I snap. "They could help."

"No," he answers, pouting.

"We'd be walking from one fight into another. No way," Axion agrees. "They'd never help us."

"Who else is there?" I ask. "Humans can't take on the Fallen without a lot of explaining first. We have nowhere to go – unless we want to hide indefinitely. We have to consider it."

"We?" Brue repeats. "You're staying?"

I laugh gravely. "You want me to go?"

"Of course not," he answers, grinning.

This could be a really bad idea. I look at Axion, tall and lean, the male version of me. My brother.

"You got any warmer clothes?" I ask him.

"Why?" he frowns.

"Because it's going to get cold."

# · Five ·

We leave the ship moored in the Indian Ocean after sunset, when the women and children have settled below decks. Convincing Brue to stay behind was a war in itself. The twenty-five remaining male crew members have orders to leave if anything happens, though the engines had to be turned off to conserve fuel. It's a risk, to leave them floating, but we need help and nightfall is the best time to approach Celthia – I hope.

"You'll remember where we parked it?" Axion asks as we head for China. He's more relaxed now, calm even. Whatever boundaries he was holding up while I was his prisoner have been pulled down.

We soar through the air under the cover of darkness. "It was between the seaweed and the floating thing," I answer, smiling. "You know, you talk a lot like a human..."

He laughs. "I know. We spend a lot of time with them – not like the angels."

"You speak English too," I comment.

"Yeah, it's the most widely spoken language in the world. It made sense to learn. We don't use ours anymore, except for the Fallen, of course."

"The symbols on the throne room door," I confirm. "Can you read it?"

He nods his affirmation. "Yeah."

"That might be useful," I sigh.

He looks at me questioningly but I shake my head. He'll see what I mean when we get to Celthia.

We land in the first large city we find, close to the mountains that form the border with Bhutan. "Smash and grab?" Axion smirks as we walk the streets, looking for a clothes store.

"Just find a climbing shop or something," I grin. "It's colder than sub-zero where we're going. You'll freeze."

"What about you?"

I smirk. "I'm built for the cold – hot blooded."

We make our way through the still well-lit and well-populated streets, both wearing the black cloaks of the dragone to hide our wings. It was the only thing suitable on the ship. We look odd compared to the crowds, but not as much as you might think.

"Here," Axion says. "Mountain climbing gear."

"Get thermal briefs," I grin as he peers through the window.

"It's shut," he comments.

"Smash and grab," I whisper, silently horrified at how low I've stooped in the last few hours. Murder and theft.

"Bad girl," Axion smirks, and then rips the door from its hinges and wanders in. The alarm blares, speeding up his illegal shopping trip. He grabs an armful of clothes, actually stopping to check sizes. I roll my eyes, watching him from the doorway.

"Hurry up!" I hiss. "People are running this way."

"Long johns or thermal leggings?" he shouts.

I don't know the difference. "Both!" I yell.

"Okay, okay." He hurries out, grabbing some new boots on the way.

"Oh, boots," I exclaim. "Get me some too, size seven."

"These aren't labelled in English sizes," he yells.

"Just guess!" I yell back.

He grabs a pair and shoots out of the door. We run toward the nearest alley, sirens serenading us in the background. "Forty-two," he grins as he hands them to me. "We should probably fly before they follow us."

I pull the cloak over my head, freeing my wings then grabbing an armful of his pilferings so he can do the same. We leap into the sky and disappear into the hazy darkness above the neon glow of the street lights. We land briefly, so Axion can apply layers – lots of layers. I use my dagger to modify his coat and thermal vests for his wings. "There's a breeze on my back," he complains as we fly toward the mountains.

"Be glad it's just your back. At least you look cool." He chose a black coat with luminous pink stripes and matching trousers, I would have picked it too.

"I'm roasting," he whines.

"A dragone feeling the heat," I laugh. "Whatever next?"

"A dragone flying toward a city of angeli, for help," he smirks back.

He's right. This is probably my worst idea yet, doomed to end in a hail of silver arrows, and I've brought him along for the ride. He follows me over the range until the landscape becomes familiar. I know these mountains. I've lived on these mountains – in these mountains. I start my warning call early, well aware that the angeli Guard will be at their outposts, protecting the city. The angelian language is birdlike and limited, I send out a series of cheeps and whistles. I hope it's enough to prevent being shot down by arrows. I keep repeating the calls as we soar toward the giant gray rock, snow-capped and angular.

"Don't freak," I whisper to Axion as we head for the massive steel hangar doors hidden in the side of the mountain. I can hear the angeli moving, see their shadows as they follow us silently. No one responds to my call but no one attacks either. The hangar doors pull open slowly, leaving only a small gap.

"In there?" Axion stutters. He hasn't noticed our silent followers. I decide not to inform him.

"Yeah, I imagine it'll be full of Guard by now. Try to look peaceable."

He raises his eyebrows at me and I bite my lip. God I hope I haven't just got us both killed.

We glide into the vastness of the stone walled hangar and land in the limited available floor space. Figures encircle us, filling the atmosphere with nervous energy and tension. No one moves. A mass of armed angeli Guard watch as the doors pull closed behind us, trapping us in.

"This was your idea," he breathes as his eyes roam the crowd. Caged again.

I spot Plyrian, Liam's second in command, in one of the front rows. I make eye contact, begging him to listen before he orders any attack. I can't see Liam. Plyrian shakes his head in silent answer. I guess Liam's not here.

I talk fast, smoothly and quietly. The angeli can hear a pin drop in a hurricane. "Plyrian, first trust me and listen. We've been deceived. The dragone are our enemy, but they aren't all guilty. Their island has been lost, their king captured and their women and children left stranded and homeless. Some dragone are innocent, their attackers are the guilty ones. This is Axion. I've brought him here for your help."

Axion stares at me, confused. Dragone hearing is more limited by volume and pitch. I don't think he heard much. I give him a reassuring smile.

"Aquila," Plyrian answers, slowly, loud enough to make Axion flinch at the sudden noise. "Guardian. Welcome back." His voice is emotionless as he assesses my sincerity and inspects Axion. "We have missed you," he adds.

Plyrian is a friend. Instrumental in my training and high up in the secret rebel alliance movement beneath the city.

"And I you," I state sincerely. "I returned as quickly as I could."

"With a guest," he comments. I relax slightly at his use of the word. He could have said any number of things: prisoner, traitor, sacrifice. I watch as the angeli in the room glare in Axion's direction, studying him. None have failed to notice his wings, obviously. "An interesting guest," Plyrian muses.

I nod. "He needs our help to protect his people."

Gasps ricochet around the room, angry murmurs. I cringe but keep my eyes on the Second.

"An audience with Victus, then," Plyrian suggests. Razor sharp noises bubble from the crowd at the insane suggestion. "We are a fair people," he states, his eyes calling for calm. "We can hear him speak before judgement is made."

I exhale. Plyrian is a good man, over thirty years my senior, experienced and loyal. He smiles at me briefly, and I feel… better. I haven't been written off as a defector by everybody here. It's a start.

Plyrian orders the Guard out, sending reinforcements to the outposts on the range. The room clears slowly, far more slowly than necessary as the Guard watch us warily.

"Aqua," he greets me less formally once the vast hangar is clear.

I exhale. "Plyrian, thank you. Are they safe? Aaron and August," I clarify.

"Your humans are well, but you are hurt. Victus would not begrudge us a short detour to the Medics." His warm eyes cool as they flick to Axion briefly before resting back on me.

"He hasn't hurt me," I assure him. "He helped me."

Plyrian nods slowly. "Forgive me," he says, "but I must know. We were friends, you and I."

We were? I'm not offended. His voice increased in pitch with the question he posed. Are we still friends? The trust I worked so hard to obtain from the angeli has been tested, tainted, and maybe lost. But I have not broken or betrayed it. Yes, we are still friends.

I nod, and answer humbly, "And we will always be friends, you and I." I pull my dagger from the sheath at my thigh, glance at the copper staining on the blade, and hand it hilt first to Plyrian. "He is unarmed," I state as an afterthought, referring to Axion who, in turn, eyes me suspiciously. Plyrian nods in affirmation. He too glances at the remnants of lost life, still clinging to my once pristine steel, before handing it directly back to me with a sad smile. Sad that he believes me? Sad for my soul?

"Your leg?" he asks. "Liam…"

"Where is he?" I interrupt, concentrating on re-sheathing my dagger much more stringently than necessary. My leg twinges at the thought of Plyrian's words. My leg. Liam. Plyrian was there, at the clearing. He must have seen what transpired. Would Liam have offered an explanation? He's never felt the need to justify any of his actions before.

Plyrian stutters as he attempts to change his sentence to answer my question.

"Never mind." I almost whine the words. I don't really want to know right now anyway.

"Guardian." A warm and welcoming voice drifts toward me, followed by the familiar smiling face of a Medic. If there's some kind of intercom system in Celthia, I missed the memo. Yet news always travels like lightening through the city.

I huff a smile and return her greeting. "Hello, Halen."

This Medic, Halen, has patched me up more times than I can remember. She helped save Aaron's life. I will always be indebted to her.

She looks me over. "Come," she instructs. "These need cleansing. You have taken your rations?"

"I had none left," I admit.

She lets out a sound akin to a tut as we head toward the medical wing. Plyrian escorts Axion behind us. Axion's posture is stiff, guarded, as we walk through the double doors and follow the corridor.

The medical wing is on the same level. The way is lit by familiar beeswax candles. The orange light flickers along the polished rock walls, which are not built but carved into the mountain. Medics in green robes watch us walk past, their faces frozen in whatever expression they managed to form before their muscles seized. I ignore them.

Halen's assistant grimaces when we enter the treatment room, but he says nothing. Just as well, I suppose. I'll be hoarse before I get to Victus if I have to explain Axion's presence to every angeli we encounter.

I sit wearily on the stone examining table, as my wounds are cleaned and bandaged, the pain controlled with the sweet pink liquid reserved for members of the Guard. The Medics ignore the dragone like he's a bad dream. Perhaps there's only so much even Halen is prepared to accept. Although, she doesn't comment when I pick up some of the extra bandages and vials she just happens to have on the tray.

Axion inspects the vial of purple liquid I offer, like he can judge whether it's medicine or arsenic simply by looking at it. Rolling my eyes, I tip a little in my own mouth before offering it to him again. He hasn't spoken yet. He's reverted back to the reserved persona I first met. I attempt a warm smile of reassurance. It could well have ended up looking like a sneer.

He holds the vial, not drinking it, while Halen finishes my treatment. She touches her fingers lightly to my cheek before flicking her eyes to the dragone, back to the spare bandages in my hand, and then at Plyrian. I nod. Halen's instinct is to heal, maybe her acceptance isn't as limited as most of the beings here.

After jumping down from the table, my pain extinguished, I gesture at Axion's arm. "My turn," I muse, "to do this for you."

His first words, in what feels like hours, come out croaky. "So we're even?" he mumbles.

Plyrian frowns hard, making eye contact with me from behind Axion's shoulder. My gaze moves to Axion slowly. "No. Because we are equals," I correct.

"Guardian," Plyrian utters incredulously as I wrap Axion's arm tightly. He regains his composure before continuing. "Victus will not wait indefinitely. We should hasten this... discussion, and head to the library."

"There's no discussion," I state as I secure the bandage and tap the purple vial implicitly until Axion relents and swallows it. "I'm just stating a fact."

"Regardless," Plyrian retorts, "we must hurry." He eyes the hand I leave resting on Axion's arm, before turning and marching from the room.

I stuff my medicine pouch with as many vials as I can and thank Halen before leading Axion back into the corridors of Celthia. He slips his fingers through mine, taking my hand in a tentative fashion. It's strange but not unwelcome. It also makes me think of my favourite brother, August. He did exactly the same thing once he'd accepted me. I squeeze Axion's hand lightly before freeing myself from his grip.

My heart flutters with the effects of adrenalin as we climb the stone spiral staircase at the centre of the mountain. Victus' office, the library, is one flight up. We walk through the empty school halls, the younglings in their beds at this late hour, to the end of the corridor.

Victus' golden office entrance is etched with the image of an open book. I don't knock. He's expecting us, and frankly it would be an unexpected change of character if I did. I push through into the library, keeping my body between Plyrian and Axion and immediately look up at the double-story ceiling. The broken glass has been replaced, the mahogany desk returned to the centre of the room. Evidence of my escape eradicated. Victus leans casually against said desk, drumming his fingertips on the wood. His red tunic and trousers always make me think of Santa Claus.

"Guardian," he greets me, his voice and expression guarded.

I surprise him, and myself, by crossing the room to embrace him. He stiffens before wrapping his arms around me in response.

"Victus," I grin before releasing him and stepping backward.

Axion paces forward reluctantly, stopping at my side.

"Victus, this is Prince Axion." I let him in on his full title, which perhaps Victus already knew because he doesn't look surprised. "We require refuge for his people." My eyes survey the room, checking the alcoves above our heads in case of listening ears. "For the people of my mother," I add. "They have nowhere safe left to go."

Victus taps his finger to his lips, which are almost hidden behind the thick fauna of gray beard he has rooted there. "Refuge for the dragone Prince and your people," he repeats insipidly. "And you felt they would be safe here?"

My people? "No," I clarify. "But I hoped you could help. I trusted that you would try."

Victus' eyebrows quirk at my statement. Axion shuffles uncomfortably beside me. His rank as leader really doesn't suit him. Brue would be demanding a squadron of angel fighters to avenge his father by now.

"We should discuss this once the Master of the Guard is present," Victus states, and my stomach flips. "His arrival should be imminent, a Tail was sent to announce your return." He speaks the words nonchalantly, but his eyes watch me in his unique, speculative manner. I attempt to swallow but my mouth has abruptly dried, like a grape shrivelling into a raisin. "He has become somewhat nocturnal," Victus continues. Nope, still can't swallow. I manage a blink, though, it's quite an accomplishment. "Fortunately, he informs me of his intended trajectory," Victus states.

That felt like a dig at me. I let it go, I probably deserved it. After I spent an entire evening swimming happily in the Atlantic, while Liam had half of the Guard searching for me, Victus forbade me to leave the city alone again. He grounded me, as much as you can ground someone with wings, and I broke the rules by attempting a lone rescue mission for my mother.

"Which Tail?" I ask. My dry throat sucks the words into a whisper.

"The best, of course," Victus exclaims exuberantly.

The Tail are messengers and spies, trained in tracking and subterfuge. And my friend, Lucas, is the best.

"What about his honeymoon?" I ask meekly. If Lucas has been sent for Liam, then they will be back much sooner than I'd like. Lucas found me, a stranger, by sniffing a single lock of hair, snipped from its ignorant owner seventeen years before. Liam's scent is familiar to him, and they can both travel fast.

"Lucas and his new mate elected to postpone their mating moons," Victus answers, "in favour of a more... unselfish quest."

That too, felt like a dig at me. "Quest?"

"The search for their Consort, Guardian." Victus mocks me with exaggerated arm movements, his composure slipping slightly. I haven't seen it break before; it's made of missile-proof glass. "There's been an almost vicious rumour circulating through these halls, that the dragone were responsible for the disappearance of their best friend. Of course they sacrificed their mating moons, to do all they could, in the search for that friend."

"Ironic," I retort, "that that friend was simply doing the same thing in the search for her own mother." I can't stand Victus' inclination for belligerent words disguised as intelligent ramblings. "If you've got something to say, or accuse me of, then just do it and stop patronising me with abstract criticism!"

A smile twitches at the Overseer's lips as he watches my outburst. Plyrian rolls his eyes at my show of disrespect. But neither of them is surprised. Axion doesn't move, or comment, or breathe, like a toddler he's hoping no one can see him if he pretends he's invisible. At least that's how it looks. I know now that there's sterner stuff in him, when it's needed.

"Ah, there you are, Aqua," Victus chortles. "For a second I thought they'd sent me an imposter. I don't recall a time that you simply *hoped,* and not demanded, I do something to help your latest..." He twirls his wrist, looking for a suitable word. "... stray," he decides finally. "Of course, this one took quite the impudence on your part." He tilts his head back quizzically, waiting for my reply.

"I know," I agree. "But not without good reason."

"Then perhaps you should enlighten us," Victus decides, "before we are interrupted."

"We'll need chairs," I grunt. Victus has his inquisition face on.

"Start talking, Aquila," he instructs me while nodding at Plyrian.

Plyrian disappears in search of chairs from the school, winking at me before leaving the room. If Victus is happy to be alone with me and Axion, then it appears the dragone prince is safe here for the time being. I knew Victus often listens to me, and perhaps even appreciates my views, but this is more than I had expected.

"Axion led the operation to abduct me from the woods," I explain.

Victus accepts my revelation easily. "For what reason?" he asks the dragone prince directly. I feel my eyes widen. Accepting his presence in the room is one thing, actually engaging in polite conversation is quite the other. In actuality, it's more like probing, but I shrug it off with a nod in Axion's direction.

Axion clears his throat with a small cough, to compose himself, before talking. "The king was informed that the Fallen were after a girl. I was sent to find her, Aquila, first."

"The Fallen?" Victus questions. "What are they?"

"Dragone, trained to fight," I answer. I slowly pull the arrow from my sheath and hand it to Victus. "Led by a madman with a sigil."

I watch the Overseer as he inspects it. His eyes remain glassy and distant. I know he knows it's Liam's sigil, Liam's arrow, yet still he asks, "His name?"

I answer with more certainty than I feel, "Rennison Jarik. And he's a crossbreed, like me."

Victus turns whiter than the petals of a daisy. He actually has to steady himself against the mahogany writing top. I wait for him to clutch at his chest as he reaches the height of his cardiac episode, but it doesn't happen. He simply stares into space, his eyes unfocused like they're glimpsing another dimension.

"Victus?"

"You're sure?" he questions. "He's still alive?"

"Yes," Axion confirms. "As sure as we can be. He leads the Fallen against us, and you."

"The sigil?" I question, hoping for some kind of explanation.

Victus looks right through me, not even acknowledging he heard me speak. I don't have time to repeat it. I hear the footsteps then. Fierce and fast, and I immediately stiffen.

"Do not speak of this until we are alone," Victus commands, as a fresh yet familiar scent hits me like a bomb blast. His aroma is strong. It causes me to stagger before he even enters the room. Liam...

I don't feel better anymore. I feel sick.

He storms through the door, a muscular, leather clad Adonis with chocolate hair and hypnotic caramel eyes. My mouth dries out again like a furnace. My blood heats and my heart takes off like a humming bird.

Liam – gorgeous hateful Liam.

Liam who sent me into the ground with an arrow in my thigh.

This should be interesting.

His face is fierce, his eyes focused on Axion and his sword drawn as he strides straight across the library toward him.

"Liam?" Axion asks me as he skitters backward.

There's no time to reply. I dive between them, my dagger drawn.

Liam attempts to sidestep me, like I'm a stray dog in his path, he doesn't even glance down. I counter it, drawing his reluctant eyes to me. His caramel pools are hard toffee as he looks me over, his gaze lingering slightly on my newly bandaged wounds. There's no reasoning with him when he's like this, no chance to talk things through. Liam has issues with his temper, and a grudge owed to the dragone. I push him, hard. I'm stronger than him because of my mixed heritage, but he's the strongest angeli in Celthia.

"Justice," Liam states, "will be mine upon his death."

"No," I hiss. I don't have time to process his warped thinking. It's me who needs justice. I glare at him. Liam doesn't answer, or acknowledge I've spoken. He raises his sword and again tries to stalk toward the dragone prince.

"Nice knowing you, again," Axion rushes in a whisper, attempting sardonic humour and failing dismally.

I don't answer, I can't. I counter Liam's attack with my dagger. "He's under my protection," I yell in his face.

Liam's eyes widen briefly at my audacity and then he responds with ferocious indignation. His fist hits my ribs and I wince, winded. For whatever reason, he didn't use his blade. I don't have time to dwell on that fact. I kick him, wearing my new boots, and he flinches.

Where is Plyrian when you need him? Or Victus and his baritone orders to *cease and desist*? An order from the Overseer is like a decree direct from God himself, yet nothing interrupts us.

I force Liam back faintly and counter with my own attack. I've fought him many times, he pushed me to learn, and he taught me how to defend myself against him. I may not have beaten him, but I can stop him hurting Axion. Plus, I'm owed my own retribution, my own justice, for the leg that he used as an oversized pin cushion, and for my heart, which he shattered simultaneously.

We fight. I engage him with my eyes, keep him moving away. I dodge his sword and kick him whenever

I can. I use my dagger to defend myself: kick... duck... punch... fake... counter... lunge. I screech in frustration, my rage rivalling a volcanic eruption. Anger is good. Anger I can work with. I land a fist square on his smug jaw. Hah! How satisfying.

Axion's voice, asking someone to help me, lingers on the edge of my perception. My ears focus on the sound, like sonar, a natural instinct of self-preservation honed throughout my childhood. My mind flits briefly to happy and surreptitious hours spent soaring around the Course on Saturdays, always staying below the tree line.

"Only they can stop this," Plyrian answers. He must have come back at some point. His words banish the first tendrils of melancholy seeping in with my memories. I huff. That's so not true. Why should I stop this? Liam started it. Stupid angeli, thinks he knows everything. Stupid Liam, always fighting first and thinking later. Stupid dragone, taking my stupid mother and locking me in a stupid cage. Stupid me, my concentration may have waned somewhat.

I miss a foot plant and stagger to regain my balance. A mistake like that should cost me my life. Instead, Liam raises an eyebrow at me. It's so minute, so small, that I could have imagined it, except it's followed by the hint of a smile. My brow drops in confusion. Why's he smiling at me? He stops moving and abandons his crouched position. I falter, and then slap him hard across the cheek, before doing the same. It's a cathartic, adrenalin fuelled release of tension, a stinging smack that makes us both wince, though he makes no other movement.

I watch in morbid fascination, as the smooth skin of his cheek changes colour before my eyes. When the blush stops developing, settling on a brilliant shade of ɔuce, I shift my gaze to his eyes. They burn with heat, the heat of anger. Though perhaps, if I were not as wise as I am now, I might believe they burned with love. We stand rigid, like bookends, storing a shelf-full of encyclopaedias between us: ancestry, biology, history, politics. The whole damned A-Z of our messed-up relationship.

"Aqua," he sighs, and his tone is unfathomable.

"Liam," I reply, in the same breathless manner.

"What did I miss?" Lucas asks from the doorway and my gaze shoots to him. He's grinning like a Cheshire cat.

"Lucas!" I shriek, glad to break the awkward Liam moment. I abandon the traitorous Guard Master and rush into the arms of my beautiful, white haired guardian angel.

"Aqua," he laughs, wrapping me in an embrace. "Thank the Mother you are safe. Never do that again, ever." He kisses my forehead, holding my face and inspecting me. "Something happened," he declares, looking in my eyes. "You are hurting."

I nod.

"It was necessary," Liam whispers spontaneously.

His voice was loud enough that he meant for me to hear it, though I can't understand why. I roll the word around my head, like a marble on a plate. *Necessary?*

Victus calls for order, interrupting any chance of Round Two.

I rub my forehead. A tension headache is already building behind my eyes. I think I prefer the physical fights to the politics.

"Aquila," Victus commands. "Please encourage our guest to explain the meaning of this... circumstance." No mention of what we just discussed. No indication that Victus has already communicated directly with the dragone prince.

All eyes on me, I focus on the only luminous yellow set. "Axion, please explain..." I frown at him, waiting. "Start at the beginning, when my mother was taken," I encourage.

He slits his eyes toward me, ignoring the chairs as he moves closer to my side. Liam paces to the periphery of the room, fuming, while Plyrian moves to guard the door. Lucas, ever protective, flanks my left shoulder while Victus leans back against his desk, his finger tapping ferociously against the grained wood. He appears to watch Axion implicitly, his eyes uncharacteristically tight.

Lucas moves closer, sensing the atmosphere but remaining relaxed. It's Liam that Victus is watching, his eyes look through us like we're transparent, focusing on the Master of the Guard whenever he stomps into his line of sight. Lucas is so close that when I reach back I find his hand already waiting for mine. Robotically, I locate Axion's hand hung at his side as well. He presses his fingers against mine, like it's an instinct, and I feel him relax.

His voice comes out with more confidence than I felt in him before. "We were patrolling the tunnels when we sensed Fallen. I had my strongest men, so we pursued them. They went above ground. They were quicker. I thought we'd lost them but when we got to a farmhouse five of them were dead. We followed the others. They had a human with them, kicking and screaming. They weren't hard to find. They attacked first, but they had injuries. We lost men but only one of theirs survived. He came with us and we took the human as a guest."

The room stays silent as everyone processes his version of events. Lucas was there, with me and Liam when the Fallen stole my mother. He squeezes my hand in reassurance and I return the gesture gratefully. I nudge Axion's fingers and he continues.

"He told us they were after a girl. There was something special about her," he glances at me, "and they needed her. He convinced us that if we didn't find her then the Fallen would. He suggested using Libby..." He glances at me again, and for some inexplicable reason, I feel his guilt before it shows on his face. "She suggested the woods."

Huh, my own mother. Well that officially sucks. *Beware the Trojan horse?* Beware my treacherous mother, more like. She's a regular day *Ephialtes*. I scowl and Axion shifts uncomfortably.

"The Fallen?" Victus echoes again.

Axion smirks. "The Fallen are a sect. Actually, we're the sect now, since there's only a few hundred of us and thousands of them. They're systematically wiping us out. This morning, they attacked our island. Aqua saved us," he adds. There's reverence in his tone, but that, too, I felt before I heard it. How strange. "Today, the Fallen killed most of our men and our king was captured. We only escaped because of Aqua."

Lucas squeezes my hand more tightly with every word Axion utters. Axion's tone is casual as he refers to me with my shortened name. He's comfortable, obviously familiar with me, and Lucas doesn't like it.

Victus' scrutinising gaze shifts to me. "Your mother?" he asks after a short silence.

Which one, I wonder? "Libby is alive," I confirm after a beat, and then I grimace. "The women and children escaped with us." My voice comes out hushed as I remember the ones we lost. A reassuring jolt of support from Axion pervades my skin, and I move closer to him reflexively. I shake the negativity away and take a deep breath. "They are vulnerable and isolated. They need protection, Victus. A safe place the Fallen can't find them."

"Gravinwart?" Plyrian asks from his position at the door. "It is abandoned?"

Axion turns to look at him and snorts. It's a nasal gust of incredulity. "Gravinwart is not abandoned," he answers. "It is the stronghold. It's completely impenetrable."

"Then why seek our aid?" Plyrian retorts snidely.

"Because it is the stronghold of the Fallen," Axion answers. His voice resigned and monotone and, quite frankly, heart-breaking.

"We'll offer them protection," Victus agrees unexpectedly, turning all heads back to him. "We have room here. It will be hard of course, there will be intolerance. It can only be a temporary measure."

I nod. It is not a confident nod of thanks. Although this is what we asked for, what we wanted, Victus has just dramatically trivialised the extent of the loathing between the angeli and dragone.

This could well be suicide.

Victus issues his orders calmly, ignoring the tension.

Axion and I will return to the ship while it's still dark, Lucas will accompany us, and the Guard will ready the cells at the base of the city for a hundred new guests.

The cells are hot and dark, avoided by all except the Guard, and, more recently, the revolution. The longer the majority of the city's residents are ignorant of the dragone's presence, the safer everyone will be.

"I want to see August and Aaron before I leave," I mumble to Lucas.

He shakes his head in response, as does Victus.

"I need to," I reiterate. "I can't leave without knowing they're safe." I have to see my humans, to at least smell them, before I leave the city again.

"Why wouldn't they be safe?" Liam scoffs from behind me. He's keeping his distance. Good. I'm furious with him.

"Because there are weapon wielding morons living in close proximity," I snipe.

"It is too dangerous," Lucas interrupts. "His scent already lingers in here, the school corridors, the medical wing. We may be able to attribute the odour to a chemical experiment gone awry, but we cannot risk him being scented or seen in the residential wing. I am sorry, Aqua."

"I'm not leaving him alone here," I state, moving closer to Axion. "I swore to keep him safe."

Our hands brush again, lightly, and I feel his faith in me flow from him. It's like an electric current, a nerve impulse, something once dormant now recharged by a spark. I glance at our hands bemused, yet, somehow certain that it's innate, another undiscovered piece of me, whatever the hell it is, inherited from my mother. My gaze flits to Axion's jaw and then returns to Lucas. His gaze is downcast, lingering on the skin contact between me and Axion, he looks disappointed.

"Aqua," Lucas rebukes, his voice low.

The ambient temperature cools a degree at his tone.

There's a hiss of air through teeth, followed by the unmistakable ring of steel as a blade slides from its sheath. I spin like lightening, pushing Axion aside in the process. I'm across the room, pinning Liam's defiant wrist against the eclectic rainbow of book spines which line the library walls. His dagger glints in the pale moonlight. The silver glow of a million stars filters down. They are dazzling, shimmering eyes, watching us intently through the circular glass skylight. I blink at the stark realisation that we're nothing more than entertaining specimens in a Petri dish. A sample... Cultured? Perhaps not.

"Enough," I command. I lock my amber eyes with Liam's. I can almost see the caramel flames of his hate, dancing hypnotically around the black hollow in the centre. *Hollow*. I smirk. Hollow seems like such an appropriate euphemism for everything we shared. No one else moves, not even Plyrian as they stare in stunned silence.

"You disappoint me, Guardian," Liam sneers. "Two weeks in the presence of a demon and your true nature emerges. You choose *him* over your own family?" He lets his vehemence cling to his words like venom, and beneath it, there's a scent of something more. Something toxic, a putrid black stain, leaked directly from his tainted soul.

"Don't speak to me about *true nature*," I seethe. "You..." I stammer with fury. My brain demands I screech so many profanities at once, that my tongue quivers like an inebriated slug. It trips on a curb and lands in a puddle of stagnant saliva. I swallow, bracing myself, regaining control. I hiss, "You shot me in the leg with an arrow! You wounded me, literally. You sent me to the demons, vulnerable and broken." My voice cracks on the last word, an infuriating loss of composure which I stifle with a growl. "I trusted you."

I refuse to release his arm. Our conflict holds the power of *Medusa,* and we all succumb to its influence. An oppressive silence descends as we turn to stone. A singular moment in time, carved in granite.

All but one of us, "Um... We're not demons," Axion interjects, breaking the suffocating effigy spell. "And Aqua is one of us," he adds. I flinch. Regaining control of my motor skills, my grip on Liam gets tighter. "You know," Axion continues, uncharacteristically talkative, "considering you're supposed to be her brother, you're acting like an ass."

I choke, flabbergasted. My voice returns, though it's somewhat higher than I remember. "Ax," I snap. "Don't." My voice breaks, like a pubescent choir boy's, and I cough.

"Why?" He questions me as I hear his boots approaching. Why did he choose now to start acting like a pompous royal pain? "That's not how brothers act, Princess."

Liam pushes me away with resentment, and I'm glad. I block Axion's body from him and attempt to put more distance between them, forcing Axion backward.

"What are you doing?" I hiss at my dragone brother. Yes, brother. I'm pretty sure of it. It's not the instantaneous sense of kin I felt when I met August. I'd known he'd once existed. My mother had turned August's absence into a constant presence, planting a memorial rose bush, crying at any mention of him. But this, me and Axion, this feels instinctive.

"What do you know about brotherhood?" Liam asks. His voice is quiet and deadly, like the exquisite predator he is. "What do you know of our *relationship*? Our bond?"

He slinks forward with fluid grace, his eyes blazing. "What business is it of yours, Demon?"

"Ax," I warn.

I want to say *'don't do this'*, but I don't. I'm more frightened of his next words than Liam's reaction to them. Voicing our assumption, no matter how sure I am that it's accurate, feels like an unexpected fork in the road that the roadmap says shouldn't exist. The GPS is telling me to continue straight on along this path, except there is no straight on, there's only left or right. And I want to pull a U-turn.

"I know your *bond* has nothing to do with brotherly love," Axion states.

It's then that I realise, whatever this ability is – this direct line to his emotions that I've managed to acquire – it is obviously a two-way thing. He can feel the depth of my emotion and I blanch at the thought of Axion eavesdropping on the shattered, excruciating adoration I know still burns inside me for my infuriating angeli *brother.*

"I know," Axion continues forcefully. "I know, because *if* you were actually her brother, then you would share the same bond that *we* do." He lets the words hang there, suspended in mid-air, like a bomb falling in slow motion. I can see its trajectory, but before it hits a blur of white obstructs my view. My guardian angel.

"Liam," Lucas warns. "Disengage and move away."

I hear Liam scoff in response.

"That is an order," Victus commands, his voice travelling like cannon fire. And everyone, even Axion, steps back a pace instantly.

"I should have seen it immediately," Lucas huffs quietly, chastising himself.

"Well," Victus stretches as he rises and assumes the formal posture of the Overseer. "This is quite a situation." He strolls forward confidently, like he'd been in on the secret all along. He never ceases to amaze me. I narrow my eyes but say nothing. "Nevertheless, it changes nothing. It seems you're amassing quite a collection of brothers," he muses, his eyes on me. "However the sky is brightening and I still have a laboratory experiment to go awry. Perhaps we should reconvene at a more appropriate time." He waves his hand dismissively and I know it's our cue to leave, before the situation billows beyond even his control.

"Come on." I tug Axion and Lucas from the room, my eyes lingering on Liam. He doesn't look in our direction, his muscles strain with the effort. It's an unpleasant feeling, the clash of sensation. I thought my love for him would have transformed to hate after his betrayal. I should hate him. I want to, I think, but against my better judgement, I'm disappointed he didn't look around.

We rush back through the city to the hangar. Lucas was right; Axion's scent is like a luminous streak through the corridors. The dragone's scent is so different, like a square peg in a round hole. I can't imagine any of the angeli will believe the cover story.

"How are we going to hide a hundred of these scents?" I grumble mordantly.

Lucas smiles at me, his bright eyes warm. "Have faith, Aqua." He unfurls his wings as we reach the large hangar doors, which the Guard swiftly open. "I am starting to believe you can perform miracles."

# · Six ·

The ship is in darkness. My heart leaps into my throat as I envisage the worst case scenario. Providence has made me a pessimist.

"They are below deck," Lucas assures me. "No signs of an attack."

I nod and we land quietly.

Two yellow eyes appear, as if by magic, followed by a tenacious voice. "Hey, fake-angel."

Lucas whirls around, clearly surprised. There's a first.

"Hey, Brue." I stifle a chuckle. "Where did you spring from?"

He shrugs noncommittally. "Nowhere."

He assesses Lucas shrewdly, wrinkling his nose at his white tunic and trouser combo, and then bursting into hysterics when he notices Axion's new pink trimmed attire.

"Come on," I grin. "I need to introduce my mother to an angel."

"Where are the lookouts we posted?" Axion mumbles.

Brue snorts. "Asleep in their cabins."

I rub my temples in despair as we climb down the narrow metal staircase into the hull. Asleep! "That's excellent."

"I'll talk to them," Axion states, and he disappears along a different passageway.

"Who are you?" Brue scoffs at Lucas with disdain.

"Brue," I caution him indulgently. "Please try to be polite." He doesn't seem to be having any problems with his confidence in an angel's presence. Brue in a city full of angeli. The thought makes me queasy.

Lucas smirks at him, his head shaking infinitesimally. "I am a friend of Aqua's," he answers. "Call me Lucas."

Brue huffs, mumbling under his breath. I don't think he manages a coherent word but the tone sounds derogatory. I shrug apologetically at my angeli friend. Brue is a force unto himself.

"Aqua!" My mother bounds over a mass of snoring bodies as we enter the ship's cargo hold, which is now housing an impromptu slumber party. It's full of too many little refugees and their widowed mothers. I try not to dwell on the thought but my eyes moisten anyway. My mother's carrying a battery powered torch, which is struggling to emit a dim beam with the little juice it has left. She comes to an immediate standstill before us, her expression full of wonder as she gazes up at Lucas like he's the archangel himself.

"Oh my," she exclaims eventually.

"Mum, this is Lucas." I push the torch's beam down and out of his squinting eyes. She doesn't even acknowledge I've spoken. Honestly, she's almost drooling. "Well, I'll let you introduce yourselves." I kiss her cheek before wandering further into the hull of the boat. Lucas is better off staying near the only source of light, they're the only two here that are blinded by the black of night.

The few cot beds that were on board were reserved for the injured. They are arranged at the bow end, and all are full of casualties. Some are asleep but most are weeping in pain, sorrow or both. I check over my shoulder before opening my medicines pouch and pulling out the vials I pilfered from the medical wing. I spend the rest of the night doing what I can with the little supplies I have. I ease their pain with medicine, re-bandage their wounds with any clean fabric I can find, encourage them to drink their rations of fresh water.

Axion takes control of the guard duties, ensuring each shift is covered. My mother succumbs to sleep when the torch batteries finally expire. Brue searches the vessel for anything of use, distributing whatever he finds to the people who most need it: food, water, blankets and more. I smile each time I see him with armfuls of his bounty.

Lucas joins me in my nursing duties, relaxing as his vision improves with the sunrise. The first light of day goes unnoticed by most, as it streams through the few small portholes of the ship. Obviously exhausted, it is long past midday when the majority of dragone begin to stir. The women comfort the children, and each other, as they wail. My mother takes over from me, fussing over the injured like a mother hen.

Lucas tolerates being the centre of attention about as well as I did, especially when the restless and bored children start playing dares. The highlight of the competition, and the most amusing thing I've ever witnessed, is the challenge to retrieve a white angel feather. He eventually plucks one himself and hands it to a jubilant little girl, no older than five. She skips off merrily and is instantly surrounded by her energised cohort. Lucas sticks by my side after that, accompanying me each time I leave the hold. The queues for trips above deck are endless. We guard each group as they emerge for fresh air and bladder relief. Lucas and I watch the horizon expectantly. Fortunately, the attack we expect doesn't come.

As night falls, he kisses my temple before taking off alone and returning to Celthia. It's this bit that has me most nervous: a fleet of angeli Guard, trained to kill the dragone, led directly to a ship, full of the stranded and vulnerable beings they despise, by the angeli who may or may not have tried to kill me.

I stay on deck, waiting and watching with Axion. The tension radiates from him, too. It makes for an uncomfortable silence.

"So," I mumble. "This thing, where I can somehow feel..." I blush and wish I'd never started my question.

Some silences don't need to be filled.

Axion glances at me slyly, without moving his head, and then smirks. "I'm not good at biology lessons," he states, his voice remains low. He huffs through his nose before continuing. "We have hormones in our skin. Other dragone can detect them if they touch us."

I contemplate his words for a while, reflecting. "That's why I've never felt it before?" Honestly, nothing surprises me at this point. Wings? Check. Gills? Check. Direct line to a dragone's emotions? Check.

He weaves his fingers through mine and frowns in thought. "Our skin excretes our emotions, different chemicals for different feelings." He finally turns his head toward me. "I felt it from you, after Nicholai." His Adam's apple bobs as he turns his face away again.

"But I didn't start feeling anything from you," I state.

"Or you just didn't realise it."

"Yeah, perhaps." I mull it over in my mind. My mother taught me enough biology to pass my final exams. The nervous system – receptors on the skin send messages to the brain, chemical codes, encryptions of perceived stimuli, transmitted along nerve fibres like electricity. Yet another dormant part of me brought to life. "Is there anything else I should know?" I mutter.

"Like what?"

I smirk as I try to remember every comic book I've ever seen, concentrating on the villains of course. "Like x-ray vision or telekinesis? Can we spit acid?"

He gives a blasé shrug. "Some of us have poisonous spines down our backs, and retractable claws like *Wolverine*." He glances slyly at me again and I laugh.

Skin contact, the inbuilt dragone lie detector. "Liar."

He grins, and we relax into a more comfortable silence. One I'm determined not to break while we watch for approaching wings.

We are downwind of their flight path. The sweet scents of the angeli reach me before my night vision detects their stealthy movement. I don't need to tell Axion they're here. He drops my hand the second he registers my spike in anxiety and stands to attention.

"This should be interesting," he murmurs.

I'd have to agree.

We watch them draw increasingly nearer, looming down on our suddenly claustrophobic vessel like fighter jets. A whole squadron of Eurofighter Typhoons, locked and loaded. It's a confusing mix of sensation. They are my colleagues, some are my friends, yet I feel... torn.

Liam lands first, leading his battalion from the front as always. It is a battalion, one angeli for every refugee. Fortunately, most remain hovering well above the height of the deck. A handful land behind Liam, it is him that has me most torn.

"Aquila," he sneers in greeting.

My heart constricts painfully but I hold the evidence of it down like a sinking sandbag. "Liam." I hold his glare, which is surprisingly accurate in the dim twilight. He looks infuriatingly stunning in my colourless night vision, a timeless snapshot of Adonis himself, all leather and steel and loathing. We could probably stand here hating each other, for an eternity.

"Worst idea ever," Axion mumbles, answering my unspoken thought. We weren't even holding hands.

Liam scowls in Axion's direction, his focus broken. He finally signals the Guard and they begin.

It takes hours, at least it feels that way, to wrap each refugee in an insulating silver blanket that looks about as comfortable as tinfoil. They also each, with encouragement, swallow a vial of red liquid. Lucas guarantees that it's safe, but still I insist on trying it first, like a modern day food taster. I learn, first hand, that it tastes like chilli sauce and dramatically increases body temperature. Great for the colder blooded dragone, not so great for me who inherited my father's warm blood. I sweat. Then I pant like a Newfoundland in a sauna. Thank God I didn't swallow a whole vial. Lucas gives me his *I told you so* look before offering me his water flask.

"I feel like a burrito," Brue complains.

I'll be carrying him. I wish I could carry all of them. I can't help feeling anxious. No, not anxious, sick to my stomach. I don't trust the Guard. More accurately, I don't trust Liam. That's the root of the matter. He's completely obliterated my trust in him. I scowl at his back, trying to quell the fire in my stomach by gulping down water. He's still on the deck, barking orders. He must sense my eyes on him. It makes his dark wings ruffle and his shoulders tense, but he doesn't give me as much as a cursory glance. He's infuriating.

I blow out a breath, ensuring flames aren't about to burst from my mouth when I speak. "Well, kid." I wrap Brue in my arms. "Better to be a burrito than a cryogenic experiment."

He groans as we take to the air. I hook his legs in mine and we fly for Celthia. We're the last to leave, me and Brue, Axion and a small boy named Cole, and Lucas and my mother. Her cheeks are a rosy red, and it's not from the chilli sauce. For someone who's never stepped foot on an aeroplane, she's surprisingly relaxed to be eight thousand feet above sea level secured only by Lucas' arms. Apparently we can't take them much higher unless they're used to altitude, which they aren't, and even then they could pass out. It makes the night-time journey even more vital. Any human glancing upward may wonder why two hundred yellow fireflies just shot past. Fluorescent orbs in a haze of neon light, like a blazing trail of fireballs, are streaking across the sky. Perhaps we should have asked the dragone to close their eyes.

The flight, however nerve-wracking, is mercifully uneventful. The hangar doors await, opened, like a gaping mouth in the mountain ready and willing to swallow every soul whole. The Guard do not waste time.

They deliver their air mail directly to the cells and then retreat to the barracks. The tinfoil and chilli sauce go some way toward masking the dragone's spicy scent. Even so, the cells rapidly acquire the tang of a Michelin-starred chef's fully stocked spice rack.

Mattresses litter the stone floors, jugs of water sit in alcoves, and one small room is full of stone buckets. Brue demonstrates their usefulness immediately in the way only a pre-adolescent boy can. I shake my head in wry amusement. I'm sure as hell not emptying that.

"Guardian," Plyrian calls me gently. His voice floats behind the glow of a beeswax candle as he approaches. "You should rest. I'll accompany you to your room."

The other Guard have vanished, including Liam. "I want to stay with them."

He sighs in response. "Victus would not allow it. You are the Guardian of Celthia and news of your return yesterday has already spread."

His tone is clear.

Damn, August and Aaron. I nod, climbing to my feet. I am exhausted. "Where's my mother? She's not here."

Plyrian offers me his arm for support and I take it. "Robyn is helping her settle into a room," he answers.

"She gets a room?" I question, my eyebrows lifting.

"She's human," he smiles. "We do not hate her by association."

I grimace. "That's incredibly species-ist of you." I mean to sound indignant, but I'm too tired.

"It's a hard habit to break," he whispers quietly.

"Brue, Ax," I signal them. "I've got to go." I look at Axion poignantly. "You remember what we discussed."

He nods solemnly. The same dragone sailor guarding patterns will continue in Celthia, this time the focus will be on a threat of a different kind, of a different species, the angeli.

I squeeze Axion's hand and plant a kiss on the top of Brue's forehead before leaving them. Brue's shaggy black hair has grown since I met him. What did Liam say? I've been gone two weeks? Now's not the time to question them, and quite frankly, their time keeping is so poor they probably have no idea how long it's been either.

"Goodnight, I'll be back as soon as I can."

They nod in unison and I smile. Unfathomably they both feel like family, like we've always been together.

Plyrian tightens his hold and urges me to move, though he tries not to make it obvious. When we are clear of the cells he relaxes slightly. "You did well, Aqua," he praises me.

I'm not sure what he's referring to, so I just smile lazily. I feel sleepy, like I'm already balancing on the edge of a dream. The events of the last few weeks, and the after effects of my adrenalin come down, are taking their toll. I really need sleep.

"I'm glad you're back," he adds, regaining my attention. "Relatively unscathed," he comments. "Here," he hands me a flask of water. "How is your leg?"

I take it appreciatively. "Thanks." Water drips down my chin as I swallow a greedy mouthful. I wipe it away with the back of my hand. "Fine," I lie.

My leg's actually causing me some pain, though the skin is healing quickly with the aid of the angeli medicine. I look at the area, contemplating.

"Did he tell you why?" I ask, perhaps too morosely. I sound pathetic.

He pats my shoulder blade powerfully, like he's uncomfortable handling my display of emotional weakness. Or perhaps just to comfort me in the way the Guard comfort their comrades. "Whatever his reasons, Aqua, he is a good man and he cares for you like no other." He accentuates his words, *'like no other'*. Plyrian knows of mine and Liam's secret love affair.

I swallow reflexively but do not comment.

"Our other project is going well," he smiles, changing the subject smoothly. "My nephew is quite keen for us to push forward. I believe your brother may have something to do with it."

"August," I smile warmly. "I've missed him."

"He missed you, too."

"I should go there now," I decide. "Walk me?" August is going to be furious with me. Putting off our reunion, even with the excuse of this ridiculous hour, will not go down well.

"My pleasure," Plyrian grins.

"So how is Oberon?" I ask. Talk of his nephew and my brother piques my interest. Oberon is the angeli responsible for the formation of the rebel alliance.

"In love," he whispers conspiratorially. "Eager to be rid of the Script."

I nod. "And Gloria?"

"Glorious," he grins. "I am a lucky man. And she is a lucky woman." He winks smugly but there's pure devotion behind his expression.

I laugh aloud, glad to see that he's still the Second I know as my friend. I still trust him. It's an unexpected fact I find reassuring. The noise of my laughter bounces along the walls as we descend the male wing of the city. August's door opens before we reach it. In its place, three surprised faces peer out. I smile. My brother and my best friend, and Oberon.

"I told you it was her," Oberon exclaims, but he doesn't sound convinced despite staring right at me.

"My God," Aaron breathes as August bursts into tears and barrels along the remaining corridor and into my chest. A tension I knew weighed on my shoulders releases as I take them in, all of them. They're here and they're safe.

"Hey little brother." I grin as I hug him. "Missed you."

I press kisses to his matted hair. He smells of August, and my coconut shower gel. I scowl. I bet he's been stealing my human bathroom products the whole time I've been gone.

"You said you wouldn't leave," he sobs, talking into my shoulder, and he's immediately forgiven. How can I begrudge him a bit of soap I wasn't here to use? At least he washed.

"I'm sorry I was gone so long." I drag him back toward his room, wishing Plyrian goodnight as I pass. He's having a quick exchange with his nephew about discretion and arithmetic. Three males plus a two-bed room does not a balanced equation make. I hug my brother tighter. "So spill. New roommate?"

He's still too emotional to respond but he manages a genuine smile. We stumble into his room and flop onto his bed. We don't speak. I curl up in his arms, holding him tight while he sobs. The others follow us in, sitting quietly on Aaron's bed, watching.

"I'm angry with you," August manages to whisper.

I nod, understanding. "In the morning," I reply. "Hate me then." I rest my head on his chest.

"I'll never hate you," he responds quietly, stifling a yawn.

"Sleep," I suggest, "I'll stay here tonight." I glance at the other two, who are still staring. They peek at each other, and then down at the single remaining bed they're on. I smother a smile. I know it's not them who've been sharing.

"You're staying here forever," August answers, but his voice drifts off at the end. I kiss his warm skin, listening to his heart beating.

"He's barely slept since you left," Aaron whispers, still staring at me. His features are blurred by the orange glow of the candles in the room.

I nod, acknowledging his tone. He's angry at me too. "Tomorrow," I tell him. Everyone can shout at me tomorrow. For now, I just want to close my eyes and hug my human brother.

I close my eyes, a content rumble vibrating in my chest.

August's snoring is the first thing I'm aware of. That, and I'm feeling overcrowded. I open my eyes in the dark, waiting momentarily for them to adjust. I lift my head, confused until I realise that I'm sandwiched between a scorching mass that wasn't there before. Aaron is asleep behind me, his arm wrapped tightly around my waist, his breath gently wafting my feathers. August has shifted over marginally, his leg is draped over mine. Oberon is stretched behind him, squat between my brother and the wall, his face nuzzling my brother's neck and his arm resting across his chest. I smile at them. I can't move. I'm wedged and still exhausted. I entwine my fingers with my best friend's and drift back to sleep.

The door slams. I crack an eyelid. Heavy, aggravated footsteps clomp below the floating orange light. The scent hits me as strong as ever, a masculine aroma full of pheromones. I inhale sharply as my eyes focus on Liam's face. I freeze, not sure what to do. If I'm the rabbit, then he's the headlights of a ten tonne steam roller.

"Three men this time," he comments, his face still hard.

His voice, however, holds a note of amusement and I risk a diminutive smile. He's caught me in bed with August before, only sleeping what with August's preferences, but he said he was jealous then. My smile drops into a frown. He has no right to be jealous now. He shouldn't even be in here. He shot me with a god-damned arrow.

"They missed me," I answer belligerently, "and I missed them."

His face darkens as he realises that I have no intention of moving from my spot in this thermonuclear sardine tin. "I have work to do," he states. "We will talk when you are less hostile." The flame of the candle disappears as he turns away, like a solar eclipse of the cranial kind. The door slams more loudly on his way out.

And I get that familiar and unfathomable urge to follow him.

I shake the feeling from my head and shut out the world again. *Me* less hostile? Ha. He started it.

My dreams pull me down, down into a dark and hollow place. A nightmare filled with a kaleidoscope of tainted images, of feelings, of moments.

A catastrophic ode to Liam.

"Breakfast," Aaron murmurs in my ear. "Wake up." His voice is so soothing, for a second I could believe we are somewhere else entirely and this has all just been an inconceivable dream.

Except it wasn't, and we aren't. "Not hungry," I complain, scrunching my eyes. "Sleep."

His chest rumbles with laughter. "You need a shower."

I slap at him with my eyes closed, achieving a groan of dissent, but I can't deny he's right. "Agreed," I sigh, pulling myself up to sitting.

The room is already busy. August is stumbling about, grabbing relatively clean clothes and eyeing us pensively. Before I left, they'd both known Liam and I were together. August accepted it. Aaron was not so supportive.

August had told Aaron I was in love with him, and I was before I met Liam. It disfigured our friendship, created tension that was never there before. Aaron hadn't wanted me when he found out I'm not human, but he didn't want to see me with Liam either. I sigh and smile weakly at him, before looking away. I'll need to talk to them both at some point, to explain. But not right now.

The shower is running. Oberon must be using it. "I'll go to my room," I suggest as I clamber from the bed.

I ignore any response they produce as I make a quick getaway. Spending the night in Aaron's arms was not well thought out. If my dreams last night revealed anything, it's that Liam is still a vine of ivy wound around my soul. There isn't enough weed killer in the world to remove it. I don't think I want there to be.

Speak of the devil. I raise an eyebrow.

"I'm never letting you out of my sight again," he explains nonchalantly as he lounges in the hallway. His winged back is pressed against the smooth rock wall, his bare foot planted below his buttock. I get a distinct sense of déjà vu and gasp involuntarily. I'm sure my face must display the sudden flush of warmth.

"Well I'm going for a shower, so mission failed already," I retort. What is he playing at? I glance around, deciding on my escape route should I need it.

He shrugs but his lips twitch into a hint of a wicked smile. "I've never failed a mission," he answers huskily.

I'd blush at the implication, except I'm too furious at him. Really, truly angry. I'm semi-aware I've zoned out. I can't help losing an indeterminate length of time while I process every ache my mind and body holds for this man. By the time I regain focus, his face has lost its amused edge. My head tilts with defeat as I relent to my own curiosity.

"Why did you do it?"

He blinks. He has the grace to look remorseful. Although, I know he can put on a good act. *Fool me once, shame on me.* "Because you left," he answers, his eyes darkening.

"Excuse me?" I gasp. "*Because I left?*" My voice goes annoyingly squeaky so I stop. I need to calm down. I'll only embarrass myself by ranting.

"No, Aqua." He takes a step forward and I take one back. "Not just because you left." He flares his arms in exasperation. "It was the only hope I had." His hands fist at his own words, until his knuckles crack in annoyance. "You were running toward a trap!" he exclaims and I flinch. "Of all the idiotic, stupid, selfish things I've seen you do I think that was the worst!" His eyes blaze like dual suns. "I wasn't trying to kill you," he yells. "Can't you see, you infuriating... woman." His hands flail like windmills again while he decides what to call me. My eyes widen but I take another step back. *Fool me twice, shame on me.*

I can't face this right now. I need a shower. I need time to think. I spin on my heel and march off toward the female wing.

"Aqua!" he yells, marching after me.

"I'm still feeling hostile," I snap. I'm relieved my voice maintains its volume. I sound as angry as I feel.

"You didn't look hostile last night," he yells back, matching my ferocity. "You are meant for me, Aquila. That human is nothing more than an annoying pet. I won't let you use this as an excuse to rush back into his arms."

I whirl on him, and slap him hard across the face – again. I could get used to this. "How dare you?" I'm too angry, too incoherent to form a proper argument. I blink and then spin again and march away. This time he doesn't follow.

My room smells of men. It's infuriating. I stomp across it to my bed, which smells of August, Aaron, Lucas, even Liam. What the hell have they been doing in here? The lack of locks in Celthia is an issue I feel needs addressing.

I pull the stone dressing table across the room so it blocks the door. At least if anyone else feels like letting themselves in while I'm showering then I'll know about it. I don't ignite any candles, the room is devoid of a single speck of light, but my vision is fine. I peel off the leather that I've been wearing *for two weeks* and drop it on the floor. I shudder. Finally, I can put on clean clothes. I smile as I step into the shower's stream. The water in the small stone bathroom is icy cold, pumped directly from the underground river. I stand under it, letting the freshness wash away the grime, the sweat of the fighting, the salt of the ocean, and the blood of the Fallen. I must have really stunk. I lather my coconut shower gel, of which only a little remains. I should have taken the time to acquire some more whilst playing shoplifter in China.

I close my eyes and let my mind wander. Autopilot takes over all essential duties, like shaving my disgraceful legs, while my psyche flips over a 'Do Not Disturb' sign. For a while, for a very short while, I feel content.

The Grand hall is exactly the same. Rows of circular stone tables fill the impressive space. Large statues of golden birds of prey edge the room. A long counter full of food sits below the bus-sized hole which leads onto the veranda. I'm hungry, really hungry. I haven't eaten anything other than grapes for days. I rush toward the buffet, and start to load a plate before Aaron catches up, smirking. "Hungry?"

I make a noise of agreement while stuffing roasted crickets into my mouth.

His expression turns dark, almost anguished. "Did they look after you? You look like you've lost weight."

"They kept trying to feed me meat," I moan. I shove in another handful and move on to the hazelnut stuffed mushrooms. Hmmm, iced tea with berries. Rice and curried ants! I pile a spoonful onto my already full plate.

He watches with wry amusement. "Fiends," he comments, his mouth morphing into a cute pout, "I want meat." His despondent tone makes me laugh.

"These are meat, sort of." I wave a roasted cricket under his nose, which he bats away with a disgusted flick of his hand.

"I'd rather have bacon," he grumbles. "Or steak. Or your mum's braised lamb." His stomach grumbles like an earthquake.

"Well, she's here somewhere so perhaps you'll get your wish."

"Really?" he asks sceptically. Our eyes roam the Grand hall together, searching. But there's no sign. God, I better not have misplaced her again.

My eyes stop at our usual table and I groan. It's crowded with eager faces. We walk toward them slowly. I sit on the stool August is tapping ferociously and dot a kiss on his cheek. "Hi little brother."

"Everyone's talking about you!" he exclaims, already breathless. "They said you killed the king to escape."

"I heard that you brought his head back as a trophy," Lielan interjects, her eyes bright. Lielan is not my biggest fan, since I humiliated her during our youngling trials. But even she'll talk to me if it involves the latest scandal.

"I heard you stole a cruise ship and sailed off with a load of hostages," Oberon adds, laughing.

"Who spreads all this stuff," I groan. "I didn't kill the king, I assume his head is still on his shoulders, but can't be sure. And I borrowed the ship to save refugees – not hostages."

August gasps. "The ship thing's true?" He sounds incredulous.

I shrug. "I had help, they wanted to escape, too, you know. And it wasn't a cruise ship, it was a cargo ship. A small one."

The whole table stares at me, bewildered.

I'm saved by my guardian angel, who drops his hand to my shoulder from behind. It's a comforting gesture. I rub my cheek against his skin gratefully.

"August," Lucas reprimands him. "Aqua has just returned." His voice holds a note of exasperation but I don't think it's aimed at August. I glance up as he glances down. His blue eyes are clouded, like there's something on his mind.

"Where are the refugees now?" Aaron asks.

I drop my eyes to him, my expression blank. His head is tilted back, so that he's looking down the length of his nose at me. He looks wary.

My gaze flicks to the table. Do I tell them? I don't know how Victus wants to handle this. I don't want a lynch mob descending into the mountain when they hear that dragone are hidden down there.

"They are safe," Lucas states, not looking at Aaron. "Victus is planning an announcement." His voice is still strained.

The man in question strolls in then, like he has in inbuilt radar alerting him whenever someone mentions his name. He strides to the centre of the room and clambers onto a table top. I've never seen Victus fly, I'm not sure if he can. His wings are greying like his hair, his belly more rounded than most here. He's wearing his burgundy ceremonial robes. I sense another epic speech and groan. Lucas squeezes my shoulder and smirks down at me.

"Angeli of Celthia," Victus addresses the already silent room. Eyes tear from their gaze on me to study him. "Last night, our Guardian returned to us..." All eyes back on me. I sink into my stool, longing for invisibility.

"You may have heard whisperings and tales of her endeavours. I bid you appreciate not all are accurate, but you can be assured that Aquila the Guardian has overcome many obstacles to return home. The city welcomes her back, grateful for her re-established safety within our walls."

I cringe, squirming in my seat. I hate it when he does this – words as weapons to assert his dominance. It's lucky they're generally words in my favour. I feel my blush and Lucas' reassuring squeeze in response.

"There have been other rumours circulating, rumours I bid you put to rest today." He raises his arms as he delivers his speech. You can never tell with Victus if it's rehearsed or spontaneous. I watch him in silence, my face still burning. "Tales of hostages are inaccurate. We are not a violent race," he exclaims.

I stifle a cough of incongruity, which he ignores. I know he heard, the room is completely soundless.

"We do not kidnap or kill indiscriminately. We are honourable and just. We are above acts of hate or fear..."

You've got to hand it to him, he knows what he's doing – even if I do dispute most of his last statements. I watch in fascinated trepidation. I have an awful feeling growing in my gut, which I can't quite put a name to. Foreboding perhaps?

"There were no hostages, but there were refugees. Innocents caught up within a war we had no knowledge of. A civil war. It is our duty as honourable people to protect the innocent. We have been given an opportunity, to make amends and build relationships. We have accepted into our midst the guiltless victims of the dishonourable dragone."

I blink. Yep, definitely foreboding.

"I understand the fear you harbour. I understand your prejudice. But as a city, as a race, you must overcome it now. Today is a monumental day. A day that will be recorded in our history as a climb in our evolution."

The doors open. Plyrian leads the entire group of dragone into the Grand hall, straight through the deafening force of a collective gasp. The city freezes, tension crackling in the air like a thunderstorm. I stare shocked. They're wearing angeli clothes, the children in yellow and the adults in blue. What is Victus thinking?! I thought he was preparing the city gradually, not striking while the iron was hot. So much for keeping their presence a secret. The silence is piercing, but at least no one's staring at me anymore.

"Angeli of Celthia," Victus continues, even though he doesn't receive the attention of anyone this time. "I introduce to you our guests. These individuals have sought our protection and we have accepted. They are to be treated with kindness and respect and, in return, they will integrate within the city to work loyally alongside us. Allowances will need to be made, by all of us. Some compromises will be necessary, but I trust you all capable.

"Today we are all ambassadors of the angeli race. We will display courtesy. Plyrian, show our guests where they may help themselves to breakfast," he commands, and even Plyrian flinches.

My mouth's getting dry. It's only then that I realise it's hanging open. "Did you know about this?" I ask Lucas, my eyes locking with his again.

He nods once, his mouth a grim line.

"He's lost his mind," Aaron hisses.

The angeli stare, as the shuffling feet of the dragone move toward the buffet. They must be starving. I watch, feeling disconnected by my shock.

"Deep breaths," Lucas whispers. "I am out of smelling salts."

I actually feel a tug of a smile on my lips and I take his advice, drawing in a large lungful of air. Urgh, the smell of roasted animal flesh. My eyes snap to the buffet. Shaking Nesters appear from the kitchens with trays of bacon and sausages. They drop their platters, with teeth clenching clangs, onto the polished stone counter before hurrying away.

Only Gloria, Plyrian's unofficial mate, stays to greet the dragone as they inch nervously yet fervently toward the food. It would be comical if it wasn't so horrifying. The dragone mothers hide their children between their legs. The angeli shuffle away, moving entire tables to distance themselves from the queue. I spot Axion and Brue, standing with my mother. She waves, oblivious to my horror-struck expression. I raise my hand stiffly, awkwardly returning the gesture. Axion and Brue scowl at me.

Victus watches everyone, scrutinising reactions. I realise I'm feeling a slither of admiration for the crazy old man. This can't be easy for him.

I hear Oberon speak softly, his voice full of scorn. "We need to push ahead," he comments. "He's evidently going senile. Now is the time to act, while the city is divided and confused."

My attention reverts to my friends at the table. "I agree," Aaron answers. "He's just made the entire city reconsider his leadership. We'll never get a better opportunity."

"We have the perfect deal to offer. Accept the destruction of the Script and we'll rid the city of the abominations," Oberon suggests.

Grunts of approval circle the table, stopping steadfast at me. I shake away the cobwebs of bewilderment.

"You what?" I gasp. "No, now is not the time for revolution." God, there couldn't be a worse time. The dragone need protection, they are innocent. And I have friends among them.

"Come on Aqua," Aaron hisses. "This is perfect! Victus would never see us coming. We could take over peacefully – burn the rules. You can't agree with him, surely. Those people kidnapped you and your mum. They nearly killed me! They're evil."

"None of them had anything to do with any of that!" I exclaim. Everyone in the room turns to stare but I don't care. I scowl angrily. My wings ruffle in frustration. I drop my voice to a whisper, but my tone is firm. "Victus needs to control this situation or there'll be a bloodbath. They're women, children and a handful of sailors. None of them have ever hurt an angeli." Probably. "I rescued those people, and I didn't do it for you to use them as blackmail."

I'm so shocked and angry I can't think. I stand up, furious. I'm the only person standing, in the whole room, except for Victus and the dragone. I shake on my feet, debating what to do: run, cry, sit back down? Angeli stare at me. Even the dragone, who probably didn't hear my outburst, watch me. Most are smiling in recognition. God, stop smiling at me. Stop staring at me. What the hell am I doing?

"Aqua?" Aaron says hesitantly.

I don't answer. I'm still scrambled inside my own head. Brue spots me as I stare over at them. I'm trapped, wavering between being happy they're here and wishing I'd thought of somewhere else to take them. I can't smile back, my face is paralysed. Brue frowns at me, concerned, before striding confidently in my direction.

He weaves between tables. Every angeli in the room starts to yell their objection. It wakes me up, jolting me. These people are grown adults.

"Look at yourselves!" I shout impulsively, glaring across the room. "Look at your proud and honourable race!"

I'm furious. Brue brings out as many protective instincts as August. I stare at anyone who looks at me in the eye, daring them to respond.

"He's a boy, an innocent boy." Brue scowls but I continue, wrapping my arms around him when he reaches me. "You sit at your tables," I shout, "passing judgment, discussing attack." I don't glance at my friends, I'm sure every table was having a similar discussion. "These people have lost their homes, through no fault of their own. Most of these children have lost their fathers, these women their mates. These individuals are innocent! They're innocent of the crimes of their species, of the crimes of their ancestors. Hell, they're innocent of the crimes of other dragone who they've never even met; just as you are innocent of your ancestors' crimes before you. I will not hear your snide judgements and malevolent statements. I will not hear you speak ill of the guiltless. Victus is right."

I almost faint.

"You all have a chance to make amends for your sins. You have a chance to prove to everyone you have honour, you can forgive and rise above prejudice." I look at Brue, my impulsive nature taking over. Without asking permission, I lift him onto my shoulders so the entire city can see him. "This is Brue. He is funny and smart, the cleverest kid I've ever met. He is innocent of the crimes of his species." I lift him back down, ignoring his grumbling.

I make eye contact with Axion and he grimaces. My lips twitch at his expression but it doesn't break my focus. I gesture toward my embarrassed dragone brother. He steps forward slightly. "This is Axion, twenty years old, and now the head of his house. He is honest and reliable. He is a hero, risking his life to protect his people. He is innocent of the crimes of his species." He nods at me, and I return the gesture.

"Mum," I shout. She waves spastically across the room, beaming. I smile back. "This is my mother, Libby. She's human. She was taken by a small group of rival dragone four months ago. Yet here she stands, happy in their company because she understands, first-hand, that you cannot blame an entire species for the actions of a few guilty individuals. My mother knows these people are innocent of the crimes of their species.

"I ask you all to listen. I myself have been the target of your malicious rumours. I know how it feels to receive harsh and inaccurate judgements." I spit my words out, more aggressively than I intended. Lucas grasps my hand, silently supporting me, while my other arm rests around Brue. I take a deep breath. "I am an inhabitant of this city. I am your Guardian. I am a member of the Guard and I am the daughter of Marcus the Protector. I pledge my protection to everyone inside these walls, whether you are angeli, human or dragone." Or any mixture of the above, I add silently.

I stand, holding on tightly to Brue and Lucas, as the entire city processes my outburst. My heart is hammering, obviously audible to most of the angeli around me. No one moves for so long that I start trembling, until, quite by surprise, a noise echoes around the space. I'm not sure what it is at first, my eyes have to seek out its source before I can process it. Gloria, standing alone behind the counter top, is clapping. I stare dumbfounded as she smiles at me. Plyrian joins in next, his hands making twice as much noise as his lover's. When the noise starts at my own table I jump. August, Aaron and Oberon have joined in. I gape at Aaron and he grins, shrugging.

Around the room, tentatively, the movement grows. The sound of clapping builds into a crescendo. Not everyone participates; in fact the clappers are the minority. However, the sound fills the room and ricochets from the walls, humbling me. Victus stares down from his perch upon the table, tapping his chin thoughtfully, always speculating. My eyebrows quirk inquisitively, to which he nods. In a show of solidarity, he strikes his hands together, matching the rhythm of the city.

The city bursts into conversation around the room, voices less sharp than before. Nevertheless, there is no miracle cure for generations of hate. Nothing as simple as a speech is going to fix a great deal.

"Brue," I sigh. "Never walk off alone again. You must stay as a group. There are people here who would hurt you if they got the chance, just because you're different."

"But you'll protect me," he shrugs confidently, ignoring my concerns. "Stop calling me kid. The whole city thinks I'm a kid now." He tugs at his clothing, scowling. "Look at this stupid yellow shi…"

"Brue!" I interrupt. "Watch your language."

"Shirt," he moans, still pulling at his clothes. "I was going to say shirt. Where have you been? You left us sleeping in the dungeon."

I snigger, exasperated. "Sorry about the cells but I had to catch up with a few people, here," I point at

August, "this is my brother, August. August, this is Brue. He kept me sane while I was gone."

"Hi," August stutters, lost for words for a change.

"Alright?" Brue replies, unbothered.

"Aaron," I say, pointing.

"The human," Brue nods. "The one the Fallen killed." Aaron blinks.

"Nearly killed," I clarify pointlessly. "Oberon, Lielan, Keera, Theon." I introduce the rest of the table. "And you know Lucas. Go get some breakfast. You can sit with us."

"You want me to walk off alone?" he smirks. "Through all these angels?"

"Gah," I groan. "Fine, come on." I put my arm around his shoulders and push him back to the group, ignoring the stares as we pass tables.

"Hi, Mum." I kiss her as we get there.

"Hi honey, nice place you have here," she jokes. The peyote has long worn off and she's obviously handling the existence of a city of winged beings better than Aaron did. "Who were your friends? Is that Aaron over there?"

I open my mouth to reply.

"And her brother," Brue adds smiling. My mother turns deathly pale.

My face catches fire. Oh my god. I have to introduce my mother to August, her biological, deceased, son.

"Um, Brue." I shake my head, sending a silencing glare. He's an astute kid. He shuts his mouth but I know he'll be roasting me for information later.

"No, honey," my mother waves away her tears with a waft of her hand, "I'm fine. I should have expected that you had family here. You found your father? Mark-something?"

"Marcus." I exhale and rub my temples. "He has two sons here. Come and sit with us once you've got your food."

"Of course, sweetheart."

I glance at Axion before I turn around. He's watching me intently, mystified by my mother's reaction. I shake my head. I'll explain later.

I sink back onto my stool when I get back. The table is silent. Lucas has wandered off and suddenly I'm vulnerable again.

Aaron moves closer and, in an unexpected show of affection, presses a kiss above my ear. My gaze moves sideways, searching his stormy gray eyes, and he flushes. I really shouldn't have let him sleep beside me. My emotions are too wrecked to deal with any of this.

"How do I tell my mother about August?" I whisper.

"Gently," he suggests; his only words of advice.

I heave a sigh, "Thanks."

The silence at the table drags on.

"What?" I bark, frustrated.

"You meant all of that," August says. "You care about them." He sounds more confused than upset.

I nod. "Of course, they're innocent." I frown. "Our mother's coming over in a minute, I haven't told her about you yet; this is the first time she's been coherent. I don't know how to handle it..."

"Coherent?" he asks.

"Yeah, but that's not important right now. The fact is she's going to freak when she sees you." I groan again.

"Then we should do that in private." August springs up too eagerly, nervously, dragging Oberon with him. "We'll vanish and meet you later." He smiles weakly at me and they dash off. I stare after them, unseeing. I'm still derelict, a shell of disorder.

"That'll be interesting," Aaron comments. I grunt in response.

How do you explain what Marcus did? Telling her August – Harry – was dead and replacing him with me. It's creepy in any language.

"I need to apologise," Aaron continues, shoulder bumping me. "For the last time we spoke. I was stupid."

I glance sideways at him. "I shouldn't have let you walk away before we talked it through."

I was too wrapped up in my new boyfriend, too selfish to consider the feelings of my best friend. I practically abandoned him in a foreign land. I should have followed him that day, instead of running off to the barracks to find Liam. I might have never seen Aaron again and that's how we would have remembered each other, angry and neglectful.

He shrugs. "I didn't really feel like talking. Look, I still don't like him, but I saw what you leaving did to the guy. He was a mess. He obviously loves you. Just don't let him bully you. He's a sexist swine. You're too good for him."

I gulp and feel myself pale. "Well, I'm not sure that we're... together... at the moment." I rub my temples again. I guess the city remained delightfully clueless while I trundled off to Hantiem with Liam's arrow in my leg.

"Aqua," Aaron murmurs, his voice low.

Thank God my mother arrives at that moment and flings herself at Aaron, saving me from his turbulent gaze. "Oh Aaron, thank the lord you're alive. I was so worried."

I don't correct her. She probably was worried, in between doses. My mother sits on Oberon's vacated stool while Axion stands awkwardly, holding his plate. Brue drops cheerfully onto the stool next to me.

"Sit, Axion," I command the hovering dragone. "Axion, this is Aaron. Aaron, this is Ax."

They exchange strained greetings. The other angeli on the table disperse quickly as dragone fill the spaces. In fact, the whole hall empties of wings rapidly as the dragone start to sit at tables. Only Aaron stays.

Dragone frequent the human world. They actually own TV's and mobile phones. He has more in common with them than he does with the angeli. As he relaxes, they start talking sports and movies. I ignore the looks he keeps giving me. He's desperate for information about Liam, about Hantiem, about the Fallen. I tell him a little about the island. I concentrate far more than necessary on eating.

"So you all slept in the cells?" Aaron asks, shocked.

"The dungeon," Brue grumbles. "Not exactly five star."

"It's temporary." I hope.

"So what now?" Aaron asks. And he's not just talking about right this second.

I heave a sigh.

It's a good question.

What now?

# • Seven •

Victus calls a meeting that's what, announced by a nervous messenger who promptly vanishes. Aaron leaves reluctantly, still watching me.

I relax once he's gone.

"Could you loosen up a little?" Axion asks.

"Huh?"

"I can feel your tension from here. It's unnerving."

"Sorry. It's harder being back here than I thought." I give him a tight smile.

"Seriously? It feels more dangerous here than on the island. These angels will never accept us," he states. "Your idea sucks."

I smirk, and then nod. "Perhaps."

"Axion, you're such a coward," Brue snipes. "Aqua saved everyone by bringing us here. What did you do? You fell on your butt and waited for her to save you. We'd all be dead or Rennison's prisoners if it was up to you!" He clenches his little fists as he glares at his brother.

"Shut up, Brue," Axion snarls. "You have no idea what it's like to fight. You're just a boy."

"I'm more of a man than you will ever be!" Brue yells back. "I would have gone back for the king. I would have protected the island, not run away."

"You got in the boat fast enough," Axion snaps.

I stare at them both. Their voices are so loud the whole city must have heard them. "Ax. Brue. Stop, please. Brue, sometimes it's better to run. I know you're brave, and courageous. But that only means something if you're wise enough to use it properly. Axion did the right thing." I swallow, lowering my voice. "Never mention that name again, especially while you're here. Please, there are things you don't know."

He opens his mouth but I silence him with a glare. I can hear feet approaching.

Lots of feet.

The Grand Hall is swarmed by a fleet of Guard, who systematically remove tables and create rows with the stools. We watch in silence, herded into a group like sheep. Liam is here, I can smell him. I'm sure I can feel his eyes on me, though I can't see him. I resist the urge to look.

Victus is already greeting everyone, and I mean everyone. He's wandering through the group, shaking shocked hands. The younger children hide between dragone legs as he passes, staring at him with wide eyes. He's changed clothes. He's now in his usual red pyjamas.

"Sit, sit everyone," he commands gently. "We have much to discuss, I think. Guardian Aquila, I thought you may have been entertaining our guests."

"Victus," I reply. "I will be *protecting* our guests for the duration of their stay."

"Today," Victus corrects. "I believe you will be expected to attend training tomorrow."

I blanch. Training tomorrow, with Liam. No wonder he's staring at me from somewhere. "And in my absence, what will become of our guests?" I snap.

"Excellent question, Guardian, as always. In your absence our guests will work and learn." He walks away with his arms up, until he's patrolling the front of his dragone audience like he's playing a tree in an amateur operatic presentation.

They gradually sit. He's created a mini-auditorium and he's the B-list star of the show. I stand at the edge, scowling at the Guard encircling the room. "The younglings will attend school," he states confidently. "They are expected to start tomorrow." He watches the dragone as they process his statement. They mostly look horrified.

"You're splitting them up?" I ask, incredulous.

"I'm giving them an opportunity," he responds. "A free education and a chance to learn the truth about our race. A chance to make angeli acquaintances and friends. A chance to integrate."

"A chance to be picked off one by one," I snarl beneath my breath. Loud enough for only the angeli ears to hear.

"The Guard have pledged their protection, Aqua. They will never be alone to be *picked off*." Liam's breath tickles my ear as he responds to my comment. I stiffen. No wonder I could sense him, he's right behind me. I don't answer. I most definitely do not appreciate this newfound ability he has to sneak up on me.

Victus keeps talking. "Lessons start after breakfast. You will be accompanied by Guard at all times. Classes are divided into age groups. Garven will collect names and ages."

He points to the tall Guard sitting at a table with paper and an ink well, complete with quill. "Form a line now, younglings, anyone over three years and under seventeen years. The rest of you will be expected to labour for our city." He launches into a speech about the society and roles within it. I switch off slowly as I watch the children. They move cautiously, eyes on their mothers or the threatening Guard at the edges of the room.

I huff and walk over; leaving Liam, whom I can imagine is frowning at me. I help the children state their names and ages, encouraging them to speak when it's their turn. Brue blatantly lies but I don't comment. I don't see the point of any of this. These aren't foreign exchange students. They are the angeli's generations-old enemies, and Victus is making them vulnerable.

"This is a mistake," I say as Liam saunters over eventually. My eyes flick to his cheek. I'm furtively expecting to see the red outline of a handprint, but it's faded away without so much as a bruise. "Why do this? We should be getting them their island back."

"We will," he answers. "You think we want them here? You know our history."

"Then why? Why all of this?"

His jaw tightens. The silence drags on until I'm almost convinced he won't answer. My eyes flick away from his face and I focus on the far wall.

He sighs quietly. "Victus thinks we can learn from them, if we watch them interact."

"So you're using them," I retort bitterly. "That makes more sense." I force my eyes back to his assertively. "I don't like it and I don't agree with it. These people are villagers. They won't give you an insight into the Fallen."

He blinks slowly, contemplating perhaps, though his face shows no hint of a discernible emotion. "That remains to be seen."

I shake my head. I feel drained, exhausted. This situation, this argument, this whole thing feels like a helix. Round and round we go, on a spinning top, never moving forward, never achieving anything more than dizziness, confusion and nausea. "We know more about our enemy than ever before. These aren't the dragone you're at war with. I believe them."

"I can see that." His gaze lands on Axion and his eyes flash with rage.

I grab his arm reflexively, and then drop it just as fast. Why should I explain myself to him? Why do I feel like I want to? "Axion protected me. We fought together. Do not lay your anger on him." Would it be petty to mention the arrow, again?

Liam glares, like he knows what I'm thinking. I turn away, disengaging completely from the conversation.

"I understand the camaraderie of battle," he whispers. I ignore his words as I wander off.

The last of the children rush back to their seats. I follow them quietly and Liam follows me. Tension is radiating from him, I studiously ignore his presence. Victus assigns positions in the kitchens, school and Nester crafts to the women. The men are all assigned to the Guard. I literally choke. Even Liam gasps. Axion blanches spectacularly.

"God, we'll be burying the dead tomorrow," I hiss. He's split them completely, men from women. Why? I wonder. Male and female angeli are not treated quite so chauvinistically, both sexes work within every profession.

"So little faith in my self-control, Aquila?" Liam asks snidely, breaking his silence with a bite of venom.

I sigh. "My faith in you bled out through a hole in my thigh." There it is. His crime. I might as well wave the steel shaft of his harpoon around in front of him, except I can't because Victus never gave it back, the crook.

His breath hitches audibly. "I'm putting you in charge of their training," he snaps. "You are good enough and it will prevent any accidents. They only spar with each other, do you understand? If any one of them hurts you I will kill them."

He storms off, too angry to converse rationally. I watch his tight back as he approaches Victus. His words are too quiet to hear but his tone is obvious. He marches out of the room and Victus beckons me over.

"Congratulations on your promotion, Guardian," he says as he shakes my reluctant hand.

"Is that what it was?" I reply.

"Regardless of his reasoning, you are capable and perhaps the most qualified for the task."

I scowl. "You know the Fallen will make a move soon. They saw me at the island. They know I helped in the escape. I still have no idea why they want me. And as for the sigil of their commander, I can only assume something crazy is going on." I wring my hands in frustration.

"Aqua," he sighs. "I'm not the dictator you make me out to be. I know you disagree with the structure of my rule. You favour equality and freedom. You favour democracy. Perhaps you are right, but for now I am the Overseer. When I choose not to inform you of something, I am acting in the best interest of this city and its people."

I gasp at his statement. It feels more like a confession of guilt to me. He's just admitted that he knows more about this.

"Don't trip on your own power, Victus." I back away from him. "It's a long way to fall." He knows I won't break his order, but it doesn't mean I agree.

He laughs. "Take your new charges to the barracks tomorrow morning, their uniforms will be waiting. I look forward to witnessing your endeavours," he bellows, his belly jiggling with amusement.

So do I. I have no idea where to start.

I follow the dragone around for the rest of the day, and Liam follows me. I can sense him but he stays out of sight, like a shadow in the dark.

Brue is like a bird in a glass cage. If I don't watch him he tries to fling himself against the invisible boundaries I've set. He watches the angeli around him like an anthropologist studying a rare culture and he asks questions constantly, more questions than Aaron ever asked when he first arrived.

I fall into bed, once everyone is settled for another night in the cells and after wishing my mother goodnight. She is in the room next to me, Robyn's old room. I warn her not to use the shower. Human's don't cope well with water as cold as liquid nitrogen. There's going to be one hell of a queue outside August and Aaron's door for a warm shower. Perhaps we should draw up some kind of rota.

My consciousness sinks slowly this time. I'm not eager to repeat the dreams of last night. It's hard to believe so much has changed. Liam was my happy place. As if to torment me, my delusions take me back in time. Not so much a dream but a memory, filling my unconscious mind. I can feel Liam's arms wrap around me. His scent swamps me.

"Hi," he whispers. "I missed you."

Dream me smiles sleepily. She remembers *my* today, her future. He shouldn't be here but instead she laughs. "You were following me all day."

He laughs along with dream me. "I still missed you." He presses a kiss to her temple and I feel it, like the heat of a match.

"Stay," dream me pleads softly. And I'm not sure if it's her or me imploring.

"I'm not going anywhere. I'll be the only man sharing your bed from now on." He kisses dream me gently.

"I love you," I mumble.

"I'm in love with you," he answers quietly. "Go back to sleep."

"I am asleep," I mumble.

But dream me looks at me questioningly as I feel myself drop over the waterfall into the land beyond dreaming. Where there's nothing but a vacuum of time. Where you close your eyes one second and open them hours later with no sense of the in-between.

A land where Liam's scent shouldn't be able to linger.

I wake with one thought, still waiting to be processed. *Go back to sleep?*

I better have been asleep.

My eyes roam the room, inspecting the shadows, though I already feel I'm alone. Liam's scent is strong, but it was here before I fell asleep. I tell myself, over and over, that it was only a dream. Until, eventually, I believe it.

After a shower, and a tense breakfast, twenty-eight male dragone follow me to the barracks. The dragone, twenty-five sailors, Axion and two seventeen year old lads who had somehow been rounded up with the women and children, are my new recruits. I look around at them as we walk. The men are tanned and muscled; they look weathered. The lads are smaller than Axion, identical twins. They're both spindly, very little muscle. They definitely don't look like fighters. We have a lot of work to do.

"The Barracks," I say as we push through the doors. The Guard inside freeze as we enter. I sigh. They've been stabbing weapons into the black dummies – they're all over the room, painted with bright yellow eyes and speared with handfuls of steel.

"Subtle," Axion whispers, taking in the scene.

"At least they didn't use any of you," I lament. "Stay together and stay close. This way." I lead them to the classrooms. I don't use mine and Liam's, somehow that place feels off limits.

The classroom is dark, no candles are lit. It makes it easier to see. The men file in, uncertain. There are desks but only the twins sit at one.

Uniforms. They're stored on the other side of the gym, next to August's workroom. He maintains the weapons. I decide to wait until the gym is empty before taking them back across it.

"You should sit," I suggest. "We're going to be here awhile."

They do, reluctantly. I watch them. Their expressions are like neon signs: loathing, anxiety, impatience.

"You don't want to be here," I state. "You blame me for bringing you. You want to be with your women and children, or back on your boat, or back on your island. I understand. I accept the blame. But you are here, and you are all in danger, and I am your only line of defence.

"In here we learn, you give me the information you know about the Fallen and in return I will teach you. We will practice. You will learn to fight. You will learn to defend yourselves. You will stay alive because I didn't bring you here to be target practice. A war is coming. A war that will divide or unite us. The angeli are not the enemy, but that does not mean they are not a threat. I tell you now, do not trust the Guard. Do not turn your back on them. They are as bitter and blinded as you."

"Why should we trust you?" a man with long hair, tied at his nape, asks. "You're a Guard are you not? You're angeli."

I nod. "I am."

"But you ask us to believe you will protect us? A wench, no older than the twins. What do you know of war, and fighting? What've you done to deserve our trust?" he scorns.

"She's proven herself to me, your king. While my father is missing I am the king. I trust her," Axion answers. "And she knows how to fight."

"We're being ordered around by infants," another man mumbles. "We should've stayed on the ship."

A fresh voice speaks, a tall man with bushy gray eyebrows and age lines. "Ye know we wouldn't have been safe on the boat, Art. The Fallen would've taken the chase and we'd all be feeding the fish." He has a thick accent, I have to concentrate to understand, but his face is kind and he smiles warmly at me, winking when he catches my eye.

"We don't know that," Art answers. "She's a clipper."

"Ours was the last island," bushy gray eyebrows continues. "Ye're addled if ye think they would've left us alive. I say we listen ta this young angel. She's got guts." He winks again and I smile in response.

"And they'll be spilled when she meets the Fallen," the man with long sleek hair sneers.

"Well, we're too late for that," I answer harshly. "I've already met them. So, if we're all ready we'll start with a bit of history... well... history as the angeli know it. Perhaps you may have conflicting accounts. I would be very interested to hear them."

I ignore their protests and start to talk. I plagiarise Liam's early lessons with me. When I first joined the Guard he spent hours rattling off his accounts of the angeli history. I start with the Battle of Scar. It doesn't take long for my pupils to stop moaning and start objecting. It turns into more of a debate than a lecture. They interrupt rudely at regular intervals. One thing is clear: no one knows what started the war, though the dragone are convinced it was the angeli and the angeli swear it was the dragone.

I flop next to Aaron at the lunch table, exhausted. My ears are ringing from the constant arguments of the morning. Axion doesn't look much better, though he hovers at my shoulder nervously instead of sitting.

"For God's sake Axion, sit on the stool and eat. They're not going to bite you," I snap.

The angeli at the table exchange glances, like they might consider biting as a suitable form of attack.

"Are you?" I glare at Oberon and Theon, who are obviously still contemplating it.

"Not bite," Theon replies. The sentence doesn't sound finished but he shuts his mouth.

"Have either of you had any experience with a dragone?" I sigh, fed up with the constant prejudice. "Have any of them done anything to you personally? Were you stabbed? Kidnapped? Anything?"

They don't answer.

"I was." Aaron grins. "Not by him though. I don't mind him sitting with us."

I dot a kiss on his cheek as a thank you, except he flicks his head and I hit the corner of his mouth instead, and promptly turn the colour of beetroot. I cough. "Er, thanks."

"For what?" Aaron laughs. His gray eyes spark dangerously, full of heat. I look away to avoid his gaze.

"Where's August?" I ask, still trying to calm my erratic heart.

"Working in the school," Oberon answers. His voice is still slightly tighter than normal. "Helping with the new... students."

"Really?" I smile. I'm glad someone I trust is with them.

The angeli leave as soon as their plates are empty, some before. My new trainees all attempt to sit around our one table. It makes for a very cramped lunch. Though it gives me a chance to watch them acting as they naturally would. I feel like *David Attenborough* as I observe them. They are a group of men, regularly laughing at each other's expense and eating like they've never seen food before. I really don't see how they are any different from humans or the angeli.

I attempt to learn their names as they talk. I already know Art's name. Bushy eyebrows' name is Reuben. I like him. The long haired man is Cain. I don't like him. The twins, neither of whom seems very bright, are Nev and

George. The rest blur into a muddle. I'm going to have to find a marker pen and some post-it notes to stick to their foreheads.

Aaron and Axion engross themselves in a conversation about some TV show Aaron's been missing and Axion seems to be an expert on. It must be on *Sky* because I've never heard of it. We've only just got a Digibox after the analogue signal was turned off. My mother doesn't do modern inventions. My childhood entertainment was broadcast over the wireless, as she still calls the radio. She eventually invested in a television so she could watch *Countryfile*.

Without warning an odd pain clenches in my stomach and my head screams: *Brue*. I'm on my feet, my stool scraping backward. I don't have time to consider how or why I unexpectedly know my little companion is in trouble, I just do. Axion obviously does too. We run, the rest of the dragone hot on our heels. I hear Aaron shout my name but we're already running through the door.

"Who is it, lad?" Reuben shouts. I take the lead. My gut is driving me. I don't know the destination but I can feel I'm getting closer.

"Brue," Axion answers as we sprint. We spiral down the staircase like falling Sycamore seeds.

Axion must be following the same instinct as me, because he dives from the spiral staircase onto the landing at the same moment I do. We tear along the corridor toward the museum. The feeling is getting more intense.

"What is this?" I yell.

"He's hurt," Axion answers.

"I know," I snap. "How do I know?"

He doesn't have time to answer. The museum door is approaching fast, and outside of it two angeli in brown robes stand guard. Their faces fall when they see us careering up the corridor, though they must have heard us coming.

My stomach cramps with a fresh bout of pain and nausea. Brue... I can feel him inside me, like a piece of me.

"Move aside," I scream. When they don't move quickly enough I assist them with my fist. "Grab them," I instruct my trainees as I push through the door.

Axion follows me in. Brue is on the floor, while two full grown angeli males assault him. They are so engrossed in their attack they don't hear us until we're on them. I grab the wings of my target, yanking him away from Brue with obviously excruciating force. He screams in agony as I plant my still new boots into the back of his knee. I hear a crack as he falls. My fist connects with the side of his jaw as I follow his descent, kneeling between him and Brue.

My little friend is silent, his eyes rolling in his head. His chest rises and falls slowly, far too slowly. I pick him up, as carefully as I can, and run. I don't know how I get to my feet. I'm just aware I'm moving. Axion follows, his opponent left face-down on the cold stone.

We pass the dragone and two unconscious angeli as we fly from the room. Liam is barrelling along the corridor toward us. I don't slow and he doesn't turn to follow.

The medical wing is a few flights below us, it barely takes a minute at our speed but it still feels like an eternity. I shout for help as we enter. Medics rush toward us. I don't fail to notice the ones that stop and turn away when they register the species of the casualty.

"Arrogant pigs," I yell at their backs.

"Let me take him, Guardian," a gentle voice says. Halen holds her arms out for my Brue. "I will care for him."

"I carry him," I answer. "You fix him."

She turns quickly and leads us into a room I haven't been inside before. It's not like the room Aaron was in. It's more like a theatre, with a slab of an operating table and an actual light. Angeli fuss around, grabbing various implements as I lay Brue down. I refuse to leave. Axion stands in the doorway. The Medics swarm around the table, injecting, prodding and assessing. I hear words shot around: broken ribs, pierced lung, internal bleeding. My legs give way and I drop but I fight to keep my eyes open. I don't shift my gaze from the small figure already being operated on. The Medics don't acknowledge me. They step over me whenever they need to.

I watch, detached and powerless, but I have to trust them. They saved Aaron... they'll save Brue too.

They just have to.

# · Eight ·

I'm eventually dragged from the room. It's Lucas. He picks me up and holds me while I soak his tunic with tears – this is a regular occurrence for us.

"Let them work, Aqua," he soothes calmly. "He's safe here."

"Safe?" I screech. "Are you blind? Look at him! They nearly killed him!"

Lucas pulls me into a nearby room and Axion follows, visibly dazed. "What happened?" Lucas asks. "Liam sent me here. He has your trainees captured in the barracks."

"He what?" I screech again.

"They attacked angeli," Lucas answers.

"No! The angeli attacked Brue." I run again, with Axion and Lucas following my hysterical cursing. Liam! I should have guessed he'd assume the dragone were to blame. Silly me.

My feet clatter along the cold stone. I burst through the barracks doors to mayhem. My sobs are lost in the deafening riot. Aggravated wings flap like turbines but the yelling rises above it like gunfire. The words are mangled and incoherent but the messages are clear, they're a step away from a full scale battle.

I find Liam easily. He's at the front, like always. His shoulders are tense, his voice hushed as he confers with Plyrian. Liam grabs my hand as I reach his side but doesn't acknowledge me in any other way. For a second it feels normal, and then I remember that I currently hate him.

I pull my hand away. "You have to stop this," I yell.

No blood has been spilt yet but my trainees have been herded against the back wall. George is face down but breathing. None of the dragone's attention is on him. They're all watching the angeli Guard, who have arrows and blades pointed in their direction.

"They were defending themselves, not attacking." Liam continues to ignore me. "Liam," I snap. He's an infuriating man. "Stop being such a child and listen to the facts." I've had enough. I don't wait for his response. I stomp past the ignorant Guard into no-man's land, the only vacant space between the two sides... sides... I'm fed up of sides. It's always us versus them: Angeli versus Dragone, Dragone versus Fallen and us versus the Script. When will it stop?

"Drop your weapons!" I scream, facing the Guard with my back to the dragone. They won't listen, obviously.

Liam saunters through the mass with Lucas, Plyrian and Axion, who hurries to my side. Oops. I kind of abandoned him in the middle of a crowd of furious angeli. "Hi," I mumble.

"Nice knowing you," he whispers absentmindedly. I guess his head's still in the medical wing.

I stare at my angeli brother as he stops in front of me. "Liam, tell them to get their steel out of my men's faces."

"Your men?" he sneers. "Your men attacked four angeli in our own city! You're lucky your men aren't all face down."

"Stop being such a pig," I shout at him. Mouths pop open but I keep going. "If you waited to listen then you would know that isn't what happened. But no, of course not, fight first think later, the Guard Master's motto." I pant in my anger, fidgeting on my feet. "The Foragers cornered and attacked a defenceless child and my men retaliated to defend him. It is exactly what you would have done. What any of you would have done!" I yell, my eyes roaming the faces of the Guard. "You are all blind in your hatred of these people, but it's not them you need to fight. It's the Fallen." I don't know how much information has been passed down through the ranks since we arrived. They're going to get it now though. "The Fallen are dragone. They carry the same traits, the same abilities. They are fast and they are strong, but the similarities stop there. They've been trained. They know how to fight. They attack, and they ravage, and they take what they want from whoever they want. They took my mother. They took Sierra. They took these men's home and it's safe to say they probably took Marcus. My men are sailors, family men who just want their island back. They came here for your help and you're too full of hate to give it. A child is dying right now because of your prejudices, and because of you I stand here defending innocents instead of being where I should be, with him. How many times does this need to happen before we're all dead at each other's hands? And who killed George?" I scream.

A few Guard snigger. Most drop their weapons to their sides. "We should have known when he fainted that there was more to this."

The Guard who spoke steps forward. I don't recognise her. She's never been a sparring partner but she smiles at me before turning to Liam. It's not a warm smile. "I should have known you would withhold most of the facts, Guard Master. The truth is always something you found difficult to speak. I say we listen to the Guardian." Her voice is bitter as she bellows. I frown at her as I process the way she's looking at Liam.

"Rae..." He warns.

His eyes are hard, his mouth firm. I stare vacantly, my eyes beginning to fill with water again. Not because of Rae and whatever's going on with her and Liam, which I absolutely do not care about. Not even because of the fight I find myself standing in the centre of again. My tears are all for Brue.

"Sort this out," I snap, tearing Liam's eyes away from his and Rae's silent exchange. "I'm taking my men and we're going to Brue."

"It was Brue?" Plyrian asks, startled. He staggers forward, too. "You didn't mention the child involved, Guard Master." He glares at Liam as he walks to my side. "I will escort you and your men, Aqua, to avoid any more unnecessary unpleasantness."

"Thank you, Plyrian." I leave Liam and Rae standing there as I march through the parting Guard. My men follow at a brisk jog. Reuben flings the still unconscious George over his shoulder.

"I'm sorry, Aqua," Plyrian mumbles as we hurry back down the staircase again. "I didn't know it was Brue, but that should not have mattered."

"You like Brue?" I smile, emotionless. Of course he does. Brue is a force of nature.

"He is quite a character," Plyrian answers. "The Medics are good, Aqua. He will make it."

"This time. But then what, Plyrian? What will happen next? How long until the Fallen knock on the door looking for blood? Although, at this rate, the floors will already be saturated with the stuff."

"We'll take the fight to them long before they reach this city, before they reach any of our cities. Liam is suffering a period of... idiocy, but he will defend you and your men in a fight. I'm sure of it. He sees you as his mate, Aqua, regardless of it not being official."

I beg to differ, for many reasons. But my tongue utters the wrong words. Traitorous tongue. "Then who is Rae?" I glance at him as we slow our pace, the door to the medical wing a few steps ahead.

"Liam should be the one to explain." He avoids my gaze.

"She's the one he was courting," I answer. It's a fair assumption but I already sense I'm right. Angeli don't move cities or change professions. I should have realised she'd still be here, and that she'd be a Guard. He told me he had a previous relationship. I was jealous at the time, maybe I still am, but she's welcome to him. Let him shoot *her* in the leg.

"He told you? I am surprised, I believe he was attempting to keep you two apart."

"When did they break up?" I ask quietly, grabbing the door handle.

"I believe the end of their courtship coincided closely with your arrival."

I push through the doors and follow the corridor. My ears are already straining ahead, blanking out the footfalls of my men as we approach the operating room. Brue's still in there. His scent is strong. The lack of beeps still unsettles me, though they must have a form of power available because there was a light on. I don't bother replying to Plyrian. I don't want to know anymore anyway.

"Lucas." I smile as my white haired angel appears from Brue's room.

He pulls me into a hug, reading my face. "He's doing well, Aqua, just like you. I heard the start of your speech before I came back to watch Brue. You remind me so much of your father. You are a natural leader." He pulls back slightly. "Should I get the salts?" he asks, looking over my shoulder.

"George." I laugh. What fierce warriors I have. "Reuben, follow Lucas," I instruct. "He'll bring George around."

Axion inches closer as we crowd around Brue's firmly shut door. No one speaks as we wait. I don't have the energy. I want to ask Axion about the pain when Brue was hurt. I want to know how I knew, why I felt it, how I followed it to the museum. But now doesn't feel like the time. I have a feeling I'm not going to like the answer, or maybe not want to believe the answer.

George reappears. He wobbles back toward us, leaning heavily on Lucas. The dragone greet him with laughter and back-slaps. Nev just slaps him.

"Thank you."

I look at Axion. He's leaning against the wall beside me but his voice was so low I'm not sure who he was talking to. "Ax?" I question.

He coughs and rakes his hand down his face. "Thank you," Axion says again.

He looks pale, tired. I can't imagine what he'd want to thank me for at the moment. I haven't exactly put them in the best situation. I grasp his loose hand in mine, tentatively. He responds with a slight squeeze before closing his eyes and exhaling harshly, his head tilted back against the wall. I watch him for a while, leaning next to him. The purple veins of his eyelids look more pronounced than usual. He's obviously exhausted. He doesn't move again or open his eyes. He may have fallen asleep on his feet. I keep hold of his hand and move closer, resting my head on his shoulder. It's comfortable. He's just the right height to not crick my neck painfully. I let my eyes drift closed too, listening to the gentle murmurs floating from Brue's room. I sense Lucas as he moves to my other side but he maintains our silence. The noise gets deeper and more muted as I drift. My brain hovers at the edge of unconsciousness but I can't let myself shut down completely.

I hear his approach before I smell him. I sigh. The mockery of Plyrian's words wasn't lost on me. Liam is an idiot and I'm most definitely not his mate, either officially or unofficially. Strong hands grab me, lifting me against a hard chest. It's warm, and it's not Axion or Lucas.

"Forgive me," Liam whispers lightly, his breath soft in my ear. "I love you, Aqua. Please forgive me."

This time I'm sure I'm not asleep. I battle to open my eyes, fighting the tears that are already there. I step away, too muddled to be angry, or confused, or anything other than breaking for Brue.

I shake my head, my gaze downcast. "I can't do this right now."

Lucas, still hovering at my side, secures me into his comforting grip. Guarding me. It's all too much. I close my eyes again, knowing that Lucas will protect me. There's a tight silence, full of the unsaid, before Liam and Plyrian start talking quietly. I don't try to listen. Their words jumble around the boundaries of my comprehension. Lucas speaks occasionally, his chest vibrates around me. I feel the increased warmth as my men crowd around us, listening. Art's voice is followed by Reuben's. Then Liam speaks again.

I force my eyes open. My head is pressed into Lucas' neck. I don't have the best view so I shuffle us both around. His chest rumbles slightly as he realises what I'm doing. "Better?" he asks, his chin pressed into my hair.

My answering nod is tempered by our position. "What's going on?"

My eyes lock with Liam's as he turns in our direction. I hadn't directed my question at him but he answers anyway, his voice strained. "We were just getting the facts. I may have jumped to an incorrect assumption."

"*May?*" My head shakes minutely, wobbling Lucas' jaw in the process.

Liam looks unrepentant. The imploring tone he used to beg my forgiveness seems like a distant echo of my memory. My hand rises to my temple, but the effort is draining and it drops again before I can soothe my piercing headache. "What are you going to do?"

He doesn't break his stare from me. "There will be a trial for the Foragers involved. They will be given opportunity to explain their actions and they will be sentenced." His words are spoken blandly, emotionlessly. "You know the sentence."

"Death," I lament "It's always death."

Liam echoes my groan. "And you always disagree with it. What do you propose we do, Guardian? They have disgraced our city and our species." The exasperated tenor his voice holds feels very familiar. And apparently I'm back to being Guardian.

"Spare them," I suggest. "We'll need men to fight against the Fallen. Let them die facing the real enemy instead of a ten year old boy."

My blasé attitude to death, specifically the Foragers' deaths, takes him by surprise. It's not really the case, it was no more than an impetuous thought verbalised. Still, Liam looks at me as though he's considering it. "He's only ten years?" he asks eventually.

I hitch a shoulder in a half-hearted attempt at a shrug. "It's a guess. He won't tell me."

"You're right." Axion opens his eyes and pushes himself away from the wall. "He's only ten, regardless of how old he thinks he is."

"He was put in with the fourteen years," Liam states. His disapproving frown is aimed toward Brue's closed operating room door.

This time my hand makes it all the way to my temple and I rub furiously, until my vision wobbles and flashing lights appear. "What was he doing on his own?"

Lucas gently retrieves my hand, before I bore a hole into my skull, and dots a cool kiss against the heated patch of skin. Liam glares at him. Is Lucas' affection odd? It's never felt it. Our relationship is entirely plutonic.

"Knowing Brue," Axion replies. "He snuck off to look around."

"Exactly what I told him not to do."

"It shouldn't have mattered, Aqua," Plyrian interjects. "He should have been safe anywhere in this city, even alone. Victus is furious. You're missing one of his city-wide lectures at this very moment."

"It is why we should make an example of the Foragers," Liam snarls. "No one would dare act again."

I could laugh at the hypocrisy. Honestly, he only wants to convict the Foragers because they have dishonoured the angeli. I'd like to think that they wouldn't harm a child, but I can't help wondering that, in any other situation, they may have been revered.

"Like no one would dare rise against the Script?" I ask. "Or break its rules?" *Like we did.* "This union is an opportunity for angeli, dragone and humans to try living together in peace. Is it so wrong to yearn for a place where everyone is free to make decisions, or mistakes, that don't end in beheading?"

"Change is slow, Aqua," Lucas murmurs from my cranium, placating me. "The Script is the backbone of our people. Our past is full of pain and bloodshed. It is a romantic notion, world peace, but I cannot imagine it is feasible. The angeli would never rise against the Script."

Lucas isn't in the resistance.

"Liam is right in one respect," he continues. "People will learn from example. I do not suggest we should dwell on Brue's attack. I advise we set a positive view. We will all involve ourselves amongst our guests. Work alongside them, eat and socialise with them. We will encourage our friends and families to do the same."

"I thought that's what I was doing," I mumble.

"We will all do it."

"Look around us, Lucas. It's just you and I jumping on that band wagon. The Guard Master is here because he does what Victus tells him. Evidently, the Foragers do not."

Liam's eyes blaze. My own amber irises likely hold the same fire as I stare at him, imploring him to dispute the fact. He doesn't.

Plyrian, whose presence I neglected a moment ago, steps forward purposefully. "Perhaps we should attend to the Great Hall, Guard Master," he suggests. "Victus required our presence."

Liam's mouth strains to stay closed, his throat bobs with unspoken words as he glares at me. The dragone sailors, my men, have not commented on any of our exchange. I easily avert my stare from the hypnotic caramel pools in Liam's head. They no-longer leave me mute and dazed. Instead, I scan the dragone, surveying their postures. The older men stand with their arms crossed resolutely in front of their chests. The younger men hold their hands on their hips, or hooked into their waistbands. The orange candlelight of the corridor flickers sporadically, casting moving shadows behind their rigid forms.

My gaze passes over their darkened skin as I assess. Some are darker than others, I realise. Many are a natural, genetic brown. A few are merely sun-bronzed, their pale skin pigmented into light ochre under the ultraviolet rays of their little island and the open ocean. I stare at them, cataloguing their appearance, while ignoring the burning eyes I still feel on me. It takes a very long time, and the sense that everyone might be feeling a little awkward, before Liam silently turns and strides away. He takes the tension with him, like a tailing parachute still attached to his back, and everybody relaxes.

Lucas and Plyrian follow him soon after, having sought agreement via a questioning head slant. I nod. They're better off watching him than me, and their absence will be noticed by the city if they remain down here too long.

We settle back against the corridor walls. The dragone spread themselves out. The hallways are relatively wide but it's nice to have a bit of space to expand and stretch. I stand next to Axion, most comfortable in his presence.

"Do dragone get tattoos?" I ask.

He shrugs. "Sometimes. We're like humans, it's a choice. Why?"

My eyes linger in the direction Liam took off. "I mean, do the Fallen get tattoos? I don't know, like an emblem, with your language or something?"

"I'm not normally looking for tattoos when I bump into one, Aqua," he mocks. "Maybe. They still use the old language. Why?"

"Why could I feel Brue?" I ask.

"You do that all the time," he laughs.

"What?" I look back at him and he grins at me.

"Avoid answering a question by asking one of your own. Maybe I should try that."

"Won't work for you," I taunt. "Tell me about the weird pain."

"It's part of the feeling thing," he answers. "A kind of dragone perception."

I'd guessed that. "But how? I wasn't anywhere near Brue."

Axion's reply is cut off by a deep voice, Cain's voice. "Pardon? Say that again," he stutters.

I grimace when I realise what we've just done. How stupid of me. None of them had questioned why I led the pack to the museum, perhaps they'd assumed Axion was leading. They're going to question it now, though. I try and formulate an answer while Axion nonchalantly informs them of my mixed heritage by saying, "Her mother was dragone." He doesn't have the same thought processes as me. I could throttle him. "What?" he asks me innocently.

"Maybe ye should've told us this afore," Reuben says softly. "We need'ta trust ye if ye're going t' be our leader, Lass."

"Leader," Cain scoffs. "Like Rennison Jarik."

I blink my brain clear. "Right, in here."

I direct them all into an empty room and shut the door. Angeli hear too well to have this conversation anywhere, but this is better than the hallway. I take a deep breath. "Firstly, very few people know what I am. Me and a handful of others, until King Axion opened his mouth. And I've only known for a few months. My parents must have known, obviously, but since we're not sure who my mother was and my father was taken before I came here, I haven't been able to ask. Brue knows and it doesn't bother him. I didn't tell you for the exact reason Cain just said. I'm not related to Rennison. I don't want you to compare me to him." My words come out hurried.

"We don't," Reuben answers. "But we need t'know where ye came from, Lass. T'is too coincidental, like someone's runnin' a rig."

"Jarik," Cain scoffs.

"She said she doesn't know," Nev pipes up. "How can you find out where she's from?"

"Test her," Cain shrugs. "Prick her."

"Pardon?" I blanch.

"Blood test, Aqua." Axion pats my back.

"Test it against what?" I ask.

"Against us, Lass," Reuben answers. "T'is a start."

"I think the chance that any of you is my mother is slight," I murmur.

"You're funny," George grins. "You could be our sister."

I'm convinced I'm Axion's sister.

"Don't be daft, George." Nev slaps him again. "We'd have wings, too."

"Not if our dad was our dad but not hers," George mumbles.

I groan.

"I think we all know who the lassie's mother was," Art interjects helpfully. "The question is what we're to do about it."

"Who?" the twins ask in unison.

"My mother," Axion answers quietly.

"Your mother what?" Nev frowns.

"It's obvious my mother was her mother," Axion states.

"If your mother was her mother, then who was your mother?" George garbles.

"My God," I exclaim. "How do you cope with this?"

"They grow on ye," Reuben smiles.

"Yeah," Axion agrees. "Like warts."

"Or fungus," Art laughs.

"Scurvy," someone suggests. The other men in the room shout out random diseases. It's the first thing most of them have said, and they get more outlandish with every new voice. I shake my head.

"You sure we're right?" I ask Axion, attempting to blank out the others.

"It makes sense," he agrees.

"Do ye claim her, Lad?" Reuben asks over the noise.

"Claim me?" I question.

"Yes," Axion states confidently.

"Stop!" I scream, finally overloading. The room hushes slowly. "What have you just claimed me as?"

"As family, Aqua." Axion shrugs. "I claimed you as my sister."

"Just like that?" I exclaim. "We don't even know if I am."

"Test her blood," Cain shrugs again.

"Do any of you actually know how to test blood?" I ask sharply.

No one responds.

"Great," I groan. "That was all pointless then. Can we get back on track? I'm still me, and I'm still your leader. Can you all deal with what I am? And keep it to yourselves? Let's stun this city with one revelation at a time, shall we?"

"Why're ye hiding it from them, Lass? Wouldn't it be better t'show 'em what ye are? Ye could bridge the gap," Reuben suggests.

"Like the missing link," Nev jokes. It's the most intelligent thing he's said since we met.

"Or they could assume I planned all of this to get you in here to murder them in their beds," I counter.

"Did you?" George asks.

"Yes, George. I planned to live seventeen years as a human hiding my wings, find a city of mythical creatures who I thought were like me, watch my mum get kidnapped by Fallen who I thought were like you, get captured myself by you, and end up back in the mythical city with you as my guests. All so I could help you wipe out the mythical winged beings I thought I was like in the first place." I wheeze to catch my breath.

"Begad!" Reuben laughs. "T'is catching."

"Ay, she's poxed lads!" someone yells merrily.

"Geonevitis," Axion grins. "Fatal."

"My God," I exclaim. "Kill me now."

The whole room laughs at me, even Cain.

"Scupper that," Reuben suggests. "We'll accept you as our leader and our princess, Lass. T'is the least we can do, in the circumstance." He glances around the room, focusing on the few uncertain faces he finds. "What say you?" he asks his shipmates. "All in favour say, Aye."

"Aye?" I whisper to Axion. "They sound like pirates."

He shushes me and my eyes widen. I was joking but his look is guilty. Pirates?

"Aye!" the room agrees in a chorus of baritones.

Excellent.

# · Nine ·

I feel like I just stepped out of the pages of *Treasure Island*. My head is throbbing. Voices rise around the room, genial conversations about my, and Axion's, parentage. I pull him out of the door, into the corridor. It's too noisy to concentrate.

"They're pirates," I hiss. "Why didn't you tell me?"

"They're not pirates, Aqua. Well, maybe but not like you're thinking. They're not all, *Yo ho ho* and *pieces of eight*."

"Then what exactly are they?"

"We're not human, Aqua. We don't pretend to be. Sometimes, when we want something, Reuben and his men go and get it. Food, supplies, modern items we can't make on the island…" he drifts off.

"Smash and grab," I groan. "You steal things from humans. That's how you all have mobile phones and watch *Breaking Bad*. You send your pirates." I shake my head. "You know, there's a reason why you're always mistaken for demons."

He grins, unashamed. "Why not enjoy the label?" he asks. "Who's going to think better of us if we don't steal? The humans don't know we exist."

"I'd think better of you."

"You're one of us, Princess, whether you like it or not. And I don't see any guilt over those shiny new boots of yours." He shoulder bumps me as we take up our vigil at Brue's door.

"You sure you're okay with this?" I ask, his comment changing my train of thought. "With me being your sister... possibly."

"Probably," he corrects. "I don't mind, and even if you're not, you feel like you are." He takes my hand in his and smiles.

"Okay." I can't think of anything else to sum up how I'm feeling. "Okay," I repeat.

"The pirates like you," he whispers. "Reuben obviously likes you."

"Is Reuben the pirate captain?" I ask, smiling. I like Reuben too, when I can understand him.

"Yeah," Axion laughs. "They call him Old Salt. He's been around a long time."

I stare for a while but he doesn't elaborate. "And what about the gut wrenching pain?" I question sarcastically.

"You're linked," he answers. "Have you touched Brue a lot?"

"Excuse me?" I cough. "What do you mean? I don't go around touching young boys." My face burns as I glare at him.

"Not like that," he laughs. "I just mean his skin, like this." He squeezes my hand.

"No." At least I don't think so. I was locked in a room for most of my stay. I guess he jumped on my back a lot, but we were both dressed. Well, he was bare-chested. "In the cage," I cogitate. "I was stroking his hair while he was asleep, and he jumps on me a lot."

"The cage probably started it, especially since he was hurt."

"So explain the link," I offer. "I get the chemical receptor thing, it's not hard to believe, but I don't get how we ended up linked so that I could feel him."

He shrugs. "I don't either. It usually takes much longer, and lots of touching." I blush again. "Families are linked because they touch regularly. Couples end up linked because of the whole naked cuddling thing..." He laughs at me again as I fan myself to cool the flush in my cheeks. "Don't worry, Princess, I don't think angels have the same chemicals. That bigoted Guard Master you call a brother is safe from your excreted desires." He squeezes my hand again. "Don't worry about touching me. I'd like a family link with you."

My brain lingers on his previous comment. I drop his hand to run my fingers down his leathery wing. "So, how do you break a link?"

"Break a link?" he asks. "Why would you want to break our link?"

"Not ours. I'm being hypothetical." Sort of. I'm curious.

"Simple. Stop touching and it wears off. The link needs regular chemicals to stay strong." He eyes me warily then grasps my hand in his. He doesn't speak as he leans back against the wall, pulling me with him. I stare at our entwined fingers.

"What are you doing?" I ask with my lip quirking upward.

"Feeling you," he grins. "Think happy thoughts." He grips my hand tighter when I try to pull away.

"Fine," I huff. Happy thoughts? I think about swimming. The water around Hantiem was beautiful. The island was beautiful. I imagine being there, swimming there, and not just to escape the Fallen, swimming there because I live there.

"What are you thinking about?" Axion asks. "You're blissing me out."

"Is that even a word?"

"Definitely." He smiles lazily.

"Hantiem," I answer. "Swimming."

"We'll see home again, Princess. You're superwoman. I have faith you'll get us home." He squeezes my hand and closes his eyes. "Do it again."

I smile. Hantiem, my home? Yes it could be. I close my eyes and take us back to the ocean: flying above the waves with Brue on my back, following the dolphins as they played around the island. Then I go back to the Southern ocean, the night I swam with penguins and a humpback whale. We both get lost in my blissed out chemicals.

"Are you two okay?" August asks. "Aqua? Is he hurting you?"

"Hey little bro," I slur. "No, we're fine." I don't open my eyes. I must be feeding off of the chemicals Axion's producing too.

"Aqua!" August shouts. He pulls my hand away from Axion's and slaps my face. Actually slaps me! My eyes fly open.

"August!" I exclaim.

Axion springs to action beside me, grabbing August in a death grip where he quickly turns purple.

"Jesus, Ax, stop!" I pull them apart. August pants to catch his breath. "What the hell is going on today? Ax, he's my brother. Christ. August, are you okay?"

"What were you doing?" he stares at me accusingly. "First Aaron and now him. Are you cheating on Liam?"

"What? No, of course not. Axion's my brother," I state. "And things with Liam are complicated."

"Your brother?" August's eyes bug out and he stutters, before shaking his head. "So is Liam," he says finally. "What's he done now?"

I grimace. "He shot me with an arrow."

August's mouth drops open like a broken hatch. "When?"

"The night I left."

"Why?"

"Who? What? Where?" I snap. "Ask him, perhaps he'll tell you. Look, I kind of brought back two new brothers."

August sighs. "Two more?" I guess he expects crazy things from me.

"Axion and Brue. Axion and I have the same mother, we think. And Axion and Brue have the same father, possibly." I glance at him, and then his wings. He doesn't comment.

"A real brother this time?" August asks tetchily.

I grin and pull him into a hug. "You are my real brother." I kiss his cheek. "Liam, not so much."

"How is Brue?" August asks, sliding his hand into mine and frowning at Axion. "How is Brue your brother?"

"He's Axion's brother, so he's mine too. They're still in with him. No news. How was the lecture?" I ask to change the subject. We're not dwelling on Brue, neither me nor Axion.

"Long," August whines. "First Victus yelled at us, and then Lucas came in and yelled at us, and then Liam came in and yelled at us even louder. I was expecting you next, but you never came." He looks at me again, and then at Axion.

I smirk. "You missed me yelling in the barracks. You think the city will listen?"

"They listened," he shrugs. "I don't know if they agreed."

"Will you wait with us for a while?" I pull him closer, leaning on his shoulder. He's shorter than Axion, my neck cricks.

"Yeah."

We all lean back against the wall. Conversation is slow to start, but August can talk. Soon he's jabbering for all of us. I listen and comment occasionally. Axion watches bemused. August catches us both up on everything I missed while I was away. He even fills me in on the revolution, which has swelled in number since my last meeting. Axion grabs my hand halfway through August's rendition and I get a stab of confusion.

"August, you're confusing Ax. Remember when the revolt was a secret?" I laugh at my little brother. Secrets are not his speciality.

"Oh." He flushes. "You won't tell though?" he asks Axion hurriedly.

Axion shrugs. "I have no idea what you're talking about."

I squeeze his hand in thanks. August scrutinizes us with a scowl, so I start talking. They both listen as I tell August about Hantiem, the dragone, my newly discovered ability, my pirates. Only my low mumblings fill the void of the corridor. Neither of them interrupts as unload the last few days like a dump-truck.

Axion must be feeling everything right along with me, but he tightens rather than loosens his grip. It feels strangely comforting, to not have to explain how the most recent revelations have affected me. I avoid thoughts of Liam, and Rennison Jarik, and my turmoil over Victus' secrets.

When Brue's door finally opens, I've finished my cathartic monologue. Halen emerges, looking tired but wearing a smile. We all deflate slightly as we relax. She nods before we even ask, and steps aside so we can go in.

Brue is wearing a white gown, like the one Aaron had on while he was unconscious. "He'll love that," Axion smirks when he takes it in. We all crowd around Brue's bed, our hands resting on his small arms. The Medics continue to move around the room, writing notes and checking drips. I ignore them, watching Brue like a hawk. His chest expands gently before drifting back down. I watch the process as it repeats: up, down, air in, air out.

I don't lift my eyes when I speak. "How long until you wake him?"

"He is awake, in theory," Halen answers softly. "He is no longer sedated. He will wake when he is ready. He will be sore and weak for a time, but his recovery is unprecedented. We do not know if it is his nature to heal quickly, or if our medicines are more effective on his species than on our own, but either way he will be on his feet in a few days if he continues healing at this pace." She places her hand gently over mine on Brue's arm. "He was very lucky you brought him here so swiftly."

"Lucky," I mimic quietly. "Thank you. Thank you for saving him."

"He will have a few scars, but he is young, I find children are often more resilient. And it was what any Medic should have done, without a thought." She squeezes my hand before moving away to confer with a male by the door.

"Scars," Axion comments. "He will love that."

"He feels so vulnerable." I run my fingers along the smooth bronze skin of his forearm.

"He's hurt and asleep. It's natural," Axion soothes. "You heard the angel. He'll be running around again before we know it, driving us both crazy."

I snort. "Driving you crazy. I enjoy his wildness, when it's not getting him into trouble. Tenacious and astute Brue." A happy tear drops from my cheek.

"You love him," Axion announces suddenly. I hadn't realised we'd clasped our free hands while standing here. I pull him closer and wrap my other arm around August's waist as he stands at my side.

"I love you all," I confirm. August wraps his arm around me and claps Axion on the shoulder. It seems symbolic, the weird pieces of my life, coming together and accepting each other. I have four brothers: a human, an angeli, a dragone and a possible hybrid – three abstract brothers, one flesh and blood. I squeeze them tighter. "I know we've only just met, Ax, but I feel like I've known you forever. And you, August, I *have* kind of known you forever." I sigh. "We need to tell Mum soon. She'll think we've been hiding it from her."

"Yeah," he agrees. "Tonight? I could come to your room. No wait, I'll knock on your door. I don't want to disturb you and Liam." He shudders. My heart clenches.

"What was that?" Axion asks, waving our hands around.

"Nothing." I pull my hand away glowering. Maybe our emotional connection isn't a good thing.

Why would August assume Liam will be in my room?

My strange dream last night comes back to haunt me.

# · Ten ·

We eat quietly. The pirates squeeze around the closest table, all laughing loudly now that they know Brue will be fine. August and Axion flank me, with Oberon sitting on August's left and Aaron sitting on Axion's right.

The Grand hall feels different. Perhaps I'm just taking more notice of feelings. Perhaps I'm imagining it. Regardless, something feels different. There's less tension in the air, though it's still lurking, and the angeli didn't rush to leave when the dragone arrived. Some of the dragone women are sitting at tables with angeli Nesters. The dragone kids and the angeli younglings are almost completely mingled: laughing, arguing and joking like normal children. The Medic was right, children are more resilient.

"Weird day," Aaron muses as we watch the city. He's cut his hair. It's still his usual scruffy dirty blond style, just shorter.

I throw part of my bread roll at him, smirking. "When do we have a normal day anymore?"

"With you? Never." He throws half a sausage back at me, grinning. He's got meat on his plate now that the dragone are being catered for. I laugh and retaliate with a handful of dried crickets. He picks up a mound of mashed potato.

"You want to swap seats?" Axion groans at me. "I'm being pelted with flying food."

"Sorry mate." Aaron drops the potato back onto his plate, but reaches around Axion to wipe his hands on my wing.

"Gross!" I moan. I ruffle it to try and shake the starchy remnants off. "You'll pay for that, Coles."

"Bring it on, Vickers." He laughs.

I consider lobbing my whole plate at him, but the table has fallen silent as they watch us turn back into the juveniles we used to be. I blush.

"Vickers?" Axion asks. Probably to break the strange heaviness that's rising around us.

I swallow and lick my dry lips. "My name, Aquila Raven Vickers." I gesture at Aaron. "Aaron David Coles."

"What was my name?" August asks suddenly. "Did I have a name?"

I glance around, checking my mother isn't about to appear at the wrong moment. "Yeah of course, you're Harry, Harry Clarence Vickers. Clarence was our dad's name."

"His dad's name," Axion says, puzzled. "Your dad was Marcus?"

"Technically," I confirm. "I guess it's confusing but I can't stop thinking of them as my parents. Libby raised me. I think of her as my mother. Marcus raised August and he thinks of him as a father."

"They're like a hospital mix up," Aaron adds, laughing.

"That's got to mess with your head," Axion muses.

Aaron nods. "Wait until you hear how they got swapped."

I grimace at August. We know *how*. We don't know why. Why Marcus told our mother Harry was dead, or why he dropped me off and left me with her a week later. I thought for a while that he'd planned it, killed my father and hung around until my mother went into labour, but that would make him evil – and August loves him so he can't be evil – maybe it was a coincidence, a serendipitous opportunity to hide me. I blank out Aaron as he rehashes my life to Axion. August pulls his mouth to the side, and then sticks his tongue out to make me laugh. I shake my head in amusement.

"Weird day," I repeat to myself.

I go back to the medical wing to kiss Brue goodnight before going to my room. Except Liam's scent is drifting under the door when I get outside. My heartbeat accelerates. I stare at the golden door like it's a dangerous animal, before wimping out and knocking at my mother's bedroom. I exhale when she opens it, relieved she's in. I can't face Liam yet.

"Hey, Mum." I kiss her on the cheek before inviting myself in.

"Hi, honey. How's Brue?" She pulls me into a hug, and a dam I didn't know existed bursts. She lets me sob. Her vacant expression and emotionless responses are long gone. She's my mother again: caring, nurturing and warm. She comforts me while I explain what happened, that he'll be fine, that I'm fed up with everything.

When I finally stop crying she kisses my tear-lines. "Oh, honey. No more of these. I'm so proud of you. I always knew you were special. My special girl. Now look at you." She pulls back and looks at me like she's seeing me for the first time. "You're not my baby anymore. You've changed, Aqua, into such a beautiful woman, inside and out. You've matured since I've been away and 'm so sorry I missed it. You've handled today so well. You are strong, and brave, and allowed to take a break," she scolds. "You have been running here and there since we got here. I've barely seen you."

"I know, I'm sorry. I'll spend more time with you, I just…"

"No," she says, putting her arm around me and sitting us on the bed. "I knew this would happen one day. You're a grown woman with friends, responsibilities. I don't need you to spend more time with me, I know I'll see you. I hope you'll remember I'm just next door."

It sounds more like a warning than a reassurance.

"And one day I'll go home and you'll have to decide where you want to be. I just want you to slow down, relax a little, and stop carrying knives around with you." She points at my dagger. "No more fighting. I want you to live your life."

I rest my head on her shoulder. "Well, I can't promise about the fighting. I'm sorry, Mum, but sometimes you have to fight for peace. The dragone need their island back, and we're going to get it for them. I did mature while you were away. I joined the army." I laugh humourlessly. "I'm finding out who and what I am. The angeli have made me stronger, the dragone have shown me somewhere I could call home. I've made friends. I've got family, more family," I correct. "I need to talk to you, Mum, about something important. I need you to be strong."

"Me?" She laughs. "You have changed. No more fighting," she states bluntly. I roll my eyes. No mother would want their child fighting in any war. I can't imagine how she feels about one involving the Fallen.

August chooses that moment to knock on the door. I gulp, and then jump up when my mother starts to rise. "I'll get it."

"Aquila?" she asks sternly. I'm already at the door. I crack it open slowly, only a fraction.

"You left without me," August moans on the other side. "Liam is friggin' grumpy." My face twists into an odd half smile half grimace.

"Aquila?" My mother asks again. "What are you doing?"

I turn around, shielding the door. "Okay, Mum, remember when I said you need to be strong?" Of course she does, it was only a second ago. "I met someone when I came here. I wanted to tell you before, but there were the drugs and the Fallen and then Brue. Please don't freak out, Mum."

"Aquila?" Her voice is getting tighter. "Just let whoever it is in. I'm not going to freak out. Is it your father?"

"No." I shake my head, pulling the door open gingerly. "It's your son."

August steps into the room slowly, looking uncomfortable. I grab his hand for support, not sure if it's for me or him. He puts his other hand up in a little wave and my mother drops to the floor, out cold.

"Damn." I rush to scoop her up and lay her on the bed. "Did you bring any salts?"

"Why would I bring salts?" he snaps. "We were meant to break it gently. You're so dramatic. *It's your son*," he mimics.

"I panicked. It just came out." I fan my hands over my mother's face. "Should I get a Medic?"

"Lucas!" August shouts, making me jump. Lucas' white-blond head appears around the door seconds later.

"Trouble?" he asks. I should have known he'd be nearby.

"Aqua decided to shock her to death," August explains.

I groan. "I didn't decide to do anything. It was an impulse."

"You are rather impulsive," Lucas laughs, pulling a vial of salt out of his white tunic pocket. "Luckily I come prepared." He waves the salt under my mother's nose. "Perhaps I should get you one of these?" he suggests as my mother starts to blink.

I ignore him. "Mum? Are you okay?"

She doesn't answer immediately. Her eyes roam the room and settle on August. They gaze at each other for a very long time. So long that me and Lucas move away and start chatting.

"You need to come and see Robyn," he urges me, "she has been asking about you constantly."

"I know. I want to. I will. Tomorrow night after dinner." I study his face, frowning. "What aren't you telling me?" I ask finally. "You look like you're going to burst."

He raises his eyebrows in mock innocence. "I have no idea what you are referring to." His mouth ticks up into a smile and I grin.

"I don't believe you. Robyn will tell me."

"I am sure she will," he beams.

"How is mated life?" I ask wryly. "Has it changed you?"

"Only for the better, Aqua."

"I'm happy for you, Lucas."

"So am I," he replies. "Should we intercede?" He points at my mother, who is still staring at August. At least she's smiling now.

"You doing okay, Mum?" I ask, moving back to her side.

"Now let me think, Aqua," she starts mockingly. "Am I okay? My dead son is standing in front of me, looking more handsome than his father, and the only warning I get is a command from my daughter not to freak. I'm just rosy."

I smile. Her words are sarcastic but her tone is the opposite.

"I should return to my mate," Lucas says from behind me. "You will be alright." It's not a question. Even I can read my mother's body language right now.

I thank him by the door and then sit back on the bed, pulling August down with me. He starts talking, perpetually – like verbal diarrhoea. My mother listens indulgently as he tells her his name, and his favourite food, and about his job in the barracks, and about Marcus, and Liam, and anything else that apparently pops into his head. His rendition is disjointed and largely confusing, jumping from present to past and back again. I'm not sure my mother, our mother, is even listening but she smiles like *little miss sunshine* as he blabbers.

I get up to use the bathroom, twice. Then I lie down on the bed, still listening. Our mother eventually starts asking questions, like she's just realised this isn't some strange noisy apparition. They talk about his schooling and my trial, and I drift off around Aaron's arrival. When my eyes open again August is talking about Liam. I try to go back to sleep but he's jumping about on the mattress like it's a trampoline. The candles have dimmed, almost burnt completely down. I busy myself lighting more. I don't see August stopping anytime soon.

"So Liam is your brother?" My mother suddenly exclaims. "Aqua? I'm talking to you."

Oh. I look up from the orange light I was igniting, a black spot dances in my vision until my eyes adjust.

"Liam is Marcus' son," she exclaims.

"Not genetically, Mum. He's adopted. We're not related." My voice sounds flat.

I can't muster the enthusiasm to explain this again. I wander back over and flop down next to her. She watches me like she expected me to say more. I don't. I think maybe my mother has a kind of sixth sense, her gaze tells me she's figured out there's something between Liam and me. Something intense.

"Well he sounds like a strong young man," she offers. "Very..." She can't seem to find the words. August's explanation of our brother contained a lot of fighting and regular irritability – pretty much spot on.

"He is," I grunt. What else can I say?

She watches me shrewdly before turning to August. "And what about you, sweetheart? Do you have a girlfriend?"

He blanches and looks at me in horror. I laugh gruffly. "Tell her, she's not an angeli."

He still stutters slightly before spitting it out. "Actually, I'm gay." He looks so worried I soften slightly. What's wrong with me? August is my favourite human brother and I'm too busy wallowing over Liam.

"Well then," our mother states simply, "any boyfriends?" And just like that the tension vanishes.

August beams at her and I find the energy to shuffle over and kiss his cheek. He launches into a description of Oberon, who I'm assuming has reached full boyfriend status now. I settle back down, listening to his voice drift away as I close my eyes.

I wake up wrapped in my human brother, with our mother sitting on the edge of the bed watching us. My heart skips when I see her.

"Christ, Mum. You scared me."

"You may not be an angel, honey, but I will not have you taking the Lord's name in vain." She smiles and pats my leg. "You look so good together I couldn't help it. My children." She shakes her head. "It's like a miracle."

I untangle myself from August's arms and leg. "So you're okay?" I ask. "Really okay?" I examine her face.

"I'm happy," she answers. "It's no use dwelling on the past. We have the future together, the three of us. And after last night, I don't feel like I've missed a fraction of his life."

"You're amazing," I say in wonder. I'd feel cheated, and furious.

"Well, honey. You may need to remind me to be forgiving if I ever see *that man* again." She rubs my hand before walking over to her dresser. "You'd better get up if you want breakfast," she suggests. "We've overslept."

"It's a wonder we slept at all. When did August stop?" I glance at him, spread across the bed. "How do you know we overslept?"

She holds her wrist out to me. "I learnt to tell the time, honey."

"A watch!" I stare at it like she just invented the wheel. 'Can I have it?" I beg. I'm not opposed to dropping to my knees if she says no.

She laughs. "Yours is here somewhere." She gestures around the room. "I asked Robyn to get me some things from home. They dropped them in yesterday."

Get my watch from home! Why the hell didn't I think of that? I dig through her floral overnight bag. I liberate a bottle of shower gel and can of deodorant from my mother's care. I also find my watch and my dead mobile phone in the bottom. The charger isn't there, not that there are electrical sockets in Celthia.

"Modern technology!" I hug it to my chest. "This is a miracle."

"Gosh," my mother exclaims. "I quite like the lack of modern day contraptions. Doesn't it feel nice to talk to people instead of all that twerping?"

"It's tweeting, Mum, or texting. Either way, I don't think twerping is a real thing. Unless you mean twerking, and I definitely don't do that."

I use her bathroom before pulling August out of bed. He grumbles all the way to breakfast about his lack of sleep, rather than his failure to use sanitation this morning. I've seen him wear the same outfit for four days in a row before now.

"Busy day today?" my mother asks, like this isn't a complete change to our usual routine at home.

"Training all day," I answer. Lots of training.

"Well, no fighting," she warns.

I grunt in response, then rush off when she tries to make me agree properly. I yell over my shoulder as I make good my escape. "See you later."

She yells back. "I'm next door, remember!"

I grab some fruit and some mixed nuts before avoiding a glowering Liam and instructing my pirates to follow me to the barracks. I eat while we're walking. I was very late. I feel Liam following, but pretend I don't.

"How was Brue this morning?" I ask Axion as we climb the spiral stairs.

"Good. Still asleep but I feel him, he's doing fine."

I shiver. "Do you know how weird that sounds? Can't we call it something else, like you recepticate him?"

He laughs. "That's a made-up word, and it sounds worse."

"Well we need to think of something. We can't all go around feeling each other." Liam pushes past us at that moment, stomping into the barracks. I watch his back, my heart spluttering.

"We always call it feeling," Axion shrugs. "I sensed him, then. Okay?"

"Okay," I agree distractedly. "Uniforms."

"What?" he frowns. "Are you okay?" He tries to grab my hand but I pull it away.

"I'm fine," I snap. "Let's get everyone Guard uniforms." I march off to the right, my pirates following me.

Their uniforms have been piled neatly in one of the storerooms. I pass them out, black leather trousers and vests, steel armour and sheaths for weapons. They change in the classroom while I wait outside.

I groan when I finally walk in. None of them are wearing the vests. Most of them have cut their trousers into shorts. Thigh sheaths are attached upside-down and one of them has his armour on back to front... George.

Axion saunters over. His armour's on correctly but one trouser leg is cut slightly shorter than the other. "You like the modifications?" he grins.

"You look like an idiot."

"Ouch." He laughs. "We aren't angeli, Aqua. They wanted to make a statement."

"I'll remind them of their statement when they're freezing their butts off and getting their bare skin shredded by swords." I walk to the front, ignoring the piles of wasted leather on the floor. "Right, no more stupid classroom," I state, gaining their attention. "We're going to the gym. And I'm going to teach you to fight. You're right. You're not angeli and I don't want you to be. Let's go." I storm back into the corridor. "What weapons have you got?" I can only imagine they used some kind of cutlass on their uniforms.

"I got me guttin' knife, Lass," Reuben boasts. I suppress a shiver.

"It's for fish, Lassie." Art laughs from behind. "Not great on leather we found."

"We'll start with short blades then, if that's what you're used to."

I lead them across the gym. The Guard move aside, watching. I consider going straight for the real thing, like Liam did with me, but grab the blunt blades out of common sense. They pass the practice daggers around, grumbling. Only Axion watches me with a smile.

"Get into pairs," I order. My concern seems to have abandoned me. I can't shift the dark mood that's been building since yesterday, so I decide to just go with it. "Ax, you sit this one out." I eye Cain as they slowly pair up. "Watch George and Nev don't kill each other," I suggest when Axion protests. "Cain. We'll demonstrate shall we?"

He smirks in surprise, pulling his long hair back into a ponytail. He looks around thirty, muscled from years on the sea. I watch him approach. My training tells me what to look for: his gait, the way he moves, which side he favours. He's quick on his feet, like all dragone. I'm going to wipe that smug look off of his face.

"You sure about this, angel?" He sneers as we start to circle. The pirates form a circle, murmuring.

"Do you feel prepared to fight an angeli Guard?" I ask. "Have you studied the way I move? The way I'm preparing myself?" The circle gets more dense as some of the Guard join it, intrigued. "Are you anticipating my first, second and third moves?"

He laughs, though it sounds slightly forced. "Enough words, angel."

He lunges, and I sidestep so that he barrels into the wall of his shipmates. They laugh as they right him and push him back toward me. "Nice trick," he scoffs. "Anticipate this, angel." He lunges again, keeping his balance this time. I spin, his blade gets nowhere near me but mine slaps him gently on the shoulder. Liam was a tough master, fastidious in his training. He taught me control.

Cain spins again, but not quickly enough. I've already anticipated it. I move in the other direction. He turns his back to me and I slap my blade across his neck. He growls in frustration, and kicks his leg out – which I jump easily. My kick lands on his lumbar spine and he staggers forward. I land lightly, ducking when he swipes his dagger at my neck. I twist my blade quickly, jabbing him in the ribs with the bulbous handle, hard enough to leave a bruise. He puffs out his air, wheezing. I swipe his feet out from under him and he falls, beaten.

"Do you feel prepared, Cain?" I refrain from kicking him while he's down.

The circle stays silent, watching Cain as he struggles back to his feet. I watch him too, waiting to judge him. He spits on the stone floor, glaring at me. I look at the noxious substance with disgust. He adjusts the grip on his blade and I smile. Round two.

I move first. I was holding back before, teaching him a valuable lesson about pride. Now I just want to pummel him. He doesn't see me coming. I knock the blade from his hand in one move, spinning him and holding my blade to his throat like a madwoman. I snarl in frustration. Where's the fun in fighting when there's no competition. I push him away, annoyed.

"Axion? Want to show him how to fight?"

"No way." He shakes his head.

I growl a guttural, feral noise from deep in my chest and the whole circle takes a step back.

"Are you looking for a fight, Aquila?" Liam strolls through the ring holding a dagger of his own.

I take a millisecond to forget that I'm ignoring him. I take another one to realise his blade is real. And I take one more to register his first attack. I drop and roll, discarding my dulled blade in the process. When I regain my feet, my own dagger is in my hand. His smile is brief, and then we're fighting. I put everything into it. Our blades clash as we both attempt the same attack at the same time, their connection causes a visible spark. I leap before him, engaging him in the air before landing on his other side. The circle have all frozen, stunned. Watching Liam fighting is like watching *Yoda* or *Bruce Lee*, except Liam's better. He moves like water, fluidly and streamlined. I've never beaten him. The only times our bouts have ended in a draw is when he's forfeited. I don't even trust him not to hurt me anymore, so I stop thinking and let instinct guide me. I spin and kick and then change direction. He counters my every move, but not as easily as usual. I fake a feint to the right. He moves left, falling for it. Before I realise it I'm behind him, my arm wrapped around his chest and my dagger pressing lightly into the soft skin above his jugular. He freezes, breathing hard.

Did he let me do that? Or did I just beat him? I blink but don't move. He taught me that: wait until your opponent is unarmed or dead.

He stands like a statue, unwilling to drop his weapon. Perhaps he doesn't know how. I consider letting go, preserving the Guard Master's dignity. I consider letting him disarm me. I consider just walking away and hiding in my room.

"Guard Master," Plyrian commands from the now massively swollen crowd. "Concede defeat or attempt to redeem yourself."

Liam doesn't move. I make the decision for him. "He won't concede," I state. I pull my blade away to re-sheath it, forfeiting the match. "It was an honourable thing, Guard Master, to allow me the illusion of your defeat in front of my men. I thank you."

I walk away, calling my pirates with me. My hands are shaking like jack-hammers. I pretend not to notice as I put them back into their pairs. Axion partners Cain and I wander between them, plastering on a fake scowl as I watch their haphazard sparring. My mind isn't on any of them. Liam stormed off toward the classrooms. Plyrian stood and studied me. The Guard slowly formed another ring around our group and then started joining in, showing the dragone their techniques. Murmured conversations stop when I pass, though from what I overhear, opinion about Liam's defeat is divided.

Lunch is quiet, until August arrives. "Is it true? You beat Liam?"

I sigh. "No, he let me win." I'm so miserable that it doesn't sound like a lie. I'm not sure it is. The more I think about it, the more likely it seems. I just can't figure out why.

"That doesn't sound like Liam." Aaron turns on his stool to study me, frowning. I stare at his chest, avoiding eye contact. He's wearing my favourite faded black *Kings of Leon* t-shirt and dark denim jeans.

"When did you get your clothes?" He's been borrowing August's up until now.

"Changing the subject," Axion whispers under his breath.

"The Guard," Aaron answers, ignoring him. "They raided my room while my parents were milking." His voice cracks at the end. I grasp his hand automatically, offering some pathetic comfort. Aaron loved his life in the country. It's my fault he's here and not home on the farm with his family.

"You could always go back," I mutter.

He shakes his head, his mouth tilting into a smile. "I prefer it here, with you..."

"So," August interrupts loudly. "How's Liam handling it?"

I grimace.

"What's his problem," Axion questions. "He let you win, why did he storm off?"

"Liam never loses," Aaron bites out angrily.

My eyes snap back to his face, shocked. "Are you okay?"

"Fine." He gets up. "I'll see you later."

"In a while..." I start but don't finish. He didn't say alligator.

"So what have you got planned for this afternoon?" Axion asks, moving closer and attempting to grab my hand. I pull away. He's not very wry in his attempts to feel me... sense me... whatever.

"Knife skills." I shrug. "Maybe I expected too much this morning. They looked like they were playing tag, not sparring."

"Maybe you scared them all too much to think," he laughs.

"Me? Scare a group of pirates? I don't think so. Maybe Cain, but that was the point."

"He's not so bad, you know." He shoulder bumps me, making sure his hand touches mine. My eyes roll as I move away.

"I'm going to see Brue." I stand up. "Meet me in the barracks in ten." I glance at my watch. "Amazing."

Brue has been moved to a different room. When I walk in he's sitting up on the bed, eating a bacon sandwich and chatting with a male Medic.

"Wow, you look better." I hurry over. I thought he'd still be asleep. "Should you be eating yet?"

"He is doing very well," the Medic comments. "I shall allow you to talk. I will be back to check you in a few measures, Brue." It sounded like a warning. I raise my eyebrow questioningly.

"I tried to leave," Brue grins, his mouth stuffed full. "Now I've got my own keeper. He's like a full-time slave." He waves his sandwich around. "It's cool." He spits saliva and mushy bread in my direction. I grab him in a hug, ignoring the red sauce dripping down his chin.

"Never scare me like that again, Brue. Promise me."

"It wasn't my fault, Aqua. Those stupid angels followed me." He pushes me away to take another bite of his food. "It was their fault."

"Okay, Brue." I smile indulgently. "It wasn't your fault you snuck off when I told you not to."

"Exactly," he mumbles around a huge bolus of bacon and bread.

"Well you got out of two days of school," I comment. "Looks like you'll be well enough to go back tomorrow, though." I try to sound serious.

Brue suddenly has a relapse. "Um... maybe I got up too quickly." He lies back on the bed, still clutching the remnants of his sandwich. "I should stay in bed for another week. Or sleep in your room, and go to the barracks with you so you can watch me. I could help you. School is rubbish anyway."

I almost agree. "School is important. Knowledge is power, Brue. You know that, but you don't have to go tomorrow. You were really sick. We were all worried and you do need to stay in bed, for at least a week." I kiss his head.

"Yuck," he grumbles. But he wraps his arms around me and squeezes before letting go to start eating again, his relapse obviously forgotten.

"I'll send your keeper back in. It's off to work I go," I sing in a very poor impersonation of the seven dwarfs. That reminds me about a princess. "Oh, by the way, Axion claimed me as your sister." I grin as Brue's mouth pops open. "See you later little brother." I blow him a kiss and shut the door.

"Aqua!" I hear him shout. "I'd already figured that out!"

I grin as I walk along the corridor. Shrewd Brue.

# · Eleven ·

"Again!" I yell. "You fight like old women! This isn't knitting class. If you don't disarm or kill your opponent you're dead. D. E. A. D. So do it again, properly!" I patrol around my pirates as they practice. I'm channelling Liam, or Hitler. I occasionally pull out my dagger to demonstrate a move or a counterattack but I mainly just shout. Now I know why Liam enjoys it so much. It's therapeutic.

"Aye, Lass," Reuben pants. "I'm an old dog. T'is an 'ard day's work, t' teach I a new trick."

I pat him on the back as I pass. He's learning more quickly than the rest, and he's obviously used to handling a knife.

"Many a good tune played on an old fiddle." I quote one of grand-mama's mantras. "And I hear you're the oldest of them, Old Salt."

"Aye, Lass. T'is I should be teachin' ye. Yer a scoundrel, I'll give 'e that," he laughs. "Aft' this war's won, Lass. I'm retirin' t' me island t' eat till I'm fat and drink till I'm drunk."

"Aye Aye," his sparring partner agrees, pouring sweat like a waterfall. Tomas, I recall, but Reuben calls him Plank. He's a shorter, rounder version of Reuben with slightly more black than gray in his hair. I'm learning their names as the pirates get more vocal. Personalities are coming out as they acclimatise. It helps that they keep cussing each other's names like swearwords.

I send them for dinner when they start pretending to be in deep conversation, rather than practicing. I follow slowly, hoping to see Liam, or at least scent him nearby. He doesn't materialise. Axion grabs my hand from behind, latching on like an incubus.

"Hey, Princess, can you make sure they write *Murdered* on my gravestone. I want everyone to know what you're doing to me."

I tug his arm in response. He's got a direct line to my emotions, so I don't bother pretending to laugh.

"You want to talk about it, sis?" he asks, genuinely concerned. "Something's bothering you. Is it this?" he asks, lifting our hands. "Because I'd stop feeling you if you'd just tell me what's the matter."

"If this was the matter," I snap, wiggling our hands, "then stopping feeling me would solve it."

"But that's not what's the matter, obviously," he prompts.

"I'm just miserable." I wave him away, disentangling my hand. "There's a lot going on and I'm getting swamped. Sometimes I just wish I was back in England, you know, a year ago none of this was even an issue. I was just a normal teenager. I only had two other people to worry about. I actually flew for fun. I can't remember the last time I had fun..."

"Flying with Brue," Axion answers automatically. "Or your food fight yesterday. You have fun with Aaron."

"Yeah we used to, a lot. Now it's all awkward."

"Yeah, I don't need to feel him to know how he feels about you." Axion nudges me, sliding his fingers around mine again. "But how do you feel about him?"

I let him feel my turmoil. I love Aaron. I've always loved him. My feelings for him are just dwarfed by my feelings for Liam. But Liam ruined it all.

"Whoa." Axion pulls his hand away. "Sorry I asked." He grins at me. "Talk to me, or talk to someone."

"Did you know Brue's awake?"

"Did you know you're changing the subject again?"

"Yes."

He smiles. "Yeah I know. I felt him."

"When?"

"When he woke up, and when you went to see him. He blasted me with happiness, the little weirdo."

"How?" I ask. "You weren't touching him."

"We're linked, Aqua, I don't need to touch him to feel him. He's just always there. Can't you feel him? I thought you... you felt him get hurt." He frowns at me.

"No, I don't think so..."

"Maybe it's just weak? It was fast, it normally takes weeks to link with someone."

"What does that even mean? What's so amazing about feeling everyone else's emotions? How do you know what's real and what's just chemicals."

"All emotions are chemicals. Everything you feel is real, Aqua. The link doesn't create feelings, it intensifies them, brings them to the forefront of your mind. It normally relieves confusion, creates openness. I've never met anyone as resistant to it as you."

I study him for a second, my head ticking to the side involuntarily as I consider what he said. The link intensifies feelings. Makes them stronger? I don't like the sound of that.

I keep my promise to Lucas after eating and seek out Robyn. She's in their new quarters, a family room on one of the lower floors. They have engraved their new conjoined sigil into the door. I'm pretty sure you're not meant to do that. I suppose that if a Tail and a Nester are allowed to mate, then anything is possible. I stare at the design before knocking. Lucas' sigil is a feather inside a quarter moon. Robyn's looks like an elaborate maple leaf. They've put Lucas inside Robyn. I shudder when my subconscious takes me somewhere I don't want to be. I knock quickly.

Robyn is beautiful, with long blonde waves and slender wings. Her face lights up when she sees me. "Aqua! Where have you been? How is your mother? Does she like the room? Oh, tell me about your awful experience. Is Liam looking after you? How is the little boy? I'm nesting. Did your mother get the items she ask..."

"Hold up!" I cut her off. "Rewind to the nesting comment."

She glows like a full beam.

"Does that mean what I think it does?" I stare at her in anticipation.

"Yes!" she exclaims. "A youngling. We're having a youngling. It hasn't quickened yet, but I begged Lucas to let me tell you."

I attempt the math but I've lost track of the days again, I glance at my watch but that doesn't help. "How far are you?" Her stomach is flat, flatter than mine.

"Do you mean when did I conceive? After our mating ceremony of course."

She must mean literally, like that night, it can't have been more than three weeks ago.

I pull her into a hug. "I'm so happy for you both." My head is throbbing with questions. "Tell me everything," I command. "I mean everything."

"Aqua," she squeals. "You are so brazen." She laughs and pulls me over to their sofa. They have a sofa? I glance around for the first time. Their room is huge, with a double bed and living space. There's even a table.

"Nice room. I didn't mean tell me how you conceived, just tell me what it was like and how you already know you're pregnant? I'm not exactly an expert but I thought it took longer, you know, to realise."

"Oh, I forget you know so little about yourself." She shakes her head. "Our nesting periods are shorter than the human's. Our youngling will arrive in twenty three weeks." She rubs her still flat belly, smiling. "I can feel the change in my body."

"Well, way to go Lucas." I hug her again. "Just tell me one thing. You aren't going to lay an egg?"

She laughs like a hyena, a snorting hyena. "No, Aqua! We stopped laying eggs generations ago. You do say the strangest things..." Her words are lost in her giggles.

"I've been told that, a lot."

I slouch into the softness of the seat. I'd like a room this large. It's much less claustrophobic.

"Now you tell me," Robyn says. She holds my hand affectionately. What is it with all the hand-holding? Everyone's doing it. Maybe there's a sign pinned to my back... *Please hold my hand.* "What is bothering you, Aqua?"

She doesn't press me for information. She just waits, her eyes soft. I groan and thump my forehead with the palm of my free hand. My mood must be blatant if someone riding their own euphoria can see it.

"It's Liam," I mumble eventually.

"What has he done?" she asks sympathetically.

I smile humourlessly. A mundane piece of gossip can fly around Celthia in an instant. Something huge, catastrophic, like the breaking of my heart, I have to relive over and over again.

"If you won't talk to me I could find Lucas..."

"No, sheesh. Okay..." I take a deep breath. "Has Lucas ever told you where I came from?"

She rolls her eyes. It seems too human a gesture on her angelic face. "England," she answers. "From the humans."

My shoulders heave. "I'm not half human, Robyn." I swallow and glance at our entwined fingers.

"Is that what has you so forlorn?" She places her other hand on top, sandwiching my hand between hers. "There is a book in the library. I have read it countless times since we met. A human named *Christopher Columbus* set off in search of a new world. Do you know the story?"

I nod.

"Do you know what happened?"

"He discovered America," I answer, confused.

She smiles. "He discovered what he thought was The Indies."

I frown.

"Sometimes," she muses, "what we think we know and what is actually true are the opposite."

"Are you telling me the world isn't flat?" I smirk.

"I'm telling you that I know you are not half human. We were wrong about the dragone." She shakes her head. "We were blinkered by our assumptions." She squeezes her fingers around mine. "You are the New World, Aquila."

"Are you being metaphorical?"

She winks. "You are the gateway to possibilities: like peace and freedom. You are the start of the revolution."

"Revolution?"

"You think I didn't notice the change in Gloria? She and I have known each other for many measures." Her voice drops to a whisper. "You have given them all hope. It isn't just what you represent; it is *you*. You are gifted with compassion and they all see it. Soon they will see that we cannot continue to blame an entire race for our history." She clears her throat. "Liam too, will eventually understand..."

I catch her eye, assessing her. It's a valid conclusion, that I would be worried about Liam's reaction. But her voice cracks like she's lying.

"You don't believe that," I grin. "You're just trying to comfort me."

Her eyes widen slightly. "Well, it is true that he may find it difficult..."

"He knows," I interrupt. "He knew before we started courting."

Her mouth forms a little O. Her eyelashes flutter as she takes that in. Then she coughs daintily. "Excellent," she squeaks. She shifts and her posture changes slightly. "So what in the Mother's name has got you so miserable?" Her voice is reprimanding.

So I tell her, "He shot me just before I was captured. The worst thing is, I don't understand why. Why would he do that?"

Robyn opens her mouth to speak, and then closes it again several times before finally finding her voice. "So Liam wounded you..."

"Yeah," I confirm.

"Well," she exclaims. "I still do not see the problem."

"Did you not understand?"

"Oh I understand," she says, sounding frustrated. She wipes the tear from my cheek before it drops and tucks my hair behind my ear. "Do you know how long you were gone? How long he searched? How long he brooded in that room of yours? Aqua, he loves you."

"He shot me!"

"Did you die?"

"No, of course not."

"Then he did it for a reason, and if I know Liam it was to protect you in some convoluted way. That man is entirely too strategic." She furrows her brow disapprovingly.

I raise an eyebrow. "You mean like *the enemy of my enemy is my friend*?"

"Yes, I suppose."

"Well that's stupid," I state.

"He should have informed us. No wonder you're acting like this." Her disapproving look doesn't fade. I can't help but feel it's been redirected to me.

"How do you expect me to be acting?"

She flicks her shoulder in a tight shrug and pouts. "Like an adult. Sometimes we're forced to make tough decisions, Aqua. We make mistakes. Liam's mistake was making you think that he'd betrayed you."

"And what was my mistake?"

"Believing it."

I gawk at her. "I spent two weeks agonising over this and you just expect me to accept it and move on?"

"And I imagine he spent two weeks imagining a lot more painful outcomes than your wrath, Aqua. You knew you were still alive, he did not."

I rise from the sofa, irritated. "So is this your idea of an intervention?"

"If you like. I believe it is what friends do." She rises to her feet far more gracefully. "I think you should talk to him."

"We'll just end up fighting."

"Then use Victus as a mediator, Aqua. Honestly, you're both as bad as each other." She pushes me toward the door. "Go on."

"Now?"

She pulls the door open and pushes me out. "Yes, Aqua. Now."

The door shuts behind me and I huff.

Robyn's voice is muted by the metal. "Start walking."

I huff again and stomp away, exaggerating every step like a child in a tantrum. I'm not even sure where she expects me to go. I have no idea where Liam is. I head for the library nevertheless. Victus is always happy to engage in a verbal tirade with me. The door is closed but I walk in anyway. I expect Victus to question my etiquette, instead I jump when Axion slams a book shut guiltily. My eyebrows quirk.

"It was empty when I got here," he states.

"What were you reading?" I walk over and pluck the book from his hands. It's a journal, its pages worn and smeared. I flick to a random entry. "Deceiving Death?"

"Interesting title," Axion comments. "Almost as nteresting as where I found it."

I wait, flicking through the handwritten notes. "Where?" I mumble when he just stands there. My eyes skim the words but they make little sense.

"Hidden in here," Axion grins. He pulls out Victus' drawer and lifts the panel in the bottom. I wander over. The secret compartment is small. I recognise the shimmer of silver, my arrow.

"What were you doing?" I ask him, pushing the drawer closed again.

"Looking," he shrugs.

"For a secret compartment in Victus' desk?"

"Yes, of course. There's always something important hidden in a secret compartment. Don't you watch movies?" He tries to grab the book from my hands. "I wasn't finished."

I whip it behind my back. "I want to read it," I smirk.

He sniggers. "I found it." He moves fast, catching me off guard. Before I can react he pushes me against the shelves in his attempt to grab it. I growl in annoyance. He shouldn't have been able to do that. His arms wrap around me, searching for my hands which have been pinned. "Give it back."

I shake my head and a small snigger escapes. "Get off you moron." I consider lifting my knee into his groin.

He grabs my wing and tugs playfully, initiating an unexpected laugh from me. "Are you actually laughing, Princess?" He digs his fingers into my sides and my knees buckle.

No not tickling! I can't stand it. "Ax, you're a... royal pain... in my..." I'm laughing too hard. He holds me up, still tickling until I'm hysterical. "I'll wet myself!" I screech. "Stop!" My stomach is aching.

"Wow." He steps away grinning, "Too much information, sis."

"You're such a freak." I groan, holding my stomach. He snatches the book from my hands while I'm incapacitated.

"Did you wet yourself?" he asks, flicking through the pages of the journal.

I snatch it back and jump onto the desk. "Nope." I open the book and start reading obnoxiously. "*What fools these insignificant mortals show themselves to be. I see no benefit of the existence of lesser men. Let them scorn me now. For in the winter, they shall watch my triumph with glassed eyes.*"

The journal vanishes as Axion jumps the desk in one leap. "Thanks, Princess," he smirks.

"I was getting into that," I moan.

He flips open the book and mimics me. "*A female! Her usefulness has faded. I have no choice. The time has come so it must be Tylis. The mark is fresh upon his skin. Beware the winter, you righteous fools.*"

"Shh." I jump from the table. "Footsteps."

Axion attempts to stuff the journal into his shorts. I grab it from him and hide it inside the back of my leather top, under my wings.

He watches me, frowning. "That's why we wear cloaks."

"It's Liam," I say as I realise I can sense him approaching. "Act normal." I don't know why I said that.

"I am normal," Axion whispers as the door bursts open.

"*That* is a matter of opinion," Liam states as he strides in. He stares at me, unblinking. "You were laughing. Why?" His face is hard but his eyes are burning, hurting. He doesn't look at Axion.

"We were reading." I step toward him. "I was looking for you."

He stiffens. "In a sealed room with another man?" His voice is bitter.

"No, I got distracted."

"In a sealed room with another man," he repeats sourly.

"Liam..."

He spins to leave.

"Liam!" Axion shouts.

Liam is in front of him instantly, towering above him. He doesn't touch him but Axion still takes a defensive step back. "Do not address me. I will not let you take her from me again."

I tug his arm sharply, pulling him away. He doesn't resist.

"Him?" he asks me harshly. "After everything, you choose him? You hold his hand and laugh, while I watch from the shadows." He takes a deep breath. "I will not surrender without a fight, Aquila. You are meant to be mine."

I draw my dagger. He startles and takes a step back. It's the opposite reaction to the one I was expecting. "I do not choose him," I spit. My tone leaves a bitter taste in my mouth. I step forward, pointing the dagger at his chest. "You lay claim to me? Like a possession, after everything?" My dagger touches the leather of his vest. I run it down his abdomen. He doesn't move, eyeing me warily. "You don't trust me to stand in a sealed room, with my only birth-brother, and not be unfaithful to you, after everything?" I slide my dagger under the material of his vest. I'm too angry to admit that I just confirmed we're still a couple who are required to be faithful. "You think you have to fight to win me from him, after everything?"

In one move I lift my dagger and slice through the leather, splitting his vest open like a shirt. I re-sheath my blade and pull open his ruined top. My fingers trace the circular outline of his tattoo. The language is familiar, though it is Axion who will have to read it.

He moves slowly when I beckon, watching me. "You're being weird," he hisses as he reaches my side.

Liam hasn't moved, still watching me without expression. "What is this?" I ask him. I notice Axion become rigid as he registers it. He starts to speak but I elbow him roughly. Perhaps I am acting weird.

"A tattoo, Aquila." Liam nearly growls when he speaks.

"And its significance?" I ask. "Why did you get it?" I lock my eyes with his. The hypnotising flecks of gold twinkle in the eerie moonlight, which is pouring through the glass above our heads.

He doesn't answer. He raises a hand to lightly touch my curls before dropping it again. "You're angry," he states.

"Furious," I amend. "Tell me about the tattoo, Liam."

"I don't remember," he snaps. "It was a long time ago. Why are you concerned with it? It's just a mark."

*A mark.* "Axion," I sigh. "What does it say?"

"It says nothing," Liam argues.

"It says, *Son of the Fallen*," Axion corrects, his voice slightly higher than usual.

I exhale. Goddamned Rennison Jarik.

"You're trying to deceive her," Liam yells in response. "That is your attack on me." He grabs me, pulling me toward him. "It is simply a tattoo. It holds no meaning, Aqua. They are attempting to steal you to their side." He draws his sword. "Your welcome here has been withdrawn. Run, vile scum."

I groan. Liam can be so hostile. "For the Mother's sake, stop this, Liam. Get the arrow, Ax."

"What?" Axion mumbles.

"In the drawer." I point in the direction of Victus' desk, not taking my eyes off of Liam. He smells too good to be legal. I think about kissing him, lightly, on the lips. Then I shake the absurd thought from my head. He's still not forgiven. His eyes stay planted on Axion as he moves.

"Here," Axion offers the arrow.

"Take it," I urge. "Look at it."

He narrows his eyes at me before he studies it, plucking it from Axion's grasp. "What?"

"Is that your sigil?"

"You know it is," Liam snaps.

"Is it unique?"

His eyes flick quickly away before glaring back at me, an involuntary admission. "Sigils are always a unique adaption of a family emblem. You know that."

I ignore his attempt to avoid answering my question. "Is yours?"

"What does it matter? My father is dead." He pushes me aside, storming from the room with the steel shaft still clutched in his palm. I turn to follow automatically.

Axion grabs my arm. "What's going on, Princess?" He moves his grip to my bare hand, feeling me.

Good question. I rub my free hand down my face, exhausted. "I've got to go after him."

"No, you don't." He grips me tighter. "Aqua, I don't trust him. Think about it. Why would he have that tattoo and not remember? He's lying to you."

"He doesn't remember because he was only a boy." I pull my hand away. "You don't know him, Ax. Stay out of it." I turn again and stomp to the door.

"He changes you!" Axion shouts behind me. "Every time you're with him, you act differently, you talk differently. You become one of them!"

I ignore him. "You don't know me, either."

# · Twelve ·

L iam can vanish. If he doesn't want to be found, he won't be. His scent disappears as if by magic, until I'm convinced that he's somehow developed the ability to walk through walls. I work my way down through every floor, stopping at my room to hide the journal, before abandoning any idea of finding him and stomping back up through the city. Where the hell did he go?

"Aqua!" August shouts from behind. I stop and lean against the wall, waiting, staring up at the smooth rock ceiling like it may hold the answers I want. August catches up, panting.

"Mother, you move fast. Victus has sent for you." He stops to catch his breath. "Something about a tattoo." He studies me questioningly, still clutching his sides like his lungs might explode any second.

So I guess that wherever Liam is, he's with Victus. "Where?" I ask, annoyed.

"He'll meet you in the library."

I'm sure he will. "Are you coming?" I offer hopefully.

He shakes his head. "Nope, he was very specific."

"About?"

"About you going alone," August grimaces.

Great. "Can I pretend you didn't find me?"

August's laugh is strained by his still protesting lungs. "Yeah, but he sent Lucas after you too, so you won't have long."

"Damn," I curse. "How'd you find me first?" Seriously, it's like a miracle.

"Axion did his freaky locating spell for me, which is so cool by the way. Being human sucks," he grumbles.

"Being human isn't such a terrible thing, August. And what do you mean, freaky locating spell?"

"I checked the cells first and he told me exactly where you were, said he could feel you." He studies me again.

"Perfect." I march back toward the library, stewing. So apparently Axion has a direct line to my emotions and location now. I let my annoyance build like a hurricane in my chest. Suck on that, *Your Highness*.

The library is full. So much for insisting I come alone. Liam and Plyrian are having another loud discussion while Victus watches on. A select few of the Guard stand in groups, murmuring to each other and watching the commotion. Tarcus, a short, bald Guard ambles over when I enter. I guess his hair used to be a burnt umber, like his wings. "Guardian," he murmurs. His smirk doesn't drop.

"Tarcus."

"Good to have you back." He gestures toward the raised voices of the Guard Master and his Second, still smirking. "Never a dull moment when you are around."

His words are emulated by the noisy arrival of Lucas and my pirates. They wedge themselves through the door in twos, like a herd of buffalo embarking the Ark.

All eyes turn in their direction, including those of the bickering duo that purport to be in charge.

"Indeed."

"Princess," Reuben addresses me. "T'is our understandin' ye'r discussin' our next move."

"Princess?" Tarcus echoes from my side, as the rest of the room erupt in indignation to their unannounced arrival. I can't hear myself think. This is why I have never harboured a desire to be in government. Who wants to spend all day in a room, arguing opposing views? That's Victus' thing. I'd rather be swimming.

"SILENCE!" Victus screams in a sudden burst of vocal prowess that crashes above the timbre of the crowd. Of course, everyone but the dragone obey. It takes me a few seconds to realise I should probably issue the same order, and a few more to actually do it. A simple raising of my hand does the job. Liam scowls at me.

"Guardian," Victus continues at a more normal volume, "name your representatives and dismiss the surplus." He flicks his finger at my men like he's trying to dislodge a persistent ball of dried snot. It irks me. Liam's scowl morphs into a wry smirk which irks me even more and a growl rumbles in my throat. Victus follows my line of site. "You as well, Guard Master."

Liam stiffens as his face blanks out. His head tilts back a degree, hooding his eyes as he stares at me along the length of his nose. It doesn't make him look any less attractive.

He fires his list of names through a clenched jaw. "Myself, Plyrian and Lucas."

I scowl at the last one, as does Victus. Lucas is a Tail, not a Guard, he answers to the Overseer, not the Guard Master. Liam's making this personal.

"Myself, Axion, Reuben," I state calmly, and then impulsively add, "and Tarcus."

"Excellent," Victus interrupts, before I include any more names I expect, and orders the extra bodies from the room.

My men don't move until I give them a nod, a fact I find smugly reassuring. "Get some rest," I instruct them, "we're training again in a few hours." They mumble as they shuffle from the room, most are already nursing fresh bruises and aching muscles from earlier.

"Well done," Lucas whispers as he passes. "You are setting an example by uniting both species."

Tarcus shuffles awkwardly beside me. I'd almost forgotten he was there. I wasn't trying to unite anything; I was being petty and impulsive. However, in retrospect, species unity is an added bonus.

"You feeling like a pioneer, Tarcus?" I glance at the Guard as Lucas moves to stand beside Victus. A move which appears to be a direct rebuff of Liam. Tarcus arches his lips into a dry grin. I imagine this is the first time he'll be witness to talks involving the top ranked of the angeli hierarchy. I hope he's not expecting to witness an intelligent exchange of ideas. If this is anything like my usual run-ins with Victus, there'll be shouting, insubordination and lots of eye rolling.

As if on cue, Liam starts off in a tirade of verbal assault aimed mainly at Axion I think, although he doesn't appear to be too fussy about whom he insults. Victus eventually cuts him off with a dismissive flick of his wrist.

"Enough, Liam. You've stated your opinion." Victus focuses on me expectantly, waiting. I inhale a lungful of air and blow the entire lot out through my nose before glancing at my representatives.

"Our first priority is the island. We need to reclaim it. Whatever clues the Fallen may have left are more likely to have vanished the longer we leave it." Reuben and Axion nod in agreement, Tarcus imitates them.

"Accepted," Victus states. "You will form a reconnaissance party. Choose a handful of your most equipped men," his eyes flash to Liam, "you included." Victus' finger starts its persistent tapping as he surveys the room. "Plyrian and Lucas are to stay here for the protection of Celthia, you may include any other." He looks at me and I nod. "Inform them tomorrow that you'll fly at sunset," he adds.

"And in the meantime?"

Victus leans back against the desk, his eyes bright. "In the meantime, we discuss a plan of attack." He gestures at the dragone. "We'll start by learning the layout of the island."

I let Axion do the talking. After all, he's the king and it's his home. Then I send them back to the cells when the arrangements are set. Axion suggested Cain and Art come with us to the island and I agreed. Art is a good guy and Cain would make good cannon fodder. My reasoning, not Axion's. Reuben and Tarcus will come as well.

Now I find myself wandering the eerie flickering corridors of the city, unsure of my destination. The smoke of the beeswax candles creates a fetid haze that seems more pronounced at, I sigh, four o'clock in the morning, according to the little hands on my wrist. I should probably give into the fatigue and head to my bed, but instead I gravitate toward the male residential wing of the city.

The conversation with Liam never happened, he actually high-tailed it out of the library faster than I did when Victus eventually excused us. Lucas and I both watched him go, like two fat cats debating whether to chase the mouse, except neither of us think of Liam as a mouse.

The door I eventually halt before is barely different from the others in the row. It's gold plated, etched with markings as familiar as my own. I run the pad of my finger along the lines, following their design. This room used to be Liam and August's, now it belongs to my brother and my best friend. Aaron. I'm not sure which of the two my subconscious has brought me to see.

I don't knock to announce my presence. Although I probably should, in case Oberon's ignoring his uncle's instructions and still sleeping over.

The room is warm, heated by the constantly stoked wood burner in the corner. August's bed is empty, his blankets strewn lazily across the surface of the mattress. I cross the room silently, aware of the soft snores emanating from Aaron against the left-hand wall. He's alone, deep in slumber. I watch the gentle rise and fall of his bedding, which is obscuring my view of his face. He's curled into the foetal position, one arm overhanging the bed.

August's mattress is cold, obviously yet to be slept on tonight. I'm not worried. He can make his own choices about where he lays his head. I curl up on August's bed, inhaling the scent of him that lingers on the bedding. I'm tired. Perhaps dream Liam won't find me here and I'll get a few hours of peaceful sleep. I wrap my wings around me like a feather quilt and close my eyes.

My watch beeps at the stroke of seven. I shut it off immediately. I'd never once overslept before coming to Celthia. I don't even have the excuse of the thick mountain walls obscuring my internal alarm clock. I always used to be up long before the sun arrived to climb into the sky above England. Funny, how things can change in such a short space of time.

Like my relationship with *that* man, I think as Aaron drags himself from his bed. The room must be pitch black to his human eyes, yet he finds a candle and lights it without any difficulty. I preferred the black and white show he was providing me before the bright flame seared a blind spot in my night vision. Aaron is a sight worthy of a place amongst the wonders of the world. Shirtless Aaron should be somewhere on the wonders winner's podium with a shiny medal around his neck.

"August!" he yells in my direction. "Get your lazy ass up."

I give a small chuckle. "August isn't here."

"Jesus!" Aaron jumps and his voice hits a peculiar pitch.

"He's not here, either." I sit up, swing my legs over the side of the bed and stretch my wings out to their maximum span. Ruffling the feathers, I tuck them back in. I always keep them tucked in, years of conditioning I guess. "Morning, sunshine."

"Aqua?"

"Hey."

"Hey," he answers. "What are you doing here? I mean, it's great, but, I mean how long... Were you here all night?"

"No, just since four."

"Why?" he asks. His hooded gaze assesses me with suspicion.

I lift and drop one shoulder in quick succession. "I wanted to talk to someone, but you were sound, and August wasn't here, so I fell asleep."

Aaron's head ticks back. "What's wrong?"

"Huh?"

He purses his lips and frowns. "Is something wrong?"

"Nothing new." I used to be able to talk to him about almost anything. I hate what's happened to us. I stay sitting on August's bed, my hands wedged under my thighs. "You okay?"

He stays standing, his thumbs hooked in the waistband of his sweatpants. "Fine," he answers. "What were you doing until four?"

"Sitting in the library, discussing tactics."

"War talks?" He drops his antagonistic pose and strides forward. "Aqua, you don't need to do this. You don't need to fight for them. This isn't our home."

I attempt to swallow the dry briars that curl in the back of my throat when he says, *our home.*

"I know it isn't." I stand up. "This isn't our home, but it is mine, for now at least."

He crosses the room slowly, closing the distance. My first reaction is to step backward, except there's a bed behind my calves. "It's not too late for us," he implores huskily. "For the life we would have had together."

"Aaron." My voice comes out as a plea. I don't want him to do this, to try and kiss me. I can feel it. The atmosphere charged in an instant. We're toe to toe. His fingers skim along my arms to trace the profile of my neck, threading into my hair and tugging gently.

've seen this look on his face before: concentration, ntensity, longing.

I should never have encouraged him. Sleeping here was another bad idea. His warm breath puffs against my cheek in rapid bursts. It causes a physical reaction, one I can't control. He's still Aaron, the only boy I'd ever fantasised about before Celthia. My tongue skims my teeth reflexively while heated blood courses around my veins, like molten lava. He tugs my hair again and my head tilts back in response.

"Just try," he begs before his lips cover mine, slowly, softly. He's far gentler than Liam ever was, his taste is different, and he doesn't try to force his tongue through my teeth. It's sweet and chaste but it doesn't feel... right. There's no triumphant chorus of cherubs, trumpeting their fanfare. I draw back quickly, slightly embarrassed, and extinguish the kiss before it gains enough momentum to crush us both. The silence lingers as he studies me, his lips rolling against each other like they miss the contact with mine. I was wrong. That was the worst idea ever. I shake my head, unable to voice the word, no. After everything we've been through, he still means something to me. I love him, just in a different way than before.

He eventually drops his hands to his sides in defeat. "Am I not enough?" he asks as he rakes his hand through his hair. "You are everything I want. We could have an amazing life, together."

"In England, where I'll spend the rest of my days hiding feathers under sweaters to keep them hidden? Or the life here, where you spend your life stuck inside a mountain? All the time, waiting for me to return from the latest mission or the latest fight?"

He looks lost for a moment, pulling his hand through his hair again. "But, I love you."

My blood turns icy-cold. My face must pale dramatically because he raises his hands like he's going to catch me. I'm not going to fall. I already did that, and picked myself back up again. My gaze drops to my wringing fingers. Aaron was always the one. I planned him into my human future. Aaron. His dirty blond hair, his stormy gray eyes, the pop of his dimple. My love for him was born during a childhood of experiences, of feelings, of memories. *Now* he decides to love me how I'd hoped he would. But, the future changed, my dreams have changed. I don't have to have a human future anymore. I can be me.

"I'm sorry, but I want..."

"Your misogynistic angeli brother," he cuts in bitterly.

Well, yeah. "Yes, I want Liam. I'm in love with him. Only him."

He winces. "Ouch."

"I'm sorry, Aaron. I choose him."

He shakes his head in disbelief. "But, he hurt you, he hurts you, constantly. Physically. Mentally. Do you think I can't see it?"

"He's not the only one who's ever hurt me, Aaron."

His face darkens. His mood has changed in an instant. "But he's the worst," he snaps. "Why him, Aqua? You're so... strong, independent. Why let yourself be abused by such a pig?"

"Abused?"

"He hits you, Aqua. If that's not abuse then I don't know what is. I've seen the bruises."

"Bruises from training. I'm in the Guard."

"He shot you with an arrow."

"I haven't forgotten."

"But you've forgiven?"

"No, not yet."

"Then why?"

"Why?"

"What are you, a parrot?! Yes, Aqua. Why?"

"I don't know why, Aaron!"

I fume a few heaving breaths before I continue.

"I'm not a martyr. I don't just put up with his attitude. I challenge him about it, constantly. I'm the first to tell him when he's being an ass."

"Doesn't stop him being one though, does it."

"Apparently not."

"So you're just going to put up with it, for the rest of *his* life? Because you know, he's going to piss off the wrong person eventually. He's headed to an early grave and then he won't be anyone's problem." His eyes flash with amusement.

I raise my eyebrows at him.

He shrugs, unrepentant. "Just stating a fact."

"Look. I've still got a very firm hold on my grudge for the whole arrow debacle. I didn't come in here with my love life all planned out. I wasn't even sure Liam would feature in it anymore. But you're right, the fact is, I haven't given up on him yet."

He flashes his dimple without smiling, his gray gaze whirling like a tsunami. "Don't look at me like that," I snap. "I'm not being submissive, or wearing blinkers, or just putting up with him. The fact is, I'm choosing to give him a second chance because I want to. The fact is, I'm choosing to give him a chance because it feels right. The fact is, I haven't spoken a civil word to him since I returned. I've avoided contact with him, and for some unfathomable reason my head is still full of him. My heartbeat seems to fall into time with his whenever he's near. I can smell him, constantly, even in my dreams."

"That's a lot of facts," he states.

I rub my temples with the heels of my hands. "Yeah."

"Possibly a bit too much information," he adds.

"Sorry." My hands drop to my sides and he steps forward again.

His mouth, the mouth that was on mine a minute ago, pulls up into a sad smile. "Don't be. Truth hurts, I guess."

We both watch as his hand snakes forward, wrapping around mine. "I always thought it would be us," Aaron whispers.

My mouth pulls to the side in a humourless smirk. "I did, too."

"So this is it?"

"This is it," I confirm.

"I think I want to go home," he says quietly, "to England. I think it's time."

It feels final, like he's cutting me off. I'm a gangrenous toe, better got rid of completely than attempting to revive it. I wrap my fingers slightly more tightly around his. "I don't want to be that friend you used to have. My mum will be going home, too. I want to be able to come see you, to visit. I want to be your friend, always."

"Yeah," he sighs as he moves closer, "I can't imagine not being friends."

I feel the finality of the moment. The strings break and any intimate future together floats off into the cosmos, to join all the other lost moments and missed opportunities that will never be: the moments that will never happen, the lovers that will never meet, the children that will never be conceived, the fame and fortune that will never befall. Because it's not fate who dictates our future, it's us. It's our decisions, our choices that change our course.

"Don't leave yet." I step away. "When this is all over, when we're not at the brink of a battle, I'll take you home." I need to know he's safe.

He nods slowly, raking his hand through his hair in his oh so familiar way. "I'm happy for you, you know." His eyes dart to the floor, like he can't quite believe he means it, or said it.

"I know," I answer anyway.

He takes a pace backward, allowing me to sidestep him. "So, what's next?"

"I need a shower," I answer, increasing the distance between us and heading for the door. I'm not running from him, I'm taking the first decisive step to moving on. "We leave for the island tonight."

Aaron follows me, his demeanour resigned. "Is he going?" He says *he* like it's a dirty word.

I stop, my hand already grasping the handle. "Yes."

I feel his fingers, lightly stroking the feathers of my wing. "Then watch your back," he warns me softly.

How quickly time passes, how things change. I close my eyes and nod, taking a ragged breath before answering. "Always do."

He leans in and whispers three more words into my ear before he steps back. I swallow, tilting my head slightly in acknowledgement.

I blindly push open the door, lifting my eyelids and stepping straight into a familiar wall of muscle. My vision follows the profile of his features until they meet his seductive caramel gaze. "It's my front I seem to have trouble with," I grumble.

Liam crosses his arms and glowers. "You kissed him."

"Yes." I pull the door shut behind me, hoping that Aaron didn't see, yet knowing there's no way he could have missed it. I really need a shower. I start in a fast and stubborn clip toward my room.

Liam matches my stride. "You told him you choose me."

I keep walking. "Yep." Not that Liam was meant to be listening.

He stops abruptly. "Were you ever going to tell *me* that you chose me?"

I take a few more paces before I also halt and spin to face him. My vision is slightly visored by my furrowed brow. "Eventually."

His lips tilt into a wry grin. "Do I get a choice in the matter?"

He's teasing me. I fold my arms across my chest. "Do you want one?"

His elflike grin, the one he always reserved for me, is back. "It's generally the custom, when deciding on a mate, that you inform all parties involved. Or so I've heard."

I rake my gaze across him, shamelessly checking him out. His feet are apart, the tight leather of his trousers pulled taught across his thighs. The defined muscles of his abdomen, evident beneath the black leather of his vest, form deep grooves in the surface of his skin. His dark brown wings, their feathers warm and inviting, are held away from his body ever so slightly. I can hear his pulse racing, his heart pumping like it's taken a hit of ecstasy, although you'd never think it to look at him.

True to form mine speeds up too, which sends a flush to my cheeks.

"Well," I purse my lips in mock contemplation, "consider yourself informed. Now, I'm going to my room, to have a shower, alone. I'm still majorly pissed at you." I turn again and continue toward the female wing.

He follows me. "We need to talk, Aqua."

Talk? I spin again, stopping him dead in his tracks. Talk? Whenever we try and talk we argue, and right now I've had enough of arguing with him. Wounds don't heal overnight, unless you've got access to some pretty talented angeli Medics, and even then there are scars to contend with. Scars are something we all have, whether they're on the surface or buried deep within. Scar tissue is rigid, inflexible, even painful, but to shun something because it bears the scars of the past can only be detrimental to the future.

My eyes lock with his again. His gaze is a mix of longing and bewilderment. He's the dominant, the Alpha, yet I can see through him, through that tough outer exterior to the lost boy within. I'm not the only one who understands that the layer he keeps on show is nothing more than a shroud, a pretence.

Lucas sees it, August sees it and I'm pretty damn sure Victus sees it too. "Victus told you, didn't he."

The lost boy, the one wrapped up so tightly in the centre of the parcel, stares back at me through burning caramel. Silently, the shutters come down. Liam nods and the young boy is gone, replaced by the sculpture, the mask of who he's grown to be.

"My father is alive," he states. It's a simple sentence, hiding so many repercussions of the fact.

"Then we really should talk," I agree in a breathless whisper.

"Later." He mirrors my breathless tone, in a direct contradiction of his reasoning for chasing me along the corridor. "I am annoyed," he murmurs, "that the human was the first to kiss you."

I tease my bottom lip with my teeth, hiding a grin. "First since I returned or the first ever?"

"Both," Liam almost growls.

I silence him with my lips, pressing my mouth to his with unnecessary force. And I swear to God, somewhere a trumpet sounds. I can feel desire, pouring through the pores in my skin, igniting my synapses, carving a direct path to my heart and somewhere a little lower. Not imagined, not fabricated, simply intensified by my dragone abilities, and Liam's, I realise. Whether he likes it or not, he is the son of Rennison Jarik. His DNA is a quarter dragone, and I can feel his emotions as clearly as I can feel my own. Perhaps I always could, I just never understood before.

Human, angeli, dragone – it's not race, creed, colour or species that dictates our nature. There is light and dark in all of us. With knowledge of *what* I am has come the gradual understanding of *who* I am. The human veil that cloaked me for so long, stunted me in ways I never realised, has already blown seven sheets to the wind. The naivety of ignorance and youth has been dispelled by my life experience. I am not afraid of the dark. I live within it. I plough a line through it, every day of my life; I am not a product of it.

I pull back, extinguishing the kiss and extinguishing the link our skin contact provided. Lucas was right about one thing when he described the angeli histories. *These are all relics from our past. We use them to guide our future, that we may learn from our mistakes.* Liam and I made mistakes. We fell hard and fast, like a runaway mine train our relationship took off at the speed of light, exploding in a ball of fiery destruction when the ground disappeared from under me. Intensified, it seems, by each of us. I'm not making that mistake again. Plus, I've just kissed the two men I love, in quick succession, without brushing away my morning breath.

"You are nothing like your father," I reassure him, aware of the fear he's harbouring. His eyebrows arch and I smirk, leaving it hanging. "I'm going for a shower." I turn and amble away, heading for my room.

His voice follows me, his feet don't. "How do you know?"

I keep walking, turning only my head to address him over my shoulder. "We carve our own paths, Liam. You are the product of your own choices, your own destiny. Don't fear the place you came from." I pivot my head back, staring forward as I open my wings to their full span. Their feathered tips brush along the parallel walls, wafting the swirling smoke so that it dances in tendrils around me. "I will never fear it again," I state, "because it makes me who I am."

"What happened to you? To the girl who left me?" His voice holds the sound of a smile, a note of adoration.

I tuck my wings back in, rolling my shoulders but maintaining my pace. "She came back, older and wiser." My voice is low but not below angeli hearing range.

Liam's answering edict echoes the last words Aaron said to me.

"Happy Birthday, Aqua."

# · Thirteen ·

Yes, eighteen today, according to Aaron, Liam, and, judging by the noise coming from my room, my mother. I can hear her voice, and August's, as I approach. So, apparently it's not acceptable to be late for your own surprise birthday wake-up call, or more accurately, it's not acceptable for your mother and brother to find your bed still made and obviously not slept in on the morning of your eighteenth birthday. I grin at the rare normality, the glimpse of teenage angst and rebellion that doesn't involve an entire city. I'm still grinning when I saunter into my room.

"Aquila!" my mother exclaims, glaring at me above the waxy remnants of eighteen small candles, their flames barely hanging onto life. I inhale, savouring the smell.

"You baked!"

"Of course I baked," she snaps. "How often will my baby girl turn eighteen?" Her voice softens, slightly.

"I helped. It's called a carrot cake!" August adds. It's then that I realise he's already had a slice, my mother is shameless in her indulgence of him. "Happy Birthday, little sister."

He has a soppy smile adhered to his face. I'm the worst little sister ever. "I'm sorry we weren't here for your birthday, August."

"Don't worry," he dismisses my blatant act of insensitivity as I realise that his birthday was a week ago. It only takes two steps to cross the room and hug him.

I add, "You know, we celebrated your birthday a week before mine every year, by sending a balloon up to the angels with a note attached." Our mother folds us into a hug, silent tears in her eyes and a carrot cake balanced precariously in one hand.

"We didn't celebrate. We can have a joint celebration today, with more cake." He looks at our mother adoringly. "Anyway, you brought me the best gift ever."

"Suck-up," I mock. "Have you never had cake before? Where did you get the stuff for this anyway?" I take the plate from our mother's hand and cut myself a slice, and another slice for August who's leaning over my shoulder salivating.

"In the kitchens," he says. "We just put things in a bowl, cooked it, and this came out." He stuffs the slice, the whole slice, into his mouth like a hamster. Yes, my mother does make baking look that easy.

"Well, I need a shower." I dust the crumbs from my top and head to the bathroom. I kiss my mother's cheek as I pass. "Thanks, Mum."

"Where were you?" Her voice is deceptively light.

I pretend not to hear. The shower water blocks out the second edition of her lecture, although I can hear the tone of it. She's still rambling when I walk back in, wrapped in a towel. I shake my wings to dry them, sending a spray of water around the room. August complains with a mouthful of his fourth slice of cake. He complains even more when I extinguish the candles they've lit, so that I can dress within the modesty of total darkness.

"You want to take the cake to breakfast?" I ask him. "We could share it with the table." Not that there'll be much left if August gets anymore alone time with said confection. The look on his face says sharing is the last thing he wants to do with it.

"Yes." Our mother re-joins our conversation, abandoning her attempts to question the status of my virtue. "Aaron will want a slice, and Oberon," she suggests.

I open the door, bathing the entrance of my room in the orange glow from the hallway, an orange glow with the elongated shadow of the Guard Master. "And Liam," I add, amused. August grumbles his protest, shielding the cake like he's auditioning for the role of *Gollum*.

"My precious," I tease as I pry the plate from his grasp. It's a reference completely lost on everyone within earshot. Aaron loves *The Lord of the Rings*. He and I had a marathon all-nighter when he first bought the box set of DVD's. My mother didn't question my chastity then. I guess all these wings have got her feathers ruffled.

"You're so strange," August comments as we head to breakfast. Liam gravitates to my side, matching my stride. I hand him a slice, smirking. If I give the plate back to August, no cake will make it to the dining hall.

The enormous room is more noisy than the angeli are used to, what with the ruckus of the hundred new residents of the city. Heightened angeli hearing usually results in a more harmonious volume of conversation. As t is, the noise now is similar to a riot. I head straight to our usual table which sits, island-like, surrounded by the black sea. My pirates have commandeered the closest seats, and surrounding them the Guard sit furtively attempting to prevent their classified conversation reaching civilian angeli ears. It's rather comical.

I place the remnants of the cake in front of Aaron, an act swamped in tension, and then turn my attention to my men. "Old Salt."

Reuben acknowledges my tone and the course of conversation changes fluidly to waters less turbulent. Not quickly enough, it seems, for my mother to not have comprehended the ramifications of their previous topic.

"Aquila, you are not going back to that island." The assertion is that of a mother, the command is that of a civilian. Cain sneers at me from my peripheral, as do a few of the Guard. I wonder idly if *Napoleon* had this problem.

"Okay, Mum. We'll talk about it tomorrow." I drop into the seat beside Axion and he nudges me playfully, hiding a sly smile. As long as I'm back in one piece by the morning, she'll never know. "How's Brue?"

Axion gestures with a nod toward the buffet, rolling his eyes at our youngest brother. He's there. He hasn't bothered with a plate. He's simply walking around the counter eating as he goes.

"Should he be out of bed?" I ask, smiling despite my misgivings.

"He said he's training with us today. Apparently you insisted on it, for his protection." Axion grins at me, not believing Brue's account for a second.

"Remarkable." I shake my head benevolently. Brue looks over at that second, like I called him personally.

Perhaps I did? Whatever part of the link that allows them to feel and locate each other at distance, doesn't seem very prevalent in me. He grabs another sausage and heads over, unashamed. "Hope you didn't overeat. We're doing cardio this morning, and blade work later, after some weights that is. I was thinking low weight high reps? Or maybe power lifts? Yeah, Ax?"

"Yeah," he agrees.

"Don't be facetious," Brue pouts.

"Don't swallow dictionaries," I counter.

"Can I train with you or not? Because otherwise I'm going back to bed." He folds his arms and glares at me.

"Not. You just had major surgery and no matter how fast your recovery, there's no way in hell you're completely healed. But you're staying where I can see you, you can watch."

"Then I'll watch, too." I spin my head to lock eyes with my mother who's glaring at me, daring me to challenge her.

"Fine," I shrug. "We'll set up a spectator bench."

Liam laughs from my shoulder, making me flinch. Jerk. His fingers purposefully brush my hair as he leans across the table to grab the last slice of cake, before leading the surrounding Guard in the direction of the barracks.

"Yuck," Brue grumbles, watching him leave.

"I'll teach you how to block it off," Axion whispers, although he's staring at the table so I can only assume he's talking to me.

"Let's go," I command, before anyone puts too much thought into the disjointed exchange.

Aaron rises to his feet, glaring first at Liam's disappearing figure and then at me. "I assume that's an open invitation." A muscle in his jaw ticks at me, like an ominous countdown.

"Of course it is," my mother answers, looping her arm through his in the process and then doing the same to August. I can almost envisage them skipping off to Oz to see the Wizard, except Aaron has never been the skipping type.

Brue smirks at the younglings in yellow as we pass. I quirk my eyebrow at him. "You're a smart kid, Brue, so tell me, when has gloating ever been a good idea?"

He shrugs, but doesn't rearrange his features as we ascend the spiral staircase to the barracks. Dorothy, the Tin Man and the Scarecrow prancing along beside us.

The gymnasium is unusually bright when we enter, and there's the scrape of stone on stone as the Guard drag an obviously heavy item across the floor. Liam is already assigning training exercises, issuing orders, and staring in my direction. My eyes flick around the room, to the domed mirrors currently diffracting the candle's glow, so that they light the ether like halogens.

The Guard push the heavy object against the wall and rub their calloused hands together. I frown. "Where'd you find a bench on short notice?"

They both turn to smirk at me, obviously amused, as my mother sits down eagerly. She's still giving me her confrontational glare. August sits next to her, experiencing a bout of amnesia as to the fact that he should be working. Aaron lowers himself slowly into the spot next to him, his hands clasping the front edge of the polished stone seat and his gaze vacant, like his mind's elsewhere. Brue is eyeing a climbing rope, which hangs from a bracket on the ceiling, like he may actually attempt to scale it. I'm about to threaten homicide if he takes one step toward it when Liam appears at his side holding a basket of blunted blades, two small whetstones and a bottle of oil.

"Make yourself useful, Brue," Liam states, almost kindly. "August will teach you." He leads the young prince back toward the bench and deposits the basket next to August, with his eyebrow raised. Brue's eyes light up as he stares into the basket greedily, before pulling out a dagger with a clip point end. The blood drains from my mother's face. My mouth pulls across my face in concern.

"He'll be fine," Axion says, watching as Liam marches off to yell at someone. "That should keep him amused for days."

I guess he means Brue. "It's not him I'm worried about. Now might be a good time to practice in the dark," I suggest, thinking aloud. "My mother is heading toward some kind of aneurism, or a haematoma."

"You mean a stroke?"

"Yeah."

"Possibly," he agrees. "Do you want Plank to give her another dose?"

His back hits the floor hard, a whoosh of air escaping as he's winded. I regain my footing almost instantly after my sweep kick. "No," I answer sharply. The pirates snigger around us, drawing my attention to them. "Old Salt with Art, Me and Ax, Tarcus," I beckon the Guard over, and he reacts instantly. "Partner with Cain," I instruct. "The rest of you form pairs and warm up like last time."

Warming up should involve some kind of structured cardio and stretching to warm the muscles, unless you're a lifelong pirate, then it simply involves a bit of bare-knuckle boxing and a mouthful of profanities. Axion regains his feet quietly as I watch Tarcus flinging himself at Cain like a pitbull.

I almost miss the faint air current as Axion's fist flies toward my back, targeting my kidney. I drop forward, onto my hands like a plank and opening my legs in a scissor kick as I log roll onto my back. He jumps my attempt to take him down, but my sideways impetus puts me back onto my front. I plant my hands and pull myself into a cartwheel to regain my stance quickly.

"Sneaky," I quip as Axion follows me with a sloppy flying kick. It contains a lot of power, but it's uncontrolled. I steal his energy, turning it against him as I catch his leg and flip him with his own momentum. He lands behind me with a dull thud and a curse on his breath. The speed he comes at me again is worthy of some respect. The speed in which I lay him flat on his back for a third time is not. I smirk at him.

"Funny," Axion wheezes as he jumps up again.

He plants his feet, abandoning his attempts at poorly directed kicks, and raises his fists. He takes the first swing, aiming high. I block it with my forearm and return a jab of my own. He blocks it easily, shuffling his feet like *Ali* and moving like a blur. Dragone are naturally fast, and so am I. His fist appears from the left, glancing off my shoulder as I shift. Taking the hit is a small concession to make, considering he didn't notice my right arm extending into position, ready to grasp the follow-through jab he throws with his left. My fingers wrap around his tight flesh, anchoring my grip just below his elbow. His weaker arm is caged in my strongest. It's a defensive advantage, one Liam taught me during our hours of training. His answering blows will be harder than mine but he won't be able to escape my clutch.

I don't waste a portion of my consciousness wondering if Liam's watching now, if he's assessing the effectiveness of his lessons. I jab hard with my left, a quick succession of powerful hits that focus Axion's attention on deflecting and retaliating with his right arm. And while he's aiming his clenched right hand toward my face my leg wraps through his. I could just knee him in the groin with enough force to make him female, but I need him on my team tonight. So instead I twist my hip, winding my calf around the back of his knee, so that when I push, forcing my entire weight forward, he trips backward and his fist flies wide and wild. The force carries us both down. I secure his other arm on the way and we land together, him pinned immobile beneath me.

The smirk returns to my lips as I feel his disappointment through his skin. "Thought I had you, Princess."

"Maybe next time, Ax." I jump up, dusting specks of nothing from the leather of my halter top. "You're too predictable, and your moves are sloppy and unstructured."

"Well, let's hope we can avoid hand to hand combat at the island then," he grumbles as he shakes out his dragon-like wings. They took a few hard knocks when he landed, though they look undamaged as he stretches them to full span before tucking them back in. A simple ruffle of my feathers loosens the muscles of my back sufficiently, the advantage of inbuilt padding can't be denied.

"So," I state as we assess the sparring pirates. "Who's taking the twins to the Medics this time?"

Axion laughs as we watch Nev and George pound each other like *Rock 'Em Sock 'Em Robots*. They each go for brute force, neither one willing to concede to the other, until one of their heads inevitably pops up with a small explosion of blood and spittle.

Axion holds his hands up in defence. "It's not my turn."

The high-pitched squeal of airborne metal pulls an instant reaction from me. As easy as taking my next breath, I pluck my axes from the air above my head. Axion's laughter falls flat as he notices I'm suddenly armed and my weapons are raised like flags atop parallel posts.

"What the..." his mouth pops open as Liam saunters up behind me, fully armoured by the smell of him, lots of metallic steel and the added sweat of excitement. Axes are my party trick, something we worked on rigorously after my display in the youngling trials. I split the wooden shaft of an arrow in half, with my eyes closed, quite by fluke while Lielan was hiding behind a wooden rack like a coward. Although, if I'd have thought of it first, I'd say she was utilising the environment to gain an intelligent and tactical advantage, but I didn't.

"Suit up, Guardian," Liam breathes huskily against the curve of my neck. "Two weeks on an island and you have dropped your fitness." He tugs on the rise of my right wing, until I relax and stretch it out beside me. The familiar leather strap of my back harness slides over my shoulder, and a hand tugs my left wing until I stretch that one out too.

Another leather strap winds its way over my other shoulder, dropping like a snake over my chest. Axion's eyes widen in front of me, and I realise with a blush that he's getting a huge dose of whatever emotion Liam is eliciting from me right now. Even I can't put a name to it. I just know it's definitely not something I should be sending to Axion, or Brue. Christ. I drop my arms, which are still in the air like two demented goalposts, and grab the straps hanging from my chest before Liam does. Holding the axes in my palms, I use my fingertips to cross the straps between my breasts and then hold them out behind me so that he can secure the buckles under my wings. I hear his soft chuckle.

"I'm not unfit," I mumble as he takes the axes from my grasp, the axes that he just threw at me with no warning, and secures them in their holsters under my feathers. I love the design, hiding them completely from view but still within easy reach. Axion mumbles something incoherent.

Plyrian walks over, his arms piled with steel. "Here." He hands me my armour with a sly grin on his face, assessing Liam's performance with a hint of approval. "You seem to have settled some of your differences," he says in a whisper.

My eyes roll automatically. I hand the armour right back, taking one piece at a time from his arms and securing it slowly, methodically, partly to annoy Liam, who is getting increasingly impatient now that he isn't buckling me in, and partly because I haven't put this stuff on for weeks and I don't want to make a fool of myself by doing it wrong.

"Get the shields," I state when I'm finished. My chest is protected by a moulded Y plate, my arms and legs are covered by various segments of steel armour, secured with straps, the same black leather as my uniform. Weapon sheaths reside at various points around my body, some visible and some not. I walk over to a weapons rack while the ring of Guard form, and peruse the selection of blades on offer. My own dagger is already at my thigh. I take my time choosing blades to slot in other locations, checking their weight and balance before selecting or returning them.

When I turn around Liam is pacing in the centre of the ring like a circus lion, long caged. The Guard have the huge wooden shields secured in their hands, creating an impenetrable wall of wood to protect innocent bystanders. My mother, one of those innocent bystanders, is standing on the bench and craning her neck to see what's going on. As are August and Aaron. I give them a quick grimace, hoping they'll manage my mother, before striding into the ring and feeling the walls close behind me.

"Were you deliberately slow, to test me. Or are you scared, Aquila?" Liam cracks his knuckles as he readies himself, eager for the bout.

I have milliseconds to decide which show I am going to put on. The show where we're two siblings who can't stand one another, the show where I'm petrified of the big bad Master of the Guard, or the show of confidence I displayed when I managed to maybe beat him. He'll be out to rectify that, I'm sure. I go for scared, letting my knees quake with silent tremors, too small to be faked, yet not entirely real. Real fear leaves me statuesque, frozen.

This fear, this rush of adrenalin, is under my control. It comes from the years of pent up anxiety, of the dread that a human would discover my feathers. It's no longer applicable, no longer perceivable as a problem, yet I can still use the memory of it to my advantage. I swallow, the noise exaggerated slightly to imply my throat has dried. And then my throwing knife is striking the wood directly behind him. Its blade would have sliced his jugular, if I hadn't aimed slightly off.

"One kill, Guardian," Plyrian bellows. The rest of the Guard remain silent, waiting in shocked silence.

Liam cocks his head at me, amused and angry and possibly slightly baffled. His hand traces the line my knife would have made in his throat. Eventually his lips curl upward, his eyes darkening with the challenge.

"Best of Three," he commands, and then he lunges at me.

I fake right, and then follow through with it, except it's a trick I've used before and he spots it.

"One Kill, Guard Master," Plyrian bellows before I know what happened. "Next kill will name the victor."

There's not a mark on me, of course, but there's a blade against my throat. "Not good enough," Liam growls against my cheek. "One kill and you let your guard down. It's no good to slay one foe only to be slaughtered by the next." He steps back, re-sheathing his blade. "That trick may save you from the first," he adds. "But the rest will not be fooled. And now you are a weapon down." His eyes flash with mirth. He loves the tactics of a fight, the thrill of mortality, the knowledge of his prowess.

"Two kills," I breathe below a whisper. Whether he likes it or not, I have two kills against him now. His mouth quirks slightly, the only acknowledgment he heard me. I pull the axes from my back, swirling the handles like a majorette. He makes the first move, putting a fair portion of his power into a two-handed downward swing with a sword. I catch the blade above my head, in the centre of my crossed weapons. I crouch and spin, retreating a few paces before he can slide his blade back and chase it with a swift jab toward my ribs.

During the fraction of a second that he's in his lunge position, I leap to his left, diving over his blade and attempting a strike on his achilles. I miss. He spins on his knee, reacting instantaneously and I barely have time to execute a belly flop onto the hard rock floor. His sword whistles over my neck, close enough to give me an impromptu haircut. Had my tight ringlets been pulled into a ponytail he'd have lopped the whole thing off right then. Thank God I French plaited it this morning.

I rock up onto my hands, in a poor interpretation of dancing the Worm, and tuck my chin into my chest. My wings cushion the impact of the forward roll as I tip over the zenith of my almost-handstand. I cross the axes again, blocking the next strike of Liam's blade as I finally regain my feet using the momentum of the roll. I stick the sole of my foot into his gut while it's unprotected, but his left hand comes from nowhere, wrapping around my calf and lifting it so high that my other foot leaves the floor. I'm suspended in the air, like a slow-motion video image, until gravity remembers it's got a significant role to play and drags me back toward the earth's core like a magnet. I land hard, winded, my leg still firmly encased in Liam's grasp. Too late, I realise that his last swing of the blade was one-handed. I may be able to survive the slice of his dagger, currently pressed against the back of my ankle, if this was a real death match. I may still have a chance at this point, against a real attacker. But for the purposes of training, I'm dead. Damn.

"Victory to the Guard Master," Plyrian announces, and the atmosphere fills with the pressure of the mass exhalation. I thump the heel of my hand, my axe still held in my palm, against the stone as I pull myself to sitting. Liam laughs at my look of disgruntlement as he finally releases my leg, and then offers me his hand to help me up. I take it out of respect and tradition, leaving my axe on the floor like a flaccid symbol of defeat.

"Don't look so disappointed, Aquila." Liam fills my head with his pheromone laden scent as he helps me to my feet. "You gained the first point."

He stoops down to retrieve my axe, offering it to me with a small smile tugging his lips. I take it with more dignity than I feel in the moment. "Teach them to shoot," he orders, his voice taking on the hard edge I'm used to. And then he turns away, beckoning the Guard and their huge wooden shields to follow. I watch them follow obediently. Paint clubs on them and they'd look like a line of *The Queen of Hearts'* playing cards.

"Now you're swapping to guns?" Aaron mocks. His voice comes from behind me, far enough away that he feels the need to raise his volume, despite knowing damn well I could hear him from the corridor outside. I heave a sigh as my mother, her footsteps moving at the same pace at his, starts shrieking nonsensically.

I turn in time to watch their final approach. August looks sheepish as he follows behind. Brue is still by the bench, blissfully happy, submerged elbow deep in the basket of blades.

The surrounding angeli, even the dragone, turn to stare at Aaron like he just suggested the Queen of England will now be using paper plates instead of *Royal Doulton*.

"Humans," a Guard spits out in disgust.

My eyes shift from Aaron to my mother. "For God's sake, Mum. Stop screeching."

"Aquila Raven Vickers!" Her tone is indignant. Nothing centres my mother like a touch of blasphemy.

"You promised me you would stop fighting. You could have killed your brother with that knife and now you're going to be shooting guns at each other. It's ridiculous."

"The angeli don't use guns, Mum. He's not my brother and he was talking about arrows..."

"Because that worked out so well for you last time," Aaron murmurs, his tone petulant. "Why wouldn't you take a gun with you? Sure as hell the dragone might and you'd be stuck with a knife at a gun fight. This isn't the *Charge of the Light Brigade*, Aqua. You don't have to just go running whenever Liam decrees it."

"Technically, I do."

"Because you're screwing him?" he states, disgusted.

I gasp. How incredibly crass. And untrue. "Because he's my commanding officer," I seethe.

I'm glad that human idiom is mostly lost on the angeli, who are still listening intently to our small group, the dragone aren't quite so ignorant. The twin's eyes bug out of their heads at Aaron's proclamation.

My mother gasps, followed by a gag and a drawn-out cough. "Aquila..." My name stumbles from her tongue like a curse. Aaron has the gall to look contrite as her face pales. She spears me with a look of pure horror. "What is he talking about?"

Cain sniggers in my peripheral. I can feel the red veil descending.

"Is that where you were last night?" she gasps, her eyes widening.

"Actually I slept in August's room last night."

August blanches, trying to shush me over our mother's shoulder. I ignore him.

"And Aaron knows damn well I'm not, so he had no right to say it." I shake my head at my best friend, angry and baffled at why he would say something like that when he knows it isn't true. The angeli don't have sex before marriage.

"They're together," Aaron retorts. The bitterness is evident in his voice. It's made easier to hear by the fact that the entire gymnasium has fallen deathly silent. It stays that way for a very long time.

Well this is awkward.

My mother purses her lips as she processes the situation. I sigh, resigned to whatever fallout occurs from this. "If you slept in August's room last night," she stares at me, "why didn't he know where you were this morning?"

Oh. Now August's expression makes sense. I shoot a look at my little brother. "August wouldn't know if a herd of tap-dancing elephants were in his room at night. He sleeps like the dead and snores worse than that old *Massey*. Hell, that thing sounds like an angry bear whenever I start it up."

My distraction works. The mention of her father's old tractor has my mother in instant melancholy, her eyes watery, and I feel like the world's worst daughter for causing it. August owes me big time.

The silence fogs us again, thick and heavy it hangs in the air, waiting. I sense Liam beside me. The silent steps that brought him here were evidently watched by our audience. Most eyes are on him when I glance around. Confusion. Anticipation. Disdain. They are all expressions I can read, though the thoughts behind them are a mystery.

Our relationship was never public. To Celthia, we are brother and sister. To the majority of the Guard, we are the thorn in each other's sides. Everyone seems to lean a little closer as Liam crosses his arms and turns to stone, glaring icily at Aaron. To Aaron's testament, he doesn't flinch.

"Don't halt your conversation on my account," Liam announces, his voice eerily serene. "I'm sure we're all eager to hear your definition of *together*."

I gulp, watching Aaron's reactions.

It takes me a while to realise the attention isn't on him, but on me. My head whips around to Liam in surprise. "Me?"

His answering smile doesn't reach his eyes. If anything, I'd say the overriding emotion in residence there is insecurity. Is that possible? Or have I completely misread him? Perhaps I should try feeling him...

"Yes, Aquila. As you so eloquently put it, *Aaron had no right to say it*. I want to hear what *you* have to say." His mouth pinches tight and I gape.

I can't think of anything to say. I'm not even sure I'd be capable of forming sounds. I manage to croak out one word. "Why?"

"Why not?" he counters, his voice still cool.

I swallow. "You want me to define *together*, now?"

He smirks as he glances around before settling his eyes back on me. "Well, you could do it later, but I can't guarantee we'll have such a rapt audience."

"Sarcasm? Really. Can't you recall what happened the last time you spoke to me like this?" I can. I'd thrown my weapons at his feet and stormed away, until he'd come grovelling at my feet, literally. My mouth ticks up at the memory.

"I remember," he answers, his voice more hoarse than before. His gaze is lingering intently on my lips. A fact no one but the blind could miss, and I'm sure the visually impaired could still pick up on the chemistry he's emitting.

"What happened before?" August seems to have recovered. He gawks wide-eyed at us, as enthralled with our display as the rest of our audience.

"He worshipped at my feet," I answer.

My words float from my mouth, buoyant and carefree. Something's changed. In this moment, I can feel it. Liam wants everyone to know. Surely it can't just be because I'm now eighteen and therefore eligible to find a mate. Although, if this is his way of staking a claim on me then he's going to pay for it.

"Why now?" My voice stays soft, merely inquisitive.

"Because yesterday I was sure I'd lost everything I'd never known I'd wanted. I'd *needed*."

He takes a step toward me, his hard exterior crumbling before me like old mortar. His speech is hesitant, his expression guarded. Yet his words flow from his heart, in front of the stunned onlookers.

"Love is a risk I never envisioned in my future. Love makes you vulnerable and exposed. At least that's what I always thought, until I met you." He raises his hand to wrap my curls around his fingers, playing with my hair so tenderly that my breath stalls. "When you've loved another person, so fiercely that they've claimed a piece of your soul, losing them is like having your heart ripped out in shreds. Getting it back, feeling it heal, is a chance that not everyone gets. I refuse to squander it. Every measure I have with you is precious." He tugs gently on my hair, his eyes full of anxiety. "Define together," he repeats quietly.

A languid smile spreads across my face. My breath comes rolling back to me in gentle undulations. Screw secrecy, and opinion, and Rennison Jarik, and the Fallen. Screw the arrow and the mistakes of the past. Liam's right. Finding love with someone once is a blessing, but finding it again, after it's been lost, is a miracle.

"I think you just did," I answer.

# · Fourteen ·

"I think they've forgotten we're here."

August's assumption is the first noise to fill the void Liam's declaration created. The angeli seem to have solidified, suspended in time. Confusion and tension surrounds us all, like an unanswered question, they're waiting for the punch line. My mother has gone mute.

Liam's mouth curls into a relieved smile.

I don't want to break the spell but this really is beginning to feel awkward. Not to mention, we only have a day of training before we fly for the island. I chew my lip, to prevent myself from kissing him, and glance around his shoulder. Ever felt like you're a living shop-window display? I have.

"I think we should get back to work."

He grins at me. "Who's preventing you?"

"I don't know. He kind of looks like the authoritarian, slightly bigoted angeli Guard Master I remember. Except now he's gone all soft and started making proclamations of love and devotion in front of his horror-struck troops."

"Only in front of a fraction of them, and of that, they can't all be horror-struck. Most are merely stunned.

Perhaps you should be more concerned about your mother. She seems to believe I am your brother." His eyes gesture toward the pale swaying form of the woman who raised me, his brows arching in amusement.

"She knows we're not related." I watch her gasp for air, like she's trying to eat the atmosphere. "Perhaps I should remind her."

"August," Liam yells.

Our brother looks over briefly in-between his attempts to stop our mother hyperventilating. He appears slightly harassed. I grimace an apology.

"Take her to your work room," Liam suggests. "Answer her questions." He turns back to me. "You're right. We have a lot of work to do. Gather the team you've enlisted for tonight, we'll train together. The rest of your men can join with the Guard drills today. I'll rally my horror-struck troops."

He smirks as he morphs into Leader mode. I nod my agreement. If this recon mission is going to have any chance of success, it'll require us to work as a team.

I glance at the spectator bench, aware that Aaron has regained his seat there. He's staring at Liam with a look of contempt, his hands steepled under his chin. Brue is still sharpening blades like he's on commission.

"Ax, Old Salt, Art, Tarcus, and Cain," I command. You're with me. The rest of you will be training with Plyrian." The Second appears at the sound of his name, his face stoic. "They are in your charge."

I confer command to him, grateful that not a single one objected, and beckon my small team to the side. Cain looks wary but doesn't complain as I hand them all a bow from the rack.

"We're flying to Hantiem, tonight. We will need to be able to defend and attack from the air." I glance around. "The winged beings will be doing the heavy lifting, so non-wings will be their gunners." I smirk at the term. "Arrows are most effective. They're light, accurate and have a decent range. They'll be our best bet."

"Aye, las," Reuben agrees. "But what happens when we're all on th' ground?"

"Then your guttin' knife will see some action, Old Salt." I hand out a quiver of arrows each and lead them to the target range Liam has set up. He's already waiting with two of his men. His initial choices of Lucas and Plyrian didn't count. He's chosen their replacements well. I know Rhyan and Kav. They are both highly trained, ranked uppermost among his elite forces. They have rarely acknowledged me before, but now they stand to attention when I approach, and bow their heads in respect. Liam smirks before ordering them to demonstrate. I frown and he gives me a *get used to it* look.

"Guardian!"

I turn as Lielan's high pitch osculates across the room, followed, it seems, by a swaying heap of black suspended upon a Nester-blue skirt. I step away from the range and toward the talking fabric. "Lielan?"

"Mother, Aquila, are you going to stand there gawping or help me with this?" I'm pretty certain she can't see me, let alone that I'm gawping, over the huge pile of... something... that she has in her arms.

"What is it?"

"A peace offering." She hands me a pile of fabric, with a little grunt of displeasure that sounds like a contradiction.

There are so many questions that I can't decide on one. I let the silence hang there until she regains her breath. Admittedly, this peace offering would qualify for the WWE heavyweight category.

She eventually elaborates, slightly. "It's a gift from the Nesters of Celthia, for your... people."

My frown deepens.

"Your dragone sailor people, so they don't freeze up here. Mother, Aqua, just act like you are grateful and I will tell Gloria you appreciated the hours they have spent slaving over needle and thread to please you." She rambles without a breath, her frown matching mine.

"Again, what is it?" I can't move my arms. They're laden with the gift that Lielan so unceremoniously dumped into them. It sounds more like the product of a sweatshop than the delicately crafted items associated with the angeli Nesters.

"Cloaks." She lifts a sheet from the top and opens it like a matador. "Modified, of course, to insulate the cold-bloods when they leave."

And in that one sentence lays the truth of it, of common opinion, they want the *cold-bloods* to leave. Regardless of the reason, the Nesters have worked wonders with the silver foil, insulating the dragone's hooded cloak so that it shimmers as it drapes elegantly from Lielan's grip.

"How?" I can't see the benefit of foil unless they're wrapped in it.

"New fasteners. I am sure you will figure it out. Here," she throws the cloak back on top, "they will still require the thermaide vials. You will find them in the pouches supplied by the Medics." She points vaguely at the pile, indicating, I assume, that the pouches are somewhere within my arms. After a beat of silence, and no new information offered, she turns to leave.

Then she stops herself, almost reluctantly. "I meant it, you know. It is a peace offering, from me to you. I never pretended to like you..."

I can hear her thought process. She never pretended to like me and now I'm the commander of my own little army, not to mention the probably rapidly spreading gossip that names me as the Guard Master's affianced mate. It was okay to openly dislike me when it felt like I was a nobody, now she thinks I'm a somebody. I laugh at the absurdity of narrow-mindedness. We're all a somebody.

"I never expected you to."

I don't need her to like me. I just need her not to stab me in the back whenever I turn, surely that's all any of us really need.

"Thank you, for this." I raise my arms and flash a quick smile before turning back to the range. She doesn't attempt to stab me.

Axion is the first to inspect the pile, which I drop on the floor at my feet as soon as Lielan leaves. He throws a cloak to Reuben and Cain, smirking. "Look," he grins, "sleeves." I give him my best disappointed head shake as he ridicules the frankly impressive modifications.

"Put it on," I state. I'm intrigued.

I want to see how they work, if they'll work. Axion flexes his chest and narrows his eyes in my direction. Cain throws his cloak back at him, with the same smirk Axion wore a few seconds ago, so I pick up another and hurl it toward tonight's cannon fodder. "You too."

Liam nudges my arm as he moves closer, reminding me he's still there. "Feels good, doesn't it."

"What?"

"The power to command an army." His voice drops to a seductive whisper, "To control a man, to have your bidding done with just one order from your lips, to cater to your every whim."

I watch Axion and Cain as they envelop themselves within the ebony cloaks. Their arms fit snugly into the tight sleeves, leather gloves protect their hands, their hoods drape down low, masking their features, fasteners pull the material around their legs like jumpsuits, keeping them warm until they decide to release the catch so that the cape can billow free. The dragone look impressed, and Reuben and Art shimmy into theirs without a command from me.

"Don't be weird, Liam." I turn to face him. "There's a difference between leading and dictating."

I step away to pick up a bow, taking my turn at the firing range. Arrows are not my speciality. Perhaps I should have omitted my turn in favour of maintaining my dignity and illusion of warrior-ness. I miss the target completely with the first arrow. I take aim again, ignoring the eyes on me.

Liam's right, I suppose, in a small way. It does feel good when someone listens and acts on my instructions. But my whims? I release the arrow, hitting the target slightly off centre, and then reload. Have I asked anyone to do anything on a whim? Or issued an order that couldn't be contested by the recipient? Are Axion, or Reuben, Art or Cain the type of men who wouldn't challenge me if they thought I was out of line? Hell, sometimes I feel like they're just humouring me anyway. I release the next arrow, finally hitting the centre of the target. I string the next one, pulling it back to my ear, my gaze running along the wooden shaft. When did taking charge of a situation become such a moral minefield? Is it wrong to use the power you're handed? How do you tell if you're using or abusing it?

Axion joins me at the line, loading his own bow. I release my arrow as I exhale my breath, hitting just left of my last one.

"Don't over think it, Princess." Axion aims at his own target, hitting the centre with his first shot. "Liam wasn't questioning your leadership technique."

I load and release my next arrow in quick succession, quirking an eyebrow at him in favour of seeing where my shot lands.

"Really, Aqua. Have more faith in yourself. Liam's a guy, I'm a guy, trust me, he wasn't questioning your morality."

"Oh?" I watch as Axion hits another bulls-eye. Two for two. He's good with a bow. "Then what was he questioning? And you can be chief gunner tonight." I re-rack my bow and discard my empty sheath. "I suck at archery."

"That's why no one questions you. You use your strengths, our strengths, to gain the advantage for the greater good. And if you can't figure out what was on his mind then I'm afraid I can't help you." He releases his next arrow. Three for three.

I watch him fill the centre of the target with his arrows, mulling over our plans for tonight, our conversation, the craftsmanship of the shimmering cloaks.

"But for whose idea of the greater good?" I ask eventually. It's a philosophical, rhetorical question. Ultimately, the answer is: mine. It was for my idea of unity and equality, not that I lay claim to the whole principle of course, that I joined the movement to overturn the Script and eradicate the role of the Overseer. To get rid of the hierarchical system in which I currently reside, somewhat reluctantly, in the region of the summit.

"You know, Aristotle once said that it should be only one who governs. Even in a democracy, the power is distributed unequally. My father may have been flawed, and tainted by his hatred of the Fallen, but he always fought for what he believed in. So do you. It's admirable."

We move aside so Tarcus and Cain can take their turn. "You don't strike me as an Aristotle buff," I jibe. "So are the Fallen admirable, then? They are fighting pretty hard too."

"Ah," he laughs. "Pythagoras had a theory about that. Apparently, it is just as dangerous to give a mad person a sword as a dishonest person the power. I'm guessing R.J. is pretty dishonest."

R.J. Rennison Jarik. "Did you swallow a copy of *Philosophy for Dummies?*"

"Do you think I haven't pondered these questions before?" He glances at me, searching my face for an answer. Quite honestly, no, I hadn't. "I've grown up first in line. Since the moment I took my first breath I had the power to rule. I didn't want to be a warrior, Aqua. I'm not a great fighter, or a great leader, but I can ponder with the best of them. And I figure, if I don't use the power, then someone else will. I don't want to be responsible for unleashing another R.J. on the world."

I watch his face as he speaks. It's a moment of sincerity and openness. "Fair enough." I stretch out my arms, releasing the tension caused by awkwardly wielding a bow. "I don't want to be responsible for that either."

So for now I'll just go with it, and hope that I make it through the other side with my principles intact. "Let's get back to work."

We spend the day working on our strengths. We don't have enough time to do much else. A lot can be achieved in a day, apparently. Well, whoever determined that has obviously never needed to organise antagonists into a single unit within the restricted deadline that is *day*.

Aaron watches us the entire time, adhered to the bench like a waxwork while Brue empties the dulled basket and goes in search of more. August leads our mother to lunch while we're still working. I nod my appreciation, which he returns with an energetic August-like wave. We eat later, from plates brought to us by Nesters, at Liam's request. I've never been more grateful for take-out. I don't see my mother again and I'm glad, I know she'll be safe in the city with my friends around.

Celthia is silent when we leap through the hangar door, and I hope it remains that way until we get back. Aaron walked us to the hangar, staying quiet as we hung back. I don't know why he felt the need, if it was to comfort me or him, but I appreciated his presence. He squeezed my hand and pressed a kiss to my temple before he walked away. I can't help thinking it's what Lucas would have done if he'd been there too. Yet, it felt different coming from Aaron, more profound, like he was really saying goodbye rather than good luck.

I sigh and shake off the memory of his expression. I have other things to concentrate on tonight, like getting to Hantiem without dropping Art into the ocean. Axion's long leathery wings glide silently beside me. Reuben scans the earth from Axion's arms, his hand already clasping his bow. Cain is in Tarcus' arms, doing the same thing though looking more sour about it. Their new cloaks seem to be keeping in their body heat, protecting them from the sub-zero altitude. Gloria has personalised Axion's for him, complete with hidden openings for his wings. It was thoughtful of her. I sent word with Plyrian to tell her as much, because I'm still not sure Lielan would have passed on my gratitude with much enthusiasm. After all, I didn't really muster any for her at the time.

The angeli are at the front, leading, although they have never been to the island before. Axion and I drive from the backseat, turning a fraction before the leaders because they have no idea where we're going.

The island appears on the horizon like a mirage. A dark mass of angular shadows, frayed at the edges as the sea breeze wafts the trees. The waves are rough tonight, pounding the shore like they're attacking the shimmering sand. The paleness of the beach makes for an eerie sight in the moonlight and I tense in response. Axion registers the movement.

"Are you detecting something?" His voice is low but does not waver with uncertainty.

"No. Nothing yet." The *yet* hangs in the breeze like an omen, the fateful last words of the hapless victim in a horror movie.

"Me neither," he confirms. "It looks deserted."

"Appearances can be deceptive, Lad." Reuben doesn't lift his eyes from the terrain. His voice carries his years of wisdom like a medal.

"Stop talking," Liam orders from the front. "Circle the island."

We do just that, dividing instinctively into a patrol formation. The dragone know every inch of the terrain below us. They point out the areas most likely to be hiding any Fallen preparing for an ambush. The angeli's superior senses give us an advantage, but none of us detect anything.

Liam signals in angelian and we all land quietly on the red roof of the building around the main courtyard. Me and Axion exchange glances briefly, both of our thoughts jumping back in time for a second. We follow Liam's silent command to move forward, cresting the ridge of the roof to survey the courtyard below. A sharp whistle of air through teeth is the only sound that accompanies the scene.

I've seen a fair amount of blood in the last few weeks. I've seen the vibrant red of it as it paints the ground, stains the water, marks my steel. I haven't before seen the putrid black sludge of stale blood, that has congealed and solidified around the bodies of dead men. The Fallen have not cleaned up the mess they made. They have not bothered to provide their victims with a sacred final resting place. They have simply left them to rot amongst the potted plants.

"I don't see anything," Tarcus comments as we all stare at the picture below us.

"We can't leave them like that," Axion states.

"If we disturb anything the Fallen will know we've been here." Liam, ever the voice of tactical reason speaks quietly and authoritatively. "I understand, but we must leave them for now. Search the island. Leave everything as you found it. Overlook nothing."

Liam gives me a long and conflicted stare before he turns to start his search. I can understand. I feel the same way. I want him by my side, where I know he's unharmed.

"Princess," says Reuben as Liam disappears over the side of the roof and into the courtyard. He seemed to sense that the location would be too hard for the dragone to search.

"Old Salt, you and Art head to the coast, search the shoreline. Cain, take Tarcus, search the tunnels and along the tracks. Ax and I will head to the throne room."

"Into the valley of death," murmurs Axion as we scale the rooftop toward the main building.

"You think this is a bad idea?"

"Tennison," he answers. "Charge of the Light Brigade kind of bad."

Has he been talking to Aaron? "Good to know."

We jump from the roof when Axion indicates, landing outside the double door that leads to the throne room. We exchange a silent nod before going in, weapons drawn.

The building is silent, signs of the Fallen's ambush are everywhere. In the turned up furniture, in the deep gouges in the mortar of the walls, and in the scent of death that lingers in the air. We make slow and silent progress through the corridor, down the steps to the wooden door with the black symbols. The door is closed, which somehow makes it feel more menacing. Axion draws his bow, ready to release an arrow if the room harbours any hostiles. As I push the door open, the thought that this is a world apart from sparring and training exercises runs through my mind.

"Empty," comments Axion as we enter through the gaping mouth of the doorframe.

"Not quite," I correct while my eyes sweep every inch of the room. "Check behind the door, Ax."

"You do watch horror films." He smirks as he checks out the only area obscured from my view. "Clear," he confirms.

"Looks like it's just me, you and him then." I point to the throne. A figure, slumped awkwardly and secured with thick black rope, sits scowling in our direction. His face is marked with dry blood, his lip appears swollen and there's an odd bend to his nose

He doesn't look overly pleased to see us. His mouth pulls to the side in a painful looking sneer as he acknowledges us in a mocking tone. "It would appear so."

I take a reluctant step forward. "What are you doing here?"

"I live here," he answers with a throaty laugh. "Welcome home, cousin." He stares over my shoulder at Axion. "Took you long enough."

"Clyst," Axion nods. "You look good."

Clyst laughs again, a dark, humourless laugh that finishes in a fit of dry coughing. I almost feel sorry for him.

Axion strolls past me, pulling out a short blade as he goes. "Hang on a second."

"Ax, wait." I take another step forward. My eyes remain fixed on Clyst. Something doesn't feel right.

Axion stops next to his cousin with his blade ready to cut Clyst free.

"Ax," I repeat. "Hang on a minute."

"What?" He slices through the rope in one easy movement and gestures at me. "You know Aquila."

"We've met," Clyst scoffs toward me as he rises to his feet. He cracks his knuckles as he runs his eyes over me. A cold shiver travels the length of my spine in the process.

"Really?" I tighten my grip on my dagger. "I don't remember."

Axion laughs, smacking Clyst on the shoulder in the process. "She's quite entertaining. You'd like her. So what happened? Where's my dad?"

"Ah, about that," Clyst says, turning toward Axion in an instant. His fist hits Axion's jaw like a pneumatic hammer, sending a rainbow of blood and spittle in an arc above Axion's rapidly crumpling form. He lands hard on his back, slamming his head on the floor. Pain burns through my skull: a tingling, neuropathic pain. It also comes with an almost irresistible compulsion to help him. My eyes narrow and my teeth clench as I stave off the impulse.

"There you go, Aquila, ruining all my plans again." Clyst turns and stalks toward me. "Unluckily for you, I know how to adapt." He stops his advance, watching me with interest, waiting for my reaction. "Good teacher, you see."

"Then we have something in common." I lift my wings slightly, preparing for the inevitable.

He laughs again at my response. "I sincerely doubt that."

"You've wasted your advantage." I indicate toward Axion. "He'll be pissed when he wakes up."

"Depends on your perspective." He slides his sword from his hip slowly. I knew something seemed wrong. He doesn't look like someone who's spent days tethered to a throne. "If he wakes up."

"What do you want, Clyst?" I move my fingers, slowly, into a throwing grip around my dagger handle.

He beats me to it. A small, sleek throwing star hits me in the armour on my right arm, knocking my dagger from my grasp. It clatters to the floor. He raises his hands sympathetically. "I'm not one for rambling monologues. They never work out so well for the bad guy."

His strength is immense. I can feel the trickle of blood dribbling down my arm. It's a flesh wound, from the star piercing right through my protective steel. I inspect the damage briefly, leaving the star where it is. My eyes dart back to him, my mouth forms words around clenched teeth. "So you admit you're a bad guy?"

"You're tough, I'll give you that." He stalks forward quickly now that I'm unarmed. "Let's see if you scream like a girl."

I duck, not very productive as tactics go: unless you're avoiding the half crazed love of your life as he dives onto your would-be attacker. Liam hits Clyst like a wrecking ball, lifting them both off of their feet. He's joined by Rhyan and, between them, they make Clyst scream at a pitch I don't think I would have achieved.

"Guardian, are you hurt?"

"I'm fine." I shake off Kav's attempts to help in order to get to my brother. Axion is still out cold, his jaw looks dislocated. "That's going to hurt in the morning. Where are the others?"

"There was no sign of anyone else in the buildings. Your men haven't returned to rendezvous yet." He gives me a once over gaze and then turns his attention to Axion. "That will need resetting."

"At least we're keeping Halen in business." I glance back down at my arm as Liam walks to my side. His fingers follow the trail of blood along my hand and then up my sleeve to the protruding star. "I'm fine," I repeat. "We need to find the others. Whoever tied Clyst up can't be far away. He hadn't been there long."

"Kav and Rhyan will take your brother and the prisoner back to Celthia. We'll find the others." He plants a hard and fast kiss on my mouth. It tastes like a promise of more to come. "Stay beside me."

"Is he alive?" My eyes land on Clyst, limp and silent in Rhyan's arms. Clyst's arm is obviously broken. The bone is climbing through his skin like a blood-stained tooth.

"Barely," Liam admits. "He won't be for long."

"But?" There sounded like a silent but.

"But, he may have useful information." He leans in close, his breath heating my neck. "He's lucky he only wounded your arm."

I watch the heat in his eyes as he gives Clyst a final glare and issues the order for the Guard to leave. Axion groans as he's lifted but his eyelids stay firmly closed.

"Did you know him?" Liam asks as we head out of the throne room and into a small courtyard behind the main building. I haven't been this way before but it's the entrance the Guard appeared from, so I figure Liam knows where he's going.

"He's Axion's cousin." I leave it at that. Brue was never specific about the genetics of their lineage.

"Do you trust him?"

"Clyst?"

Liam shakes his head, pursing his lips while he rolls his eyes at me. It makes for quite a dizzying gesture.

"I trust Ax. He feels like family."

Liam huffs out a short breath as we turn right, following a narrow alleyway between two high walls. They shimmer a dusky white in the moonlight. "You can't always trust family."

"I trust you."

I'm not sure why I chose to declare my trust in him right at that moment. I know he's not family, but it felt right so I said it aloud.

In the throne room, when I saw him barrelling through the door behind Clyst like a man possessed, I realised something. Liam is a person. An entity, made up of millions of cells that have experienced millions of seconds of a life that I have not witnessed. He is another being like me, and like me, like everyone, he is trapped inside his own head. He thinks the way he thinks, and he acts the way he acts, because that is who he is. And I know him. I can't look inside his mind to decipher what is going on behind those stunning caramel irises of his, but I do know him. My perception registers him as part of my own little universe. It is attuned to his wavelength and it identifies him as part of me. I knew he would come for me, protect or avenge me, because that is what I would do for him.

"Aqua?"

"Yeah?"

He's stopped walking. We've cleared the buildings while I've been inattentive. The treeline sways like a crowd at a concert, their arms moving in time with the slow rhythm of the wind. The dust beneath my feet has the last hints of sharpness as the island begins to give way to beach. Liam is silhouetted against the starry night sky, the lights twinkle around his head like a cosmic halo that extends past infinity. His breathing is shallow, making his leather-clad chest rise and fall in a hypnotic display of clavicle and muscle. He gently places his fingers onto the same spot at the base of my throat, like seeing the vulnerable meeting place of airway and ribcage does something to him too. I swallow reflexively, making his hand dip softly.

He's moved in close, so close that his body heat mixes with mine. The warmth intensifies as he brushes his feathers against me, around me, until we're cocooned within a tender embrace of wings. My hands rest against his breast, rendered immobile by our proximity. His other arm wraps around my waist and holds me still. Holds me like it will never let me go.

"Please," he whispers, he pleads, "be my mate."

I nod my answer, waiting to ensure my voice won't break before speaking. "Yes, Liam, in every way possible."

Our kiss, the kiss that seals our promise, is slow and sensual. Our lips linger against each other, revelling in the moment, building a memory that will last for our eternity. And then I'm spinning around, still locked inside Liam's hold, and we're laughing like idiots. He eventually lowers me back to the ground, letting me slide unsteadily down his body as my equilibrium returns.

"Tomorrow?" he asks earnestly.

# · Fifteen ·

"**W**here are my men?" I repeat as we walk along the edge of the train tracks, shielded from view by the first line of trees.

We left the purity of our romantic moment behind us, agreeing to seek Victus' blessing as soon as we return to Celthia. It's a formality. He's already given it once, albeit unofficially. Now we're looking for Reuben and the others, and I'm getting increasingly anxious for their wellbeing.

"The tracks look clear," Liam states. "If they came along here, then they flew."

"Tarcus and Cain were headed this way. Maybe they did." But it doesn't sound likely. Cain loathed the flight here.

"They could have taken another route," Liam suggests. "Cain knows this island." He glances around and then up through the canopy above. "It still amazes me."

The knowledge that the dragone have been visible and living in the open for generations has taken him a while to get used to. Hantiem is nothing like he envisaged the home of the dragone to be. Yes it is hot and humid and there's a network of tunnels that circumnavigate the whole planet, as far as I can tell, like their own personal subway system. It's also full of vibrancy and life, at least it *was*. There are still signs of it as we walk. Signs of children's play things, of tree houses and dens, the odd football lost amongst the undergrowth.

I shrug. "You can only know what you know, until you learn something new."

"Poetic," he grins.

"You don't think we'll find them, do you." It's not a question. Liam, Master of the Guard, would not be wandering along in the moonlight, conversing like teenagers at the back of the classroom, if he thought we were anything but alone on this island.

"We could do another lap from the air, to be certain," he placates. "But no, I don't."

"Why?" I look around, searching for something I can't see. "What do you see that I don't?"

"Open your senses, Aqua. You rely too heavily on your sight in the dark." His voice takes on the condescending edge he uses during training. I roll my eyes reflexively.

"How can I smell anything else when you're right beside me?" I'm teasing but surely I do have a point?

He smirks. "Compartmentalise."

I inhale in response, filling my sinus with the powerful smell of him.

"Everything, every living thing, has an effect on the world around it, immense or slight. But every effect is significant. Sense, process, make a decision. Trust your instincts. You are naturally talented, it is impressive, but you must not be complacent. Tell me what I can see that you cannot."

Our feet have stopped moving. The sand shifts and alters beneath the weight of us. The air swirls around us, creating mini currents in the wind. Our scents travel with the breeze, changing the perfume of the island and mingling with the smell of the ocean, of the plants, of the blood.

"You cleared the main buildings without searching them," I assume. "The windows are open, glass free. Your senses are more defined than mine." I turn to face him, hypothesising. "It's how you got to us so fast. You registered Clyst's presence, smelt Axion's blood, right?"

"Correct. And your men?"

I have to compose myself before I can answer. I go worst case scenario first, hoping it's not true. "Dead, or captured, I assume. I can't process a whole island, Liam. I'm not the same as you. But we would have seen signs of them by now, if they were here, affecting the world around them."

"No blood is a good sign."

"We should check the tower before we leave. It's the only room with glass. There might be something there."

"Then let's go," he agrees. I take the lead, launching into the air and heading for the tower. "And I can't process a whole island simultaneously, either. It's like a puzzle not a photograph. One piece at a time until you see the whole picture."

We circle the tower once, high in the sky, where arrows would do well to reach us. With no signs of life, we move in closer and secure ourselves by grasping the same bars that prevented my escape before. I look into the room with the same focus that I used to look out of it.

"Feathers," I comment. "Lighter than mine."

"Tarcus?" Liam suggests, pulling closer beside me to look for himself.

"No." I sigh, swinging myself around so I'm watching our backs. "The arrows you carry, the steel ones with your father's sigil." I glance at Liam as he stares through the window, his eyes on the feathers laid out on the bed. "They're old. Recycled. You've used your ration of steel on the multitude of fancy blades you keep hidden at the back of August's workroom."

Liam glances at me and then back to the room, his jawline flexing with the tick of a straining muscle. "It was an act of rebellion," Liam murmurs before turning away from the window and unsheathing his sword with one hand. "I kept his sigil to hurt Marcus." His eyes flash toward me briefly before he draws his arm back, forces his sword in a swift jab through the bars of the window and shatters the glass. It cracks like the ring of thunder. "I was four and it was a stupid idea." He inhales the scent of the room through the broken pane, cursing under his breath.

"He's been here," I comment, picking up the waft of male emitting from the room.

Liam finally makes eye contact, staring at me like he's trying to read my mind. He nods solemnly. "And now he has your scent."

Something that was going to happen eventually. "And we have his." I glance one more time through the window, to the feathers on the bed: chocolate brown feathers arranged in a triangle, with burnt out candles around the edge. "By how much do you think we missed him?"

Liam lets out a noise similar to a growling bear while he sheaths his sword. His eyes blaze with something hot and angry, perhaps at being so close and so far from finding out the purpose of all of this. The fact is, we still don't know what Rennison is after, apart from that he's after me, and why he's doing all of this.

Liam finally offers an answer, or a guess at one. "He probably did this, tied your friend to the throne and then went underground."

Liam lets go of his perch on the bars and lifts himself back into the air. I take it as his cue to return to Celthia and follow, climbing quickly into the clouds. The stars are beginning to diminish as the night draws on. Dark clouds are on the horizon. An ominous omen if ever I've seen one.

"Perhaps Tarcus and your dragone found something before their tracks were covered," Liam suggests quietly as we leave Hantiem.

"I don't like leaving without knowing if there's something we could have done. If we could have helped them." I understand it would be crazy to stay searching the island and the tunnels on our own. But it feels like we're abandoning them to their fate.

"Leadership means making decisions for the good of the majority, Aqua. I will not let you risk your life, again, for the sake of a few men." He pushes on, flying hard and as straight as an arrow.

"Is that a decision based on the good of the majority? or on our relationship?" I challenge.

Liam does have a point, even if somewhat skewed. We need to report our findings to Victus. We can come back, with a larger team. We could cover more of the tunnels if the majority of the Guard deploy.

"Both," Liam snaps back, regaining my attention. "Losing you drove me to the brink of insanity. I would drag every last man down with me if I lost you again. The entire Guard, of every city, would not be enough to satisfy my quest for revenge. Do you understand how much you mean to me? What I would do for you? I love you more than Tristan loved Isolde, more than Paris loved Helena."

He's silent for a few beats after his tirade. I can't see his face because he is ahead of me, using his advantage of speed. I can't help thinking that the epic love stories he's just compared us to never worked out so well for the couple in question.

"Speed up," he commands. "We need to return by daybreak."

I have the feeling that, if I hadn't been here, he would have done the opposite and gone after his father alone. Anyone moving this quickly isn't doing it to beat the sun. Besides, they fly in the daylight all the time. No, he's doing it to get away from what's behind us. Or to stop himself going back.

The return flight is the opposite of the flight out. Liam doesn't speak again and neither do I. We're both cogitating. I'm replaying scenes of the island, worrying over my men and my brother, attempting to hold Rennison's scent in my nose until it's ingrained in my evil'o'meter.

It takes a long time before we see the first peaks of snow-capped mountains. I've slowed Liam down even though I've maintained my top speed. My muscles are aching and all I want is a shower to wash away the pain and the grime. But I need to check on Axion first, and then report to Victus, and then it will be morning and my mother will expect me at breakfast, and then I'll have to explain to my men that we've lost Old Salt and Art and Cain.

Liam calls my name gently. He may have already called it once. He's reduced his speed so that we're gliding level as we descend toward the hangar door. My eyes flick to his wearily. "We will visit your brother together and then we will rest. You are exhausted. Everything else can wait a few measures."

I couldn't agree more. "Won't Victus want an immediate debrief?"

Plyrian is waiting alone in the hangar when we land. He greets us kindly, an edge of relief on his face. Liam acknowledges him with a nod.

"We have the prisoner under interrogation," Plyrian states as we all walk toward the doors that lead to the medical wing. "Victus is in there with him," he adds. Of course he heard my question. "The casualty is out of surgery, his jaw has been wired. He is not...amused."

"Where?" I ask as we enter the corridor, a corridor that is getting all too familiar.

"Halen's room," Plyrian answers.

"Go ahead, Aqua. I'll catch up," Liam suggests.

My step falters slightly in a brief moment of indecision. I thought he said we would go together. He turns to face Plyrian directly, effectively cutting off any answer I may have given him. It doesn't matter, I suppose. I can still face things on my own. I just like having him beside me.

Halen's door is open. The Medic, looking exhausted, is just leaving as I walk up. "Halen."

"Guardian," she replies warmly. "It has been a long night, I gather. The casualty, Axion, has been asking after you since he awoke."

"Damn right I have," Axion growls as he follows her out. His words come out disjointed and mumbled, hindered greatly by his immobile jaw. He has two surgical incision sites, secured with a neat row of stitches, and a split lip. He's obviously been pumped full of heal aid and pain relief. The swelling is reducing.

"Looking dashing, Ax." I step in to his chest, wrapping my arms around his waist. "We lost them." My words come out just shy of a sob. He stiffens but wraps his arms tightly around me before responding.

"I could feel you, when I woke up. You must have been on your way back here, but I knew something had happened. No one here knew what was going on." He releases me from his embrace but leaves his arm around my shoulder as we walk toward the cells. I thank Halen, again, for her expertise before she goes back into her room and closes the door. "Tell me what you saw. I'll relay it to the others."

"In that voice? It's not a comedy, Ax. I'll tell them myself, if they're awake. Then I'm going to get some rest." We descend the spiral staircase slowly. He's still groggy from the medications and I'm not eager to get to where we're going. "He was there, you know, at some point. Maybe even at the same point. I think Clyst was working with him." Axion growls again, rubbing his jaw with his free hand. The other arm is still wrapped around me, his skin on my skin, sensing each other, strengthening our bond. "I felt you get punched. It hurt. I think I got screwed over when it comes to long distance feeling. I only get the painful stuff on my wavelength."

"Happy to share," he answers in an attempt at humour, which leaves him grimacing. "Can't smile," he grumbles. "I'm going to kill Clyst."

"Not if I beat you to it."

The debrief with the pirates doesn't take as long as I was expecting. They take one look at Axion and me and assume the worst. It can only get better if you assume the worst from the beginning, I guess. They take the loss of the three men hard, cussing and swearing until their energy for words wanes and they start demanding action.

Axion is the muted voice of reason, forcing his words out slowly in order to make them clear. "The island was deserted. They are obviously using the tunnels. Aqua knows *his* scent now, right Princess?" I nod. "I am going to talk to Clyst, directly. The Fallen left him there for a reason. Perhaps he'll tell me. He always liked to prove how superior he is."

"And I'll talk to Victus when he emerges from wherever they're holding him. We'll discuss our next plan. We won't let them get away with this. Reuben, Art, Tarcus, they were good people."

"Cain," Axion whispers loudly.

"And Cain was one of ours. They were our people and the Fallen deserve our retaliation. There's far too much people-taking going on. They came to Hantiem looking for a fight and then they lured us back to take more from you, from us. Next time we take the fight to them."

"We're all with you, Lass." Plank, Tomas, steps forward. "Old Salt had faith in you, called you the Angel of Deliverance. Tell us what you need and we'll do it."

I look around the dark, dank space at the earnest faces of the dragone. They're each in agreement, each pledging their support. Even Nev and George seem to have grown a foot taller as they straighten up and puff out their chests. I don't want to lose another one of them but we can't spend our lives hiding, waiting for Rennison's next move. What kind of life is a long life lived in fear? If my life is to be short, I want to live it in liberty.

"The war is drawing closer. I can feel the fight brewing in each of you. Be prepared. Live the life you want or die trying. But for now, rest."

"Princess." Plank turns back to the dragone. "You heard our orders, lads. We'll be summoned when we're required."

"You know," Axion mumbles, "if I die first, I want you to write my eulogy. When you speak everyone takes notice."

My mouth pulls into a smirk. "When you speak you sound like a lawnmower."

He shakes his head like he's laughing inside his head. "I'm not the one walking around with a metal snowflake in my arm."

I look down in response. "It's a star," I correct. "Clyst put it there." I'd forgotten about it. "He's a jerk."

Axion sighs in agreement. "It's not something we use. I guess we know where he got it. Go and get it removed proper...No, stop!"

"Too late." I remove the armour and the star together before inspecting the wound. It's a short clean slice through the tissue with a pool of dark blood. The armour protected me enough to prevent any life altering damage. "It'll be fine."

"Meet you at breakfast," Axion offers as I head for the stairs alone. "You think they have straws?"

"I'm sure you'll manage," I answer as I round the corner and travel out of sight.

My room is empty when I get there. It's a disappointment, considering Liam's been holed up in here every night until now. It figures that as soon as I decide to commit my eternity to him he vanishes. I place the star, still impaled in my arm plate, onto the dresser. Peeling off the rest of my uniform, I head straight to the shower. The water runs along my arm, across my wound, and turns rosy as I cleanse it of dirt. My shampoo makes it sting as I wash and rinse my hair. I'm lathering my coconut body wash when I sense Liam in my room. What I don't expect is the very naked form of said angeli to wander through the bathroom archway, place his burning candle on the sink, and climb into the shower behind me. I face the wall automatically, keeping my eyes up... up... up... up.

"Do you mind?" he asks. I'd swear he's trying not to laugh.

"Do you?!" My voice does a weird octave jump that sounds like a scratched record.

"Not at all." And now I know he's laughing. "Shall I do your back?"

I panic, naturally. "Um...no... I've feathered my shampoo...uh...shampooed my wash...urgh... I. Have. Shampooed. My. Feathers."

"You could do mine."

Eyes up. "I...this is new." Eyes up. Eyes up.

"This is natural. You know, we'll have to share a bathroom when we're mated," he leans in, pressing his body against my wings and heating my neck with his words, "and I like to shower. A lot."

"Cold showers," I agree. "Lots of cold showers are the way forward." Eyes up, I slowly turn around. His eyes don't stay up. "Gah, Liam!"

"What?" He still doesn't look up but at least he's not laughing now. He is staring, intently.

271

"I'm getting out."

"You're still covered in coconut foam," he comments. His eyes finally find a more suitable level at which to look at me.

"Ever observant."

I rinse quickly while he watches in amusement, his eyebrow quirked. "Why does nakedness make you so flustered, Aqua?"

"You want to discuss this now?" I scramble from the shower, slipping around like *Bambi on ice* as I grab a towel and cover my modesty. Talk about uncomfortable. No one else has ever seen me like this. Except my mother and that was pre-puberty.

"We could discuss it at the beginning of our mating moons, if that makes you feel better."

"No, it doesn't." I pull the towel tighter.

Liam's brow drops as he stands in naked glory before me. Eyes up. Eyes down... Holy hell! Eyes up. Eyes up!

He tilts his head to the side like a forlorn puppy. "Am I displeasing to you?" He sounds insulted. "This is all of me, Aquila. It all belongs to you."

"It's all any girl could ask for, probably all any guy could ask for as well. I just... have never been so... so vulnerable in front of anyone. It's unnerving." I shrug and pull the towel so tight it begins to look like a second skin. "I know I shouldn't, but sue me, I care what you think."

"I think you are the most beautiful demonic angel I have ever seen. I'd be honoured to see you naked every day for the rest of our lives." He turns around to reach the shower gel, at which point my eyes immediately gravitate to his bottom. It's very athletic looking.

"Okay. I mean good, that's good. Thank you. I... er... same to you. It's good. Lovely. Good chat."

I spin and dash from the bathroom before my skin melts from my bones with the heat of my embarrassment. Jesus Christ. I could slap myself, stupid prude, running out on the gorgeous naked guy in the shower. I'm eighteen. I'm a friggin' mythical being. I'm a sexually inept moron.

"Make sure you take heal aid for that arm," Liam shouts from the bathroom, "an antimicrobial one."

"Yes, sir." I follow his advice and swallow a vial before putting on fresh underwear. I'm being indecisive over my choice of outfit when Liam comes in, still dripping. "Oh, here." I overlooked the fact I only have one towel. Not usually much call for two. I hand him the damp one I used. "Sorry it's wet."

"You should be resting," he comments.

"I'm just getting dressed." I indicate toward the open drawers.

"So I see." He drops the towel and closes the distance. "I sleep better like this."

His demeanour is giving off a challenging vibe. I must have offended him. I really didn't mean to.

"Like this?" I ask, attempting for alluring. "I like you like this."

"You're sure? I don't intimidate you? Make you uncomfortable?" His eyelids droop in a languidly attractive way. "You like what you see?"

"I love what I see." I reach up on my toes to place a kiss on his mouth. "I love you, Liam. All of you." I'm careful, however, to place my hands on his abdomen and not any lower. "You know, most men would be happy their mate had never been seen naked before."

He kisses me back, more roughly than mine. "Believe me, I am."

"Bed."

"Pardon?"

"I said I want to go to bed, to sleep." I take his hand and pull him and all his nakedness toward my mattress.

He follows willingly, almost eagerly, and climbs under the covers. Holding his arms open he waits for me to scramble in beside him. "You are timid one second and confident the next. You never fail to keep me chasing my own wits around you, Aqua."

"It's part and parcel of being female, I'm told. Hormones, you know." I snuggle down with my head nestled in the crook of his elbow. "You're still wet."

"I hope you'll provide me with basic essentials and comforts when we're mated, like dry towels." He wraps his arms around me, sniffing my hair in the process.

"This is an equal rights relationship, remember." I yawn as my eyes close. "Get your own damn towels." Being awake for hours takes its toll, especially when a large proportion of those hours are spent flying and fighting.

He presses his lips against my shoulder. I can feel his gaze on my face. His words are muted against my skin. "Then why aren't we equally naked?"

I manage a smile before I fall asleep.

# · Sixteen ·

Liam sleeps longer than we planned. I was relying on him to wake me up. Instead, it's August who strolls in, carrying a lit candle, expecting me to be ready for breakfast. It wouldn't be so bad, if he hadn't brought our mother as well. She's also carrying a flame, illuminating mine and Liam's position in a romantic glow.

Liam throws our pillow at August while my mother gives me her most dissatisfied glare.

"Morning, Mum." I climb ungracefully from under the sheets, attempting to protect Liam's modesty by not lifting them more than absolutely necessary. "August."

Our brother looks mortified. His cheeks flush as he registers the compromising position he stumbled in upon.

"Aquila," my mother reprimands. "Did you spend the entire night with that man?"

"Yes. Yes I did. The whole night." I discreetly pull my arm behind my back, hiding my newest injury from her sight.

She seems to realise she's being rude and turns toward Liam with a quick apology. "Good morning, Liam. Do you mind giving us a minute?"

Liam gives a perplexed frown. I stifle an inappropriate giggle at his expression until I realise he's actually considering it. Christ. "No can do, Mum, he's a little exposed."

"Oh, sweet Lord," my mother exclaims. "Stay where you are Liam. We'll give you both a minute to make yourselves decent."

"Thank you, Libby." Then he adds as an afterthought, "Pleasure to finally meet you."

"Likewise. August," my mother commands as she pulls him from the room. "Honestly. If it's not you sneaking off to your boyfriend's room it's your sister, right next door."

"He's been doing what?" Liam asks as the door shuts behind them.

"When was the last time you slept in your own bed? You can't talk," I warn while I'm pulling on the outfit I chose last night.

"Perhaps not. But we can make it official." He jumps out of the bed like it's an Olympic springboard.

"You're sprightly this morning." I watch him get dressed in record time. He appears to have stocked a drawer with his own clothes. I wander over in interest and inspect the uniformly neat piles he has laid out inside. The drawer used to contain my human clothes. "Huh."

"For convenience," he responds as I give him a questioning look.

"How very presumptuous of you, my love."

"So sue me," he mimics before placing a hot kiss over my lips, which I immediately deepen. He responds, threading his fingers into my curls and cradling my head with his palms. When I open my eyes he's watching me, his gaze creates a sweltering heat under my skin.

I pull back slowly, feeling exposed even though I'm fully dressed. "Do you even know what that means?"

"No, but you used it with such passion it seemed appropriate."

"It means to prosecute someone for a crime in order to be awarded compensation."

Liam steps back, regarding me quizzically. "Humans are strange beings."

I flash him a smile and head off to placate the strange beings in the hallway. My mother is waiting with a contrite expression. "Please lock the door next time you have company sweetheart."

"With what, my willpower? You know there's no lock on the door, Mum. You were gushing about how wonderful it is to have no crooks around and how everyone trusts everyone not to enter without reason."

She acts like I haven't spoken. "August explained what happened with Aaron. I'm sorry things didn't work out between you two. You seem happy with Liam though. You love him?"

"With everything I've got." When my mother blanches I laugh. "Not literally, Mum. The angeli are very strict about sex before marriage, at least Liam is."

"Which is why we're having our ceremony as soon as possible," Liam declares as he strolls out of the door. "This afternoon perhaps."

My mum gasps. "Aqua?"

"He's joking." *Possibly.*

"We're on our way to discuss it with Victus right now," Liam continues. He seems to be enjoying himself.

I like to see him so carefree. Just not at my poor mother's expense. She's probably thinking about all the possible reasons for such a quick ceremony to occur. "We might miss breakfast."

"Aquila!"

I flash my mother a grimace as Liam drags me off toward Victus' office. "It won't be this afternoon, Mum, I promise."

"I'll talk to Gloria about a dress!" she yells back as we turn the corner.

We traverse the corridors of the city toward the library. Liam's pace seems to increase the closer we get, his brow drops lower the more determined he gets, until I'm not sure if the purpose of our visit to Victus has morphed into something more. There's an unfamiliar scent in the air. It's not unusual for me to smell someone I can't identify. After all, Celthia has three thousand inhabitants and is visited occasionally by traders from other cities.

Liam, however, is marching with a determined glare toward the source of the smell. He's not the only one, it appears. As we round the corner of the school, we hit a large crowd of angeli congregated at the library entrance. The door is shut tight. Plyrian stands, arms crossed, like a cherubim before the gates of Eden. He just needs a flaming sword.

"Plyrian," Liam commands and he moves aside to let us pass. "How long?"

"Victus summoned me after I had returned to the barracks. They have been in there ever since. I expect the crowd to multiply. They cannot be expected to ignore his presence." He nods at the expectant faces of the surrounding angeli. Some seem to be worshiping with their heads bowed in respect as they whisper adoring words toward the door.

"This corridor is too restricted and the younglings are due to begin classes. Send them and any other arrivals to the harbour. Avoid the Great Hall and the barracks for as long as possible." When Liam's finished issuing orders, he turns to look at me. His eyes burn like he wants to speak but his mouth pinches closed. I shrink back an inch as I imagine who could possibly make him and the rest of the city act this way. There's only one person I can think of.

"August?" Plyrian asks Liam. It's a quiet whisper, the whisper of a friend to a friend.

"He's with his mother. Perhaps it would be better to wait."

"Very well," Plyrian agrees in a tone that suggests he doesn't.

While Liam and Plyrian have a brief staring competition, I slip into the library as silently as a shadow. I close the door tentatively and press my back against it, staring contemplatively at the two men in the room. Victus is standing in front of the desk, looking back at me with the same expression. The man I can only assume is Marcus, due to his piercing green eyes and the wildfire of hair on his head, is sitting in the Overseer's chair.

"I see your descriptions have been accurate," Marcus states in an impoverish tone. He looks exhausted in the way a suave businessman might look after a long-haul flight. His clothes are sophisticated yet creased around the edges. He is not wearing traditional angeli garments. Instead, he has a fine knit sweater with the collar of a button down shirt folded around his neck. His wings, which must protrude through a modification in his clothing, do not shimmer like rubies, as I was led to believe. They are, however, the same colour as his hair.

The door I'm leaning against tries to buck me off without warning. My immediate and natural response is to push back. The force ceases immediately with a muted curse. I move aside quickly before Liam bursts through like a battering ram, which he does a moment later. He stands stock still for a second, taking in the figures at the desk, before turning to search for me. I'm pressed against the back wall of books, wondering why Marcus used a plural.

"Are you okay?" Liam asks as he walks over. He puts his body partly behind mine and wraps his arm around my waist. He scrutinises my face until I nod in response.

"Neither did you exaggerate," Marcus comments as he rises to his feet. "I believe that's a first."

The room falls quiet then as Marcus makes his way around the desk. Tailored trousers and wide leather loafers, I muse. There is also a long trench coat style jacket draped over the back of his chair. Not really the outfit I'd expect an escaped hostage to roll up in.

Liam glares at him. It is not the relieved expression of a son reunited with his father. In that silent exchange, I can see the years of resentment and defiance that hangs between them. Liam told me once, a lifetime ago, that he became Marcus' son so that he could be August's brother. Perhaps he used to revere the man, when he talked of his leadership and legend he was admiring, but my existence punches holes in Marcus' stories and his legacy. Now he's back, obviously well-kept and well fed. I wonder what his story will be this time. It's an echo of a thought I've had before.

"You elected to summon Plyrian before me?" Liam asks.

Marcus leans back against the desk in the same way Victus often does. My eyes move to the greying Overseer as Marcus answers with an air of arrogance in his tone. "I was informed you were resting after your mission."

Liam doesn't hold back the argumentative tenor in his voice. "And August? You did not visit him immediately. You know he will be disappointed."

Marcus scowls. "Your brother's sensitivities are his own issue to overcome, as you well know. I cannot be expected to inform him of everything I do at every moment. It is just not feasible to care for a grown infant when you are the spearhead of an entire city."

"Self-righteous twit," I comment. I've decided I hate Marcus more than I thought I would. He's more of an arse than Victus.

Liam squeezes my waist and pulls me closer. "Aqua."

"Well he is." I pull on Liam's arm until he releases his death grip. "If you didn't want to care for a child, then you would have done better to not abduct one." I step closer and Liam moves with me, trying to shift his body from behind to in front of me. "Who do you think you are?"

"Apart from the fact that I am the Overseer of this city," he retorts, "I am also your father and you will address me as such."

"I will do no such thing. You're no more of a father to me than you are to Liam. As for August, he deserves better than an egotistical fraud like you. I don't know you, I don't like you and I don't appreciate the way you have waltzed in here and attempted to assert your parental authority."

I have crept slowly forward, Liam fused to me like armour, until I'm a few feet from the parent in question. "Last I heard, you vanished and Victus took over." I look up at the glass ceiling to emphasise my point. "Modifications and a vivacious red pyjama suit say he's the Overseer now."

"She takes after her mother," Marcus comments.

"Undoubtedly," Victus confirms. "She's being uncharacteristically lenient on you."

Marcus smirks humourlessly. "Well, Aquila, my child, I have never abdicated my position in this city. I have spent too long living in the bowels of this mountain to allow just anyone to upset the delicate ecosystem."

I scoff. "It's a city full of living people, not a botanical garden, and what the hell do you mean?" My eyes dart to Victus and back. Liam stays silent, radiating fury.

"Victus is my aide-de-camp," Marcus says coolly. My gaze falls on Victus, who looks a little annoyed at his declaration. He doesn't dispute Marcus' claim. "My demeanour has offended you, for which I am sorry. However, you have not lived the years as I have. You have not witnessed the malevolence of which people are capable." He waves his arms around, in a similar fashion to Victus when he's talking fervently.

My eyebrow quirks. "Which people?"

"People so sure of their superiority and ideals, that they grow intent on diseasing the world to spread them." He looks from me to Liam and back. "We should converse alone, after all, there is much to discuss and only a small amount of time to do it."

"I stay," Liam growls.

"As do I," Victus adds. "I have harboured your secrets long enough to warrant your trust, have I not? The city is as you left it, your people still loyal." Victus doesn't lose the edge of authority that resounds in his voice when he speaks.

Marcus bristles in response. "Yet insubordination appears to be rife." His eyes find Liam. "From the Master of the Guard no less." He shakes his head. "You may not stay."

I huff an exasperated sigh. Honestly, Marcus is no different than the rest of the autocrats I've met: so sure of his own superiority, convinced that his opinion is the right opinion.

"Yes you may." I pull Liam around my supposed father to Victus' chair and sit in it.

"I hear you do that a lot," Marcus states as he stares at me.

"You've obviously kept yourself informed." I glance at Victus accusingly. "So where did your mole dig you up? And why now?"

Marcus' eyes flare a vibrant green as he responds, walking back toward the desk in the process. "Rennison's campaign is gaining momentum. This last attack was the beginning of his major offensive." He stops when his designer-clad thighs touch the desktop.

The room seems to hold its breath, like a mini vacuum of silence, which ceases when I realise he is waiting for my response. "His major offensive being...?" My curiosity burns, like the fire of anger that I've held as a torch for so long.

Marcus, staring intently at my eagerness, pulls his mouth into the same humourless smirk I often use. It's the first likeness I have noticed between us and my gaze lingers on it as he answers. "Dominion."

"You were aware," I turn to Victus to include him in my accusation, "of this, of the threat from the Fallen from the start."

Victus nods, his gaze penetrating. Perhaps it is stupid, that my first reaction is to feel hurt at his deceit. After all, I had a sense all along that there was a head full of secrets behind those intelligent eyes.

"Tell me, from the beginning, was it all a lie?" My heartbeat quickens, sending chemical signals racing around my body. But, instead of letting the mix of emotions distract me, I use the feeling as an anchor. I tether myself to the moment, to the situation, so that I can focus.

"The threat existed before you came into existence," Marcus answers, trying to pull the conversation back to him. I ignore his input. My glare stays on the Santa impersonator whom I've slowly formed a tense bond with over the months I've lived here.

He responds to my question without looking at Marcus for permission. "Your existence was a secret of which I was not informed. After Sierra, when so much was lost, your father came to me with information..."

Marcus tries to interrupt as he realises Victus is going to tell me what I want to know, whether Marcus likes it or not. Liam, silent as a sentinel, moves slowly back around the desk until he is almost on top of the man claiming to be my father. Liam is an imposing figure, with the threatening physical presence and the sense of determination that only a lifetime of battles can achieve.

He stares at Marcus, a man just as threatening in his own way, with a look that could wilt a thousand flowers. "We have lost so many," Liam rumbles. "So much has been denied to us as we hide in this rock or fight a hidden enemy. Countless angeli, countless innocents, countless measures of people's lives lost so that you, our revered leader, may play a game of chess with living pawns."

Liam is tactical. He thinks like a commander, he sees stratagems with ease. He has the ability to join the dots in a way that leads him farther than the end of the trail. In his silence, while he let me do the talking, he seems to have generated a concept that casts Marcus as the grandmaster playing off against his greatest opponent. The threat that existed before I did, the threat from Rennison and the Fallen, started before Sierra.

Marcus was right. There has been a change since he vanished. The angeli are evolving, developing a sense of their own desires and seeking out their own destinies. Liam has displayed that to me, to others, by joining the resistance against the strict and archaic rules of the Script. The angeli are seeking out their own mates, building their relationships on love instead of convention. Lucas and Robyn, August and Oberon, Theon and Kiera: they are all couples that would be denied mating rights under the leadership of a devout enforcer of the Script. Yet, Victus allowed a ceremony to take place for my best friends. I wonder how informed Victus has actually kept Marcus in his absence.

Marcus finally deflates a fraction as he realises he's outnumbered. Liam and I want answers and Victus is willing to provide them. When Marcus replies, his voice is resigned. "This game, if that is what you deem to call it, was initiated before even you were born, Liam. Losses, however painful, are an unavoidable part of being alive."

"Absolute power corrupts absolutely," I quote while watching my father impassively. "There is a place for leadership, a place for authority and a place for democracy. Since I arrived, Victus has attempted to convince me that I am like you, that I'm a leader." I stand up, wanting to look my supposed father in the eye. "He insists that you are a good man, that you are a protector. I have seen no evidence to convince me of that, even now you attempt to use your leadership as an excuse for withholding knowledge."

Marcus stares at me with the same intensity as I often use. "You believe you would not do the same? You are no different. Are you not fighting toward your own goal? You hold power, given to you by my name alone, and you use it to force your own ideals."

It seems he is well informed, perhaps more so than Victus, who stares at us in confusion.

"I have allies, Aquila, trusted friends of both species. Perhaps our ideals are not so different. You are of my flesh, after all. Your mother was an idealist, as passionate as you. I made a mistake that cost us dearly, all of us. Yet it was her bravery that gave us a means to rewrite the future for the next generation."

I stare at him for a long while, processing his words and my reactions. I do have ideals, formed by my experience, my childhood, my friendships, my sense of injustice and my acceptance of individuality. It is hard to dispute a belief system without being hypocritical. Perhaps my quest to eradicate the Script is driven by my own selfish...no, not selfish...my parochial desire to impress my idea of freedom onto a society of people.

I have no doubt that the Script holds too much power. After all, it is just a book. The Script also has its place, as a beacon of hope for most of the angeli. They depend on it to guide them, they revere the word of The Mother, and they look to it for direction. The Script tells them that there is a purpose, a meaning to their lives that goes beyond the moments of exhalation or pain that living entails. I am not fighting against their hope, or their faith, but I do despise the way the Script prevents them from truly living. I am fighting for the choice to live however they choose. I am fighting for a world where devout and atheist can cohabit the planet peacefully, and accept each other has an equally relevant and deserved place in the world. Is it conceivable that Marcus had a good point. The future can be rewritten.

I smile.

"Before the destruction of Sierra," Marcus continues, sensing a change in the atmosphere perhaps, "the world we live in was a much less confusing place. I had goals and ambitions. My destiny was clear to me. The world I saw was a mirror image of my expectations. I did not see what was truly there. I did not see the danger lurking and of that I am most regretful. The night the city was raided, I sat in this very office like I was blinkered."

"You left Sierra when you were seven," I clarify. "How would you have known of a threat?"

"So you know part of my story," Marcus states, surprised. "It is true, that I was only a youngling when I came to Celthia with my father. He was in the Guard. It was torturous to stay in our home after my mother was lost. Training accident," he adds. "I left my youngling friends behind and never looked back. After Sierra, the world I knew changed. The traitors were brought before me. Rennison and his young son were among them." Liam, still standing against Marcus, stiffens as Marcus continues. "I knew Rennison as a child, although he went by an angeli title then. He had always been arrogant."

"He was accused as a traitor," I prompt. "But he didn't get beheaded."

He shakes his head. "He escaped, killing anyone who got in his way, and then disappeared."

The silence descends again. It's frustrating when there is obviously much more to be told. I already know a version of this part, Liam's version. Marcus took him in after his father was killed. I glance at my Adonis. It's impossible to conceive why he'd be abandoned for no reason. "He left Liam here."

Marcus nods. "Rennison had no need to return and risk execution, yet he did." I watch Liam as he speaks, waiting for any reaction. There is none.

I sigh. "You think he placed him here purposefully."

"It was part of his vision of the future." Marcus finally takes a small step back from Liam's intimidating glower. I'm impressed he lasted this long.

A hint of amusement is in my voice when I speak. "Yet you took him in, raised him and gave him power." I'm merely inquisitive, trying to decipher Marcus' motives. Liam, on the other hand, seems offended by my statement. His muscles coil tighter, the tips of his ears turn red and his jaw grinds audibly. "Which he rightly deserves," I clarify.

Marcus smiles, a genuine one that reaches his eyes. "He earned everything I have given and more."

I nod in agreement. I can see that. Liam, stoic in his acceptance of Marcus' praise, asks the question I was considering myself. "And what were you planning to do when Rennison came for me and requested I join him? You never told me the truth of his actions. I idolised him, moulded myself on him as I grew and resented you at every turn. Had August not been here, had I not met my mate, then I may have followed my father willingly when he returned."

Marcus blinks as Liam stuns him with an outburst of real emotion. Liam's feelings, the ones that affect him most deeply, are something he turns inward, keeps to himself and shares only on rare occasion. I'm sure it's not healthy to live that way.

Marcus takes a while to answer, thinking it through with his mouth tightened. "I would not corrupt your ability to make your own decision by tarnishing your memory of your father, turning you further against me."

Something in Liam's posture, in his face, has me moving around the desk and curling my body against his. He responds without hesitation, wrapping me in to his chest with strong arms. He presses a soft kiss to my forehead as I rest my head against his shoulder, in front of my father no less. I grin at the absurdity. Liam feels frustrated. I can sense it through his skin. "And if I hadn't fallen for Aqua, like you'd hoped?"

"I hoped?" Marcus frowns. "Such a plan, with immeasurable variables, would be ludicrous. Aqua was conceived for a purpose, yes, but not in the way you have imagined. I never expected you to have such an intense attraction to my daughter that you would consider her for mating." He steps back another pace, observing us like he's framing a photograph. "A union for which I give my full blessing."

I have to lift my head in order to hear above the contented purr which reverberates through Liam's chest as my father gives us his approval. It's a relief to know that our relationship is not some unethical product of selective breeding, but it doesn't explain what he originally hoped it would achieve.

"Then why?" I ask.

"To infiltrate the dragone royal family and prevent the insurrection of Rennison's army." He wrings his hands as he begins to pace small zig-zags within an invisible box. "At least that was the plan your mother and I agreed upon. It was straightforward, only one major risk that we hoped wouldn't occur."

"Explain it," I urge. "Please, Father."

Liam squeezes me.

Marcus produces a nasal snort at my tone. "You are your mother's daughter. She could also manipulate." His mouth pulls across in a superior sneer. "I requested you address me as your father, you refused until it was of benefit to you. It is a skill that served her well and made her connections. It will do the same for you, no doubt."

"It helps that she is surprisingly likeable," Victus interrupts while tapping his finger against his lips. "Her ability is based on her compassion for others and her understanding of what they require from her. It is admirable and candid. She does not manipulate to court favour, so do not burden her with such notions. She will agonise over it for measures."

"I'd hate to put you through that," I snap back at Victus. Anyway, I was manipulating Marcus purposefully, so the likelihood of me feeling guilty about it is negligible.

"I'll need to sit," Marcus states as he strolls back toward the chair. "Your birth, Aquila, was intended as a pre-emptive counterattack, a means to fight fire with fire. Your mother hailed from the strongest dragone bloodline, which is why Rennison also targeted her."

I think about that for a second. "Axion?"

"You process quickly," Marcus observes.

"You explain slowly."

Marcus shrugs. "Rennison courted favour from powerful females of both species, intent on producing male heirs to facilitate his dominion over all."

Liam growls. I take his hand, interlacing our fingers. "Humans?" I ask.

"Beneath him," Marcus retorts. "Humans are an infestation of vermin in Rennison's world of gods."

I nod, accepting the likelihood. "So you don't think that way?"

"There was a time that I thought exactly the same way. As a young man, I felt the desire for adventure and discovery. I used to walk among the humans, observe them, despise them. The angeli are a regimented, hardworking and loyal species. The humans are a loud and disorganised rabble, always fighting amongst themselves. I studied them for entertainment. The city ran like clockwork well before I came into power. I was privileged to have the freedom to secretly come and go as I pleased."

"How?"

"The same way I met your mother," Marcus answers. "Through the concealed tunnel underneath the city."

Liam stiffens, a multitude of emotions seeping through his skin. I absorb them all automatically. His excretions are dilute, like a drop of cordial in a litre of water, but they are there and I'm attuned to them. I must be. I can feel them like I hear a whisper or scent a fragrance.

"No tunnels exist beneath the city," Liam glowers. "The Guard patrol every cave."

"The Guard patrol past it continuously," Marcus barks back. "I ensured it when I became Overseer, to prevent its existence being discovered by any other young adventurers such as myself." He leans forward against the desk, his arms resting on the surface. "There is a tunnel. After the destruction of Sierra by Rennison's army, I discovered Queen Aschar Jarik, bride of the dragone King, Horen Jarik, waiting inside that tunnel." He relaxes slightly as he recounts the event. "Her marriage had been at the insistence of their elders, arranged because of Aschar's bloodline. We had common ground, had both been kindred spirits, both seeking a release from our claustrophobic existence. When Rennison had come to her, wooed her with romance rather than convention, she had given herself willingly. The king was unaware of her treachery. She convinced him that their son's wings were a product of evolution, a signal that the dragone were awakening long dormant genes. There are winged lizards that exist today, although they lack the capability to sustain flight. In the distant past, their ancestors were more adept."

"But she was manipulating him," I remind us all as we process the possibility.

"A necessity, but her defence was plausible."

It still doesn't make sense. "Why was she under this city?"

"A year after Axion's birth, Rennison came to her again. He had just escaped Celthia, using the tunnel. He was not a resident of Celthia. To this day, I am yet to discover another who knows of its existence. I still do not understand how it was known to him.

"When he reached her, he was gloating and energised by his success. He knew his sons were in their positions. He did not reveal his plan in detail, but Aschar was intelligent. She understood that Rennison had set in motion a desolate future for her child.

"She bade her time, still courting the man she had come to despise, as he hid from the angeli world. When Rennison had finally moved deeper underground, taking his growing forces with him, she followed Rennison's escape route all the way to the base of Celthia, where she waited.

"When I found them, she had the one year old youngling strapped to her chest. She had brought Axion with her in order to prove her association with the traitor. She took a huge risk. Had anyone else have scented them it would have cost their lives. It was fortunate, perhaps fate, that I was a year into my role as Overseer. Guards were patrolling past regularly. However, I alone knew of the tunnel's location and had been entering it regularly, searching for Rennison.

"I listened to her story, saw the child with his scaly wings, and learned that Rennison had withdrawn to Gravinwart with an army. She told me what she knew of his plan and we devised a counteroffensive. We spent many hours in those tunnels, she always brought the boy with her, and her womb gently began to round with your growth. It was a risk. I am an angeli. Rennison is a half-breed. The boy had only a quarter angeli genetics, yet his wings had formed. You were destined to be a half-breed, we laid all our hope in the possibility that your feathers would not develop."

I realise my breathing has increased as I listen to Marcus' version of events. I know he has lied in the past, to cover his actions, yet the credibility of his story affects me more than I expected. It almost seems like he's telling the truth. "I was born with feathers."

Marcus nods. "Feathers as black as tar." He leans back in his chair as he watches me. "Unable to fit within either species. Fate, however, had already interceded against us. Your mother had given birth in secret. The king believed he had fathered the baby. She could not risk him witnessing the event for fear that he would realise something was amiss. It was wise. When she saw you, no matter how beautiful you were, or how perfect you looked to her, she knew she could never convince the king that you were his. She stole you away immediately and brought you and the boy to me. I spent an hour convincing her to return with Axion to the island. She wanted us to run away together, to take Liam and raise him as our own, to protect you all from Rennison's influence. But Rennison's influence was already widespread. He was a formidable opponent when he was simply an angeli Guard. As the commander of an entire dragone army, he would be voracious in his hunt for us. She agreed to return and I never saw her again." His eyes glaze with the memory. He slowly leans forward in his chair.

I lean forward too, enthralled by details of my mother's existence. "You don't know what happened when she got back?" I ask.

"I heard pieces. There were dragone loyal to your mother, her family especially. They provided me any information they could. Rennison was waiting for her, he had been informed of the pregnancy and was curious. Her stomach was still rounded; you were little more than a few hours old. Only Rennison knows how she convinced him to leave Hantiem and take her with him. A few nights later, you awoke with such a deafening scream that it caused your custodian to come running to me in fear. Only I was able to settle you, even then it took me the majority of the night.

"I heard later, from her family, that your mother was dead and they had gone into hiding. There was also word that Horen's men had defeated Rennison during a bid to get his queen back. The story was never substantiated with evidence and I was always sceptical."

I listen, sceptical myself. I really want to believe Marcus' story and that is the only reason I am hesitant to. I don't want to be blinkered to his lies by my desire for a neat and convenient explanation of my childhood.

"What about August?" I ask. He hasn't offered any explanation for abducting my human brother from my unsuspecting mother.

He exhales a breath full of tension. Perhaps he's been waiting for someone to pose the question since my existence was discovered. He must know his lie was revealed as soon as I was. He also knows August's mother is here in the city. His voice is firm when he answers, again it rings with truth. I hate that I can't get a good reading on him, whether it's me or him that's hampering it is uncertain.

"I was travelling under the cover of darkness," Marcus explains, "having just rendezvoused with a dragone informant, when I heard the human's screams. I was inquisitive. With dragone in the area, I wanted to ensure the human had not stumbled upon one of the Fallen's spies. They were still proving themselves to be a threat, with or without Rennison at their head. I had not witnessed a birth before. It was...unpleasant...and the baby was very small. I thought him to be dead at first, but then he wriggled in my arms. The woman kept screaming at me, of course my wings had been exposed when I entered her home which may have caused that. When she asked me if I had come to take him, it gave me an idea. The child was too premature to survive without medical attention. I knew we could save him and perhaps the human could be a playmate for you, as well as a means of warming Liam to the idea of siblings. He was quite a troublesome child, always angry. I had no idea how he would react. So I brought Augustus back to the Medics and they helped him to grow stronger. Liam surprised us all by bonding immediately with the boy and so we named him as family."

"But you didn't keep me." It was meant to be a question, but for whatever reason it comes out as an accusation. I choose to listen to Marcus' response rather than examining the cause.

"Liam was incredibly gentle with August. You were not a fragile human. Your strength, even then, could have resulted in broken bones had you been allowed to interact with a human infant. You had spent an hour with the, then, two-year old Axion after your birth. That short time had involved you playfully grabbing at his fingers and reaching for his wings. You were far more advanced than the human. The dark did not hinder you. Your scent held a note of spice. I realised I could not risk raising you among the angeli, when the differences were so abundant. You were not the first of your kind, but you were the first, I know of, with your colouring. The decision to return you to August's mother seemed like the best solution. I could warn her of your strength and abilities without informing her of your true origin. I knew you would be safe. You could have a chance at a happy childhood." He swallows. Damn it, I really want to believe him. "Rennison, if he was alive, would never search the human territories for you."

"You really had no idea?" I ask Victus, who has been listening as entranced as me. He shakes his head in answer.

Marcus looks slightly contrite as he eyes first Victus and then me. "Only your custodian here knew of your existence. She gave me her solemn promise to maintain the secret."

"My custodian. Is she still here?"

"I believe you've been acquainted for some time. Her name is Gloria."

"Of course it is," I grumble. She couldn't have told me all of this?

"She is a female of her word," Marcus responds, like he heard my silent remark.

"So where've you been all this time?" I ask my father eventually.

Could his story be genuine? His version matches up with the parts that I have discovered on my own. I need to do some fact checking, talk to Axion and see what he remembers, if he remembers anything. I know he said he didn't, but he soon spoke of a princess after his father mentioned the pregnancy. And Gloria, the treacherous wench, has been a good friend while I've been here. Perhaps she will be willing to corroborate Marcus' explanation.

"I asked Victus to cover for me and went in search of information. My informants have been disappearing. Those who I could find were scared to talk to me, but I realised you were no longer safe. I sent Victus instructions to find you and keep you from harm. I have been scouring the globe ever since, seeking out remote human colonisations in the guise of a human businessman. It has taken me a long time, but I eventually found your grandparents and aunt, living among humans in the Amazon jungle."

"Oh."

"They have maintained limited contact with their own species, but were happy to see me. They had heard that the Fallen had begun their uprising and innocent dragone were being slaughtered or forced into hiding. With your confirmation that Rennison is alive, and the three of you residing within the same city, Celthia is no longer safe. Rennison could lead his army through the tunnel without notice. Victus sent for me immediately."

"Lucas?" I ask.

"Of course."

"So he knew?" That would hurt more than I can comprehend.

Marcus shakes his head. "No. He is very angry with us."

I don't think Marcus is including me and Liam in that sentence. Victus looks remorseful about the whole situation.

"Where is he?" He's normally by my side in situations like these.

Marcus shrugs. "The human you adopted requested to be returned home. Lucas volunteered for the duty."

"Please tell me you don't mean Aaron." My face pales with realisation. Aaron *was* actually saying goodbye when he walked me to the hangar door last night.

"He was quite adamant," Victus confirms softly. "He gave us his oath of death, should he discuss our existence with anyone."

"I'm not worried about his loyalty," I clarify in a screech. "I'm worried about his safety! The Fallen know where I live. They've already spilt his blood once."

"He is well aware of that. Yet, he chose to leave and he requested that you do not follow. He asked for time alone before you return your mother to her abode. You are able to give him that, are you not?"

It sounded like a challenge. "Of course I am, Victus, but I planned to do it after the war."

"You speak of the war like it's a singular event that will end all of your troubles in one instance." Marcus sits back again, shuffling in his seat. "I have been fighting in a war my entire existence, as have the angeli before me, and we are still not safe. In fact, with the three of you here, this is the most unsafe place Aaron could be."

He's right. I sigh, "Rennison took four of my men last night."

"I am aware. It is probable that he already knows where you are. By chance alone, your existence has led to his sons meeting without his manipulative control. The original plan may have failed, but you have attained your destined purpose. His sons are against him. I'm convinced he won't rest until your blood is on his hands, followed by mine. This is a personal debt which he will want me to pay."

"He has your scent," Liam adds as he emerges, exhausted, from his data processing marathon. He's never been silent for so long.

I stretch my wings as I relieve them from the tension of standing here for what feels like a century. "I don't think that matters now. Rennison was always going to come here, either for you or with you, to wipe out his only worthy adversaries. And I think we should be ready to meet him."

"No," Liam bites back. "You will not be anywhere near this city when they attack." He starts pacing as he cultivates a strategy. "The city will require evacuating immediately. Marcus, we'll need to know the location of the tunnel. We should send messengers to every city and warn them of the increased danger..."

He stops talking, sensing the lack of responsiveness. His eyes roam his small audience expectantly. I shake my head when they land on me, causing him to scowl in frustration.

"I'm not hiding," I state resolutely. "Too much is at risk. Too many people could get hurt. I want to finish this. I want to try." With every determined word I utter, Liam grows more furious.

"I will not allow it!" He storms around the room like he's swatting invisible hornets. "Your request to face Rennison is denied. You will be deployed with the refugees to the closest city, where you will remain, under the protection of angeli Guard until this situation is resolved."

"I am an angeli Guard!" I don't need dragone blood to sense how he's feeling. He's completely unreasonable when he's like this. It isn't worth the energy it would take to argue. "I respectfully refuse your request, my love, to run away like a coward while men die in my place. You wanted me to behave like an angeli, well here I am." I glare right back at him, not raising my voice above speaking volume. I feel amazingly calm. I'm sure that this is the right thing to do. My mind is made up. "Where is the tunnel, Marcus?"

I don't turn my head from Liam as Marcus answers. His voice rings with something warm beneath the surface. "Beneath the mountain, beside the underground river, you won't find it hastily unless you are shown."

"Then show me, now, while Liam organises the Guard."

"No," Liam counters abruptly. "We go together or you don't go."

"We go together then. He's coming for us both, after all. Perhaps together we can prevent more bloodshed." I lean into him, inhaling his natural scent like it's exclusive cologne. Everything about Liam is exclusive. All except one thing and we can fix that together. "There's something I want to do first."

Liam waits.

"Marcus?" I inquire, he's watching me intently.

"Father," Marcus corrects me.

"Marcus." I turn my head toward him emphatically. "I need Victus to perform a quick ceremony before we leave. If that's okay with my mate of course."

Sorry, mother. We're not even going to make it to this afternoon.

# · Seventeen ·

I'd thought I'd feel nervous or uncertain about committing the rest of my existence to one being. To acknowledge that I love someone so intensely, that I will never need anyone except for him. I'd thought I wanted a human wedding, with a get out clause.

It turns out I was wrong.

Before Liam agreed, although I know he had absolutely no intention of saying no, he asked me, *'Why now?'*

Perhaps he was concerned that this was another impulse decision. He was wrong. I want to face the rest of our lives together, and I have no idea how long our lives might be. I want this bond. He wants this bond. Why shouldn't it be from this moment on? We might not get another chance.

Marcus was not impressed that I demanded Victus perform the ceremony. I wouldn't back down. Victus is the only Overseer of Celthia that I have a shred of respect for. As he stands before us, I find it impossible to imagine any moment more perfect. With Marcus as our witness, in his rumpled corporate attire, Liam takes my hands and encases them within his own. I could have sent for my mother and brothers, they may hold a grudge that I didn't, but vows can be renewed. It's not like we're going to be locking ourselves away after this for our mating moons. Technically, we're still on duty. This ceremony is for us, no one else.

Liam's practically radiating an effervescent glow. His incredible caramel eyes are sparkling like polished topaz and his leather clad chest is inflated with masculine authority. My eyes are focused on his face, his warm and beautiful features, and his lips as he whispers his vows to me in a way that masks how impromptu our nuptials actually are. It makes my heart soar to realise how much thought he must have put into his words, in a time when neither of us was certain if this is the choice I would make.

"On my death, to you I swear. My heart is forever yours, Aquila Raven. Our bonding joins us together as one, equal parts of a single entity. I vow to value and appreciate your independence and impulsiveness, share our responsibilities equally, and provide my own dry towels. I give my life to you. I'd give my life for you. I will spend the rest of my days attempting to match the honour you have bestowed on me in this moment."

Liam's husky speech has my whole body fluttering, from my fingertips to the soles of my feet with the release of heavyweight endorphins. These are the kind of feelings that encode themselves to the memory of the moment, the kind I'll feel again and again whenever I picture this instant. Right here, right now, when love seems eternal and life suddenly has meaning.

My words are not so eloquent. I cannot hold back the emotion. It turns my words into fragments truncated by breath hitching tears, but I think I get my point across.

"I accept your oath and give you mine. On my death I vow to you, Liam of Marcus, to love you past my final breath. All that I am, all that I have, I share with you equally. You have given me the world. You asked me 'why now?' The answer is simple. We are stronger together. Like an alloy, you galvanise me. Whether we get a day, a year or a hundred years together, I will never regret a moment of our bond. I love you and I am in love with you. Always."

His eyes stare into mine in wonder, intently, lovingly, before he leans forward.

Our vow is sealed with a kiss, a kiss which is interrupted by Lucas as he storms into the room. For once he doesn't seem to read the situation immediately. "Your brothers are pacing the corridor."

I unwillingly extricate myself from Liam's embrace. "Which brothers?"

Lucas seems to cool down as he assesses the atmosphere, his brow raised. "All of them."

"Wait." Liam stops me with his arms as he presses another, longer, deeper and far more inappropriate kiss to my lips. "Now you may go."

And just like that our ceremony is over and we're back to work.

I indicate that I want Lucas to follow me as I head for the door. I also glance briefly at Victus. He's standing behind the desk, a pen still in his hand after cataloguing our mating in the city's record. Victus keeps meticulous archives.

When he catches me looking, he shifts his stance slightly. His head dips, just the smallest fraction, so that I follow his line of sight to the desk. It's a brief exchange, interrupted by Marcus calling Plyrian in as Lucas opens the door, and it leaves me pondering what he was trying to tell me.

"Are you alright?" Lucas wraps his arm around my shoulder as we pass Plyrian. My brothers, even Brue, are indeed pacing the hallway. Axion's jaw has bloomed with green bruising. The swelling seems to have gone. Angeli medicine really is more effective on the dragone. It's ironic. Lucas pulls the library door closed, as August attempts to bounce past us. "What did I just walk in on, Aqua? It looked like..." He gives me a pertinent look. August is swearing at him but he doesn't seem to notice.

"It was." I grab Lucas and a confused Axion as I take off in a jog along the corridor. Brue follows immediately. August dithers in front of the door before following as well.

"What's going on?" Axion asks as we reach the spiral stairs and I lead us all down. His speech is still hampered, but it's clearer than a few hours ago. God, we really do need more time to rest. Two hours of sleep in twenty-four hours should not be the norm, yet my life seems to consist of running, fighting and hoping I'll get something to eat before the next crisis.

I inhale the smell coming from the Grand Hall and my stomach rumbles. "Humour me for a second. I need to go to my room."

We stop descending when we reach the residential floor and they follow me, a panting August included, to my room. The wing is relatively quiet. Most of the city is likely either at breakfast or have had a whiff of

Marcus, and have followed the Guard's instructions to congregate in the harbour. I need to get the journal. It's the only thing I can think of that Victus may have been indicating to. I could be completely off base, but at least this is somewhere private to talk to my brothers.

I hid the book at the back of the dresser. Not very inventive, but I was in a rush at the time. I pull out the small leather bound journal while August collapses on the bed and Brue attempts to look around me curiously. Lucas and Axion stand by the door, their expressions bemused.

"Victus was trying to tell me something," I mumble as I flick through the pages. "I trust you four more than anybody else, other than my mate. I think there's something important in here. I've been thinking about what Marcus just told me."

August sits up when he hears his father's name, still gasping as he recovers from our run here.

"He said Rennison escaped Celthia through a secret tunnel. Except Rennison was from Sierra, so he must have been told about it by someone else. Someone from here. Victus didn't know about it and neither did Liam."

"What tunnel?" Lucas and August say in unison.

Brue and Axion ask, "Where?"

"Good question," I answer as I thumb through the pages, looking for anything that could suggest an ally from here. "I think this journal belonged to Rennison. Why else would Victus have hidden it in his secret drawer?"

"His where?" Lucas asks impatiently.

"In his desk. Axion found it. It looked important."

"I wondered what you did with it," Axion acknowledges.

I keep thumbing through, looking for anything that seems significant. "This all happened nineteen years ago. It must be someone older than you, Lucas, perhaps someone in the Guard? Rennison was a respected colleague, even after everyone thought he was beheaded. Only the dragone knew who was leading the Fallen. When Axion confirmed he was still alive, Victus freaked and called Marcus back." I glance at Lucas and then back to the journal. It's full of sanctimonious claptrap and narcissistic drivel. "How much do you know?"

"Nothing of what you just mentioned," Lucas snarls. His reaction draws my gaze to him. He really is pissed. His eyes flash an icy blue.

"I spoke to Clyst," Axion adds. "The Guard, Rhyan, let me in."

I nod. "What did you learn?"

"Clyst is a fool, but I knew that anyway. Rennison promised him power in exchange for your capture. He said Rennison is poised to wipe out anyone standing in his way. He implied there's something important that we don't know. He said we're ants, scurrying around in our ant farm while the Gods watch and laugh. We're predictable and easily manipulated, apparently."

I don't doubt it. I've felt like a pawn since I first got here. "He told you willingly?"

I'm scanning Rennison's diary for anything that could be useful. There's a lot of mention of the winter but not any indication of his plan. Liam has never mentioned his birth name and I've neglected to ask, but Tylis is also mentioned regularly.

Axion snorts. "He was rather chatty, probably because of the pain medication he was given to stop all the screaming. Your brother broke more than his arm."

"My mate," I correct him.

"What happened in that library?" Axion asks, bewildered. "It was like watching a soap opera with no sound and no picture."

"That sounds difficult," I chuckle. Nothing. Nothing. Nothing. I flip the page and keep going.

"It was exhausting."

Still nothing. "Marcus confirmed that I'm your sister. He said he encountered you as a child, our mother used to bring you when they met." I'm preoccupied by my reading but I sense him harden. "We've met before as well, after I was born. Perhaps part of you remembered me."

His next words are forced through his already rigid jaw. "Is he my father?"

I pull my head up, placing my finger on the page to reference my place. I've finally found an interesting paragraph. Axion looks nervous. Brue looks furious. It occurs to me then that Brue is the only biological heir to the Jarik throne. "No, he's not. You were already one when he met Aschar."

Axion seems to sense there's more but he doesn't question me. I turn back to the page, engrossed in the passage I've found.

'*Two sons have ascended, yet there is an essence of concern growing. I know I have chosen well. My future is assured by my closest, unseen within their walls. When they act, we shall act, and that crown shall sit atop my head. Deserved are the loyal, honourable is the fight. My war shall fuel the new era, produce a generation of Gods among mortals – superiority and power, born of the strongest and unified by blood. My brother has warned me of a threat brewing, a plot to usurp my throne. The suspects are few. Who would dare?!*'

I read the passage twice while a gentle drum of conversation creates white noise around me. There has been no mention of an 'us' in any of the other pages I've scanned. "Does Rennison have a brother?"

August has never heard of Rennison before now. Lucas shakes his head, unsure. Axion and Brue glance at each other before shaking their heads. "No one has ever mentioned a brother," Axion says. "Why?"

"It says here that his brother informed him of a plot against him." I flick through the remaining pages. There is more talk of spies and gossip but no other mention of a brother, and then the entries stop. I don't know how Victus got hold of it but I guess it was removed from Rennison's possession at some point. "I don't understand."

"Perhaps he uses the term loosely, as you do," Lucas suggests with a hint of irony. "The Guard refer to each other as brother also."

"You think? I don't know. There's no other mention of 'brother' anywhere else." I give up, my stomach interrupting my thoughts with a fresh protest. I hand the book to Lucas. "Maybe you can figure it out."

August is on his feet, recovered from his respiratory attack and ready to rush back to the library. He's probably regretting his decision to follow us at all. I grab his hand and tug him with me as I head from the room and toward the delicious aroma spilling from breakfast.

"Marcus is an arrogant twit, August. Don't rush to him after everything he's put us both through."

"It wasn't his fault they took him. I said he was smart didn't I! Did he tell you how he got away?" August is leaping along, tugging on my arm like a skittish colt. I direct him to the Grand Hall, Brue and Axion following. Lucas must have stayed in my room, he isn't behind us.

"They didn't have him, he was busy interfering with our lives some more, somewhere in the Amazon apparently." I head straight to the food and stay there, eating one handed while August fidgets impatiently. "Relax. Marcus is showing us the... you know... in a minute. If you're with me than he'll have to see you."

"Why wouldn't he want to see me?" August sounds flabbergasted and a little hurt.

"That's not what I said." I give him an apologetic smile. "It's just that he mentioned us being short on time."

"You still don't like him," August mutters indignantly. I huff and am considering a diplomatic response when we're interrupted by Oberon. August's attention switches to him. "My father's back. Aqua is being obtuse."

Oberon smiles at him adoringly. "My uncle said you would be impatient. He said you can meet with him in the library if you go now."

August gloats at me before following Oberon. I let him go.

"What's the plan?" Axion mumbles. "I take it Marcus wasn't what you'd hoped."

"He was exactly what I'd expected." I have quenched the bite of hunger enough to have the inclination to use a plate now. I start loading one for me and another for Liam. "I think I believe him though."

He drops his voice. "So you're going to the tunnel?"

"Yes." I look around, checking for nearby ears. "Can you track me with our bond? Don't follow underground. If anything happens, run the surface, use our bond. You're faster than the angeli. I think there's a traitor here.

Whoever it is has kept themselves hidden for years. It could be anyone. I trust Lucas and Liam, anyone else could be dangerous."

"What should we do?"

"Stay alive. Please be careful, Ax. I'm going after Rennison. You stay in the shadows for as long as you can. We need to end this." We take a table in the corner. Brue stays at the buffet, carbo-loading. The room seems to be filling rapidly. Perhaps the harbour got too crowded. A buzz of conversation is developing around us. "Keep Brue safe."

"I'm not a magician." Axion fiddles with his impaired jaw as he thinks. "I trust the sailors. They want revenge for Old Salt and the others. We'll all run the surface, Brue included. It's the only way."

"The only way he won't follow me on his own," I deduce.

Axion nods. "He can locate you as well." His voice lowers further. "Tell me, is Marcus my father?"

I find his hand under the table and interlace our fingers. My head shakes slowly. "He said no, Ax." I take a deep breath.

"Then who?"

I pinch my eyes closed and rub my eyelids. When I open them again, he's staring at me in horror.

"Please tell me it isn't true," Axion breathes, his face pale.

"R.J. sought out dragone and angeli females from strong bloodlines." I squeeze his fingers tightly. "You and Liam are the result."

"I told you not to tell me."

I pull my hand away. It's strange, how often we end up connected like that. It's definitely instinct. Perhaps it's evolution's way of keeping bonds strong? I should ask if he often feels the need to hold Brue's hand. But I don't. Instead I say, "I know, but sometimes you need to hear things you don't like."

He locks his gaze on mine, assessing I suppose, and then nods. "Okay, Princess. Explain it. Who is really related to who?"

My first instinct is to laugh. It seems like such an odd question. Except, he's right, and voicing it may make it easier to handle. "You ready?" I ask and he nods. "Okay. Our mother was Aschar so we're half-siblings. My father is Marcus. I'm his only biological offspring. I'm not related by blood to Liam, at all." I keep feeling the need to emphasise that but Axion just smirks so I continue. "Liam is your half-brother. You have the same father. R.J." I stop when Axion closes his eyes. "You okay?"

"Yeah," he answers, unconvincingly. His eyes open slowly, like a sunrise revealing twin burning yellow orbs. "What about Liam's mother?"

I rub my temple again, out of habit. "She was an angeli, from Sierra. His mother and sister were both killed by the Fallen when he was a boy." I drop my elbows to the table and cross my arms. "Brue, well Brue is the son of Horen Jarik, which makes him our distant cousin, not a brother. August is the son of Libby and Clarence, human, not biologically related to any of us. But Libby's the only parent I've ever known, she'll always be my mother." I finally feel brave enough to make eye contact. "Does that make sense?"

He blinks once, slowly, like he's just waking and reality feels off. Then he nods and drops his gaze back to his plate.

We eat in silence after that.

Our plates are almost empty when Liam walks over. He stands beside the table watching us apprehensively, for him at least. I push the plate I filled toward him, my brow raised in offering. After a beat he lowers himself onto the stool beside me, giving us a speculative glance before he delves in to the food. Liam knows Axion is his brother. I think he's handling it well, all things considered. I watch him, admiring my mate like he's a priceless piece of art.

"Marcus wants to address the city before we go," Liam states.

"I think he should meet us there," I counter. "If the chance of the Fallen making a dramatic entrance is as likely as he implied, then it makes sense for us to be ready."

He glances at Axion, addressing him in a semi-friendly tone. "What are your orders?"

Axion answers tersely. "Keep Brue out of trouble."

"The hardest task imaginable," Liam acknowledges.

"Okay," I interrupt, standing quickly. "Let's go, it's getting cramped in here."

Liam has cleared his plate. His metabolism could be a source of envy, if I live long enough to relax and grow fat on my content.

"I think I'll stay and get a look at your dad," Axion suggests. He points at Brue, who is creeping subtly toward a table of Guard, to eavesdrop I imagine. "And keep an eye on him."

"Be careful," I reply. "See you later."

He flicks his eyes to mine briefly, agreeing. "Same to you, Princess."

"Plyrian wants to accompany us," Liam informs me as we push through the crowd to the veranda. The ledge, accessible through the bus-sized hole in the mountain wall, is also beginning to fill with people. "He wants to discuss the information they have learned from the prisoner."

"Which is?"

"Not much apparently. Victus interrogated him but he claimed not to know anything."

We reach the edge of the drop off, the space still relatively empty. There is a breeze blowing, whipping our hair around our heads. Liam stretches out his wings, preparing to leap.

"Really? He knew nothing?" I know that's not true, obviously.

"That's what Plyrian informed me. However, Marcus was there, perhaps there is more he wanted to say. Here," he points at the winged figure gliding on the breeze across the range, "we can ask him."

We jump together.

Plyrian joins us in the air and falls into formation as we follow the mountain trail to the cave. With Marcus indisposed, Liam leads the way. We don't know its exact location, but at least if Rennison emerges from the tunnel we'll be there to greet him.

The cave entrance is unguarded. I know from previous experience that it doesn't mean there aren't Guard somewhere on the range with eyes on it. There will also be a patrol inside, stationed at intervals along the cave wall and at the underground river. Their positions during the youngling trials were not random. They know the geography of this terrain like they know the city. It is their job to know.

Liam leads us in, undeterred by the sudden loss of light. I must ask him if his dragone DNA has given him an advantage in the dark all of these years. Of course, he was unaware that he was any different to his colleagues, until recently, so perhaps the advantage is minimal. Plus, he always uses candles in the city.

We move quickly, passing stalagmites and ducking around stalactites as we gust through the damp shaft toward the audible roar of the river. It sounds furious today. I realise the level must rise and fall depending on the season, although I'm yet to lay eyes on it. The water is so cold that it must foster ice for part of the year. It's not exactly tropical here, and we're in December, but it's warm enough for moist dirt around our feet.

My new mate leads us further into the gloom, passing the Guard stationed along the route. Beyond the point Lielan, Theon and I found the fake casualty during my youngling trials, deeper into the earth, until the roar is deafening and our faces are moist with spray. The patrol on duty stand to attention as we arrive, greeting us all with respectful shallow bows. While Liam confers with the senior on duty I ponder the location of the tunnel. Marcus said he'd be here as soon as he could be. But, surely if he could find it, then we can, too.

I inch closer to the flow of water. The sound of it from further up the tunnel was misleading. The river is obviously moving fast, but the noise must be amplified by the cave acoustics. There are uneven rocks and fallen boulders, interfering with the river's steady progress. More water cascades down through the rock of the ceiling in several places, but apart from the occasional drum of subsidiary inlets the river is mainly a smooth flowing, singular body – like a crystal snake whose body is infinite.

I follow its course with my eyes, then my feet. I wander along the edge in the places I can, then turn back when the way becomes impassable. The entrance is somewhere along the route of the patrol, a hundred metre stretch. I make my way slowly back toward the group. Plyrian, who had followed me silently, turns with me and walks slightly ahead. I ignore his presence as I search the rock walls on both sides. There are no visible crevices other than the ones spewing fresh water. There is no change in the air quality, temperature or flow. There is no evidence of a tunnel of any sort, other than the one we're walking in.

"Where is it then?" I ask the ether.

Plyrian turns his head, drawing my attention to him. I've stopped walking to stare at the water as it competes against itself in a race instigated by gravity. It must be fun, to be water, avoiding resistance and continually taking the easiest course. Not having to decide which way to turn, just turning because it's the best route.

Plyrian moves to stand beside me, as I stare past the turbulent surface into the black of deep liquid. The tunnel is devoid of light, my night vision prevents it being a problem, yet Plyrian seems equally comfortable. The angeli Guard do not let themselves succumb to the disability of blindness. They use all of their senses all of the time. He turns his head in my direction, dropping his voice to a whisper that would be lost above the noise, if I took more than a step back.

"Where the water changes in pitch, look down and behind, you need to get wet. Not a problem for someone dark and deadly." He turns and continues along the path like he hadn't spoken. I watch him leave, my heart constricting with every step.

Plyrian knows.

He doesn't look back and I don't follow.

Could Marcus have been wrong? Of course he could. It's likely that the tunnel's existence isn't confidential. Rennison had known, after all. The Guard are here constantly. Perhaps Plyrian found it himself, or Marcus told him how to find it today. Perhaps the whole damn city uses it to sneak out.

I turn back toward the impassable end of the trail. With Plyrian's relaxed, yet slightly disturbing, exit I can only assume I had passed it before he revealed what he knew. I close my eyes as I walk, attempting to transport myself into the angeli's world. He said the water changes in pitch at the location. I guess a tunnel could cause that. I take every step with care, one foot in front of the other, silently. I reach the end, sensing the sheer drop that ends the path. I listen intensely, hoping and petrified that I'll hear a change. I don't.

Turning back, I follow the route at the same slow pace. My cross-bred ears are less sensitive than the angeli. On impulse, I drop to my hands and knees and crawl along the slimy rock with my sense trained on the rhythm of the river. It becomes a song, a lullaby as I process. It's a peaceful melody, a total contrast to the swiftness and forcefulness of the orchestra creating it, but there is definitely a bum note there. I stop and take one shuffle in reverse.

My body leans over the edge of the path as I listen. I keep going, bending at the waist and submerging my head, like an ungraceful swan feeding below the surface. Down and behind, with eyes open and body inverted, a crevice full of water is obscured by an overhang of rock. Well, I'm already wet. I slide in, head first, and use my strength to pull my body through the narrow passage. It's claustrophobic. I shimmy myself between protruding walls, inhaling the water because I neglected to take a large enough breath before doing this. Can this be right? I can't imagine Marcus doing this.

The passage is relatively short and I'm relieved when I finally emerge through the other side. It feels like I just experienced my own birth, for a second time, with a more developed consciousness. My head breaks the surface and I find myself in a small cavern. The water is calm in here, unaffected by the tumbling flow of the river on the other side. I expel the water from my lungs, controlling it as well as I can, and inhale the stale air. Water obscures scents, when you're beneath it. But when you're wet, and standing on a shelf a foot above someone's head, your scent smells like it's the only smell that ever existed.

I smell trouble.

"Finally," Rennison exclaims. He glares down at me, a bow in his hands. "I was beginning to get impatient."

I blink as I observe him, stunned into cerebral lock-down. I barely remember to breathe. Rennison Jarik. I know because of his scent. Most disturbingly, I know because he's Liam's father. It's scarily obvious. They have the same complexion, the same stature, the same features, except Rennison's aged face is drawn into a permanent sneer. He has a deep scar that runs from his bottom lip to his left ear. It looks like it must have hurt, and healed without the assistance of angeli Medics.

He narrows his eyes when he sees me staring. His bow drifts up, until his face is obscured and I'm staring down the length of an arrow. I take the hint and drop my eyes. He's wearing black jeans and a leather jacket, left open over his bare chest. His feet are clad in thick soled boots, the kind that add a lot of weight to a swift kick. He's drenched, like he's been jumping in and out of this water in his impatience. I snap out of my stupor.

"Looks like you've been impatient for a while," I answer as I swim to the edge, leaving as much distance between us as possible, and pull myself onto the dry rock floor. I'm not stupid enough to attack him here. His strength would force the arrow through my body and out the other side from this distance. When I'm safely sitting on the shelf I add, "You needn't have waited."

He steps slowly toward me, bow steady, foot over foot. I keep my eyes on his feet. "Be glad I waited, you'd find the alternative less favourable."

He stops with one pace between us and, although I'm trying to prevent it, my heart rate takes off like a sonic jet. Rennison is a far more imposing figure than King Horen. His muscles are like boulders beneath his skin. His wings are immense. I don't like him, at all. This was probably a really bad idea, the worst I've ever had, and I didn't think twice about it.

"You're alone?"

I nod. How long until Liam realises I've disappeared? Plyrian will know where I've gone, but will he know I'm in trouble?

"Up," Rennison orders. "Our company will be along shortly."

"You organised a party?" I scramble to my feet, my haste giving me away. He laughs at my false bravado.

"That way." He points to a narrow hole in the wall and then puts his boot into my back when I turn. Ouch. "Let's speed this up a little."

I start walking. In truth, I'd rather be out of this tunnel when Liam catches up with us anyway. Unfortunately, my motor skills seem impaired. I'm not sure what it is about Rennison Jarik that has me trembling like a civilian. My feet seem to find every uneven purchase, despite my eyes being too wide. I can tell my pace is infuriating him. I don't think he's afraid of what's behind us; it's more like he's eager to get wherever we're going. Our tempo morphs from scuffling walk, to untidy jog, to bumbling run and he's still breathing down my neck. I don't think I could outrun him in a full sprint, even if I could control my limbs.

The narrow passageway opens up into caverns in some places and shrinks to hobbit's holes in others. We squeeze through the gaps at speed, me scraping my skin on the rocks like they're cheese graters. At intersections Rennison barks an order and I turn. It's pretty simple. The air is getting hotter, the pressure more imposing. There's been a slight decline in gradient since the last few turns. We're sinking into the earth slowly.

Rennison orders me to turn right and I stumble with confusion. There isn't a turn, only a crevice. His boot finds my leg.

"Stop kicking me!" I blurt. I even consider returning the favour, but he's still armed.

"Turn. Right," he repeats.

I stare at the small hole. "In there?" It smells like a spice oven. Aromatic heat is pumping out through the gap. There are a lot of dragone in there somewhere.

He kicks me again.

"Okay, Jesus." I climb in, feet first. Forgive me if I don't want to shove my head in a furnace that may have armed guards.

Rennison chuckles darkly and pushes me down. Down is exactly how I'd describe it. The floor disappears and I fall, no, I slide against a smooth worn surface toward the centre of the earth. I hit the floor hard, when I reach the bottom, rolling to the side as Rennison's boots land solidly beside me. He must be in his late forties but you'd never guess it. He's exuding energy and strength. He reaches down and easily lifts me to my feet before pushing me onward again.

I move at a hesitant pace toward the source of the smell. Rennison doesn't push me, but the toes of his boots scrape my ankles every few paces. I grit my teeth and pretend it doesn't hurt. Sweat is dripping from my brow and my leather uniform is beginning to creak with the heat. My wings waft gently in response to the temperature, attempting to cool by blowing the hot air around me. My lungs could be on fire and I wouldn't know until the flames shoot from my mouth. I like the heat, don't get me wrong, but this isn't heat: it's an inferno. It makes me irritable. My irritation starts to overwhelm the quaking fear. I feel livid.

"Keep moving," Rennison snaps.

"What's the rush?"

He doesn't answer.

"No really? Why come and get me yourself if your time is so precious?" I practically spit at my own feet as I force myself to stay calm.

His boot scrapes the back of my ankle again.

"Goddamn it." I stop and spin, and find myself looking down the length of the knife he has in his hand, his bow is now on his back. I didn't hear him switch weapons. I glare past the blade at the older, less attractive version of Liam. "What do you want from me?"

He prods me in the shoulder with the point, not breaking the skin. "Contrary to popular opinion, the world does not revolve around the illicit spawn of the amazing Marcus and that tramp queen."

I stand my ground. "Hit a nerve?"

He presses the blade in deeper, drawing a fine line of blood. "Don't tempt me."

I shrink back, but at least I attempt to hide how much he frightens me. I growl, "Why am I here then?"

He sneers in response, and it is the most terrifying thing I have ever seen. How did someone so twisted father two rational and considerate offspring?

Rennison points me onward, looking more vicious by the second. I turn unwillingly. I'd rather be able to see him at all times. It would be nice to have at least a semblance of a chance of surviving this. I truly am a terrible mate. Liam and I have been officially unified for less than a day, and already I'm trudging toward Hell with my maniacal father-in-law while Liam is god-knows-where.

My shoulders droop and my wings cease their pointless flapping. It is too hot for water here. Instead, vents of steam break through the rock and scold anything too close. The air is thick with it, like a Swedish sauna. We push through the swirling cloudy screen until the terrain changes. The smell is overpowering. Too many bodies, most of them alive but I can't be certain, must be sweating and festering nearby. The tunnel begins to open up, become unified.

The natural rock has been worked, formed into parallel walls. It is nothing like Celthia or Hantiem. It is dark black rock, rough and irregular. There is no door, the cavity simply opens up into another cavern. It's an outpost of sorts. The putrid stench in the cavern smells of spicy meat, well past its expiration, and stale ammonia. Dragone, armed and shielded, are lounging around the space. Rennison doesn't acknowledge them. He simply kicks out at the closest figure and gestures behind us. I assume they'll patrol the tunnels, waiting for anyone who follows.

I exhale a breath, reluctant to take another. Breathing through my nose is torturous, breathing through my mouth is unimaginable. The smell brings tears to my eyes as I fill my lungs with unhygienic airborne bacteria. I'm so going to be ill if I survive this, and I'm never ill.

We move deeper into the underworld. I assume this is Gravinwart. The network of small caverns is full of beings, most are dragone but not all, and there are children with wings. Most are membrane, like Axion's, but a few have feathers. They must be cross-breeds, I can't imagine a pure angeli surviving for any period of time in this stifling and oppressive temperature.

I see my first dead body as we cross an area packed with people. These aren't Fallen soldiers, they seem to be chained in place or to each other. Civilian prisoners or traitors, emaciated to the point of being skeletons, caked in excrement. An overwhelming number of feathers litter the floor beneath them – unique feathers that could only have come from one species. The depravity is sickening. Without knowing their crimes, if they actually committed any, I can be certain they were not sufficient to warrant this. Their eyes follow me as I pass, the ones that can still control their eyes.

We keep moving. Rennison holds my arm and pulls me along. His touch sends warning signals through my entire body. I try to calm it down but he's pumping me with his own crazy chemicals. I hear his dark rumble of laughter. My squirming is giving him some kind of perverse pleasure, yet I can't seem to stop.

"I believe you know these three." Rennison chuckles as we enter the largest cavern yet. Inside, three dragone sit propped against each other like a living tepee. They are tied together, but they look too weak to consider moving anyway. Their eyes open and close sporadically. Their lips are dried and cracked. Their breathing is laboured.

My eyes linger on them, both relieved and anxious. Tarcus is missing.

Rennison pulls me on, toward an ornate wrought iron throne on a dais. He finally releases my arm and strides toward it. While his back is turned, I rip my water pouch from my belt and toss it at Reuben's feet. It flops on the floor with a slosh of liquid. I turn myself back toward Rennison and his pompous chair before Reuben reacts.

Rennison is leant against the arm of it, his legs crossed nonchalantly. His scornful expression is masked slightly by the scar. "They'll just suffer longer," he comments.

I don't have an answer. Perhaps he's right.

He laughs. "You think you can save them?"

"Why are they here?" The cavern is practically empty. He's obviously staged this. I have no idea why. How could he have known I'd be here? "What am I doing here?"

"You want an explanation?" He pushes away from the chair and ambles around it.

"Yes." How many times do I need to ask?

He runs his long finger along the metalwork contemplatively. He's considering my request like he's choosing a movie rental. He finally purses his lips and snaps his eyes to mine.

"Tell me. If you have more of your mother in you, which I suspect you do, then you must have some rather explicit views on my actions. It appears we have time. Amuse me."

Views? I need to know why he's doing this before I can form any opinion, other than the fact that he's a lunatic. I inspect our surroundings while we're *waiting*. There's no light source but I don't suppose that matters. The smell is less rancid in this room.

"Who are we waiting for?"

"Tylis."

"Tylis," I repeat, testing the name on my tongue. "Why do you think he'll come?"

Rennison stops navigating the throne to look at me speculatively. "Why don't you?"

I jut out my chin. "Because he doesn't exist."

"You're sure about that?" He perches, slowly, spreading out his wings like a demonic action figure. "A name is just a name. Changing it doesn't alter or eradicate the soul." He plays with his knife while he speaks, it bears his sigil.

Liam and I didn't even have a chance to engrave our new sigil before we left. I frown at my mate's father. "No man can truly know another man's soul, Jarik."

"He is my son!" Rennison roars as he stands, gripping the handle of his knife like he may throw it. "You." He takes a step toward me, shaking with barely restrained fury. "There are hundreds like you, sirens and witches, who warp a man's mind by feeding on his heart." His eyes flash and his scent intensifies as his heart begins pumping furiously. If I wasn't relying on my black and white night vision, I would be able to see what colour his eyes are flashing with right now. "He will remember our goal and he will stand beside me. Together we will wipe out the wretched beasts that call themselves angels. Those who stand against us will pay with their blood. Tylis is my greatest creation. I have heard of his leadership, seen evidence of his victories." He stops, his head tilted, half of his mouth pulled up mockingly, and the madness settles over his eyes. "You do have her inside you, don't you." He lifts his knife to his mouth and runs it along his bottom lip like lip-liner. I watch as he continues along the deep crevice of his scar. "I wonder, how would she react if I marked you like she did me...?"

"I wouldn't know."

"That's right." He grins like he's just remembered. "She's dead!"

I hear a cough from behind me, a dry, raspy gasp for breath. Rennison glances over my shoulder. I know it's Reuben before I turn my head just enough to check. He's got hold of the water and is trying to pass it around their cone.

When I turn back to Rennison, he's frowning at them. "Why torment themselves with a few more minutes?"

"You really don't understand, do you." In a moment of misguided bravery, I turn and walk toward my men. Rennison lets me get within a pace of them before his blade is pressed to my throat and his arm wraps around me like poison ivy. Reuben looks up at me helplessly, whilst he struggles against the ropes. I stare. He stares back. It's a surreal eternity of vulnerability as Rennison chuckles against my ear.

"Hmmm." His chest rumbles as he inhales the scent of my hair. "Careful little angel, don't get too close." He laughs as he pulls me back toward his dais.

I scuff my feet as he drags me, the knife feels like a razor against my skin. My eyes stay trained on Reuben as I'm hauled up the dais steps and thrown onto the metal seat. I scowl as I realise where he's sat me. The iron is hot and uncomfortable. "Think I preferred Horen's."

Rennison howls with insanity laden mirth. "Horen's!" He laughs until it gets more than a little uncomfortable. "That fool." He starts playing with his knife again, still snickering. Then he snaps his head up with an idea. "Let's see what has become of the marvellous King Horen." He grabs my wrist and yanks me back to my feet. He's completely cracked.

I'm dragged from the cavern like a child. Rennison points with an eager grin on his face through a hole in the next cavern's wall. Would it be shameful to admit I'm curious?

I look.

I wish I hadn't.

I know now where Tarcus is. And he won't ever be coming back. Tarcus has been hung, strung up, like a feathery piñata while Brue's father dances around him like an imp, throwing the black rock of the city at Tarcus' swinging form. The king's lost his mind.

"I didn't need to take his throne," Rennison leers in my ear, "he lost it on his own." His lips press right against my skin, causing uncontrollable shudders through my bones. "That winged lizard of mine was useless from the moment he could walk. Too much of his mother," he snarls. "Dragone genes are always more dominant." He indicates to the hole one last time as he pulls me back. "Horen is a fool, but he is brutal. That bird clucked like a chicken before his neck finally snapped." I feel my stomach lurch painfully, readying itself to unload its contents. I'm never sick.

Rennison turns and guides us back toward the cavern. I stumble awkwardly, retching. Reuben grunts with suppressed rage when he sees us. "These three haven't uttered a word," Rennison muses. "You really should have considered your allies more carefully from the beginning. Then perhaps I wouldn't have been informed of your every move since you reappeared." He pushes me back to the throne where I sit. I can't really think of anything else to do. My legs are wobbly.

"What do you want from me, Rennison?" My voice sounds meek, even to me.

"I want you to die." He crosses his arms, knife still clenched in his fist. "But first I want you to convince Tylis where his loyalties belong. Lure my son to me and I'll spare any life you request, any except for your own."

"Tempting."

"Sarcasm is undignified." He steps toward me. "Don't disregard my offer so quickly. Soon you'll be begging for me to spare life after life... after... life." His shoulders drop then and he turns to glare at the Fallen fighter, who is standing in the crude arched doorway. "What is it?"

He answers, "No one is following her, my Lord. The tunnels are empty."

The Fallen shrivels back into the shadows as Rennison roars like Cerberus. I attempt to camouflage myself against the chair while Rennison Jarik thunders across the space and lifts the man by his throat.

He spits, "Check. Again."

"My... Lord..." The man is gone before Rennison has fully returned him to his feet. His boots clomp and scrape as he runs, until the sound disappears into the drone of underground city noise.

"He will come," Rennison repeats maniacally. "He will come for her. He will. He said. He will come."

"He won't come here," I answer impulsively.

Rennison stops pacing to glare at me. He's a few steps from my men. "You know nothing." He moves toward Cain, who's sitting furthest from me.

"We're too deep. It's too dark." I inhale the retched stench of the city and grimace. I don't want to stay here, waiting. I know Liam, and he would come. "Your son is a respected leader. He wouldn't order them to follow and they wouldn't let him come alone." I try to sit up straight in the roasting hot chair. I feel like I'm being griddled. It's impossible to bear, so I stand. I must have the intricate weave branded to my butt.

Rennison grabs Cain by his hair and pulls him to his feet, slicing through the rope with his blade when it provides resistance. "Don't move," he warns me. Perhaps he thinks I like Cain. I don't move. Art and Reuben are free, I really don't want to draw his attention to it if I can help it.

"Take me to where you meet your brother," I suggest. It's a blurted thought that I instantly regret. Rennison drags Cain with him as he storms across to me in an instant. The pain explodes in my head, a few moments after, I find myself sailing through the air. The bright light of agony sears my vision. Rennison is on me, lifting my shoulders and smashing my skull against the floor. The white wobbles and fades to gray around the edges. Everything dims. I will myself to stay awake.

Rennison's laughter fills the void around me. My ears ring with distant bells. "Get up." Rennison pulls me to my feet. "That should bring him running."

It's my turn to laugh, though it hurts my head to do so. I send reassuring vibes to Axion and Brue, whom it might actually bring running. "He's three quarter angeli, genius. He can't link."

Rennison smacks me again.

# · Eighteen ·

I wake on the floor. My head is throbbing but at least I can see properly again. The cavern is quiet. I fumble my medicines pouch. It wouldn't surprise me if Rennison's fist fractured my skull, my fingers are sluggish. It takes a long time to gain control, longer to clumsily swallow heal aid and pain medicine.

I crawl over to the dais and flop against it. My pirates are sitting against each other. Their eyes are open, focused on me.

"Finally!" Rennison exclaims. I look up. He's leaning over the side of his throne, smirking down at me. "I thought you'd never wake."

He stands as I lift myself to sitting, ignoring Rennison as he scoffs. There's no use in me grabbing a weapon and he knows it. "How long?"

"We've lost most of the day, I'm afraid." He exaggerates his disappointed expression and strides toward his captives. His voice lowers to a dangerous snarl, "And Tylis hasn't materialised." He unties a rope, which has appeared around them.

Have I really been out for most of the day? Liam is going to kill me, if Rennison doesn't beat him to it. The crazy tyrant pulls a partially conscious Cain with him as he strides back.

"You have gall," he concedes. "My boy trained you well. My brother told me as much." He drops Cain at my feet and strolls back toward the others. "So he told you," he muses, "or you have been doing your research." He pulls Art up next. "Which is it to be?"

"I read it somewhere." My strength is slowly returning. My head still feels fuzzy.

Cain groans at my feet and mumbles, "You talk too much." His voice is hoarse, almost inaudible.

"I have hundreds of brothers, comrades in arms," Rennison continues. "Only one has earned the privilege to be referred to as such." He drags Art in our direction. "He was supposed to deliver you and Tylis together." Art lands at my feet, crumpled and flaccid.

I was delivered.

*Plyrian.*

I pant with shallow breaths. "Liam wasn't with us in the cave," I lie.

"Tylis!" Rennison yells. "His name is Tylis." His boot hits Art in the back and he moans in pain.

I square my shoulders and retort, "Well he wasn't there either."

"Choose one!" he shouts as he marches to get Reuben.

I don't like the look of this. "Choose one to what?"

"To beg me for," he laments as he pulls Reuben toward his new dragone pile. "Choose quickly. We have somewhere to be."

"What happens to the others?"

Rennison looks at me like I just sprouted a second head.

I was afraid of that. "What happens if I won't beg?"

He laughs his maniacal chuckle. "They all die."

I look down at my men. This is crazy. How can I choose one? What's the point anyway? He's probably going to kill us all. How can Plyrian be working for Rennison? Plyrian is my friend. More than that, he is family. I trusted him and now I'm trapped. Liam is still with him, does he have any idea what his Second has done?

"Cain." I look up, tears in my eyes. "Spare Cain."

Rennison looks stunned momentarily, but it quickly passes. "Interesting." He picks Cain up and flings him over my shoulder. "I'll consider it." Then he turns and heads out of the chamber. "Let's go."

Maybe I've got a concussion. Cain feels like he weighs a tonne. The haze in my head is lifting but I feel peculiar. "Go where?"

"To meet my brother, of course." He waves his arms around. "It's a short walk. We'll be there by the morning."

The morning, as in tomorrow morning? Oh hell, Liam is really going to kill me. Reuben touches my leg. For the first time since I emerged from unconsciousness, I think fast. My medicine pouch and a sheathed blade lands on Old Salt's stomach, I cast a silent prayer for the pirates to a God I no longer have faith in. When you've lived with angels and fought with demons, a prayer seems futile. Reuben covers my meagre offering with his arm. He's my best fighter on a good day, this might not be a good day, but at least they have a chance now.

I'm a pace behind Rennison when we leave the chamber. My feet are sluggish and heavy but I shake it off, I need to focus. I plant every step carefully as we move, Cain stays limp and unresponsive as we travel. The city is vast, twice the size of Celthia and far less structured. It is not carved into the ground, it's formed from natural pockets of eroded and porous rock. The heat is so intense in places that I'm convinced we're in or near an underground volcano. The maze of lightless bubbles, like holes in a Swiss cheese, seems to stretch for miles. Everywhere we walk, our pace fast, yellow-eyed soldiers join our parade. Cain grumbles when he stirs but doesn't comment. This feels like a march to battle, with me, Cain and Rennison at the head.

"You're bringing the troops?" My words come out in gasps. Cain is heavy, but at least the temperature and smells retreat as we leave the proximity of Gravinwart.

Rennison doesn't acknowledge me, or the thousands of thundering feet that follow us. When I look back, there are wall after wall of bare-chested, muscled Fallen. Miles of soldiers, and they're all armed, the ground shakes with their progress. How can there have been this many men in those tunnels? How do they know we're leaving? I mean, how *did* they know? Now the whole world must know we're moving. All I can hear is thunder, all I can feel is the vibrations through my bones, there are too many to comprehend. Cain shifts on my shoulder, obviously uncomfortable. "Can you walk?"

"Do I want to?" he rasps. "You understand what you've started?"

"You're being snarky with me, now? Seriously?" I put him on his feet and hold his arm over my shoulder. He takes most of his own weight, not bad for someone as dehydrated as a sundried tomato.

"I need water," he answers.

I wrap my arm around his back and support more of his bulk. "I know. We'll find some. Just hang on."

We keep marching.

"Was I really out that long?" I whisper.

Cain scoffs indignantly. "Sleeping like a baby, angel."

I frown, confused. "And no one came?"

Cain laughs, actually laughs. "Disappointed?"

"Worried." Where are Axion and the others?

The gradient gradually increases as we head for the surface. I'm too fatigued to be apprehensive. The army marching at our heels are creating a buzz of energy. It runs through them like a current. The air is thick with their invigorated scents, it's impossible to discern individuals from the mixed seasoning. There are too many bodies in too confined a space and they are beginning to get restless, infighting and squabbling breaks out behind us. Rennison ignores everything.

As we near the surface, the stone turns to mud and dirt. "Mud means water," I whisper as we trudge through it.

I'm starting to flag. My mouth is too dry to swallow. I watch the terrain for any sign of a freshwater spring but it doesn't come, soon we're shuffling through dry dust. Cain is getting heavier.

My head aches. My feet ache. This isn't like the run from Celthia to England. This is like a trek from Hell to Timbuktu. We labour on, and an aggravated millipede of dragone follows behind.

About a mile past the point I decided to give up, the tunnel takes a sharp turn and a steep incline. It's like a dirt wall. We all scramble up behind Rennison, who, incidentally, has been whimsically sipping from a flask during our entire journey. I glare at his back, imagining my dagger sticking from it.

"Water," Cain gasps again. It's a request not an observation, we've been hiking for hours and he was already dehydrated.

The soldiers have flasks. "Can you walk alone for a second?" I spin before he answers and slide back into the ranks. I don't give myself an opportunity to second guess or regret my decision. My head feels revamped, like the damage from the knock has healed and my instincts are sharpened by our circumstance. The Fallen push and shove me as I slip among them, they're all scorching and blistering with irritation. It's not the best conditions to force your army to endure before a battle, I've heard their protests for the last few hours, and we're marching through the night.

The angeli would be well trained, well prepared and as rested as possible. Who would have thought that I'd miss the rigidity of the Guard? I take a few good hits as the Fallen wrestle me, and each other, it's worth it. In the mêlée I grab a couple of leather carafes and I rush back to Cain. I hand one to him as I slide my arm back around his waist.

He stares at me, wide eyed and I shrug, "Ask and ye shall receive."

We ignore the arguments behind us. For whatever reason, the Fallen hang back from our position. It could have something to do with their unhinged spearhead. Regardless, it means we don't bear the brunt of the fallout from my unconventional water dowsing. Cain doesn't waste a drop as he empties the contents into his mouth, I do the same. It's not enough to keep us going forever, but it quenches the insufferable ache. The dragone are adapted for hot and dry conditions, Cain's tolerance for dehydration outweighs my own, and mine outweighs a human's. We have flasks now, at least, that we can fill at the next chance.

The tunnel we are in has wooden support beams, rotten with age. It's a disused mine; it must be, there's no evidence of recent human activity and anything that did exist is about to get stomped by a herd of heavy booted demons. The air is still hot. It's a baking heat that carries no moisture in the air. Where on Earth is Rennison taking us?

We keep marching.

Then, quite by surprise, because I'm sure this is all we've ever done and all we'll ever be doing, the end of the mine appears. It's an apparition in the dark, the light at the end of the tunnel. The army halts. There's bumping and cursing behind us as the waves of Fallen shunt each other like a comedy cop pile-up in a spoof but as the traffic slows at the rear, the cursing dies down at the front. Muted shouts echo from further down the tunnel as the Fallen wait, like footballers before their final cup match, standing in formation and ready for battle. Cain and I exchange a glance. Rennison's army, or a vast portion of them, are poised to burst the banks and flood whichever land we are in.

Rennison stops before the opening and waits, impatiently, for Cain and I to join him. With the boiling glare of the rising sun comes my colour vision. Rennison stands like a deadly ridge of rock before a lighthouse. His colouring is eerily similar to Liam's, but his bright tawny eyes highlight one of the vast differences. I approach warily. He has a wildly eager grin on his face. It's awfully unsettling.

It feels hotter outside than in the baking mine. We walk out, the three of us. Cain shields his eyes from the sudden glare. Everything is too bright, too overexposed, too dry. We're surrounded by endless scorched scrub, charred by heat or fire, and planes of thick red earth. It's nowhere I've been before. There are outcroppings of rocks and foliage and not much else. It's morning, I think, judging by the height of the sun in the sky. The sky itself is a stunning clear blue, no indication of incoming precipitation. Or angeli Guard.

I sigh. The start of another day and I'm being led into the open by my nemesis, like an executioner taking captives to the block. It feels like Rennison's putting on a show. I look for signs of life, panning the landscape, but it's too rugged, too vast and too hot to pick out anything specific.

I grab Cain's arm and pull him closer. "He's going to kill you first, to prove a point to whoever's watching."

Cain scoffs and shakes my arm away. "Tell me something less obvious." He manages to sound obnoxious.

"I have an idea."

"I'm enthralled."

I huff but ignore his impertinence. "What if I kill you instead?"

He sniggers quietly.

"I'm serious, Cain." Our voices are inaudible, almost to us. "It's me or him."

We're a few paces away from the spot Rennison has chosen to stand. He's facing away from us, his bow drawn and ready. His wings fan open like a statue at a cemetery. For someone so pro-dragone, he really pushes the angel of death metaphor to the brink.

"You," Cain answers solemnly. It's a word released in a breath. I react, drawing my dagger and slicing it efficiently across his throat. He drops to the floor with a dull thud. The blood smells metallic as it colours his neck like a ruby scarf.

"Stay down," I hiss quietly in his ear.

He doesn't respond. His skin is deathly pale. Perhaps he was too dehydrated? I didn't cut anything vital for life, I think. I step away quickly and take the final few paces to Rennison's side. His shoulders are tense. I stare at the profile of his face, my bloodied dagger still in my hand.

He turns his head to inspect me, before glancing back over his shoulder at Cain's motionless body. I don't follow his line of sight. If Cain is breathing, Rennison doesn't seem to notice it. He turns his face back to me, where he simply stares. Perhaps I could win a fight against him, but I doubt it. There's no way I could avoid his arrow at this distance. So I do the only thing I can, I stare back. I'm waiting for his next move. His eyes bore into mine like maggots on a corpse. I have no idea what is going on behind them, I don't want to imagine.

I inhale. My arm has started aching, but it's not my own pain. Someone's holding onto Brue's bicep, squeezing to the point of agony. He's nearby. I can feel the pull that pain creates. I exhale. They did follow me. It's a comfort. I can't scent them which means, I hope, that Rennison can't either. The fact that one of them has to be in pain for my side of the bond to kick in makes me angry, I likely send them a blast of my annoyance but I can't control it. Axion never got around to teaching me.

"You are as taxing as your mother," Rennison concedes lightly.

I wonder if whoever he is performing to is within earshot. "Why have you dragged us, and your band of merry men, through the earth like the ruddy pied piper?"

Rennison raises his bow in response, training it on my heart. His eyes flash with malice. "One wrong step and I kill her," he bellows. I flinch, not expecting the sudden change in volume. "I do understand the reason for the recent excitement."

He grabs my wrist and forces it to his nose. I shiver as he inhales my scent like a vampire before it bites. He smiles wickedly, his eyes twinkling with inhuman mirth. My blade is an inch from his throat, still in my hand, but I have no control over it. It doesn't stop me trying. He laughs and pulls me closer, one hand around my wrist and one holding his bow. I squirm but he's much stronger than me.

I kick out and he throws me on the ground at his feet.

"Now, now," he tuts. "Don't make me kill you before our companion emerges from his hole." He trains his bow on me. "This might hurry him along."

He pulls back the string, arrow ready, and waits.

A familiar silhouette emerges stealthily from an outcropping of dry dusty mounds.

"My Lord." Plyrian approaches carefully, extremely carefully.

I'm not sure whose reaction he's more afraid of, Rennison's or mine. I'm not really in a position to be exacting my judgement on him right now. I'm staring down the shaft of a familiar-looking arrow.

"Brother," Rennison answers jovially. "You seemed reluctant."

Plyrian stands a little straighter. I watch him, too detached to feel anything resembling betrayal. I had figured already that he was the one, even if I tried to deny it. It seems tactically advantageous to place yourself at the right hand of the enemy command. He would have known about my birth if Gloria confided in him. Perhaps he spoke of the plot to Rennison. Perhaps he has been relaying information for twenty years. Rennison, no matter how insane, is a revolutionary. He wants to create a race of Gods, combining genetics for ultimate power. It's completely diabolical and immoral, but he may have convinced Plyrian it was preferable to the Script. Maybe I'm trying to justify his actions to prevent the heartache.

But something, I'm not sure what, keeps me from distrusting Plyrian completely. We have built up a camaraderie, a friendship, constructed on our mutual dislike of the angeli culture.

"Not at all," Plyrian answers. "The situation was not yet under control." He looks at me, his face blank.

I'm still on my back, a distinct disadvantage. Rennison hasn't lowered his bow and I can't help feeling it's because he's currently unconvinced of Plyrian's loyalties. This could go either way, but whether Plyrian is with or against me, there is still a tunnel full of Fallen eagerly awaiting a brawl. I raise myself up onto my elbows, my face equally blank. What can I say? I know my men are nearby, as well as Brue. I don't see Liam, but then I didn't see Plyrian until he made himself known.

"Where is Tylis?" Rennison questions. His tone is light but the bow trembles slightly with unreserved fury. He doesn't look away from me. I realise that I'm his insurance, his bargaining chip to get Liam to agree to his demands. I hope Liam isn't here.

Plyrian indicates to the position he appeared from. Of course Liam is here. "He would not walk beside me," Plyrian declares. "And he will not answer to his birth name. You have his mate. He is barely controlling himself."

All three of us turn in unison, like an expertly choreographed routine, to watch Liam as he approaches. He is armed, shielded and livid. My favourite combination.

Rennison laughs. "Mate? Tylis, she is just a pretty female. There are hundreds more like her: ripe and ready for picking." He kicks my foot. "She's a clone of her mother, good for one thing and then best disposed of."

Liam moves closer, his eyes trained on the arrow threatening my life. I find the moment ironic. I look away. Not because I'm afraid. I just don't want to do something crazy, like laugh.

Cain is still on the floor behind us. Of course he's still on the floor. I have no idea if he's alive. There is a noise, like a distant engine, coming from the mine. It could be the drone of impatient conversation. It could equally be a leaf blower. The pull to Brue has subsided. He's no longer hurting, which means whoever held him has got him under control. They are somewhere behind us, hidden in the ridges and valleys of this barren land.

"Aqua," Liam states authoritatively. "Stand up and walk to me, now."

I turn back to the gathering, confused by the command. Rennison looks amused at his son's assumption that he'll just let me move. I do pull myself to sitting. It's a mistake. Rennison releases his arrow instantly. It pierces through my hand and pins me to the floor like a spike. The response from Liam is immediate. He's armed with a sword and uses it to attack his father. Plyrian falters in indecision as Rennison counters Liam's movements. Rennison also has a blade, and a shrill whistle that creates thunder inside the mountain.

Boots.

A lot of boots.

All taking off like hooves at the Grand National.

I scream Liam's name and pull my hand from the ground. The dirty arrow lifts from the earth like a root. Another arrow, and it's a damned hindrance. I rip the feathers from its end and slide it out as cleanly as possible. It hurts. God it hurts. I don't have medicine, again. I gave it to Reuben and Art. I hope it did enough good to get them out of Gravinwart.

The small benefit of the tunnel is that it bottlenecks the Fallen, slowing their charge. The more that spill out, the more vulnerable we are. We need to block that exit. Cain finally moves. He has to or else he'll be trampled. Plyrian is dithering, watching the rapidly approaching wave of dragone fighters with his bow drawn. Liam and Rennison are really going at it. I thought there may have been more conversation before Liam tried to rip his father's head off, but apparently not. I'm dithering a little too. I want to help Liam, but if we don't do something about the army, killing Rennison will be futile.

Cain hobbles in our direction. I think I would have taken door number three and headed for the hills. Plyrian has a water and medicine pouch intact. There's no way to unite those with Cain before the army strikes. There are three of us. What is a whole army planning on doing once they've finished their charge? I don't wait to find out. I grab Cain and take to the air with him in my arms. The Fallen are mainly land based.

Plyrian shouts, "They might have bows, Guardian."

The Fallen I saw had blades and throwing knives. They may have bows, or guns, or a friggin' cannon for all I know. The fact is that standing on the ground waiting for the guillotine to fall was the least favourable option. Cain is too weak to fight.

"Help Liam," I shout back. I have to have faith in the Second. He loves Liam.

I fly toward the area I think my men are hiding. I don't turn back to look for my mate. I'm too terrified of what I'll see. Cain coughs in my arms. "Down there," he rasps. "I see shadows."

I descend swiftly and land near the shade of a gnarled tree. It has a grotesque swelling on its trunk, like a boil. Cain wobbles toward it when I set him on his feet. I watch as he pulls a plug from the growth and shoves his mouth to the hole. I can't process his actions, it's too confusing and I need to get back to Liam.

"Aqua!" Axion shouts as he rushes from somewhere. The shadows move as more of my men appear. "What the hell?!" He doesn't seem pleased. "You've been underground since yesterday."

I take off again. I hear shouting behind me as I plough through the sky. "Liam," is all I manage as an explanation as Axion follows me. He catches up easily. His wings are stronger.

"You're bleeding," he states as we near ground zero.

"You might die if you follow me," I warn him in return.

"We all die, Princess."

There is no battle field. There is no opposing army. Plyrian stands between the Fallen and Rennison. Liam is holding his arm, blood pooling on the dirt beneath him, but he's alive and standing. We fly past and turn so we land behind the two men. Rennison grins at me. Liam growls. I walk up to him anyway. It's quite a sight. Men are still pouring from the mine, and then coming to a halt in confusion when there's no one to kill. Plyrian seems to be in the most vulnerable position.

"Aqua," Liam grunts in annoyance. "What are you doing back here?"

"Silly question." I stand on his right and Axion stands on his left, facing their father together.

"You're wounded," he hisses.

"So are you."

"How touching," Rennison declares as he paces between us. "And look, another of my disappointing offspring has joined us. Delightful." He keeps pacing. "Disappointments," he mumbles, "all of them. That wretched Marcus had too much influence. Waste of time. Should have just taken with force."

I glance at Liam. He seems as uneasy as me. We have limited options. Taking on Rennison and the Fallen alone would be madness. "I don't suppose you brought reinforcements?"

He looks at me from the corner of his eye, not taking his focus off of Rennison. "It appears you did." He sounds angry.

Rennison cuts in, "Fortunately, I was prepared." He indicates behind him, to where his army is still spewing from the mine like an oil spill. "My forces are stronger, larger and knocking at your door." Rennison's face lights up in elation and Liam swears quietly.

I place my hand on his arm. "We have to get back to the city, don't we."

Liam nods. "He's sent an attack. He knew I'd come here for you."

"Marcus will be prepared," I state assertively, "he knows about the tunnel."

Rennison's laughter interrupts us again. "You are so blind," he leers. "My brother has already given his orders. Isn't that right, Plyrian?"

"My Lord," Plyrian confirms, his eyes trained on me. "The revolution has begun."

"Excellent," Rennison exclaims. "You see, son? It appears you were not vital for my ascension after all. While you were busy neglecting your duty, your Second was busy accomplishing his."

Rennison keeps talking, something about Celthia being under his control. I'm sure Liam and Axion are listening intently, but my attention is on the two familiar faces that appeared over the top of the crag. I didn't notice them emerge from the mine with the army. They are both holding bows, stolen from the Fallen, I assume. Confirmation that the Fallen are armed with arrows doesn't comfort me. Rennison is still gloating. Perhaps he's stalling. He thinks he's safe here, with no Guard poised to attack.

"You're wrong, Jarik." I stare through him and through Plyrian, to his army. "Liam puts his duty before anything else. Everything he does is for the good of the colony. Whose good are your actions for? You promised them they would become Gods, am I right? Yet instead of raising them to power you drag them to Hell and call it freedom. They live in a hole, wallowing in the stink of decay while your sons bask in the light. You didn't need them to put you where you are, buried in the ground like a cesspit, but I'm sure they'll be willing to ensure you stay there."

Rennison saunters closer, an irritated glint in his eyes. "Quite the public speaker, I see. Perhaps there's some of your father in there too."

"Aqua?" Axion whispers incredulously. "We're a little outnumbered."

He can probably feel the fight brewing in my gut, the fire of anger at Rennison and his lackeys. "I told you not to follow."

"I believe you actually said, '*you might die if you follow me*,' emphasis on the *might*."

I'm not listening. My stride takes me to meet Rennison in the space between his sons and his army. My hand is weakened but my fingers still move, it's painful but fortunate. "I don't like you," I tell him when we're feet apart.

"I'm devastated," he sneers. "You have no hope of surviving, little Princess. Like the queen before you, I will extract your last breath." He pulls back the string of his bow and I roll my eyes patronisingly.

"Are you afraid I may draw your blood?" I grab my axes and hold them innocently. "A little girl like me." My heart is flapping like a fledgling.

Rennison studies me. My pulse thumps in my mouth while he considers my challenge. The Fallen behind him are getting increasingly restless. Plyrian is in some kind of silent standoff with my mate behind my shoulder. My men are materialising around the periphery of our gathering, unnoticed, and a large black storm cloud is appearing on the horizon.

"Afraid?" Rennison echoes. "My heart has not taken wing at the thought of facing you. My hand is not dripping energy into this lifeless soil. You are a fool to mock me. Your last great battle will be fought with no one to witness it," he leans closer and drops his voice to a sardonic tone, "just... like... your... mother."

He throws his bow away in his excitement, sending it skittering across the floor. In the brief second he's unarmed, I bury my axe head into his bicep and launch myself out of reach. He screams in frustration and comes for me, sword drawn. Liam is grabbing me, pulling me with him. Rennison is staggering, lurching toward me like he's wading through quicksand. He roars and turns on whatever is holding him back. Liam pulls me further away. The Fallen are initiating a chant that sounds ominous. Axion is screaming something unidentifiable and the storm cloud is getting closer.

"Happy?" Liam growls in my ear.

"Not what you imagined today would be like?" He's pouring water over my hand to clean it and wrapping it hurriedly with linen.

"No," he snaps. "I had a mated accommodation picked out and ready, yet you spent the night traipsing across the globe with a madman." His voice cracks at the end and he's either laughing or crying. Maybe both. "Plyrian needs help, get to safety." And then he's gone and Axion is dragging me further away.

Stop, Ax," I dig my heels in. "Look up."

He does. "Oh, wow."

"Exactly. Keep their attention this way, on us," I look around at the slowly approaching crowd, still chanting their foreign mantra. "What are they saying?"

Axion snorts. "Kill, kin and kingdom. It's not very original." He draws his sword beside me as we pace forward. Liam and Plyrian are taking on Rennison together. The clang of their weapons resonates across the plane and from the craggy red walls of rock. Liam's arm is bleeding. I can't watch.

"Where are we?"

"Outback, don't know exactly. It's a large place." We stop in no-man's land, staring down the gullets of the enemy as they yell. "Shall I samba?" Axion derides sarcastically.

"I'm more of a waltz kinda girl." The army are holding back, considering their vast size it's a good thing. I kind of hope they turn back completely. "Hurry up," I breathe in a prayer.

"There are hundreds of them," Axion whispers. The Fallen army marches closer, still chanting.

He's wrong. There are thousands and I have no idea where they've all come from. I let out a shriek, a war cry of sorts, which doesn't resemble the Hacker in any way, but releases some of the aggression. The pirates on the ridges do the same, and with more masculine gusto than me. There's more noise than is discernible, but some of the Fallen must notice them because the ranks seem to divide faintly as new targets are acquired.

My men stand like roman candles around a pit of vipers. Not all of them are positioned favourably. There is only so much high ground in the vicinity. It doesn't matter this time. I'll have to ensure more intense training before our next war, though. The storm cloud descends in a blaze of silver lightening and black leather. The circle my pirates have created seems to fill with feathers and screaming. The fallen are bare chested, some displaying tattoos that now mark them for death.

"Where's Brue?" I scan around, panicked. I don't recognise these Guard, not any of them. Surely I should? How do they know my men are on their side?

"He's with Cain," Axion assures me. "Not sure who's looking after who." We start moving in mutual synchronisation, toward my mate.

The scenery has changed in the space of an instant. Battle wages on the plane, noisy and frantic. Wings collide with weapons, blood is being spilled. The Fallen were eager for this, desperate for the fight, it is obvious in every roar they make. We skirt the outside, finding it strange that they are staying confined to one large patch of ground. My men, the ones I can still see since the cloud of feathers descended, are positioned at the fringes. Like shepherds, they keep the battle contained. Some are in duals of their own. I swallow a lump as I acknowledge that we are going to lose people here, but I don't let the thought linger. Liam and Plyrian are taking on the devil.

They are moving fast, blurred with velocity. Rennison has the added speed that dragone genetics provides. Liam has youth, training and pure rage. Plyrian has... I run hard, trying to pull Plyrian out of the way.

The image is seared to my brain, in slow-motion: Liam's strong, taught arms pulling, ripping, Rennison's wings in his grasp. Liam's leg, clad in tight black leather, straining with force against his father's spine. Rennison's face, distorted in pain and wrath, his back arching, his naked chest splattered with blood, his sword held out in front of him.

His sword.

"Plyrian!" I scream. I catch the Second as he falls. "Plyrian! Damn you, open your eyes!" I fix my hands to his wound, pressing, holding, cursing. "Plyrian!"

"Aqua," he rasps, coughing, spitting, blood on his lips. "I'm dead. Tell Gloria..."

Axion rushes past, he doesn't hesitate. Liam and Axion are taking on their father, together. I can hear their grunts, like boulders clashing. I can hear Rennison's glee in his maniacal cackling.

I don't look.

I fumble with Plyrian's medicine pouch, one hand still pressed against his stomach, looking for the battlefield medicine that stops bleeding.

"Plyrian!" I shout as he closes his eyes. "Plyrian, are the Fallen in the city?"

There's another loud grunt, a strange wail and a dull thump, all scored with Rennison's unique brand of background delight. It rings in my ears.

"No," Plyrian whispers. "Never. Not since... you..."

Finally, Rennison's grotesque laughter is cut off with a snap and I know it's over. For him, anyway.

I still don't look.

"Plyrian!" I'm crying now. I can't find the plunger. He doesn't have one.

He also doesn't answer.

I feel it, the moment his next breath doesn't come.

"Plyrian? No!" I shake him, hard.

I try. God I try to bring him back.

My hands pump on his chest, pushing the last of his blood around his body.

"Liam!" I shout. I know my mate's still alive because my heart is still beating. "I need the green stuff! Liam!" I can't really see through my tears. I just know I need to block the hole and stop the bleeding, like Liam did for Aaron when he was stabbed. It saved him. Plyrian could be saved.

A hand, then another wraps around my waist. I'm lifted, pulled away. Liam is there, Axion holds me. He's hurt, I can feel it. The pain barely registers as I watch Liam. He checks Plyrian's pulse, his wound, the blood and he sags. Slowly, delicately, he draws his hand down Plyrian's face, pats him on the shoulder one last time and stands.

"No!" I fight in Axion's arms, writhing and twisting until he lets go. "Plyrian!" I rush to him. I have no idea of my intention.

He's gone. I can see it. Liam can see it. I'm intercepted and pulled into an embrace – scorching, painful and completely resilient to my manic wailing.

Liam holds me.

"He's gone, Aqua." He squeezes me closer, suffocating. "You have to hold it together. People are dying all around you. Our brother is hurt. We need to keep moving." He pulls me away from the body of his Second. The shell that no longer houses my friend stays silent, motionless.

"August?" I panic. My mind is scrambled. I thought I was ready for this, for a war. I was so wrong. I'll never be ready. How can anyone be ready for this?

"Axion," Liam corrects. He grabs his brother, my brother, and pulls him further from the fighting. Without his arms to support me, I'm lost. I stumble after them. Shock. Yes, this is shock.

I can feel Axion's pain. It's muted. He'll be okay.

My feet won't move.

I give up trying.

I'm at a safe distance. The angeli Guard are overpowering the Fallen quickly. I watch the battle with a weird detachment. There are more bodies than I can count, and they *do* all count. I have to remind myself that every body was a person, a friend, a lover, a sister or brother.

I look back at Plyrian, and then at the crumpled, wingless body of Rennison. I stare. A father, I add to my mental list. I step, my resolve faltering, but I have to do this. Morbid fascination drives me forward, my eyes trained on the figure of Rennison. He looks dead. Looks can be deceiving. I keep a small distance, pacing around his detached wings. That must have hurt. He's laid on his side, his face serene in death.

Definitely dead.

Just like that. Yet the battle still rings behind us. It is quieter, more desolate as the number of dead begins to outweigh the number of living.

I want to yell, to shout and scream until they stop and look around themselves, both sides, angels and demons, angeli and dragone, people and people, all living on the same earth, breathing the same air, dreaming the same dreams, and all dying together.

Even Rennison, creator of the Fallen army, could draw my feelings of empathy at his death. He was the father of two people that I love, he was the murderer who took my mother, my friend and countless others, he was a cross-breed and he was alive. He could have had a good life. He chose to waste it on vengeance and hate.

Battlefields are loud, chaotic places but I hear his approach.

I inhale. "You tore him apart."

Liam sighs. He takes another step closer, his presence sending tingles across my skin. "He didn't deserve his wings. He wasn't worthy, and he died like the mortal he was."

My eyes flick to his. "Like we all are," I sigh, "like they all are."

"Aqua," Liam breathes soothingly. "It's over."

It's over?

"Look," he turns me slowly, away from one body to hundreds more, "they are laying down their arms. This battle is over. Their leader is dead. We are in control. We've won." He means to reassure me but my mind lingers on his word, *control*. You either have it or you're under it. No freedom.

My mind is racing, but my body is sluggish. It feels strange, like I'm numb on the outside but my brain is burning. Random thoughts, crazy ideas, a sense I should be doing something but having no idea what. Wanting to run, scream, sleep, laugh, cry, all at the same time, but being able to do nothing except stand and stare.

Plyrian is gone.

The grief is all-consuming.

The landscape is full of souls, the living and the lost. Tarcus, Rennison, Plyrian and hundreds more. Why?

"They need a fair trial," I manage to whisper, "all of them." There's so much devastation to repair. "Gravinwart needs freeing. There are prisoners, children, a king who's lost his mind and dead who need a proper committal. This isn't over." I turn to look at him.

"The Guard will handle it," he assures me. "We cannot do everything, Aqua. You have to let it go."

Let it go. How do you do that, I wonder, when it's all tied to you? I sigh. "What about Celthia? They are unprotected, Rennison said..."

Liam rests his heated hand on the nape of my neck, comforting me. "The Guard are in Celthia, they are safe.

Plyrian saw to it all, while I drove myself insane." I feel his eyes on me, emphasising his frustration.

I watch the battlefield in silence for a few moments. The Fallen are surrendering, any that put up a final fight are being taken down with sickening ease. The angeli are the epitome of organised efficiency. The dragone are herded into small, easy to control groups. Bodies are being sorted, the injured tended to.

"The angeli will not survive the heat of Rennison's putrid city. We'll have to send my pirates," I say finally. I don't see another way.

"Pirates?" Liam asks, confused.

"Tarcus is dead too." My eyes flick to his. "He was down there."

So much death. My eyes rove back to Plyrian and my heart stutters. Liam squeezes my neck in reassurance. "It is good to grieve, to remember and to hurt for them but you can't live consumed within it. Life is for living, Aqua. Never forget that."

I wrap my arm around his strong waist. He seems so grounded, but I know he's hurting as much as I am. How do some people go on with gusto and some descend into despair?

A man, older than Liam and as blond as Lucas, approaches us. An angeli Guard, not one I recognise, his uniform is askew.

"Brother," he greets Liam. "My Guard have secured the situation."

"Thank you, Jonah. We will be in contact." Liam holds out his hand, removing the heat from my neck and the Guard takes it. It's a very human gesture.

"The Mother watch and protect you." The Guard nods at me.

"And you," Liam replies, pulling his hand back.

When he's disappeared back into the carnage, Liam leads me away.

"Who was he?"

"Master of the Guard from Graven Thrall," Liam answers. "We couldn't afford to leave Celthia unprotected. Although, we should hurry back," his voice drops to a whisper, "our other brother and his... mate... were instigating a riot when I left."

My men have convened behind Old Salt and are greeting him with relieved fondness. Art is receiving the same attention. Axion is already with them, his wounds dressed.

"Riot?"

"Vive la révolution," Liam smirks.

"Seriously?"

He nods in response.

"And you're not the slightest bit worried about that?"

He laughs. "A little."

"Princess!" Reuben calls too loudly. He breaks away from the pack and draws me into his arms. When he releases me, he hands me my weapon and pouches. "These came in handy, Lass."

"I'm glad. Reuben." He looks well. They all do. The ones that have made it back.

"We're ready, lass." He looks at me sincerely. "They require rescuin' and we want t' do it."

"Old Salt," I interject. "You need time to recover."

"They don't 'av time, Lass. We're goin' t' bring 'em home." He looks around at my men... his men... and they nod in agreement.

I can't just let it go. "You need my help?"

I know what his answer's going to be. He's taking back control. He's resolute. I can feel his confidence, his desire to see this through and reclaim what's theirs. My lips tilt up with a sense of pride. He's back in control of his ship and it's where he's at his best.

"Ye've done more for us than ye'll ever know, lass." He looks at Axion. "Ye too, lad," then he bows, "Your Highness."

As they turn, Cain and Brue appear, walking confidently through the closest outcropping of red rock. "Cain?" Reuben spins back toward me questioningly. "Ye kept him with us, lass?" He pulls me into a bear hug again, this one a little tighter. "More than ye'll ever know," he repeats in my ear. Then his crushing hold is gone and he's welcoming Cain, surrounded by his crew.

Brue pushes past them, heading straight to me. "I want to stay with you," he declares feistily. "We're family."

"Brue." I grab him to me, and spin him away from the carnage behind us. "You shouldn't be here," I chastise, "we're on a battlefield." Yes, still on a battlefield, except now it's littered with Fallen cattle and carcases. Brue's skin is burning. I look at my little companion, his face smeared with dirt like the first time I met him, except this dirt is the colour of the Australian Outback. "Why are you angry? I won't ever send you away." But he has a home, and it's a world away from mine. "They're getting your island back, Brue. You'll be able to go home."

"And you'll come too," he states. "You'll live with us." His yellow eyes sparkle with fortitude. I sigh. I wish life was as easy as it is through the eyes of a ten year old.

I feel Liam step closer beside me. This really is a conversation for another day. "I'll always be your sister,

wherever I am. Right now we need to get back to Celthia."
I scoop him into my arms, managing to smile when he
protests. "I like your cloak."

"It's too big," he grumbles.

"Aqua," Liam runs the nail of his thumb down my arm
to get my attention, "I need to bring my Second home,
for Gloria." He presses a kiss to my temple when I turn.

I blink at his public display of affection. It feels
strange. We hid our relationship so carefully and now
the whole city knows, or will soon know. We're mated,
after all. Was that real or a dream? "We'll wait."

Liam nods and goes to retrieve Plyrian's body. I take
Axion's hand when he replaces Liam's position at my
side. He's been very quiet.

"You can go with them, Ax. We'll be okay." Cain is
also insisting he's well enough to travel with his crew
mates. Brue nods in agreement. Axion turns to lock his
conflicted gaze with mine.

I sigh. "Just come back alive. There's plenty of time
to sort out living arrangements later." I kiss his cheek
before I nestle my head on his shoulder, still holding Brue
in my arms.

We're not silent for long. "Our dad?" little shrewd
Brue asks. "Was he down there too?"

I answer quietly, "The man I saw down there wasn't
the father you know, Brue. Maybe. Maybe he's still
there."

"I'll find him," Axion assures him. "If he's there, I'll
bring him home." He stands straighter. "Princess," he
squeezes my hand, "it's nice knowing you. I'll see you
soon. Take care of my brother." His eyes dart to where
Liam is gently wrapping Plyrian in his own wings, ready
to carry him home one last time.

I nod. "Always," I assure him.

"I'm right here," Brue complains indignantly.

"That you are, kid." I squeeze Axion's hand again before letting go. "Let's go." I nod at the pirates as they bow toward us. I have every faith in them succeeding. Hantiem will be theirs again and Axion will rule it fairly.

Celthia is another story.

I take a run and jump whilst spreading my wings and soar into the sky. Brue pulls his hood up and his cloak around him as we ascend into the cold air of the ether. I circle, waiting for my mate to join us. Brue shivers.

"Are you cold?"

"No."

"Don't look down, Brue."

He looks down immediately and I grumble my displeasure. "Death is a part of life, Aqua. I've seen it before, you know. Stop trying to protect everyone all the time." He looks to our left. "Your boyfriend's coming."

I don't correct him. I don't tell him death is devastating whether you've seen one or a hundred. I don't tell him just how hard it is when it's someone you love.

"Okay, Brue." I turn to follow Liam as he leads us home to Celthia. "I'll try."

# · Nineteen ·

I don't have a conventional dragone bond with anyone. I've never wished for one before now. But I'd love to know how Liam's handling this flight, and how Axion is doing. There's still so much left for Liam to explain. Does he know why Plyrian did what he did? How did they arrange an attack force from Graven Thrall in such a short time?

Brue shifts in my arms, suppressing a shiver. "Drink the fire," I insist, glaring at him until he pulls the red vial from a pouch inside his cloak. It's a short flight, mercifully. My mind is doing too much work. There are too many images assaulting me.

"Is he okay?" I ask Brue. I shouldn't but I can't help myself. Brue and Axion do have a conventional bond.

"He's fine," he answers. "Why don't I just tell you when he isn't."

"If, not when," I mumble as Celthia's golden door appears in the distance. "Ax will be fine," I reassure him.

"I know." He rolls his eyes.

For only the second time ever, I enter Celthia through the monolithic golden entrance. Brue squirms from my grip as soon as we land and takes position beside me, looking solemn. It's clear to him what this has become. It's clear to the few Guard in the room, who have all dropped to their knees in shocked despair.

This is Plyrian's funeral march.

Liam waits as the Guard pay their respects in quiet whispers, and then he descends through the city with me and Brue following silently. My mate holds his head high as he heads straight to the Great Hall. The corridors of the city are scarcely populated.

He must sense my discomfort. "Everyone is being held together for protection, while the Fallen who attempted to invade through the tunnel are dealt with." He keeps walking. "Don't expect sanctity though."

He's not kidding. I can hear voices raised in argument as we near the double doors. They are protected by Guard, who drop to their knees like their colleagues when we approach. Their muffled mumbles of respect are lost in the noise coming from the room behind them. Liam waits patiently again, until they stand.

"Status?" Liam orders once they're composed.

A Guard nods and answers, "Disgruntled. The rebels are arguing their case. As usual, Marcus has turned it into a debate. Neither side was willing to employ physical hostility. There are interesting arguments, though their support seems even."

"Under the city?

"No word," the Guard responds, with a shake of his head.

"Thank you." He glances back at me and gives me his secret smile, the one that melts my heart. "Let's share our opinion on this latest debate, Guardian." He winks and turns back to the Guard. "Open the doors."

"What's happening?" Brue whispers.

"Another battle," I grumble.

We walk in. It's hard to describe. The Guard contingent is minimal. They're still dealing with the Fallen under the city. The rest of the colony is here, though, including the dragone refugees. There is a clear divide, with all of the dragone and the resistance on one side and Marcus and his followers on the other. In the middle, a natural gap has formed. Not everyone is shouting.

The instigators are at the long stone buffet table, standing atop it to get more volume. Marcus and Lucas are on the left as I look at it, Oberon and Gloria are on the right, and Victus is dead centre, either on the fence or playing mediator. Things change every day, but still there is something that remains the same; Victus is always front and centre. My eyes fixate on the tabletop performance and then scan the crowd.

August isn't there, but he's nearby glancing nervously between his partner and his father. I can see the fear on his face, my brother, petrified but preparing himself. He must have been that way for a while. The arguing has reached an exasperated tone and pitch that suggests it's hours old.

We're not noticed by the front, but the noise around us vanishes as we pass. Brue stays at my side and I let him. The small boy will be a king one day and he will be formidable. I'd like him to be next to me then, too.

We walk forward. It doesn't take long for it to happen. I know because I'm waiting, watching. Gloria turns, like a sixth sense, before the rest of the front. I see the rapid emotion-fuelled expressions as they morph her features: confusion, shock and then the worst one... agony. She lets out a primal howl, a devastating wail that silences every person in the room. It's all in slow motion. She scrabbles from the table, pushes past anyone in her way. Screaming, she runs the remaining distance.

I'm crying. I can't stop it. Her grief is my grief. Liam drops to his knees, holding Plyrian's lifeless form steadily. Gloria drops in front of him, her face pale and sodden with tears. There is a moment, a brief second, where time stands still and they simply stare at each other. That look says more than words ever will. Then Liam places her lover's head in her lap softly and they weep together. The whole colony as one, despite their current division, drop to their knees in unrestrained sorrow.

It lasts forever but is over too quickly.

Marcus wants answers and he's determined to get them. Liam stands and takes my hand. We walk around Gloria and her grief, placing my fingers on her shoulder lightly as I go. It is all the comfort I can offer at the moment and it's not enough. My mate leads me and Brue to the table, where we stand like travellers at a junction.

Liam acknowledges Marcus' impatience with a glare, but waits for the question.

Marcus is furious to have to ask. "Are they defeated?"

"Yes." Liam offers no other comment. He's angry, blisteringly so. I can feel it through our joined hands. The city is on their knees, Victus and Lucas included. Oberon has leapt from the table to join his family as they gather around their lost member. The anti-Script portion of the table is looking bare.

I squeeze my mate's hand, drawing his eyes to me. He's hot. Burning like a star he stares at me, his dark chocolate hair gorgeously tussled. I raise my eyebrow seductively. I can't help it. He does this to me, makes me forget the bad so that there's just me and him and we're invincible. He knows what I'm thinking and it's evident in his smile. We move together, both stepping right with no element of thought involved. We move like magnets, drawn by the same force. Liam lifts me by my waist as I hop semi-gracefully onto the table opposite my father. I grasp Liam's hand to help pull him up. He doesn't need it, but it works as a symbol of unity. Brue hops up too. I don't think he knows why. And then August, spurred on by our presence, clambers up as well.

We all dip to our knees silently, allowing Plyrian's family their moment of peace. Marcus takes it all in, in quiet contemplation. I don't know what he was like before my arrival, I never witnessed his interpretation of the Overseer role. Lucas told me he was a great leader. He obviously cares about the city, but he is inflexible in his preaching of the Script. He drops to his knees, too. He may or may not know about the Second's treachery. Either way, he shows his respect the same way as everyone else.

Victus is the first to stand. It initiates a ripple through the colony until all but the grieving family are on their feet. It doesn't strike me as strange that no one questions Gloria's overwhelming presence. I notice the crowd on our side swell in size as the colony registers Liam's allegiance.

Victus signals to one of the few Guard at the edge of the room and he walks slowly toward the family, before bowing in respect. This must have happened before because the family instinctively move back, allowing him to lift Plyrian into his arms. I watch them as they all leave the Grand Hall with broken footsteps. Oberon turns to look at August before he walks out. August's breathing hitches beside me at the look on his boyfriend's face.

"He needs you," I tell him.

August shakes his head, not able to speak. I loop my arm through his in stoic support and we all stand, like *Queen* singing *Bohemian Rhapsody*, waiting for the arguing to reignite. Lucas is staring at us like we've lost our minds. I scan the crowd and notice that Robyn, his pregnant – can't get over that – mate is standing near the front of our supporters. I smile at her when she gives me a timid wave. Now he's looking at her like she's lost her mind. Still, he discreetly moves a step closer to Victus.

"Any more losses?" Victus asks sincerely.

"Tarcus is confirmed," Liam answers soberly. "His family are all Guard. They will need to be informed."

"What about us?" a brave dragone female asks, looking at me. "Where are our men to mourn?"

Liam turns to answer but this is my responsibility, my obligation.

"We lost three today," I confirm. My voice is low but strong.

I close my eyes and picture the missing faces. I have only known them a short time but each loss is significant and deserves recognition. "Micah." I breathe between names, giving them their silence. "Jon." I take another breath. "And Nathan." I know the women know these men, perhaps one of them is grieving like Gloria, but none of them show it. They all close their eyes and whisper silent words.

I continue, "King Axion has led the rescue mission to Gravinwart. There are survivors there that need bringing home, home to Hantiem. When the island is safe we will facilitate your return, your chance to grieve, your chance to grow and your chance to live." That is what I witnessed from my window on the island: the dragone live every day fiercely and fervently.

"Have the three you lost with Tarcus been confirmed?" Lucas asks, his voice compassionate.

I shake my head, allowing a small smile. "Discredited," I tell him. "They survived."

He crosses the table elegantly and wraps his arms around me, which is only possible because he folds my brothers in as well. "Some good news." He steps back and joins our growing huddle. I see what he's just done there. Sneaky.

Marcus is left standing alone. A hum starts in the hall and feet shuffle around but I don't look. I don't want to see the city divided in this way. I just want them to have control over their existence.

"Daughter." Marcus addresses me as kin in front of the entire city, confirming our genetic bond calmly. "You appear to have openly defied me and corrupted your brothers along with you." He glares at me but it doesn't feel menacing or angry. He seems expectant. Perhaps he's giving me my time to talk, to outline my case. I don't know what's already been said, but I do know that my thoughts need clarifying, verbally, to everyone. When I first joined the rebellion, I had only one outcome planned – to completely destroy the Script and enforce my own ideals. But since then, I've seen with my own eyes the devastation caused by violent takeovers. I look at Victus, standing proud in the centre as always, and smile. Perhaps the old man is cautious. Perhaps he's a genius. I'm the centre of our group, so I shuffle them all with me when I move toward Victus. He taps his lips, covering the smile I see there.

"Father," I acknowledge Marcus coolly, and then I turn and address the open gap in the centre of the room. "There is no right or wrong answer to this argument. There is only my opinion and your opinion and the opinion of the person next to you. You are all intelligent, sentient creatures capable of making your own decisions. There is a Script and a set of rules that make you conform in this society. It is unrelenting and unyielding. Some of you may prefer it. Some of you may depend on it. And some of you may object to it with your entire being. I object. I object because I want to live in a colony where people can love each other freely, regardless of profession or gender," – yep, went there – "I want to be surrounded by people who don't feel the need to create secret movements, instigate revolutions and turn to violence to escape oppression. I want us all to appreciate, love or hate each other for *who* we are and not *what* we are. The Mother showed us how we might live in harmony, but she did not write it in ink and screech for compliance. The Script is a set of archaic rules, written by our forefathers. We are here, living, breathing each other every day. We are alive and entitled to enjoy it. All I'm asking for is the freedom to make the choices that define us. I do not wish to be defined by someone else's interpretation of the Mother's wishes."

There is a moment's silence as everyone, including Marcus, ponders my words. I feel our little group enclose around me, drawn together like one entity.

Someone shouts from the audience, "Rules prevent anarchy."

I'm looking for the owner of the voice, to reply, when there is a response from another voice, "Rules should evolve with us, there should be leniencies." My eyes flick left to the male on the anti-Script side.

"Leniencies lead to rule breaking," a female shouts from the right.

This vocal tennis is getting us nowhere.

"You've never broken a rule?" I address everyone, not singling the female out for her honest answer. "You've never wanted something enough that the fact it's forbidden becomes irrelevant? You've never loved someone, or wanted someone enough to fight for them? How about these wonderfully polished walls? Have you ever wondered what you're missing by hiding behind them? Have you ever thought about exploring the world? We only get one chance at living and experiencing. You may want that chance. You may not. But whether we take it should be up to us, not a book."

"That book is the backbone of our city," Marcus states. My reference to it as anything but swamps his words with irritation.

"The colony is the backbone of this city!" I turn as I shout at him.

My patience has evaporated like steam from my skin. Hypocrite. He's my father because he had sex with a dragone queen while he was sneaking out of the city. "They work through blood, sweat and tears to keep this place palatial. They teach the younglings, they feed us, clothe us, protect us. The Script is ink and paper and can be rewritten to please everybody. We do not need to be divided. We must not draw lines and distinctions that segregate us and turn us against each other. I have seen how detrimental ideals can be. We must compromise and provide equal respect to our opinions in order to resolve this conflict. I propose we scrap the restrictions on mating rights. I propose that the decision of profession is a mutual agreement between the Overseer and the individual. And I propose that everyone is free to leave the city as they wish, providing our existence will not be discovered by humans."

"I propose we continue on as we always have, united and protected," Marcus counters.

"We are not united right now, are we? I propose we employ a more democratic system, where everyone's voice is heard and respected," I counter again.

"You truly believe that?" Marcus asks inquisitively, stepping forward as he speaks. "You believe that amending our beliefs will be more beneficial than preserving or obliterating them?"

I frown. "Beliefs, no. Rules, yes." I match his penetrating emerald-green gaze with my own. How different our colouring is. Perhaps I should out myself, and him. Perhaps it's time. There are enough dragone in the room to know that the angeli's acceptance of the other species has improved.

Marcus doesn't give me the chance. "You hold our belief system in high regard, but you disapprove of the restrictive confines that it places on our freedom."

I glare. Am I speaking in tongues? "Yes, that's what I said." Are all fathers this infuriating? Then I glance at Liam, and decide I've got no grounds on which to complain.

"You want our colony to mate for love, regardless of their profession, which you also want them to be able to choose." He observes me impassively, restating everything I've literally *just* said. My eyes narrow. "And you expect them to simply accept the first change in centuries and start courting openly, rather than cavorting behind my back and remaining unmated and childless?" A gasp echoes around the Great Hall but he doesn't stop. "You don't think that they'll have a problem with two unrelated males openly declaring that they love each other?"

Silence this time. I mumble, "It'd be more of a problem if they *were* related."

Then I look around the hall at the colony. They are hesitant, glancing at each other nervously like such a thing has never been mentioned, or maybe just not mentioned in public. I turn back to Marcus and stare. "Why don't you ask them? Let them decide how they would feel if two males or two females wanted to be mated. Would they rather look at their unmated family and friends and wonder who or what they're doing in the shadows. Or would they rather live in an environment where their friends and family can share their lives with a loving mate, in an atmosphere of acceptance and openness."

Was that a little of my biological mother's passive aggressive manipulation? I hope not. I really am trying to be as unbiased as possible.

Marcus turns toward the rapt audience and gasps. I have been glaring at him too closely to pay attention to the quiet shuffling of bodies. But I do now.

I gape, taking in the positions of the colony in the expanse of the Great Hall. It takes a second of processing. Bodies have shifted, moved altogether. There is no gap of a divide, although there are some shocked and scornful faces on the periphery. It looks random, but it feels like a code of some kind, a masterpiece of design, like a spider's web connecting the dots. I see it. Everyone sees it.

They've paired up. There are three thousand angeli in Celthia. Some are children. A lot are Guard and therefore absent. I'm sure that some of them would be joining their partners in the centre right now, if they could. Oberon is absent. I pull August in a little closer. Our mother is in clear view now, standing with the dragone, since the courting angeli have all converged in the centre. Lucas jumps down and sweeps Robyn off her feet, holding her close as she giggles. Blue clothes and white clothes, brown and white, brown and brown, brown and blue, blue and blue, white and purple and every combination in-between. Is anyone *not* currently courting?

Marcus turns back to me, his mouth agape but with a hint of humour in his eyes. "You see what you've started?" he accuses. "Mayhem!" He shakes his head despairingly. "Just like your mother."

Then he smiles, turns, and walks away. He jumps from the table and pushes his way through questioning faces, until he escapes through the hole and leaps from the veranda.

I'm at a bit of a loss. It doesn't escape my notice that I ended up doing most of the talking. Victus is unusually quiet. With Marcus bailing on our debate, and nothing more to really say, the city begins to hum with quiet conversation. August jumps down and heads for our mother, who I've just noticed is glaring at the spot Marcus left from. Oh hell, I forgot. She hasn't seen him since he kidnapped her son. I wonder if he's spoken to her? I doubt it.

It's just me, Liam and Brue left, and it doesn't take long for my littlest brother to hop down and saunter over to a group of yellow-clad younglings near the back. They welcome him warmly, as a friend. I smile.

"You're unusually introspective this evening," I muse to Victus. Is it evening? The colour of the sky outside the hole suggests it's approaching. This has been the longest day of my life. "Don't you have an opinion?" I turn to the old man, in his orange robes and smile. "You looked better in red, Victus."

"That I know." His rumbled laughter makes his belly shake like orange jelly. "We should go to the library, Aqua. There are still some matters that need clarifying before your mate spirits you away."

Liam pulls me against him, his mood subdued now that the anger has dissipated. He presses his lips to my bare shoulder before nodding his agreement. I agree there is a lot to talk about, but I don't want to do it in front of Victus.

"I'm sorry, Victus. It will have to wait until my mate and I have showered and rested. I spent the night crossing the world on foot, in the dark. We have both been through the gates of Hell today and lost a few souls along the way. Send for us if the sky is falling, nothing else takes priority." I sound tired but unyielding in my determination to evade a debrief.

"The city hasn't yet been declared safe," Victus warns as I tug at Liam.

The Grand Hall is full of obstructions, bodies blocking me from a cold shower and a soft bed. I consider launching myself into the air and skipping across heads, like I did during the dance at Lucas and Robyn's mating ceremony.

"Your father will be unhappy," Victus adds. "You are both bound by your duty to this colony, not just to each other."

I turn with a confused frown, until I realise what he's insinuating. I'm too exhausted to be mad or embarrassed, I'm completely drained, now that the adrenalin has subsided all I feel is weak and shaky. My muscles and brain are mush. My heart is constricted, it's thumping but sluggish, like it knows that it needs to conserve its energy for when the pain sets in. We've lost Plyrian. I loved the man as a friend and a brother, but Liam – the man for who my heart beats – has loved Plyrian through countless years and adventures. The hardest pain is the pain of knowing my mate is hurting, and being completely unable to fix it. Some things just can't be reversed. Some things, like death, are permanent.

"We'll be in my room if you need us, Victus." I drag Liam away, more forcefully than required. He trails behind me, his warm hand clasped in mine.

"Aqua," August intercepts our path. "I... Can I talk..." his eyes skim over my shoulder sheepishly, "I need to talk to you."

I'm still walking. "Both of us?" I ask. August shrugs despondently. It's a no but I wasn't actually giving him a choice. "Come on." I squeeze my brother's shoulder and guide him from the room.

We traipse through the empty corridors quietly. Something's eating August, Liam is detached. We don't get ambushed, which is a good sign. My room is dark, so I guide August through and onto my bed. Liam, as I knew he would, heads straight to the bathroom and turns on the shower. I'm glad he hasn't had my stuff moved to our new room, this place smells familiar and comforting.

August sits on the edge, moping. I slot myself next to him and nuzzle my head against his. "Spill, little brother, what's bothering you?" I have a pretty good idea. He loved Plyrian too.

"Everything," August answers quietly. "It completely sucks. Why can't things be easy?" I scoff but don't answer. "Oby told them." August turns his face into my neck. I feel moisture and wrap him in my arms reflexively. "He told his parents about me. It was horrible. Plyrian was going to make it better, explain, but now he's gone." His tears turn into sobs. "I love him, Aqua. But they won't let him see me. You were meant to get rid of the rules. Why didn't you get rid of the rules?" He cries against my shoulder and I let him. He's in shock. Today has been a battle for him, as hard as the battle I've faced.

"It won't be like this forever, August." I kiss his head and sigh. "Things sometimes look black, empty and infinite. If you let it swallow you, you'll get lost in the dark. Find the light, no matter how small, and use it to find your way home." I fix my gaze on the bathroom arch, listening to Liam as he listens to us. "Oberon loves you, despite the ridiculous name you just called him, enough to finally come out. He's your light, little brother, so don't let anyone take it." I kiss him again and stand, letting August fall back onto the mattress in anguish. "I love you." I walk across the room, toward the bathroom, peeling off my battle-soaked outfit as I go. My steel clangs to the floor, making August flinch and groan behind me.

Liam is in the shower, fully clothed, like he's wandered in zombie-style. I'm underdressed. He turns in my direction when I enter, his eyes burning into mine. I don't know how much he can see and I'm not really bothered anymore. This is all of me and it needs a wash. I step in and he moves back to accommodate me. His smile is diminutive but it reaches his eyes. His hand lifts so that he can run the pad of his thumb along my jaw and across my bottom lip.

He whispers, "Angel," in a voice full of awe. "You are my light," he breathes, "and you shine brighter than a star." He gently, infuriatingly slowly, crushes his lips to mine. I surrender.

When he pulls away, his eyes hooded, my fingers have somehow threaded themselves through his hair. He wears his impish grin and it takes my breath away. "I'm in love with you," I tell him.

His grin widens. We stand under the glacial stream in each other's arms. Slowly, carefully, I remove his wet steel and his leather vest. He raises his eyebrow when I get to his trousers and freeze. I really don't want to make a fool of myself by attempting to tug tight wet leather trousers down his legs. He smirks and presses a kiss to my nose before removing them himself.

"I'm going to love you forever," he states calmly. "Here," he reaches over my shoulder for my coconut shower gel, "let me wash you." His eyes burn into mine again, melting me. "Please."

I nod. It's not like I'm going to say no! He squirts some into his palm and lathers it between his hands. I watch enthralled as he gently massages it into my skin, circling his hands around my body with immense concentration, then he instructs me to turn and I can't see him anymore. I can feel him though. I lift my wings when he gently tugs them, so that he can soap my back. His hands linger on my bottom, but he pretends not to notice. I roll my eyes and wait for him to finish my legs. He stands when he's done. His hard chest presses against me and I feel him smile against the back of my neck.

"You're clean." His voice is husky. I shiver as I step back under the shower head to rinse the suds from my skin. I shampoo my own hair quickly, we'd be here all night if I let him do it. When I turn, he's watching me, his eyes are dancing. I lift my shower gel up questioningly, watching him with the same level of amused adoration. He holds open his arms in invitation and I waste no time in repeating his actions myself.

This is going to mess with his usual scent, but right now I don't care. I lather every inch of his body, appreciating the feel of his skin, his muscle. When I'm finished, I gently push him under the flow. It wouldn't surprise me if we end up running the river dry eventually. "Rinse," I order and my voice is just as husky as his. I watch him as he washes his hair, and then he shuts off the water and it's suddenly very quiet. I'm not cold but our skin is dripping with beads of moisture, I watch as a drop makes a track down his torso.

"You can see me," I state quietly.

His voice is just as low. "You're blurred but just as beautiful."

"You could always see in the dark?" I know this isn't the most important line of questioning given our current circumstances but I can't help it.

"A little." He steps forward and wraps his arms around my naked back. "Here, you are clear," he kisses my nose and steps away, "blurry," he steps out of the shower and presses his back against the wall. "Invisible..." His voice trails off to nothing. He stands like a decorative wall sconce, his wings spilling out behind him, and fixes his eyes on the spot he knows I'm standing.

The silence drags on.

"Talk to me," I implore as he waits there silently. "Tell me what you're thinking."

I'm not ashamed or bashful to be standing, soaking wet and bare-butted, while my equally wet and naked mate stares into the abyss of blackness, the blackness which resides outside of his small radius of night vision. There is still so much to learn about each other, even being this comfortable there are still secrets and omissions between us. If I'm lucky, we'll get the rest of our lives to reveal them.

Liam closes his eyes and huffs out a tired breath. His head presses back against the wall and he tilts his face to the ceiling, so that I get a perfect view of his strong jaw and his five o'clock shadow. The hollow dip between his collar bones bobs as he swallows.

His voice is unhurried when he finally speaks. "I thought I'd lost you again. Plyrian said my father would take you there, but it was agony to wait." He takes a deep breath. "When Axion read my tattoo," he runs his fingers over it absentmindedly. I watch the inked skin ripple over solid muscle. I can't understand how this perfect specimen of godliness could be mine. His voice pulls me back. "It all fell into place. I knew. I just knew. My whole life has been spent preparing to avenge him, and I end up killing him instead." He lifts his hands and plunges them into his dark chocolate waves. "I had to do it." He pulls his hands down slowly and covers his eyes, still staring toward the heavens above.

"Yes." He doesn't need my confirmation but I offer it anyway. He had to. He prevented our deaths by taking his father's life. "The decisions your father made took him to that moment, that ending. It was not your fault, Liam."

He pulls his hands down and pins me with his eerily accurate gaze. Is he sure he can't see me from there? "But his shadow will haunt us for an eternity."

I nod. There are many new shadows around us now, ghosts we've created. "It might," I agree, "but we both know why. Shadows are only threatening if you allow them to be, and I no longer fear Rennison Jarik or his ghost. He created you, and because of him Marcus created me. We get to live today and tomorrow, together, because of his crazy."

"His crazy," Liam repeats. "People listened to his crazy. We have an army of dragone to deal with because they agreed with his mission."

"His mission to obliterate everyone from the planet?"

"His mission to create one perfect race of beings, with dominion over land, sea and air. He chose your mother for a reason, and my mother, and probably countless others. He wanted to breed qualities into us. If he hadn't hated you so much, perhaps he would have approved of our union."

"Maybe," I do have all of those abilities, "but he neglected to account for one thing."

Liam frowns faintly. I step from the shower and into his field of vision. He blinks a slow, heavy blink. His eyes burn and they hold me rapt. "What?"

I shrug with a smile. "Nobody is perfect. We never can be because our ideas of perfection are all... imperfect. It's an impossible goal."

I bite my lip as he studies me, his eyes elegantly skating around my face. "I think you're perfect," he whispers.

"I'm your idea of perfect and you, my love, are mine." I step in to his scorching body and he folds me into his arms immediately. "Tell me what happened."

"After you disregarded everything I've ever told you? Leaving me frantically scouring the cave for that retched tunnel..."

I burrow my head into him. "Yeah, after that."

His chest hums with vibrations, either amused or exasperated. His hands rub circles on my lower back, making my skin pimple. "You're cold," he rumbles. "We should get dressed."

"I'm never cold," I respond. "I want to hear this first, please."

"This is not how I usually hold debriefings, Guardian. But for you, I'll make an exception." He presses his lips to my head as he wraps us in his wings.

"Only me?"

"Only ever you." He relaxes back against the wall, pulling me with him. "I couldn't find it, and it made me crazy. Marcus arrived and he wouldn't tell me because Plyrian implored him not to. He told us, then and there, that Rennison was waiting on the other side of that tunnel for us to be delivered." He sucks a lungful of air through his teeth in a hiss.

"You listened to Plyrian instead of killing him?" I sound incredulous. I am.

"Marcus listened and ordered me to spare him." His head dips along with his voice. "I could never have done it, even as mad as I was. He was like a brother to me."

We stand there letting our feelings for Plyrian envelop us in silence, but I'm eager to hear more so I nudge him to continue. "Plyrian had been feeding him information for twenty years. He saw a hope in Rennison that he didn't see in the Script."

I nod. "A relationship and younglings with Gloria."

"Exactly." He sniffs my hair and exhales with a sigh. "He knew of your existence because Gloria cared for you. He told Rennison enough to remain loyal, but something stopped him from revealing all that he knew. He'd been keeping Rennison updated on my progress since then. When you arrived, and trampled all over this colony like some kind of incredible goddess..."

I slap his chest in rebuke and he laughs. "When you arrived and acted exactly how he wanted to be, free and uninhibited, he realised that he'd been blind. He said you'd opened his eyes to another possibility. Rennison gave him nothing but broken promises, but he knew that you had a chance to make this life... better. You were compassionate. You wanted to help others, not further your own position. He loved you, Aqua."

"I know," I accept with a murmur. "I still love him."

He squeezes me. "He had prepared everything. It just took a few orders to set it in motion. The rebels were rallied to confront Marcus and distract the colony, the Guard were ordered to the cave and Jonah, the Guard Master from Graven Thrall was poised to take wing. He'd arranged it, all of it, I just had to follow the stupid fool to his death."

Liam's voice is bitter with remorse and anger. I run my hand up his side and across his ribs to his heart. "You can still love him, you know. He knew you did. I know you do. It hurts more to deny your feelings than embrace them." I press my lips to his chest and whimper with content when his heart accelerates. I look up at his throat, my cheek pressed flat against his burning skin. "Does Gloria know?"

"No." He wraps his left arm around my waist and uses his right hand to pin my circling fingers over his heart. "No one knows. Plyrian was a good man who died while fixing his mistakes. He brought our family together, all of us living under the same piece of sky if just for a short time. I don't blame him."

"You love him."

"I love him," he concedes quietly.

"What happens to him now?" I don't know where they've taken his body.

"He will be laid out in the harbour for the city to honour him. Then we will set him ablaze at dawn tomorrow, so that he can join the sun in heaven." He slowly shifts us back to vertical, so that the wall is no longer supporting our weight. I guess he's told me all there is to tell, for now.

"That's beautiful, you know."

"What?" He raises his eyebrow questioningly.

"The way you intern your dead. I like the thought of joining the sun."

He stiffens, his eyes searching mine and scowls. "Not yet. I want a lifetime on Earth with you before we ride the sun to Heaven."

"We?"

He gently spins us and leads us from the bathroom. He gives me his impish grin. "Always we, from now on."

We don't get very far. There is still a figure sitting on the edge of my bed, only now he's not crying. He looks furious. "August?"

He glares in our direction, blind in the dark. His lips form an angry line. "How can you both love a dead traitor?!" He stands with his shout of fury and marches in the direction of the door.

"August, wait." I try to follow but Liam holds me back.

"You're not racing through the city like that." He crosses the room and rummages in my draw before throwing me some clothes. Oh yeah, naked. I start dressing automatically. "Go and stop him before he does something stupid."

He doesn't have to tell me twice. As soon as I'm decent I leave Liam behind, still hopping into his trousers. He'll catch up.

"August!" I run, following his scent. He's headed straight for the harbour.

# · Twenty ·

It's only because of August's head start that he makes it to the golden doors at the top of the stairs. He's gasping for breath when I grab him and pull him away from the handles. I plead despairingly, "August, you're not thinking straight. Don't do this."

He wrestles within my arms, shouting with anger. There's no way that they don't know we're out here. Plyrian might even know. "No!" August roars between cries. "Get off me! No! How can you let them remember him when they don't know the truth?!" He keeps fighting me, struggling to evade my grasp. I don't let him. My palms clamp around his upper arms and I hold him immobile.

"Calm down!" My voice comes out in a threatening hiss. "This isn't you. Walk away." I take a step toward the stairs, pulling August with me. He increases his attempts to escape.

"Let me go, you freak! Get off me." He kicks out, spewing expletives.

"August." I take a breath. "I'm taking you back to my room to calm down." I lift him, still held in undignified restraint, like a child being scolded and evacuated from a playroom incident.

"No!" He screams. This isn't my August, this is a man deranged with pain. He yells at the door as I turn us back toward the city. "They'll never let me see him again! Oberon! OBERON!"

He's probably right.

"Wait," August yells again, kicking furiously. "Put me down. I'm a friggin' adult!"

"Usually," I extend my arms but he just kicks at me with more leverage. It hurts. I pull him back into a bear hug instead, "Today you're an idiot."

He yells into my ear, a feral growl that sends my eardrum into spasm. The noise pushes me back against the wall. We end up in a sloppy rendition of a seedy backstreet embrace, all scrunched eyes and joined limbs. I drop my grip as soon as my brain catches up and push him away. He staggers backward. Clamping my hand over my ear doesn't stop the ringing. It really doesn't.

"Jesus, August. I'm deaf."

August's escape is short lived. I hear his squeal as Liam grabs him and slaps a hand over his mouth, muffling his protests immediately. Liam obviously has experience with irate August.

"Submit," Liam snarls, his face against our brother's as he presses August against the wall. He really doesn't need to. August went limp as soon as Liam got his hands on him.

"Liam." I speak softly as I step toward them. "Take it easy. Please."

I watch them as they exchange silent communication, the kind that siblings perfect in childhood.

"He's never hurt me," August finally answers quietly, his mouth partially released. He sounds completely depleted.

"Whatever you're trying to achieve," Liam insists, "you won't do it this way." His eyes are level with our brother's. My gaze travels to August's feet, which are quite a few inches from the floor. "They'll love him regardless, and you'll just be the human who tried to hurt them." Liam's voice is low but gentle. "They'll never forgive you, brother."

August's eyes are moist and his skin pale. He simpers, "They'll never forgive me anyway."

"Come on." Liam stands him on his feet and turns him toward the staircase.

We're all at the top when the click of a latch sounds behind us. We turn and freeze, wide eyed, like noisy cat burglars who've just been caught.

"My family want to talk to you," Oberon says quietly, his eyes trained on the floor at his feet, he leaves the door open as he steps away, disappearing into the room. Liam sighs, August gulps, I move first.

The room feels different than usual, the grandeur of the high ceiling and massive door feels overbearing now. I enter gingerly, my eyes scanning the layout quickly. Plyrian is on a gold monolith, a metre high, dressed in his battle armour, his body is surrounded by mounds of fresh snow and there is little difference between the colour of it and the colour of his skin. His sword is in his hands, held along his body, like a stone memorial at a warrior's grave.

Gloria is beside him, dressed in her Nester-blue robes. Oberon's parents stand clasping one another on the opposite side, they wear the brown of the Foragers. Oberon is skirting around the edge, restless and keeping himself distanced from everyone. He looks as broken as August. Plyrian was more like a father than an uncle to him. We all saw it. This seems so unfair.

There are no Guard present. It's just us and his family. Liam and August enter behind me, shutting the door with a deafening click that echoes in the quiet space.

"Guardian," Gloria summons me. "Join me," her eyes lift to mine, "please."

I don't hesitate to stride to her side. I don't know what she needs from me, what I can give her, so I simply open my arms and accept her offered embrace. "I'm sorry," I whisper.

She tuts. "It's not your fault, my girl. He made his choices." She turns her head so that she's looking at Plyrian. I follow, my eyes roving over my fallen friend's features for the last time. "He was an astute man. He would not have fought had he not believed it had purpose." She sniffs but her tears have long since dried. I gaze at her. There's an abundance of love held in her eyes, and it's focused on Plyrian. She releases me to run her hand gently along his face. "Was it swift?"

"He had a little time. He asked me to tell you..." I stop. What did he ask me to tell her? He said, *'Tell Gloria...'* He didn't finish. My mouth mimics words but none come out.

"I understand, Aqua." Gloria pats my hand and nods like she comprehends my stammered silence. "He had nothing left to tell me, just as it is supposed to be." Her grasp tightens around the hand she patted. Her skin feels hot and clammy, like she's full of fire. "He was not sorry for the route that his life took. He never regretted trying to change the world and he was convinced that the impossible task might finally be achieved, by you."

"Gloria..." I stutter to a stop, again.

"Aquila, my sweet girl." Her eyes pierce mine with sentiment. "You must keep fighting for our freedoms, do not let this dampen your resolve. When I am able, I will fight alongside you again."

"Okay." I'm at a loss for words.

"August, my boy." Gloria turns and beckons him with an open palm, releasing me, I take a pace backward. She kisses August warmly when he reaches her, her lips pressing against his cheek. I'm still close enough to hear her quietly whispered words. "No more talk. Don't let anger blind you. The boy and I love you. We will still love you tomorrow." I don't think anyone else could have caught what she said. August nods, his face still ashen, and pulls away from her clasp.

I watch in bemused fascination as he plucks a hair from his head and places it on the snow. He gestures toward Plyrian a final time, with a subtle bow, and walks from the room in a fast scurry. I watch him go. He seems to suck some of the warmth out with him. Liam runs his fingers along my wing as he joins me at the monolith. It feels like a comforting gesture, until he plucks a feather right from my back. I gasp incredulously, Gloria smiles at my shock and nods toward the snow. I notice then, that there are already four other feathers placed around the Second. Liam hands me mine and places one of his own. He nods a bow and waits for me to do the same. I do, though somewhat less fluidly. I smile at Gloria once more as we leave the room. Oberon watches us while he paces, his hands rubbing his skin from his face. His parents don't acknowledge we exist.

August is waiting on the stairs when we shut the doors behind us. I loop my arm through his automatically, shivering off the hostility I turn to him and implore, "You should rest."

August doesn't answer. He's sulking. This is the face he wore when I first informed him that Marcus isn't the saint everyone believed he was. We walk back in the direction of the Grand Hall in silence. My thoughts are of Plyrian and Tarcus, and of my brother who is still somewhere in the tunnels. How can so much happen in a day? Yesterday morning was like most others, today the world has changed forever. I don't feel elated to be rid of Rennison; how can I when it cost us so much?

Angeli are spilling from the doors when we arrive, flanked by Guard who seem relieved when they spot Liam beside me. "Guard Master," one of them calls, "the threat has been neutralised and the city released from confinement." He looks like he wants to say more, but he doesn't.

"Thank you," Liam answers without looking. He's back to moody and aloof. He waltzes into the Grand Hall ahead of us, not noticing the escaping bodies as they push wildly past him. I grab Brue as he sneaks out, his head down.

"Where are you going?"

He looks up at me innocently, like he hasn't just been caught about to do something I'm sure he shouldn't be doing. He shrugs. "Nowhere." He must sense my indecision about letting him go, because his mouth pulls up into a sweet smile and he uses his most convincing tone. "I'll stay out of trouble, we're just going to... you know... hang out, as friends." He points to the same group of yellow-clad younglings I saw him with earlier. They are pressed against the wall, avoiding the stampede as they wait for him.

I'm still suspicious. "Where?"

"Nowhere," he repeats with a cute grin.

"A hint of trouble, Brue, and I'll be dragging your ass to the cells quicker than you can say 'it wasn't my fault'."

I let go and watch him disappear into the crowd as it streams by. That kid will be the death of me. I'm convinced of it.

When August and I finally make it into the hall, it's almost empty. There are Guard milling around, discussing their experiences during the last battle. I listen to snippets as I head toward Liam, who is talking animatedly to Marcus. My mother is also nearby, shooting daggers from her eyes. It sounds like most of the Fallen fought to the death. They didn't know Rennison had been defeated. It also sounds like we've lost Guard. There will soon be more bodies laid on snow in the harbour.

Marcus watches us over Liam's shoulder as we approach. I'm stopped before we reach them by an unfriendly female voice, "Guardian."

I take a second to place her face, because it's bruised and covered in grime. "Rae." I scan her quickly. "Are you okay?" What I mean to say is, *what do you want?*

She looks briefly taken aback before her scowl returns. "I just wanted to thank you."

I don't get the feeling that she wants to thank me at all. "For what?"

She smirks at me. It's not attractive, although she is admittedly beautiful. "For running off and leaving us to deal with an invasion, while your *brother* had to go looking for you. He can't be happy that he missed such a good battle."

Seriously? That is what she wants to use to belittle me? It's not even accurate. Confirmation of mine and Liam's relationship must have spread. I ignore her, too tired for vindictive and petty, and head for my mate. August follows automatically, his head still somewhere else.

The little minx follows us. "What's wrong, Aquila? Liam fed up of courting a selfish wench? I notice he came in *alone*." She drags out the word *alone* like she's trying to stab me with it. We've stopped walking again, and Marcus is looking at us intently. So is Liam. "Did he ever tell you about me?" she purrs. Her eyes are set in a sly, narrowed mask. I just stare at her, my expression weary. It seems to rile her further. She starts with another snide comment and I put my hand up to interrupt.

"Don't bother." She stutters as she looks at my palm, infuriated. "There are more important things going on than insignificant spats with ex-girlfriends, or whatever you call yourself. Don't bother doing whatever you're trying to do, Rae."

"I'm his mate," she snarls incredulously, but her voice cracks on the word.

"No you're not. You might have been going to be, once, but not anymore. We've lost angeli today. Have some respect." I turn and start toward Liam again, who is now smirking in our direction. August's feet start moving too, and then stop when mine do. A hand has grasped my upper arm. Has she not seen me training? I could rip that hand off. Literally.

"You can't think he'll ever be allowed to mate with you, his *sister*. Marcus won't allow it," her voice drops to a hiss, "you have no chance."

I pluck her fingers off with minimal effort. "Haven't you heard? Marcus' opinion is only that, an opinion, and soon it won't hold any more power than yours or mine." I walk away, August following. "Vive la révolution."

When we finally reach our destination, irritant-free, Liam is dazzling me with his megawatt smile. "What was that about?" He's laughing because he damn well heard every word.

"Trivialities of life getting in the way of living." I pin him with a glare. "Just so you know, I don't approve of the type of women you dated before you met me."

Now Marcus is laughing too. "Woman," Liam corrects. "Singular."

I'm not sure that is any better, but I don't comment. At least he seems to have shifted his mood.

"I'm curious," Marcus probes once his grin has subsided. "Why not tell her I've already blessed and observed your union?" His green eyes sparkle with curiosity. He looks brighter now, more relaxed, and I find myself feeling curious too.

I know my answer. "Because it shouldn't be just about me and Liam. There are hundreds of couples, Marcus, that want your blessing but could never ask for it, for no good reason. Do you understand yet? Why it is so important to me, to us? I would have mated with Liam regardless of whether you approved, because I love him. He's my idea of perfect." I pull my lips to the side in a secretive smile. "But I suppose I was raised in a different world. I had the knowledge of possibility. What did they have?"

August, realising for the first time that this conversation doesn't make any sense to him, starts to shake off his sulk with a series of garbled noises. I can feel my mother drifting closer, too. There's no way she can hear what we're saying, yet.

"But you chose not to tell her," Marcus pushes. "I'm just attempting to understand."

For whatever reason, I believe him. I also notice, belatedly, that he's wearing the Lilac uniform of the teachers instead of the red of the Overseer.

"What are you wearing?" My eyes land on his abdomen, where he's tied a red sash.

Marcus doesn't have time to answer before I'm distracted by August, who's tugging on my arm frantically. Liam puts his hand on our brother's shoulder, to silence his escalating mumbling, and slots himself between us – surreptitiously freeing my battered arm.

Liam's presence is all-consuming, intoxicating, and I tingle when he presses his hand in the dip of my lower back.

"Aqua doesn't gloat," he answers Marcus' query with a diminutive pout to his mouth. "She's not spiteful. Although, we should tell everyone," he glances at my mother, "before August regains his speech."

"Augustus," Marcus reprimands quickly, "hold your tongue. I want to better understand your sister before I make any decisions regarding her demands."

I frown. "Why should it matter?" What, if anything, has him understanding *me* got to do with the rebel's objectives? They all want the same thing that I do. They just didn't have the impudence to attempt to obtain it before I arrived. "They aren't just *my* demands."

"But you voiced them, did you not? You vowed to fight for their cause."

"Yes."

"Why, when you have the mate you desire, do you still fight?" His eyes pierce through me, probing.

Is that what he thought? That I'd give up on the revolution if he allowed me to mate with Liam. "It's not just about me and Liam," I repeat, my voice displaying my anger. "The fight is for all of them."

Marcus seems to find my anger entertaining. Liam pulls me closer, his heat drawing me in willingly. I melt against him. I really am too tired for this, for these arguments. The mountain is safe, the Fallen under control and our grief raw. Liam's strong arms support me and his chest cushions my head.

"And you want what's best for the majority, not just yourself," Marcus rambles on. He accepts mine and Liam's closeness without batting an eyelid. In fact, his smile broadens as Liam presses his lips to my head. It's only after the silence has surrounded us for a good while that I realise Marcus is just gazing and smiling neurotically.

"Can I speak yet?" August asks quietly, breaking the silence. He's subdued and depleted. He seems like a different person in the shadow of his father. The conversation with Marcus is getting us nowhere and we need to talk to August and my mother, quite urgently.

"You will have to ask your sister," Marcus announces. "She's in charge."

I almost say 'who?' but I'm sure I'm his only sister. Marcus pulls a red sash from the pocket of his trousers and holds it out to me. I stare at it, alarmed. "What's that for?"

"I'm abdicating," he answers plainly, "I've had my time."

"You..." I stutter and then laugh. He's joking. I've had too long a day for unfunny jokes from men I don't understand.

He looks at me, bemused, and tries to hand me the sash again. "The Overseer elects their successor," he states, slightly irritated now. "You are my daughter. Your outlook is fresh, your blood young and your goal noble. Don't make me ask again."

"But... you didn't ask the first time." I stare at him in shock.

"I don't need to ask," he snaps arrogantly. "My decision is final, until you take this damn sash and start implementing that retched elected government you seem so keen on. Perhaps we should start calling you Prime Minister." He puts the sash in my hand. It feels quite unceremonious.

"But..."

Marcus waves his hand dismissively. "Victus will be here to guide you," he states.

"Where are you going?" I turn to Liam, who looks as pale and shocked as me. "Where's he going?" My voice is a little shrill.

Marcus answers, "I'm going home, Aquila. Sierra was my home once. It's about time the angeli reclaim it. This movement of yours, this progression, it has been a long time coming, yet there are some here who are not ready. I will offer them an alternative, a city that upholds the traditions." He stares into my eyes, interrupting my protest with his hand. "I will not divide us. Sierra is a short flight and there will be no restrictions on travel between the cities. Every angeli will be welcomed. Perhaps, in time, the other cities will join us. You can bring it up at the next meeting."

"Meeting?" My mouth is working on autopilot right now. Hopefully Liam is taking notes so I can revise later.

"The Overseer assembly. We convene every new moon to discuss our colonies." He laughs at my expression. "You'll cause quite the sensation."

"Marcus," Liam interrupts, his throat seems dry. "Is this... Have you fully considered this?" He sounds faintly panicked.

Marcus raises his brow, his green eyes still sparkling. They really do remind me of emeralds, I wonder how many people envy the colour when they look at him. He smirks at Liam and asks, "Have you lost faith in her abilities?"

Liam answers immediately with a resolute, "No," and then he follows it with, "but, Overseer? She is just eighteen, she has little experience of ceremony..." his voice drops, I don't know who he's trying to prevent from hearing, I'm standing right here, "and she's female."

I have a eureka moment. "And I'll be your boss."

I laugh aloud at the face he makes. It's a mixture of bad constipation and sheer horror. That is the crux of the issue, right there. There has never been a female Overseer, ever.

August raises his hand and waves it in front of my face. "Can I speak?"

Was he really waiting for my permission? "Um... yeah."

He explodes. "What the hell are you talking about? When the hell did you mate and are you serious?! You're the Overseer now? This is the weirdest, freakiest, most confusing day of my life."

August's announcement pitches the Grand Hall into silence, and my mother into a wobble. "Well, that handles the announcement," Marcus deadpans. "If you'll excuse me, I believe I owe your mother an audience. Perhaps I should entertain her while her claws are retracted."

He waltzes off, head high, to scoop my mother from her slow faint. Her eyes are a little too wide and her skin a little too pastel, yet she still manages to shoot me her *we'll be talking about this* glower. Everyone watches them as they leave. Everyone. And then all eyes swing to me.

Oh screw it. I unwrap the sash and tie it around my waist.

There's no real decision to be made. I never wanted power or control, but I want to see justice and diplomacy, I want peace, I want to see Plyrian's dream realised. I stifle a yawn. I really want to sleep. "Is it night yet?"

August and Liam look more than a little puzzled by my sudden change in conversation. However, they both look exhausted too. "No, but we should get some rest," Liam agrees.

"Will you be okay?" I ask August. I haven't forgotten that his human roommate has run away and his boyfriend is holding an all-night vigil. Perhaps I should share his room tonight.

I feel Liam stiffen beside me, like he's just read my mind and doesn't agree. August's expression turns wry. "Company would be nice." His face drops briefly with a memory. "You know Aaron left yesterday?" I nod. "Do you think he's alright?"

How would I know? I wasn't sure I was going to be alright, or Liam. I still don't know if Axion and the pirates are alright. My face must display my unease because Liam interjects quietly.

"He has Guard watching him and his family," his eyes shift to mine regretfully, "he's fine."

"Would you have told me if he wasn't?" I ask, because it's obvious how much Liam hates Aaron in his expression, but then my brain catches up. I register the shadow of hurt that flickers across Liam's face, and I realise that Liam didn't have to issue protection duty. The only person he's done it for is me, so that I'm not hurt by someone getting to Aaron. "That was crass, I'm sorry. Thank you for protecting him."

Liam seems to consider his response before repeating, "You're sorry?"

I agree with a sincere nod and a contrite smile.

He mirrors me. "I like it when you apologise, it's like you're admitting you were wrong."

I roll my eyes. "That's normally what an apology implies."

"So witty, Aquila." He steps forward, encroaching on my personal space with his godly gorgeousness. The atmosphere seems to change with that look. I feel the fizz of chemistry in the air. It feels incredibly decadent to bask in it, in front of our brother. Still, I can't pull my eyes from Liam's and I can't slow my beating heart.

"Erm," August clears his throat, "perhaps I'll see if Brue wants an actual bed and a hot shower tonight. Well, maybe not a shower... it's Brue after all. But he hates sleeping in the cells... so... err... yeah... I'm sure I'll find him... um... Okay, I'll see you at dawn, at the ceremony... for Plyrian." By the time he's finished rambling, I've overcome the ensnarement of Liam's burning caramel gaze and am staring at August in amazement. "Later," he repeats with a small wave and a scuttle backward.

"What do you suppose that was about?" I ask, slightly perplexed by my brother's crazier than usual behaviour. "Do you think he's still in shock or something?"

"Or something," Liam laughs. I swear I hear him sheath a blade, but when I look his hands are clasped in front of his hips innocently.

My eyes narrow accusingly. I think I know what was up with August, and it's currently standing in front of me looking apprehensive. I frown when I register his posture.

"I want to show you something," he states.

My frown vanishes. "Is it the thing I saw in the shower?" Because I'd quite like to see that again.

His lips pull up into an enormous grin, with a flash of his white teeth thrown in. "That's a good idea, but no. It's a surprise." He pulls me against his chest and lifts my feet from the floor in one molten move. I cling to him in response, wrapping my thighs around his waist and ignoring the attention that is still focused on us. "Close your eyes," he whispers.

I do, it seems like a good idea, and suddenly we're moving – racing from the hall and through the city. Clinging to a moving pillar of muscle with my eyes closed sends my stomach churning. I tuck my head against his shoulder and open my eyes, just enough to focus on the pulsing skin of his neck. I count the ticking of his carotid to calm myself. I'm just into double figures when our motion ceases. It feels like the earth decided to spin faster, just to catch us up. I press my nose against his scorching skin, inhaling his scent and regaining my equilibrium before he places me back on my feet. His eyes hold mine, and then his hand is covering my vision.

"Hey!"

"I said close your eyes," he answers.

He can't hide the amusement in his voice and I simper. He gently wraps an arm around my waist, teasing my senses with his proximity, and turns me around slowly.

His hand stays clamped across my eyes, his arm moves to wrap snugly around my stomach, and my back is pressed firmly against the hard contour of his body.

He places a hot kiss to the back of my neck before whispering, "Ready?"

"Yes." Does it matter that I'm not sure what I'm meant to be ready for?

His hand lifts, tentatively, and I can see again. We're standing at a door, golden like the rest, yet it is embellished with the most beautiful design I've ever seen.

Our sigil.

Mine and Liam's, combined.

I gasp. This is ours. It's real. This is him and I, we're a mated couple, sworn to each other for life. We have a sigil.

"It's perfect," I whisper.

He steps with me when I move forward and run my finger around it, following the curve of the flames and the sharp points of the star.

His answer is full of emotion. "I think so too."

"Can we go in?"

He nods against my head. "Every day for forever."

He releases me to open the door. He almost looks nervous as he glances at me. I step past when he beckons and venture into the room. He moves behind me, allowing the door to close on its hinges. It is the only movement he makes. I feel him watching me, waiting for my reaction. The room is large, spacious, yet it's only a room. As mating quarters go, it's unexceptional in terms of layout and furniture.

But I'm not really looking at that. I'm looking at the candles. Hundreds of beeswax candles, ablaze, on every stable surface. Trails of candles light the floor in a wash of golden colour, which still dance in the breeze of our entrance. "It's beautiful."

"You're beautiful," he breathes as he steps in to me.

"How did you do all this?"

"I delegated," he flicks his eyes around the room appreciatively, "this is all Robyn's effort."

I turn slowly, partly afraid that I'll knock over a candle and start the Great Fire of Celthia. When my gaze meets Liam's, I relax. He's bathed in an orange glow, his features more pronounced and his anxiety more evident.

I tilt my head inquisitively. "What are you thinking?"

He blinks a slothful blink that draws my gaze to his dark lashes. My heart rate spikes as he cups my cheek with his palm and runs his thumb languidly along my cheekbone.

"I was thinking," he murmurs huskily, "that I never want to wake from this dream." His eyes close again as he inhales a deep breath. His words tickle my skin as he moves closer. "I'm worried that I'll open my eyes, and you'll be gone, and this is just in my imagination." His forehead presses against mine, our noses touching, and his eyes shut.

"This isn't a dream," I assure him, moving so that I'm talking against his lips. "My imagination isn't this good."

He smiles, a slow sexy smile. "But this is my dream." He presses his lips to mine.

"Well then," I grin whilst threading my fingers into his hair, "it must be your fault that we've still not got to the good part."

He kisses me then, hard and desperate. His tongue invades my mouth and I groan. His hands burrow into my hair, pulling me closer, clashing our teeth together. His strong masculine scent fills my head and I laugh, ending our kiss. I laugh out loud, and Liam laughs too.

His eyes darken with longing.

"Time to show you that other something," he grins.

# Epilogue

The island grows before us, an oasis of green, floating regally on the pristine blue which encircles it. The straw huts that line the beach are surrounded by the vibrant foliage of summer. The green seems greener and the white seems whiter under the bright light of day. The scents are so fresh here, so much more inviting than the cold stone of the angeli city. I inhale longingly. I have missed Hantiem, yet it's only been a few weeks since we last visited.

We skim the treeline in tandem, drawing a gaggle of shining yellow eyes to our shadows. Their laughter jingles like morning bells as they skip and jump along below. When the thick leaves dissipate and the white walls of the city appear, the children scatter. Their laughing, chattering voices mark their trail back into the foliage, long after their little figures have vanished.

"Quite the welcome," my mate rumbles, his voice holds a rasp of dryness.

My eyes are drawn to his when he speaks, and, as usual, I'm rendered mute. Liam is a truly beautiful creature. The sun seems drawn to him, like it won't ever be able to bathe him in enough light but continues to try, regardless. His chocolate hair is unruly after our flight – and a brief interlude in a little secluded cove we found. He holds the same heat in his eyes right now and I blush. The man is insatiable and I fear he's corrupting me to the point of addiction.

"Keep looking at me like that," he breathes, his voice still husky, "and we'll be late for the party."

I hitch in a breath. We're gliding now, decreasing our altitude, ready to drop over the wall into the city. I have nothing to say to his statement, other than I don't care if we're late. Except I do care, because I promised Brue I wouldn't be. So I keep quiet. He laughs at the conflicting expressions on my face. His impish grin sets my heart fluttering. Looking away is the only way we'll be on time. I focus hard on my landing, setting my feet down on the cobbled street carefully. I'm barefoot. My black leather cropped leggings are trimmed with red embroidery, as is my corseted leather top, at my father's persistent request. He really is an arrogant man.

Liam lands lightly beside me and tucks his wings in. I quickly forget about looking away. His sleeveless leather vest grips to the contour of his chest. His leather trousers are tight on his thighs. He crosses his powerful arms, his eyebrow hitched in amusement as I trail my eyes over his body. I lift my hand to lightly run my finger around his newest tattoo appreciatively. He took Cain up on his offer during our last visit, to have our sigil inked on his bicep. While I'm admiring it, and the tattoo, he uses his left hand to clasp my wrist and do the same. Cain was happy to ink a matching mark on me. I'm sure that having a tattoo on your inner wrist must be infinitely more painful than getting one done on your arm, because Liam didn't flinch and I wriggled like a worm on a hook. When I look up, his eyes are on me.

He presses his lips to mine and whispers, "You look beautiful." I let him kiss me. Our brothers know we're here, so technically I'm not late. "Come on," Liam grins against my lips, "they'll be coming to find us if we're much longer."

"Heaven forbid," I mumble as Liam pulls us toward the main courtyard.

The courtyard is bustling with fruit-laden and hassled women, shouting commands at excited children and a few henpecked men. I watch them as we pass, and they bow their greeting to us. I feel the warmth of their welcome and smile. The island has been brought back to life and in only a little more than a year. There have been changes, of course. There are still scars, and a full cemetery, that remind us all of the damage they've endured. The survivors each have a different story, an individual account of their history, diverse memories, all an intricate fragment of the war we all outlasted. The prisoners that were freed from Gravinwart were the most affected, the most vulnerable and the most difficult to heal. The angeli supplied Medics, medicines and training. Physically, the dragone population of Hantiem is healthy, hydrated and nourished. Mentally, there are some things that will never heal. Like in the case of Brue's father.

"Aqua!"

I turn and catch Brue as he dives on me. He's wearing black cotton shorts. He's clean, for a change, yet his skin has tanned a deeper shade of brown in the Hantiem summer sun. His yellow eyes are bright.

"Have you grown?" He's definitely an inch taller.

"If you visited more often you wouldn't notice things like that." He sticks out his chin defiantly, waiting for me to challenge him.

"I know, Brue." I really do.

I wish I could come more often, I sometimes think about absconding completely, like Marcus did, and shacking up in one of the inviting grass huts on the coast. Waking up each day to bathe in the ocean and lie on the sand sounds like my idea of Heaven, but I have my own responsibilities and I'm mated to an angeli Guard Master. He would never be comfortable here fulltime.

"Did you get my message?"

"Yeah," Brue grins.

Being the new Overseer of Celthia has its advantages, ike inserting a satellite on the mountain. There was already a solar panel, installed by my father, to power the halogen light in Halen's surgical theatre. With the addition of the satellite, I can keep in contact with my family no matter where we all are, and we are far and wide.

"And?" I prompt him.

"Axion sorted it," he shrugs. His tone turns sour, "You're late."

I'm so glad Axion finally got around to teaching me how to block the remote connection to my emotions. I'd rather Brue didn't know the reasons behind our tardiness.

"Strong headwind," I answer, hiding my smirk by biting my lip. "So where is Ax?"

"Waiting," Brue grumbles, "Come on."

He leads us into the throne room, where Axion is talking to a group of men. Dragone. When the angeli Guard finally finished processing the Fallen, the convicts were given an ultimatum: a life in solitary or a pledge of allegiance to a new leader. One that will honour the truce with the angeli and uphold the promises he makes, one that will train them to control their tempers and focus their energy, one that will never fully trust any of them. Axion didn't want the job, he's already acting king until Brue is old enough to take over the throne. It's a job that keeps him busy.

"Master," Clyst fawns at Liam as we enter.

Liam glares at him. Clyst was related by blood to Horen and Rennison and therefore is related to Liam, too. You'd never know it. Clyst is not the man he was. He survived the angeli interrogation, just, and angeli medicine healed his wounds. Although his arm will never regain its strength and coordination, too much nerve damage, Halen said. Of all the dragone, Liam trusts him the least.

Axion has been watching closely in Liam's absences, ensuring Clyst is truthfully loyal. Rennison promised him power, but it was Liam who gave it to him. So far, he has kept his word. He enforces Liam's orders efficiently and precisely.

They all seem to appreciate his command and Liam handles them well, much better than his father did. And although there are so few adult male dragone left, after the war and the executions that they're practically an endangered species, there is finally peace. Although somewhat strained, there has been no more fighting, no more attacks or abductions, no more murder. The dragone are free. They have friends. They have liberties. They have a future.

"Ax." I ignore the dragone crowding him as I push through.

My brother has been fundamental in the integration of released prisoners and the rebuilding of Hantiem. His gentle leadership style was exactly what the frightened islanders needed. With Old Salt and the pirates at his side, he oversaw every burial, spoke with every family, catered for all of their needs. He and Liam have grown as close as Axion and I, and Brue finally has a worthy role model from whom to learn.

Axion smiles at me, his eyes sparkling. I launch myself into his arms and squeeze. "Hey," he laughs with some effort, "too tight." But he hugs me back with the same pressure.

"Happy Birthday."

"Thanks, Princess." He kisses my head. "Now, where's my present?"

"Liam has it." I drop my voice. "Is everyone here?"

He rolls his eyes but maintains his smile. "You know t's *my* birthday, right?"

I do know. "But how often are we all together?" I give him my best little sister pout. "You know I love you, right?"

I do love him, very much. I love having brothers after so many years as an only child. He indulges me with a smirk. "I know. Now where's my present?"

Liam hands him the package we brought, and used as a makeshift pillow along the way. "Happy Birthday," Liam echoes. The angeli never celebrate their birthdays, so this is all new to him.

"Thanks." They share a guy hug, all back slaps and macho-ness, before Axion rips into the paper. I guess even kings don't mess about when it comes to opening gifts. "Wow, thank you." He rifles through the piles of fabric, clothes from the Nesters, to the firm article in the centre. "This is stunning." He inspects the blade in awe.

"Liam forged it. The book, which you so gratefully discarded before you looked at it, is from me."

"Thank you, Aqua." He reads the title from its location on the floor. "War and Peace." He grins. I know he likes it.

"What else do you give a king for his birthday?"

"A list of instructions via email, apparently." He attaches his new dagger around his waist and takes my hand. "This way, my Lady."

He leads us out of the throne room and toward the beach. Liam follows a pace behind. We walk serenely through the small jungle, our way marked by flaming tiki torches. Voices travel on the breeze, joyful and exuberant. We arrived from the north, over pristine white powder. The beach on the south has the same white sand, but today is bustling with crowds of people.

We follow the trail from green to white, the tiki torches lighting a path right to the water. The cargo ship is moored in the ocean, listing gently on the horizon. My pirates are larger than life, joking and drinking around a burning fire pit near the treeline. The fire is crackling furiously. There are still hours left of daylight, but they look settled for the duration. Islanders are swimming in the water, playing ball games and jumping around on some kind of inflatable trampoline.

I smile when I spot my family. My mother and August are sampling a selection from the cocktail bar near the shore. It's a large grass gazebo with open sides and a continuous circular bar top. The barman, an ex-Fallen soldier turned barista, is shaking a cocktail tumbler exuberantly. Oberon's hand is clamped firmly in my brother's, but he's eyeing the alcohol dubiously. None of the angeli have been to the island before. I thought it was about time. I search the beach, picking out my father easily. Marcus is lounging on the sand. He's wearing shorts and a red T-shirt. His wardrobe looks more human every time I see him. He's with my dragone grandparents and aunt, who all moved back when they heard of Rennison's death. They also brought humans with them, the tribe they were living among in the Amazon. The humans don't seem the least phased by life here.

I hear a squeal of delight and I smile reflexively. Liam has stopped moving in order to gape at the eclectic mix of species amassed under the burning sun. The squeal sounds again and I turn, seeking its source eagerly. She's down by the water, laughing every time one of her parents kicks the salty spray toward her. "Thanks, Ax. This is perfect."

He squeezes my hand and lets go, just as Brue comes hurtling past like a greyhound and sprays us with a water cannon. We take chase, the three of us, tearing after him across the beach, toward the ocean. He's planning on refuelling. We splash through the surf, laughing at the squeals from the people nearby, and dive toward our youngest brother. He yelps as he's hit with a tidal wave and knocked from his feet. He disappears spluttering beneath the surface, his gun going with him.

"Brue?" Liam yells, immediately panicked, and then he growls as he's shot in the head with a steady stream of saltwater. We laugh, hysterically, at Liam's answering splash. He sends another wave through the water which Brue leisurely rides, grinning. It's nice to see Liam relax, and actually play. He missed a huge chunk of his own childhood, trying to live up to the memory of his father.

He has a lot to catch up on. I leave them to it. They play like boys and it always gets rough. There's a little girl I'd rather be playing with.

I sneak along the shore, toward my best friends. They're immersed in their game, and Rian is screeching in laughter.

"Where's Rian?" I coo when I'm a few paces away.

The stunning little angel spins when she hears my voice, and gives me her most gorgeous smile. Rian is a beautiful baby, with hair the same yellow as her mother and eyes as strikingly blue as her father's. She's not talking yet, but I'm holding out hope that her first word will be 'Aqua'. I say it to her enough when her parents aren't around.

"There she is!" I laugh as she toddles toward me, pumping her little fists for a cuddle. I lift her into the air and throw her, to Lucas' horror. Robyn laughs with me. She is such a relaxed mother. Lucas, usually so laid back, is an overprotective neurotic whenever his daughter is involved. "Relax, Daddy," I grin. "I got her." I spin her in circles, and fly her like an aeroplane along the beach. She laughs the whole way, and Lucas follows nervously. "Gorgeous Rian," I chuckle. "What's my name? Say Aqua. Aqua. Aqua."

"Aqua," Lucas mimics in a baby voice, catching up and stealing his daughter back. "Her first word is going to be daddy. That's right, Rian, say daddy... daddy..."

Rian laughs and dribbles saliva onto his face. I grin. "She must think daddy needs a wash."

Lucas glares at me, and then laughs as he wipes it off. "Thank you for inviting us, Aqua." He looks around, smiling at the scene in front of us. "This is Rian's first time outside of the city, and she is having so much fun." He shifts his daughter onto his hip. "The island is beautiful. I can see your attraction to it."

"I know." I tickle Rian's tummy, making her giggle. "I wish we could do this more often, all of us."

"You mean your family." Rian squirms in his arms until he hands her back to me. She wants to pull my hair. It's loose today, tangled in frizzy ringlets because of the humidity. "Your mother looks happy."

I smile. "She is. I thought she'd want to go back to the farm, but she loves this island as much as I do. And Brue needs a mother figure." Without either of his parents around, and with Axion so busy, she was worried he'd get himself in trouble. I watch my mother and August as they laugh together. "I just wish there was a way for August to spend more time with her."

Lucas nods, contemplating. "Give Oberon some time. He's had a lot to deal with. Gloria is all he has left since his parents moved to Sierra. I know he is reluctant to leave the city, and her side," he gestures to Gloria as she downs a shot of something at the bar, "but he will eventually start bringing August to visit."

I'm attempting to extract Rian's fingers from my hair, and the pretty little mite is just tugging harder. "I know," I agree. "At least my mother's gotten over her aversion to technology and started emailing."

Lucas leans over, trying to help me I assume. He chooses to tug my hair, to try and free her, instead of untangling his daughter's hand. I'll be bald soon. Fortunately she squirms excitedly and untangles herself when she notices Liam sauntering up the beach. I don't blame her. I squirm excitedly too.

"Aqua," Lucas rushes in a whisper. "I should warn you, Aaron's here."

My head snaps around to gawp at Lucas. "What?"

He shrugs apologetically. "Libby," he grimaces as explanation.

"Where's Rian?" Liam asks in the same high tone I use. She wriggles her way to her feet and then toddles across the beach. Show off. I fear her first word might actually be 'Liam'. She adores him.

He picks her up and swings her, prompting Lucas to scurry after them like Mr Cotton Wool. I give him a wave and head over to Marcus. He sits up when he notices me. "Aquila, you're late."

My eyes roll as I ignore him to hug my aunt and grandparents. They cluck over me, patting and kissing and prodding like they always do when I visit. Apparently I *really* look like my mother.

"Hi Nana, Gramp, aunt Arin. Are you enjoying the party?"

"Oh, don't you look just like your mother today," my Nana exclaims. And then they all start exchanging comments and memories, they keep me talking for ages.

When Liam joins us, looking sour that I've been held up for so long, I make my excuses and leave them to it. Marcus has fallen asleep on the beach, and his pale skin is looking a little pink.

"He'll moan about that at our next assembly, I'm sure."

"You'll handle it," Liam answers, "You always do." He pulls me against him and I smile. "Old Salt wants to talk to you. So does your mother." He seems flustered. It's probably the heat.

I wrap my arm around his waist and he drapes his around my shoulder. "We'll start at the fire pit and work our way around," I suggest.

Old Salt is jolly, and rather hard to understand due to the quantity of alcohol he's already ingested. Apparently, he's retiring, just like he promised himself in the barracks. He wants to spend the rest of his days like this, basking in the sun with good food, good company and a strong drink. Cain is taking over as captain when his father retires. I'm glad I managed to save them both, by some small means. It was them with the strength and desire to survive, I just gave them water and weapons.

Cain's actually an incredibly decent and loyal guy, who is awesome with a tattoo needle. He and the crew seem happy. George and Nev are joining them permanently. Together, they're like a rowdy dysfunctional family, but their strong bond is obvious. I watch, intrigued as they share stories and laughter. I've noticed, the more time I spend around them, that they all touch subconsciously: a quick hand shake, high five, back slap. I take more notice now, I suppose. Liam and I sit by the fire, sharing tales and a drink with our comrades. Until August, looking amused, requests our assistance at the bar.

My mother, it seems, has enjoyed a little too much of the vino, as has Gloria, who is not used to the effects of alcohol, they are like a pair of naughty school girls, giggling and wobbling around the bar like bees around a flower. I ask the barman to switch them to water and confiscate their cocktails. They boo me like thespians and then fall over, laughing all the way to the ground.

We all watch as they land, in a quivering heap of hoots and snorts. I notice Oberon gingerly push away the drink he was nursing, before attempting to help his aunt and mother-in-law back to their feet. August raises his glass to me and smiles. I smile back, toasting him with a fresh drink of my own. He's astounded me recently. Being there for Oberon, as he struggled through his grief, has matured him as a person and them as a couple. They are still in the courting phase and they are very happy.

Actually, no same sex couples have requested a mating ceremony yet. Nonetheless, there are a few pairings openly courting now. I've been busy, conducting ceremonies for any couple who have requested one. The angeli counsel of Celthia, chaired by Victus at the colony's request, voted on the new mating laws. There is still no form of divorce, they are all proud that we mate for life. I don't disagree. Couples are still supposed to live separately until they are mated, but the whole city feels more relaxed, and I know the rules are bent regularly. I won't be executing anyone for falling in love. I also wouldn't deny a couple an annulment, if they ever requested one.

Hearts are mending, slowly, across the whole city. Rian is like a little ray of light, filling the corridors with purity and laughter. She gives us all hope for the future. Plyrian would have adored her. Although, with the increase in couples enjoying their mating moons, there are quite a few new lives being created. There's space in the city to accommodate every one of them as they grow. Perhaps we'll need to expand one day, but for now we are all safe, secure and sheltered.

The sun begins to drift in the sky. We stay by the bar, drinking and laughing and plying the two laughing hyenas with water until they begin to sober up. Axion joins us, sharing jokes and stories and introducing his latest female admirer. Who knew? Axion is a real lady's man. He exudes a quiet charm. It probably helps that he's the king, too. We toast his birthday before someone shouts that the feast is served in the main courtyard.

I lean back against the bar, watching as the beach clears slowly. There's a gentle breeze that blows from the water, lifting skirts and feeding the crackle of Reuben's fire. The moment of silence, around the chatter from the guests, is comfortable. Liam leans next to me, enjoying the reduction in temperature as the afternoon rolls in. When August shouts from the edge of the path, waving us over, Liam pushes himself back to his feet and turns to me. His eyes search mine before glancing over my shoulder. I know what he's looking at so I nod and he presses a kiss against my lips.

Liam signals to August to wait and says, "I'll give you two a minute," before turning to stroll across the beach. I watch him. I can't help it.

Aaron moves closer, circling the bar slowly. His scent is still the comforting fragrance I spent a childhood appreciating, but I haven't seen him since he left Celthia. Over a year has passed, almost a year and a half. He's been in contact with my mother, and August and even Axion, but not me – not once.

"Hey."

I inhale before I turn, playing down the pinch of hurt that his voice causes. "Hey." My eyes lock with his. I smile. I'd feared, irrationally, that perhaps I wouldn't recognise him. It feels like my life has changed so drastically that we might not look like the same people anymore. But I am, and so is he. He smiles back, popping his dimple at me.

"You look good," he comments.

"You too."

We stand for a second, perhaps debating the same question. Would it feel weird if I hug him? He steps forward before I do, I always was the more cautious, wraps his arms around me, and closes the distance like he knew I wouldn't. After a beat I hug him back and he relaxes. He's put on a bit of muscle since he left, I can feel it rippling across his back.

"You look happy," he informs me as he straightens. I drop my arms and he eventually does the same.

"You look buff," I answer. "How's the farm?"

He scratches his head. I watch his fingers pull through his dirty blond mop and hide another smile. "Busy," he decides.

"Your parents didn't mind loosing you to the Organic farming business?"

My mother gifted him our farm. She asked me for permission first. I don't know what she thought I might like to hold onto it for, nostalgia perhaps. The memories it held for us are still there, regardless of the building belonging to someone else. There was no use in it sitting empty, and August didn't want it.

"They're just glad I haven't disappeared again," he answers, his voice low. "Well, until now."

"You didn't tell them?" I don't know what gives me the right to sound disappointed, but I manage it without offending him.

"I didn't give them exact coordinates. They know I'm visiting Libby and... you." He leans back against the bar, staring out along the sand. The barman has left his post, to satisfy his stomach I expect. I sit on one of the stools, quietly wringing my fingers. "Nice tattoo," he comments. I meet his eyes.

"Thanks. Cain's talented."

He doesn't drop his stormy gray gaze. "He makes you happy?"

I know he isn't asking about Cain. "Very," I agree softly. Liam makes me feel quite a few things. Happy is definitely one of them.

"I can see that," he agrees. "He seems... mellow."

I snort a laugh. It bursts out and takes me by surprise. Aaron's brow arches in response. "Don't let him hear you say that." I grin when I've regained my composure. "But yeah, he is more mellow. Celthia as a whole is more relaxed. You should visit."

He blinks slowly, before turning his gaze away. "Yeah, maybe. I kind of prefer it here," he adds with a wry smirk, "better chance of a tan."

"True."

He sighs audibly before continuing. "I'm sorry I left like that."

"Don't be." I shake my head. "It was my fault. I felt it, when you walked us to the hangar. It felt like goodbye. I could have challenged you, but I was too caught up in the war and in..."

"Liam," Aaron finishes.

"Yeah. I'm sorry."

"Don't be."

The conversation dies as we both stare in different directions. People start returning to the beach gradually, reigniting their conversations or games like they weren't interrupted. I don't think Aaron and I could do the same thing. Our friendship's been more than interrupted. It feels like it's been on hold and neither of us are sure how to start it again. Perhaps we'll get there. Perhaps we won't. Either way, I'll always know he's safe because he has Guard watching over him, twenty-four hours a day. I'm not sure that he's aware, but they'll be there if he ever needs them.

"I better get some lunch," he declares as he spots Liam emerging from the foliage.

"Yeah," I agree, strangely relieved that he's the one ending the reunion. "My mother's been baking. There's enough to feed an army." He laughs at my proclamation, his eyes properly twinkling for the first time, and I grin. "You know what I mean. It's a saying."

I drop from the stool when he nods. I don't have to debate whether to hug him. He just pulls me in and kisses my temple. "It was good to see you. I'm glad I came." His tone tells me this wasn't an easy decision for him and the thought depresses me.

"Thank you for coming."

"Hey," he grins, "free flight to paradise without needing a passport. It was a no-brainer." He pulls away and drags his hand again through his hair. "I'll come more often. This has been... good." He glances briefly at Liam, who is slowly making his way over. "I'd better go eat. Later 'gater." He takes a few steps backward before turning and walking away.

"In a while," I answer, almost shouting.

He glances fleetingly over his shoulder, smiling and giving me a stiff wave. He even exchanges a quick greeting with Liam as they pass each other.

"You cleared the air?" Liam asks cautiously when he reaches me, two plates of food in his hands.

I nod. I guess that's what we did. "You're picking up my idioms," I comment. "You'll be asking if I'm cool next."

"You're not cool, you're hot." He winks and I burst into flames, metaphorical, of course, although they feel blistering. He places the plates on the bar and pulls me into his arms. "Thank you for arranging this. I wouldn't have believed it, even yesterday, that we could all be in one place without another war breaking out. But here we are, all mixed together like that absurd concoction your mother was drinking earlier."

"Well she'll regret that, but I'll never regret this." I tuck my head against his chest as we watch our friends, family and the once mistaken foes all enjoying each other under the descending sun.

Liam's hand trails along my arm until he weaves his fingers through mine, causing goose pimples to prickle my skin. The pad of his thumb circles my wrist lightly, following the outline of our sigil perfectly while he stares into my eyes. I'm caught in his intense gaze as soon as I meet it. His breath teases my lips and his scent fills my body with oxygen.

"I know you want this," he whispers, "I think I could do it." I must look confused because his eyes sparkle and his brows rise minutely. "Give me," he pauses, "until next winter." A smile dances across his face, but I still don't understand. "Perhaps it will be cooler in the winter," he muses. "It will give me time to acclimatise and you time to choose your successor." Then he asks wryly, "Unless you plan on commuting to work?"

I blink. "You would move here, for me?"

"For us," he amends. "My home will always be with you. The where isn't as important as the why."

I smile, so wide that my cheeks hurt. I love this man more than words will convey. Hantiem or Celthia, it doesn't matter as long as we're together. "We have plenty of time to find our place, and every moment between now and then will be perfect," I tell him earnestly.

Life might not always allow us to relax as it does now. It might challenge us and tear us or cause us pain, but it will be ours and we'll live it together for as long as we can. I press my lips to my mate's, showing him how much I love him with the heat of my mouth.

Our kiss lingers as the afternoon draws toward evening. Our lives will be spent together. However long or short it may be, this is our small perfect part of the vast forever and we'll make it our own.

The End

# Acknowledgements

That's it for Aqua's story for now. I'm sure we'll visit Celthia and Hantiem again one day, but for now, thank you for enjoying the ride.

I have to say thank you. The support I have continued to receive, from family, from friends both old and new, and from my fans, has been inspiring. Everyone who has read and appreciated my work deserves a heartfelt thank you.

I must also mention my husband and children, who have continued supporting from the sidelines; allowing me time to write, without descending into irrevocable chaos around me, mostly.

Thank you to each of my betas: Hannah, Lauren, Karen and Neil, whose wise comments were, and ever will be, priceless.

Printed in Great Britain
by Amazon